LAKE OF SORROW

THE CURSE AND THE CROWN
BOOK 2

LINDSAY BUROKER

Kor'ruk Lands
Havartaft Estate
Strait of Torn Towers
Preserve
Port Jirador
Frost Harbor
Stillguard River
King's Highway
Evardor Mountains
North Dakmoor Sea
Justori Pass
Kingdom of Zaldor
Old Beyrok
Potato Patch
Potaraki River
Sand and Sage
Sandsteaders
South Evardor Mountains
Tirak River
L'ro Vamorka Islands
Tirak Valley

1

Fleeing proves only fear, not guilt.

~ Ranger Sergeant Mlokar

In the foothills under the Evardor Mountains, with the setting sun painting the snowy peaks pink, hounds bayed. Though rain, cold, and weariness had long since sapped the strength from Kaylina Korbian's muscles, she forced herself to stir.

"Do you think that's for us?" From a hilltop, Kaylina peered around the crumbling remains of an ancient windmill, looking for the riders that had to accompany those hounds.

"No." Her brother, Frayvar, pulled his damp cloak closer around his frail body. "I'm sure the king sent his guards out to hunt raccoons in the aftermath of a rebellion, an assassination attempt, and a plucky southerner trying to poison the queen."

"I *didn't* try to poison the queen." Kaylina speared him with the dirty look the comment deserved. Her brother might have been nursing his wounds in ranger headquarters during the chaos in the royal castle, but he knew her better than that. "I was framed, and as soon as the Kingdom Guard and rangers stop hunting us, I'm going to find that awful Jana Bloomlong and punch her in the face until she confesses that she stole my mead, laced it with a deadly substance, and had a lackey deliver it to the queen."

It wasn't fair that Jana walked free while Kaylina had wanted posters nailed to posts and trees all over Port Jirador and the surrounding countryside. *Ugly* wanted posters drawn by a dubious artist with a shaky hand who could only have caught a fleeting glimpse of her. In the portraits, her black hair stuck out oddly, like she had porcupine earmuffs, and her pouty lips seemed cruel, her warm brown eyes sinister.

"Logic suggests you'll need to cajole a confession out of her *before* the authorities will stop hunting for us."

Hunting for *her.* Frayvar hadn't been on the wanted poster, one small relief. Kaylina didn't want to have to write a letter to their mother and grandparents, explaining that she'd gotten her little brother killed.

"Is cajole the right word when fists are involved?" she asked.

"No, but you're my older sister, and I prefer to imagine you nobly pursuing victory through words and craftiness rather than physical violence."

"I'm too tired to be crafty. Or wordy."

As the hounds bayed again, Kaylina attempted to muster the energy to run. All she wanted was to curl up somewhere warm and sleep for two days straight. Enticing thoughts of her bed back home—back home and more than a thousand miles to the south—flirted with her mind.

"Springing into a fisticuffs battle doesn't require vigor?" Frayvar asked.

"The frustration simmering inside me would give me energy."

"At least the rangers aren't trying assiduously to find us. Yesterday, that taybarri looked right at us with its nostrils twitching, and the rider kept going."

"I'm out of honey. It had no reason to leave the path and veer into our bushes."

That was true, but Kaylina knew she had Lord Vlerion to thank for the rangers' half-hearted search attempts.

Thinking of him brought a pang of longing to her, and she remembered the kiss they'd shared before parting ways. The hot *fiery* kiss that made her want to do exactly what he'd commanded: clear her name and return to him.

Even if he hadn't made it a command, she would have wanted to do those things. She longed to walk freely in the city again and help him lift his curse. After Vlerion had saved her life, she owed him. More, she wanted him to be the man he could be if he didn't have to worry about losing his equanimity and turning into a murdering beast.

Frayvar pointed toward the road that passed below the sprawling country estate they were hiding on, the manor house miles from the abandoned windmill and the meandering stream it perched near. Eight men on horseback rode closer with their hounds running ahead and through the fields to either side.

Kaylina rose to her feet, careful to stay hidden by the ruins, and grabbed her pack. It had grown lighter these past days as she and Frayvar ate through the food Vlerion had given them.

The hounds turned up the drive for the estate, sniffing at the ground Kaylina had walked across before dawn.

Crouching beside her, Frayvar pointed at the stream. "That way? They'll have no trouble following our trail if we don't hide our scent in the water."

"I know." Kaylina had grown up hunting grouse and small animals in the Vamorka Islands with her grandfather and his hounds. She knew their abilities well. "But it leads..."

She trailed off, gaze drawn to the dense forest bordering the estate. The ancient trees grew thick, tangled undergrowth flourishing between the trunks, and twilight appeared to have already fallen within its bounds.

"To the Daygarii Preserve," Frayvar finished. "A spot we've been avoiding for the last three days, but it's the only place the hunters may hesitate to follow us."

"The *rangers* won't go in there—Vlerion said the preserve is as cursed as the castle we leased and hates their kind. I'm less certain about guards and bounty hunters."

But what choice did they have? They had to avoid being imprisoned if they were going to eventually sneak back into the city and clear Kaylina's name.

Frayvar only shrugged and glanced nervously toward the approaching riders.

Summoning her flagging energy, Kaylina stepped away from the windmill, descended the backside of the hill, and stepped into icy water that flowed off glaciers in the mountains. Frayvar splashed after her.

"Be careful not to brush any branches." She pointed toward rhododendrons, goatsbeard, sword ferns, and other plants she couldn't yet name. It was only because of drawings in the ranger handbook Vlerion had tucked in with their supplies that she could identify any of the local flora. As her reading had emphasized, the royal rangers were hunters and trackers as well as defenders of the borders.

"Easier said than done." Tall and gangly, Frayvar slipped on every other rock, wobbling even without a pack or any weapons weighing him down. And was he wheezing slightly? His recently cracked ribs had to be bothering him.

As the baying grew louder, the voices of men now audible, Kaylina and Frayvar fell silent. They hurried up the stream toward the looming forest, glancing back every few steps.

Ahead, a bridge arched over the waterway, its stone framework already in shadow as twilight approached. Kaylina didn't notice anyone on it until a taybarri reached the top, the ranger mounted on the creature's long back gazing downstream toward her and Frayvar.

Surprise and the immediate hope that it was Vlerion made Kaylina misstep. Her foot slipped on a slick rock, and she flailed, her pack slumping off her shoulder.

The ranger couldn't have missed the movement, but his chin lifted, his gaze shifting farther downstream. The *taybarri* looked right at Kaylina, its floppy ears twitching, its long, thick tail swishing on the bridge.

The shadows made it hard to see the ranger's face, but he had too much hair to be Vlerion. Disappointment filled Kaylina, as well as the certainty that this guy would impede them.

She lifted a hand to keep her brother from running into her and glanced toward the right bank, thinking of crawling into the undergrowth. The forest rose in that direction, but they were still a quarter mile away. It would be a long crawl. And the blue-furred taybarri had nostrils as good as any hound's. More, it could run as fast as a horse, even faster if it used its flash power. If the ranger wanted to catch them, he would.

The man shifted his cloak aside, the gesture oddly flamboyant, and drew something from his belt. A weapon?

Kaylina tensed and grabbed Frayvar's wrist, ready to yank him into the brush.

The ranger held up something flat and rectangular. An envelope. He looked like he was trying to read it by the vestiges of the sunset but shook his head, as if there wasn't enough light. He set the envelope on the stone railing, then rode off the bridge.

The taybarri trotted down a trail that headed downstream, rustling encroaching foliage along the way. As the ranger passed close to Kaylina and Frayvar, he didn't look at them, instead gazing with determination toward the hounds and horses.

Would he stop the hunters? Try to get them off Kaylina's trail?

She doubted it. So far, the rangers hadn't tried hard to catch her, but they *were* on the same side as her pursuers.

That thought didn't keep her from hurrying upstream, climbing out, and heading for the envelope. Her boots squished on the stone bridge, leaving wet prints that even a nearsighted grandma could follow, but it couldn't be helped. Kaylina wanted whatever the ranger had left. Something from Vlerion, she hoped.

The light had grown too dim to discern much, but she could make out the word *pirate* in dark ink on the envelope and grinned. That was what she called *him*, and it irked him to no end, but Kaylina had no doubt the message was for her.

After tucking the envelope into her waistband, trusting the belt to keep it secure, she climbed back into the water. Ducking low so they wouldn't be seen, she and Frayvar continued under the bridge and upstream.

The bays had shifted to whines, the hounds right alongside the waterway now and almost to the bridge. Kaylina worried their pursuers would continue into the preserve after them and she and her brother wouldn't be able to escape.

"Lord Ranger," a rider called from the path, the words barely audible over the gurgling water. "We're on the trail of the fugitive from the south."

"I glimpsed her near the manor, but she was heading into the mountains. I believe she may have caught a ride on one of the mining wagons." That voice was familiar. It belonged to Jankarr, Vlerion's handsome comrade.

"That's not what our hounds think."

"No? Then by all means, follow them. Their noses are much keener than mine."

"But not that of your taybarri."

The words grew harder to make out as Kaylina continued to creep upstream. It sounded like the speakers had stopped moving. Maybe Jankarr was blocking the path and buying her time?

"The taybarri will not help hunt down an *anrokk*," Jankarr said. "It is why we've struggled to capture her ourselves. Several times, they've led us—we believe—deliberately astray."

"What in all the altered orchards is an *anrokk*?"

"One to whom animals of all kinds are drawn. They're believed to have druids in their distant ancestry."

Kaylina halted. She hadn't heard *that* before. Vlerion had only said that animals were drawn to *anrokk*, and his mother, Isla, had implied that *he* might be drawn to Kaylina because the curse turned him into a beast, something more akin to an animal than a man.

"That girl has druid blood?" Skepticism dripped from the guard's voice.

Jankarr chuckled easily. "Maybe, maybe not. Who knows how much faith to put in the old stories. All I know is that the taybarri all like her and won't turn against her."

"Fantastic. Then you'll have to step aside so *we* can capture her. Your taybarri is blocking our hounds."

Too bad the *dogs* didn't mind turning against Kaylina. Though it was possible that once they found her, they would jump on her and lick her.

A concerned whine suggested the hounds weren't so much blocked as intimidated by the much larger beast. The taybarri might have soft blue fur and floppy ears, but their powerful muscles, rows of fangs, and sharp claws made them fearsome predators.

"Is he?" Jankarr asked. "Not by my choice, but as I said..."

Frayvar poked Kaylina in the shoulder and pointed toward the preserve.

Right, they needed to use this time to put more distance between them and their pursuers. As badly as Kaylina wanted to hear the rest of the conversation, she continued upstream as it curved, following the terrain toward the forest.

They were almost to the first trees when Jankarr called, “Best of luck to you on the hunt, but be careful in the preserve. The animals in there may aid an *anrokk*.”

“They can aid her all they want,” the guard called back, “after we’ve peppered her with crossbow quarrels.”

Kaylina glanced back. The horseback riders crested the bridge and headed toward the preserve.

Jankarr must have continued downstream because he wasn’t in view. The rangers might help Kaylina in small ways, but they wouldn’t openly attack the guards, not for her. Probably not for anyone. After all, they all served the king and were on the same side.

A feline screech came from the forest, and Kaylina whirled toward the trees, images of panthers and tigers from the south springing to mind. There were even larger and more dangerous predators up here in the north. She remembered Vlerion battling a yekizar and had heard of powerful crag cougars.

Something moved in the shadows to the side of the stream. Kaylina yanked out the only weapon she had, a sling that her grandfather had given her.

From the dark trees, yellow eyes glinted as they looked toward her. They disappeared before she could take aim, and a faint rustling sounded as the creature sprang away.

A moment later, a horse shrieked in fear.

“Malikar!” a rider cried, naming an animal Kaylina had only read about, a shaggy sabertooth cat larger than a tiger.

Hounds barked, and branches snapped as some creature ran away. A blunderbuss fired, the boom drowning out everything else.

Kaylina didn’t know if the great cat was attacking the hunters—it sounded that way—but she gripped her brother’s arm and led him deeper into the forest. Though she hoped none of the dogs or horses would be hurt—she was more ambivalent about the men who wanted to pepper her with quarrels—she intended to take advantage of the distraction.

She and Frayvar left the stream behind so they could travel faster. They pushed through the undergrowth in the direction the malikar had seemed to come from. Hopefully, its appearance would rattle the hounds, and they would shy away from traveling deeper into the preserve.

Men shouted, and the blunderbuss fired again. The twangs of crossbows were too soft to hear, but Kaylina trusted the guards were unleashing all their weapons. She was surprised the malikar was sticking around to be shot at. Or did it think it could best them all and feast on the flesh of men?

She shuddered at the idea but didn't stop moving until the sounds dwindled and her breathing grew ragged. Her leg that had been bitten weeks earlier throbbed, a reminder that the deep wounds would take a long time to heal fully.

Frayvar tripped over a root and rasped, "I need to stop."

"Me too."

They put their backs to trees and listened. They could see little, the darkness in the forest deep, no hint of the waning daylight filtering through the thick canopy. The attack must have alarmed whatever creatures lived nearby—Kaylina's and Frayvar's breathing was the only sound. Conscious of that, she did her best to quiet hers.

"Maybe you *are* an *anrokk*," Frayvar said.

"Because that cat attacked the men?" Kaylina wasn't as skeptical as she would have been a couple of weeks ago when she'd argued that the taybarri only liked her because she had honey. Too many weird things had happened since then for her to dismiss the possibility that something about her attracted animals. That great cat had looked right at her, a far easier target than the hunters, before springing into the middle of all those armed men and dogs.

"Among other things."

Kaylina eyed her brother in the dark, but she could barely see him much less consider his expression. She hoped he wasn't implying anything about Vlerion—and the beast curse. She'd promised Vlerion that she wouldn't share his secret with Frayvar, but her smart brother figured a lot out for himself.

"I don't see why, if it's about blood, I would be an *anrokk* and you wouldn't," she pointed out.

As far as she knew, animals had never taken to her brother. Which was probably good since cats, dogs, horses, and who knew what else roused his allergies and made him sneeze.

"I don't either, but you're the only one in the family grandpa's hounds follow around faithfully."

"They follow *him* around."

"Because he feeds them, but they also trail you and, I don't know, show off for you."

"If you mean they wrestle right next to me and knock me over, that's a true honor."

"*They* probably think it is. What is that envelope the ranger left? Was that Jankarr?"

"Yes." Reminded, Kaylina drew it from under her belt and eased her pack off her shoulders. "Do you think I could risk lighting my lantern to read it?"

"It's more of a risk *not* to read it. If it offers help... we need help."

"True."

2

Even the best laid camp may suffer a branch falling upon a tent.
~ Ranger Captain Bonovar

After lighting it with a cinderrock match, Frayvar held up their small travel lantern. Its glow did little to push back the deep shadows under the trees but allowed Kaylina to examine the envelope. It did indeed read *pirate* on the front. There weren't any fancy stamps or embellishments, such as she would expect from the desk of an aristocrat.

"It doesn't smell like perfume, does it?" Frayvar asked.

"Uh, no. Should it?"

"If it's a love letter from Lord Vlerion, I thought it might." He eyed it warily as if tiny paper hearts and profusions of adoration might spring out.

"I'm sure it's not that." As Kaylina opened the envelope with her knife, she noted how many pages were folded inside. Nope, it wasn't a love letter, not unless Vlerion was as verbose as Frayvar, who couldn't pen a grocery list without turning it into an essay.

"You did kiss him."

"I thought you were behind the shed and missed that."

"I went behind the shed when it was glaringly imminent. I'm observant. I miss very little."

"Uh-huh. Well, as the girl, *I'd* be the one to put perfume on a letter I sent him. Guys don't do stuff like that." Despite the words, Kaylina sniffed surreptitiously as she drew the folded pages out.

They smelled only of parchment, maybe slightly of taybarri. That made her imagine Crenoch standing over Vlerion's shoulder and watching while the pen scrawled across the page. Could the taybarri read? All the ranger mounts were young, but they got the gist of spoken words.

"If I had a lover and sent her a letter, I might use perfume," Frayvar said. "Do you think Lady Ghara would like that?"

"No. You'd get further cooking for her."

"Hm."

"They're maps," Kaylina mused as she looked through the stack of papers. All except one page showed mazes of tunnels and caverns and burial chambers. "The catacombs under the city."

When she'd gone down there with Vlerion, she'd only gotten a look at one tunnel, a couple of alcoves, and a pool near Stillguard Castle. He'd said there were miles of passageways on different levels—and that some of the deadly traps the original builders, the Kar'ruk, had left were still viable. The idea of exploring down there held no appeal.

Kaylina opened the remaining page to find Vlerion's writing. For some reason, her belly fluttered with nerves, as if it might be the love letter Frayvar had teased her about. As she *hoped* it would be?

Her name wasn't at the top. Vlerion must have assumed it could be intercepted. The words were as aloof as he so often was when he wore his mask, determined not to let his emotions out, lest the beast be roused.

Hiding in the countryside will not allow you to do as you must, it read vaguely, though she had no trouble filling in *clear your name.* The letter continued, *With these maps, you can move about under the city and travel from place to place. Traps are few on the level closest to the streets. Do not venture deeper. The more important Kar'ruk sarcophagi are down there, and they did their best to ensure their honored dead would not be disturbed. The topmost level is patrolled infrequently but occasionally by the rangers, especially if we have a reason to believe the rebels are skulking down there. You will avoid them.*

It sounded like an order rather than a suggestion, but that didn't surprise her. Vlerion *was* a pompous lord, after all.

Venture above ground only with your face hidden. In the aftermath of the Virt assassination attempt, there are more patrols in the streets. The guards should prioritize capturing the Virt leaders, but they are aware that the queen wants you dead, and they will attack you if they see you. They will shoot to kill. Do not take undue risks. When you have obtained evidence to clear your name, seek me out. I went in search of evidence of my own and have something to add to what you are able to gather. If I did not have watchers right now, I would have already brought it to you.

Kaylina re-read the last sentence. Watchers? What *watchers* would he have? Other rangers?

Maybe he hadn't been able to convince Captain Targon of her innocence, and he was keeping an eye on Vlerion. Or… Kaylina remembered that the queen and especially Jana had been suspicious that Vlerion would do something foolish because he'd fallen for her. Maybe the queen was the one who'd ordered him watched. Would Kaylina have to clear *his* name of suspicion as well as her own?

"Is there more on the back?" Frayvar asked.

"Are you *reading* it?" Kaylina scowled at him. The way he stood ensured he had to do so upside-down, but that wouldn't faze him.

"Yeah. Why is it taking you so long?" He twirled his finger to request a page flip.

"I'm *pondering* the meaning of his words as I read."

"They're instructions and straightforward." Frayvar gave her the kind of I'm-sorry-you're-so-obtuse-because-it-must-make-your-life-difficult look that little brothers had all mastered.

Exasperated, Kaylina glared at him. "I take it back. Sprinkle perfume all over your love letters to Lady Ghara. She'll adore that."

"I believe you're being facetious."

"And to think, you say you're bad at reading people." Kaylina turned the page over, angling it so that he wouldn't be able to see it until she'd pondered all the meanings. Besides, she hoped it would finish with something more than orders and instructions. Something with more *feeling*.

But Vlerion might have gotten over his attraction for her in the days they'd been apart. That could be especially likely if it was her *anrokk*-ness that drew him rather than... Well, she didn't expect him to *love* her. They hadn't known each other that long, and he'd admitted that she irritated him with her lack of respect, but she'd thought... She thought he cared. He'd sent these maps, after all. That meant something, didn't it?

"You're not reading," Frayvar said. "We can't stay here all night. The guards and hounds will regroup and come after us."

"I am too reading," Kaylina snapped, though she hadn't been. Why were little brothers such pests?

"Your eyes weren't moving."

She wouldn't admit he was right, but she did continue to the lines on the back.

I regret that I didn't stay with you the night you fled from the city. It crossed my mind as we departed through the catacombs. As I told you, Targon ordered me to return, saying he needed my help ensuring all the rebels were gone and the threat to the king and queen was past. Honor and my duty made me comply, but... as I said, I have regretted it. As I am occasionally being observed, you will avoid ranger headquarters and not come to me unless you've gathered evidence to prove your innocence. Once you have, you will come to me, and I will stand at your side as you present it.

The pompous order shouldn't have warmed her body, making her think of their shared kiss, but it did. As did the admission of regret. He *did* care.

The word *pirate* was all he'd signed it with. It was enough. More than enough.

She rested the letter against her chest, aware of insects buzzing and chirping. Frogs also croaked now. Hopefully, the threats had disappeared from the area.

Frayvar, growing bored with her tediously slow reading and pondering, was considering the maps.

"He's circled places. I *think* this access point is by ranger headquarters. We went that way when we fled." Frayvar pointed to another. "I wonder if one of these is an access point near where Jana's meadery is. Nakeron Inn was the name, right?"

"Yes, I think she said it was in the Factory Quarter."

Frayvar nodded and tapped the circle he'd pointed out. "It looks like Lord Vlerion wants us to visit her."

"For pummeling?"

"Or *cajoling*."

"I'd rather strangle her until she tells the truth." Kaylina couldn't help but sound wistful.

"Her strangled neck can't be the evidence he wants."

"Probably not." She fished in her pocket until she found the vial of poison that Jana had brought to her dungeon cell, telling her that, if she cared about Vlerion's future and didn't want him to ruin his career on her behalf, she should use it to kill herself. "Bitch."

"Hm?" Frayvar asked.

"I want to make her drink this herself, but maybe if we could find identical vials in her inn, that would be enough evidence."

"Also, if we found the poison maker who sold it to her, he might identify her."

"You don't think she makes her own poisons?" Kaylina asked.

"I suppose she could, but she would have to have bought the ingredients somewhere, so there still might be a trail leading to a person who could point her out."

"Let's hope."

Kaylina lifted a finger, about to ask if one of the circled spots on the map suggested a way into the catacombs from outside the city walls. The access point they'd used the first night had been guarded when they'd circled back two days earlier. Even before Vlerion had sent the letter, Kaylina had planned to eventually return to the city. In addition to clearing her name, she wanted to visit Stillguard Castle to see if the plant in the tower continued to glow purple instead of red—and find out what exactly that meant.

Before she could ask about the map, she noticed that the forest had grown quiet again. Was the malikar stalking their way?

"Put out the lantern," Kaylina whispered.

Frayvar drew it protectively to his chest. "I'm studying the maps."

"Something's out here with us."

He cut out the lantern. "Something or *someone?*"

"I don't know. Ssh."

In the dark, Kaylina took the maps from him. By touch, she folded them and slipped them back into the envelope with Vlerion's letter. She tucked it under her belt. If they were attacked or had to run, she didn't want to risk losing it. The letter might have started out vague, but there were enough details that someone familiar with the rangers and the situation might guess who'd written it. If Vlerion was already under suspicion because of his association with her, Kaylina didn't want to make his predicament worse.

Ears straining, she listened for the something or *someone* the silence told her was out there. The nightlife hadn't been disturbed by her and Frayvar's presence. She felt certain something more dangerous was in the area.

Long seconds passed, and she didn't hear anything, but she caught a faint musky scent. That of a predator?

"Do you think it's safe to go back the way we came?" she whispered.

Kaylina wanted neither to spend the night in the preserve nor run into the hunters who might be waiting for them to come out. She doubted the malikar had scared them into leaving the area permanently. Unfortunately.

"No," Frayvar whispered back. "But I'm familiar with maps of the area."

"Does *familiar with* mean you've memorized them?"

"Not... entirely. But I think I could lead us to the Stillguard River. The waterway cuts through this side of the preserve on its way from the mountains to Port Jirador and the harbor. We could follow it back to the city."

"Fray, in this kind of darkness, you couldn't lead me from your bed to your closet back home. And I *know* you've memorized the layout of your room."

"Do you want to stay here and sleep under this tree with... whatever you think is out here?"

Kaylina listened to the silence again, the hair on the back of her neck standing up even though she didn't have any confirmation that danger lurked. "No."

"Okay."

She let him lead, mostly because she didn't have a better idea. *She* hadn't memorized any maps.

As they crept through the undergrowth, tripping over roots

and rocks and being whacked in the face by branches, she hoped being an *anrokk* meant that nearby animals wouldn't attack them.

After they'd traveled what felt like ten miles but was probably less than one, voices made them halt. Clipped voices with a lot of clucks, harsh noises, and tongue smacking. Kaylina didn't recognize the language.

"Those aren't animals," she whispered.

But were they humans? Zaldorian wasn't the only language spoken by men, and she'd heard others from travelers, sandsteaders, pirates, and fishermen who visited the Spitting Gull, but this sounded different.

"I... think that's the Kar'ruk language," Frayvar breathed, almost too softly to hear.

Kaylina wanted to object. There was no way Kar'ruk warriors would be this close to the kingdom capital, not when the rangers patrolled the mountain passes and borders so assiduously, but hadn't Vlerion admitted they were stretched thin right now? Thanks to the rebellion requiring they help the Kingdom Guard patrol the capital and surrounding lands?

"I've only heard it spoken aloud a couple of times," Frayvar added, "but I've seen phonetical spellings of their words in books."

"Can you understand it?"

"No."

The voices grew louder and more intense. Excited. Like they'd found something.

Kaylina swallowed. Her and Frayvar? Why would they *want* twenty-one- and seventeen-year-old human commoners?

Maybe their age and status didn't matter. If the stories she'd heard were true, the Kar'ruk would enjoy killing them simply because of their race. The horned beings hated humans because they'd long ago joined forces with the taybarri and driven them into harsher northern lands.

Kaylina gripped Frayvar's wrist and took the lead, moving

away from the voices. Unfortunately, they had to go slowly. Roots and rocks weren't the only obstacles. Thick undergrowth reached past their knees, and sometimes above their hips, and they risked making noise as they pushed their way through it. The Kar'ruk might have keen hearing or be able to see in the dark. Or both.

"*Clak drok*!" a voice called.

Kaylina glanced back as the light of a torch appeared, highlighting an eight-foot-tall figure in a chainmail tunic decorated with bones and fangs. The being had a bumpy, broad, gray-skinned face with two stubby horns thrusting from its head above its brows.

She recognized the features from the statues in the catacombs. A Kar'ruk warrior. And it, probably *he*, was chasing them.

Frayvar wheezed as he glanced back, but that didn't keep him from increasing his pace. His long legs propelled him through the undergrowth.

Kaylina raced to keep up as she groped for something they could do to escape. Negotiate? Barter? She doubted the Kar'ruk spoke Zaldorian. What were his kind *doing* here?

Not caring about stealth, the warrior crashed through the foliage, gaining on Kaylina and Frayvar.

The sound of flowing water came from ahead. Maybe Frayvar had run in the right direction, and that was the river they sought. But the Kar'ruk had them in sight. Stepping into water wouldn't do anything to shake his pursuit.

Frayvar burst onto a trail and picked up speed. Kaylina barely had time to wonder why there was a cleared path through the rarely visited preserve before he ran around a bend and cursed. They'd reached the river, but only a narrow mossy log stretched across it. He stepped onto it, arms spread for balance, and cursed again when his foot slipped.

"Is this—?"

Something sped out of the darkness and lodged in a tree scant inches from Kaylina's head. An arrow.

"The way we have to go? Yes." She didn't shove Frayvar, but she did shoo him forward as she glanced back.

Several Kar'ruk with torches and axes had come out onto the trail, and there was the bowman, readying another arrow.

Frayvar hurried across the log, but he'd only made it a third of the way before he slipped again. Kaylina lunged, trying to catch him. All she gripped was his cloak, and it didn't keep him from falling and splashing into the river. It was far deeper than the earlier stream, and he submerged fully, head disappearing among white froth.

"*Davrok noft*!"

Kaylina glanced back and spotted a nocked arrow pointed between her eyes, poised to release.

Frayvar came up downriver, sputtering as the current carried him away. An instant before the archer fired, Kaylina dove in after him.

No sooner had she submerged, icy water shocking as it enveloped her, than her shoulder struck a boulder. It sent her into a wild spin into the center of the current that swept her downstream after her brother. As she caromed off another boulder, she wondered if either of them would escape the river alive.

3

The gods blessed the world with life but also filled the moon with craters.

~ Summer Moon Priestess Tya

After the river flowed out of the preserve, it grew wider and calmer. Battered and in pain from striking her shoulder, Kaylina alternated paddling toward shore and looking for her brother.

"Frayvar?" she risked calling, hoping they'd left the authorities and the Kar'ruk far behind. "Are you there?"

Even as a strong swimmer, Kaylina struggled to pull herself out of the swift current in the center of the river. Another mile passed before she neared shore, finally snagging in a beaver dam that thrust into the waterway.

"Kay?" called Frayvar from the shadows. "Is that you?"

"No, I'm a Kar'ruk maiden who fell in love after hearing that you sprinkle perfume on letters, and I leaped into the water after you."

"Funny."

"As I always strive to be." Kaylina pushed wet hair out of her eyes and used the jumble of branches and logs to pull herself toward Frayvar and the bank.

"From what I've read, the Kar'ruk females are almost as likely to be warriors as the males, though some are holy leaders, alchemists, and sacred gatherers—that's someone who specializes in finding and collecting useful parts of altered plants." Only Frayvar could give a lesson on culture while clawing his way along a beaver dam to shore. "It's too bad the Kar'ruk were aggressive. I wish I could have asked them about their people. What humans have recorded and what's reality might not be the same. Although the primatologist Denri Morvarian, after spending a few years studying gorillas in the jungles of Egorth, lived for a time among the Kar'ruk. She's believed to be the only one who's ever been permitted to do so, likely because she became the mate of one of their chieftains. She wrote a fascinating text."

"On how to make love to a man with horns?"

"It was a scientific study of their people, culture, and social dynamics."

"I bet she learned the other thing along the way." Kaylina reached the boulder-strewn shoreline and pulled herself out of the water, then lowered a hand to help her brother.

"I suppose that could be accurate."

The snort of a horse kept Kaylina from making another comment.

"How many people are out here in the middle of the night?" she whispered.

Frayvar groaned softly and flopped down on his back. Not caring if guards found them?

After being chased by the arrow-shooting Kar'ruk, Kaylina almost wanted to return to the relative safety of a dungeon cell, but her time in the royal castle hadn't been uneventful either.

"Stay there," she whispered, though Frayvar didn't look like he would move until dawn.

His second groan sounded like compliance.

Kaylina crept up the slope, lamenting that they'd lost their lantern and pack—she hoped Vlerion wouldn't be upset that she'd lost his book as well—and peered out onto a dark field. There were enough hills that she couldn't see the city in the distance, but the map in her mind told her they had to be near the highway that followed the river toward Port Jirador and Frost Harbor.

Yes, there it was. A team of horses pulled a covered wagon along it, one a white mare that stood out even in the dark. A sleepy-looking driver with his chin to his chest rode on the bench. The wagon was heading toward the city, the team ambling at a sedate pace.

Kaylina scrambled down the slope to shake Frayvar. "Up. We're getting a ride."

"Uh? With rangers?"

"No, in a wagon."

Or maybe *under* the wagon. The back might be searched, but if they could find a way to hang on underneath, this could be their way to sneak into the city.

Not explaining further, Kaylina tugged Frayvar to his feet. He groaned again, but at least he had stopped wheezing.

"Follow me," she whispered.

They scrambled up the slope, the rush of the river and clop of horse hooves hopefully drowning out any noise they made. The wagon had passed their position and was continuing toward the city. The driver was the only person visible, and none of the weary horses flickered their ears as Kaylina and Frayvar crept closer.

The darkness and a flap hid the contents of the wagon. Kaylina hoped there wasn't an army of guards or army of *anything* sitting on benches inside.

When they caught up, they gripped the edge of the tailgate,

and Frayvar untied the flap. Kaylina started to whisper her plan to hang onto the frame and ride underneath, but Frayvar slithered over the gate and inside. Nobody shouted an alarm. Good. If they had miles to go, it would be hard to hang on from below.

Kaylina pulled herself in after her brother and winced when her shoulder struck something again. Not a boulder this time but a… what? She groped about a huge stack of papers tied together. It was one of many that filled the wagon, leaving little space for them to hunker down.

"These feel like newspapers," Frayvar whispered.

"Ssh."

They couldn't see the driver, but they were close to him now. Even a sleepy man would notice people talking behind him.

"Why would someone be taking newspapers *into* Port Jirador?" Frayvar asked. "The presses are in the city. Papers might be distributed *out* of Port Jirador—we get the *Kingdom Chronicle* all the way down in our islands, after all—but *into* it?"

Kaylina, worried her brother was musing too loudly, clasped a hand over his mouth.

Frayvar huffed but stopped talking, and they rode in silence. Her hand didn't keep him from untying one of the bundles, removing a newspaper, and stuffing it into his wet shirt.

She almost said he was stealing, since he hadn't left any coins, but the wagon was slowing down, the road noise quieting, and she dared not speak. She released Frayvar and eased aside the flap to lean out for a look. Just ahead, walls, watchtowers, and lights marked the eastern edge of the city.

A guard called out to the driver. "Stop to be searched."

Kaylina was on the verge of telling Frayvar they needed to crawl under the wagon, but he'd wedged himself into a tight space between stacks of paper. She hesitated. It wouldn't take a thorough search to find them, but maybe the guards wouldn't investigate newspapers that closely. She squeezed in beside him.

A whinny sounded, followed by a *whuff* that belonged to a taybarri instead of a horse.

Two clinks followed as the tailgate fasteners were pulled out, and it clanked down. Kaylina grimaced and sank lower, afraid the guard *was* going to investigate the newspapers closely.

The wagon bed creaked as someone climbed in. A lantern shed light over the stacks, and she slumped in defeat, certain they would be caught.

"What is it?" a man outside asked.

The bed creaked again as whoever had climbed in leaned back out. "Looks like mining equipment that needs repairs."

Kaylina frowned. What?

The taybarri *whuffed* again, and sniffing noises came from the side of the wagon.

"My mount thinks there's something interesting in there."

"Might be some food too." The bed creaked as the speaker hopped down. He secured the pins and pulled down the flap. "Maybe a rat or two."

"Taybarri aren't mousers."

"Your mount ate the label off a can of beans the other day. They don't seem that particular."

The other man—he had to be a ranger—grunted but didn't ask more questions. The wagon rolled into motion, the horses pulling it through the gate and into the city.

"Fray," Kaylina whispered. "Do you see any mining equipment in here?"

"I do not."

She left her nook and opened the flap enough to peer out. A guard leaned by the gate, lantern dangling at his side, and the back end of a taybarri was also visible, its rider out of sight.

"What's going on?" she wondered.

"Shenanigans."

"That's your educated opinion based on all the books you've read?"

"It is. For now." Frayvar rattled the newspaper he'd taken.

Yeah, Kaylina wanted to see what it said too.

With no light inside the wagon, they had to wait for it to slow again. They took the first opportunity they could to climb out, slipping into an alley without being spotted.

Kaylina, mindful of Vlerion's warning, tugged her damp hood over her head. As soon as the wagon was out of sight, and they made sure nobody was around to see them, they headed for a streetlamp.

Frayvar held the paper up to the light and read the front-page article aloud. "*Mystery Beast Slays Another Innocent Commoner. Rangers Believed to Be Responsible or Colluding with It.*"

"Beast?" Kaylina whispered, fear for Vlerion rearing up.

Had something happened to cause him to shift forms again? And to *kill* someone? Even if that had happened, why would the newspaper journalist have believed the rangers were involved?

Worry for Vlerion made Kaylina struggle to focus as her brother continued to read aloud, the words detailing how a factory worker had been killed near a canal, his throat torn open by claws. Two rangers had been spotted in the area by witnesses claiming they'd done nothing while the man had screamed. People speculated the rangers might even have brought the beast to do their killing, releasing it into an area where only commoners lived.

"*The Court Cryer.* I don't recognize this newspaper." Frayvar turned the page and skimmed through some other articles. "I've read the ones printed in the city since we've been here. This isn't as thick or professional. There was a typo in the first paragraph."

"An even worse crime than the one reported."

"It might have been put together by some small organization," Frayvar said. "Some small quasi-illiterate organization."

"I'd call you a snob, but whoever wrote that is making the rangers look bad."

"And you like them now?"

"Well, I like Vlerion. And Doctor Penderbrock."

"So, two of them."

"Yeah," Kaylina said. "I also like the taybarri."

"Me too."

"I wonder where the newspaper originated." Frayvar gazed back toward the gate.

"I don't know, but we need to show it to Vlerion. And we need to tell him about the Kar'ruk in the preserve." That might cause the rangers more concern, especially if they didn't already know that the mortal enemies of humanity were lurking so close to the capital.

"I thought we were on a mission to clear your name."

"We are, but these things are more important." Kaylina waved toward the paper, but the Kar'ruk were foremost in her mind. "They could be a threat to the entire city."

"Have you noticed how complicated our lives have become since we came north to open our meadery?"

"Grandma has always said that starting a business is hard."

4

Lust grows less restrained after dark.

~ Sandsteader proverb

Thanks to the catacombs map Vlerion had given them, Kaylina and Frayvar were able to travel underground and come up near ranger headquarters. They pushed open a hidden door that led them through an oddly warm and steamy basement lined with benches around fountains. Only when they climbed stairs to an alley exit and saw a sign for the Gentlemen's Steam and Strigil did Kaylina realize they'd been in a bathhouse.

She looked wistfully back at it, wishing they could have lingered, whether it was for *gentlemen* or not. During their trek into the city, their clothes had dried, but Kaylina still felt travel-begrimed.

"Good thing it's the middle of the night," Frayvar said, "or you might have been traumatized by a lot of sweaty male nudity."

"After being chased by Kar'ruk with bows and axes, that would be a tame trauma."

"I suppose that's true." Frayvar looked at the map. "I wonder if any catacomb exits come out in a Gentle *Ladies'* Steam and Strigil."

"Probably not. Women aren't keen on strangers wandering in from burial grounds while they're bathing."

Frayvar's grunt suggested he found that statement likely.

With their cloaks wrapped around them and their hoods up, they crept to the headquarters entrance. As they approached and Kaylina noted a ranger on duty in the gatehouse, she realized it might not be as easy to reach Vlerion as she'd anticipated. Just because Jankarr had left her a letter instead of helping the guards catch her didn't mean all the rangers were in on that plan. She didn't recognize the young face that peered toward them, eyebrows raised.

"Uhm, hi." Kaylina lifted a hand but didn't get to say more.

Heavy footsteps pounded across the courtyard toward the gate—a *lot* of them. Enough lanterns burned inside for her to make out the large blue-furred bodies of no fewer than ten taybarri thundering toward them.

"Shit." Frayvar took several steps back, as if the iron bars of the gate wouldn't stop the stampede.

He might have been right, but Kaylina recognized the taybarri in the lead and knew from the bright eyes and lolling tongues that the furred creatures didn't have attacks in mind.

The ranger on guard stared at the herd, his jaw hanging open as they halted in front of the gate. Their tails thumped against each other as they jostled to see between the bars.

"We'd like to speak with Lord Vlerion," Kaylina said.

"Is he... expecting you?" The ranger didn't take his gaze from the taybarri, as if his question might be for them.

"No, but I haven't gotten a chance to call him a pirate in days, and I suspect he's bereft."

One of the taybarri—she was fairly certain that was Crenoch

—butted the gate with his broad head, then looked expectantly at the ranger.

"Well, Vlerion's *mount* wants to see you," the ranger muttered.

Crenoch whuffed, which prompted the others to do the same. Several snouts prodded the bars.

"This is highly unorthodox."

"My name is Kaylina Korbian, and I'm training to be a ranger." Admittedly, she'd only had the *one* day of training. "It'll be okay," she assured the man.

"Oh, *you're* Captain Targon's new *anrokk*?" The ranger gave her a second look. "The one the men were talking about who started training and was dumped in the pool and, uhm." He glanced at her chest before looking away. "Never mind. They mentioned a new woman started training."

"It's good to be remembered," Kaylina muttered, wishing her boobs weren't what prompted people to do so.

"I guess you can come in. I'll take you to see Vlerion." The ranger had to push aside a number of taybarri to unlock the gate. "Though maybe you should see Captain Targon first."

Kaylina would much rather see Vlerion, but she didn't object since the ranger was opening the gate. Targon needed to hear about the Kar'ruk too.

"Whatever you think is best," she said.

As soon as Kaylina and Frayvar entered the courtyard, several taybarri sniffed her—checking her pockets, especially. She regretted that she hadn't visited her honey stash before coming. Since they hadn't stopped by Stillguard Castle, she didn't even know if her honey stash still existed.

Crenoch licked the side of her head, then pranced off across the courtyard.

"The taybarri don't get that excited about the other *anrokk*—Sergeant Jastadar," their guide mused as he led Kaylina and Frayvar in the same direction. "What's so special about you?"

"Many things." Kaylina waved airily, as if she hadn't wondered the same thing.

For some reason, her ex-boyfriend's words floated through her mind: *What is* wrong *with you? You look so normal.*

The ranger grunted dubiously as he led them into the barracks, a single long hallway with evenly spaced wooden doors to either side. Kaylina had stayed there before but hadn't seen Vlerion's room, nor had she visited Targon in his. Though maybe he lived elsewhere. Would a captain lodge in the same single-room barracks as his men?

Since the door was too narrow for the taybarri, they remained in the courtyard. That didn't keep them from crowding in front of it, as if they would wait for Kaylina's return.

Their guide led them up stairs to a second level. The doors on the long hallway were spaced farther apart than below. Maybe the senior-ranking rangers had rooms up there with more space than the newer recruits. Did Vlerion count as senior-ranking? Kaylina didn't know. He wasn't that much older than she, but when he gave orders, the other rangers all deferred to him. Even Captain Targon seemed more like Vlerion's equal than his superior.

As they approached a door near the end of the hall, grunts and groans and thumps grew audible. Kaylina slowed in confusion, and it took her a moment to realize people were having sex inside. Heat crept into her cheeks. Was this Vlerion's room? Was he...

The memory of Lady Ghara leaning against Vlerion while flirting with him flashed into Kaylina's mind. Or maybe he'd found some other woman, someone he could sate himself on without worrying about growing too emotional—too lustful—and rousing the beast.

The thought of him with someone else filled Kaylina with such distress that she almost turned and ran, notions of sharing warnings dumping from her thoughts. Vlerion hadn't promised anything to her, so it wasn't like this was a betrayal, but it felt like—

"Uhm," the ranger said. "Maybe I'll take you to see Vlerion first."

A masculine roar of satisfaction came from behind the door, and the ranger skittered back.

Of course. Targon. Kaylina felt foolish for her assumption—and how distressed she'd been. By all the moon gods, was she *falling* for Vlerion? For a man she couldn't ever be with, not unless she found a way to lift his curse?

"That sounds like a good idea." Frayvar eyed the door like a viper might come out.

Kaylina pushed her meandering thoughts away and nodded to the ranger.

He continued down the hallway, surprisingly only to the next closed door, and knocked on it. A long moment passed, and Kaylina wondered if her relief had been premature, if Vlerion might also be inside with a lover.

She snorted. It *was* the middle of the night. He might be sleeping.

Before the ranger could knock again, the door opened. Vlerion stood inside, tall, broad, powerful, and... naked except for a sheet wrapped loosely around his waist.

Gaping, Kaylina couldn't keep from glancing down and noticing he was aroused. The sheet did little to hide that.

She jerked her gaze up, embarrassed heat searing her cheeks, and looked at the room behind him, anywhere other than at his lower half. His perfectly proportioned *upper* half wasn't safe to look at either.

Vlerion grunted a surprised greeting. He couldn't have expected her to come to his door in the middle of the night. He tightened the sheet around his waist, tying a knot to keep it up, and tried to cover his groin area more effectively.

Meanwhile, Kaylina noticed a violin case leaning against the foot of his bed. There was also a bookcase filled with leather-bound tomes and a small table with a deck of cards and two chairs. A side door led to an office with a desk and two more chairs, as well as more bookcases and cabinets. Maps of the city, the North Dakmoor Sea, the surrounding lands, and the Evardor Mountains hung from the walls.

The rooms weren't that fascinating, and Kaylina caught her gaze swinging back to Vlerion. She managed to look into his blue eyes instead of... elsewhere. But they were as compelling as the rest of him.

His initial surprise shifted to something else, something more intense. He didn't seem to notice Frayvar or hear the ranger saying, "This girl, uhm, Trainee Korbian, said she needed to see you, my lord."

Vlerion's charged gaze remained on Kaylina, bringing more heat to her body, heat that had nothing to do with embarrassment.

She might have been delighted and pleased by his steamy focus, at the hint of lust in his eyes, but something more dangerous glinted there before he straightened and affixed his mask, the one that made him appear cold and aloof—the one that meant he was carefully controlling his emotions.

"Come in." Vlerion clasped Kaylina's wrist to draw her into his room and close to him, his callused palm warm, his thumb brushing her skin. The gentle gesture wasn't erotic, but it raised her gooseflesh, nonetheless, and sent a tingle of pleasure through her. "I was thinking about you," he added in a low murmur. A sultry murmur.

He looked like he wanted to pull her into an embrace, but, after hesitating, he locked his elbow instead, keeping her at arm's length. That was safer, yes, and she couldn't object, even if she longed for the hug.

Why she was so drawn to him, she didn't know. Oh, she appreciated that he'd saved her life and that he'd been watching out for and helping her, even though his captain only wanted to use her. That meant a lot, especially since he had no *reason* to help her. But she'd never been around someone who occupied her thoughts so and made her crave to be close. Maybe it was as his mother had said, and she was drawn *because* of the curse instead of in spite of it. The allure of danger. The magnetism of the beast. Did it call to the *anrokk* in her, just as something in her called to Vlerion?

"Oh?" she asked, realizing she should respond.

Before she could stop herself, she glanced down again. She shouldn't have looked or *wanted* to look, especially since the sheet didn't conceal much.

Vlerion snorted, not appearing ashamed. "Yes. *Often.*" He quirked his eyebrows and brushed her wrist with his thumb again. Gods, maybe the gesture *was* erotic. It made her glance at his bed, the blankets rumpled, and imagine what he might have been doing before she knocked.

"I didn't know nobles thought often of commoners." Kaylina strove for a casual tone, aware of her brother and the ranger in the hallway.

"Certain commoners with unique attributes can be appealing." His eyes closed to slits. "Even those who come to ranger headquarters after they've been specifically ordered not to until they've gathered sufficient evidence to clear their name. Since that letter was *just* delivered, I trust you haven't done so yet."

"I haven't, but my aching need to see you meant I couldn't obey your order."

Vlerion blinked.

Kaylina smirked.

"Your irreverence remains intact," he noted. "And your inability to say *my lord*."

"Four days doesn't change a woman much."

"No? I thought they might have been fraught." Vlerion looked down and plucked dried grass off her sleeve.

Could he tell that she'd been doused in the river? Kaylina was lucky she hadn't carried more of that beaver dam to town on her clothes.

"They were fraught," she said. "We've studied your maps, or at least Frayvar has, and we'll put them to use and do as my lord ranger has commanded."

"Good. It's appropriate to obey one's superiors."

"Yes, you've informed me often about your superiority."

His lips pressed together in disapproval. Maybe she'd taken her joking too far.

A groan wafted through the wall, the sounds from Targon's room as audible in here as they were in the hall.

Vlerion sighed. "That's another reason I prefer sleeping in the mountains while on patrol to being back in the city."

After spending a few nights on the cold ground outside, Kaylina couldn't imagine desiring that. But when Vlerion camped out alone, he wasn't in danger of anyone bestirring his emotions and arousing the beast.

"It sounds lonely," she said quietly.

"Peaceful. But one does sometimes wish for company." His fingers shifted from her wrist to trail up her forearm, nails lightly grazing her skin as he looked into her eyes.

Kaylina gazed back, captured—if not *mesmerized*—by his heated gaze.

"Uhm." Frayvar lifted the newspaper. "Should I... wait outside?"

"Yes," Vlerion said promptly, not looking at him.

"No." Kaylina didn't trust herself not to do something foolish if she was alone with Vlerion. Besides, they'd come for a reason. "My brother needs to read you a bedtime story."

"A lack of someone reading to me is not what's kept me up,"

Vlerion grumbled, but he released Kaylina and stepped back, finally looking at Frayvar. "Is that one of those new rebel-friendly papers?"

"It may be," Frayvar said. "The front-page story implicates rangers in a murder and beast-wrangling."

Vlerion's face closed up, all hints of longing and lust disappearing. He studied Frayvar, his gaze long and assessing. Kaylina realized he was trying to tell if Frayvar knew the truth about the *beast*.

Of course, she hadn't told her brother anything, but Vlerion might worry that she had. She didn't think Frayvar's face showed anything but mild puzzlement as he lifted the newspaper, but who knew what Vlerion deduced?

"Let's see it." He held out his hand.

Even though Vlerion had saved Frayvar's life, and he'd spoken well of the lord, Frayvar approached warily. He held the paper out at arm's length, as if he feared Vlerion would strike him for being the bearer of bad news. Not likely since Vlerion was an expert on not losing his temper, and Kaylina doubted he would strike an unarmed person under any circumstances. He simply accepted the paper with a nod.

"Prepare a room for the boy, Lenark," Vlerion told the ranger in the hall and waved for Frayvar to go with him.

A zing of nervous anticipation ran through Kaylina. Vlerion wanted to be alone with her.

She *knew* he couldn't plan to emulate the acts his captain was engaged in next door, but... what did he want? Not to flog her, she trusted. And he didn't seem irked that she'd disobeyed his order and come to see him. Maybe he had an idea about what was in the paper and wanted to talk to her privately about his secret. She hoped nothing had happened and that he hadn't been responsible for that death.

"Yes, my lord," the ranger said, though he was likely an aristocrat as well—most of the rangers were. "And, uhm, for her? Or will she stay..." He glanced toward the rumpled bed. "Elsewhere?"

"Prepare a room for her as well." Vlerion's gaze shifted to Kaylina. "You'll have to leave before dawn."

"Because you're being observed?"

"Unfortunately, yes. The king and queen are pleased that the rangers helped thwart the assassins, but the queen is irked that you escaped and thinks I had something to do with it."

"I was afraid of that," Kaylina said.

"She was unconscious when you were helping save her life, and the king... was too busy being senile and confused to notice you. I can't fault the king for getting old, but the situation is frustrating. You fought *with* us."

"With my elite sling skills." Kaylina appreciated that he knew she'd been fully with him and had used her modest weapon to help where she could, but she couldn't help but be self-deprecating. The taybarri she'd ridden, Levitke, had been the true battle master.

His eyelids drooped as he regarded her. The word *sultry* came to mind again. Never had she applied it to a man, and certainly not one with so many scars, but his gaze heated her again, making her wish...

Vlerion set the newspaper down and closed the door. A frisson of anticipation coursed through her, but they couldn't *do* anything. They both knew that.

Yet he stepped close, slipping his arm around her waist and pulling her into a hug as he leaned his jaw against the side of her head. "Your sling skills *are* elite. One day, you can wield a more deadly weapon if you wish, but I saw you strike the man aiming to kill me." His lips brushed the top of her ear, and she shivered with hot desire, then reached up to grip his warm bare shoulders.

"You would have done the same for me," she whispered, as if it had been nothing, but it pleased her that he'd noticed. She wanted him to know she had his back and to trust her; maybe it shouldn't have, but his opinion of her mattered more than that of the king and queen. Much more. "You *have* done the same for me. In the catacombs. In the dungeon."

"I wish I could reward you for fighting with me and keeping my secret." Vlerion nuzzled her ear, sending such delicious tingles through her that she couldn't keep from shifting closer to him. What kind of *reward* did he have in mind?

Possible answers to that question made her heart pound as much with fear as eagerness and anticipation. If he let himself go too far with her, he would turn into the beast right here in the ranger barracks. He had to worry about that too, about hurting—or killing—his own allies.

"It's possible my family is right," Vlerion murmured, releasing her and stepping back.

"That my mead is wonderful?"

"My *mother* believes that. My cousin hasn't tried it, as far as I know."

Ah, yes, the cousin who'd tattled to his mother that Vlerion had been standing close to Kaylina the first and only day of her ranger training. Standing close and lusting, apparently, though Kaylina mostly remembered him being a gentleman and covering her with a towel.

"But, as my mother said, I *am* drawn to you and have a hard time being... wise."

"Sorry," she murmured, understanding the problem perfectly. Even after he'd stepped back, she longed to close the gap between them, to slide her hands over the powerful muscles of his shoulders, to lift her mouth to his for a passionate kiss. To resist the temptation, she looked at his violin again. "If it helps, I'm drawn to you too."

"That makes it worse, because I know the night would be extraordinary."

"Until..."

He became a threat instead of a lover.

"Until," he agreed, taking another step back. "I need to put on my trousers."

No, she thought silently. "Yes," she said aloud, turning her back to give him privacy—and to keep from ogling him.

"Give me a moment." Vlerion waved her into the office, handed her the newspaper, then closed the door behind her.

She poured herself a cup of water from a jug and lit a lantern so he could peruse the story she'd only halfway heard when Frayvar read it aloud. Long moments passed, and she skimmed some of the back pages of the newspaper.

When Vlerion stepped into the office with her, he was fully clothed, his mask in place. Distant and aloof, or so she'd initially believed. Now she knew better.

He reached for the newspaper but paused and glanced toward a cabinet. "I don't dare spend time at your castle, especially after it tried to strangle Targon, but I risked stepping in long enough to grab the belongings that you left there."

"My belongings? There wasn't much after the fire in the kitchen. I got the mead out."

"Yes." Vlerion opened the cabinet door. "Your bottles are in one of our cellars with a lock on it. A few young rangers—and Doc Penderbrock—thought they could help themselves to samples. I disabused them of that notion."

"I hope you didn't beat on the doctor who's bandaged both me and my brother."

"Not too much. One wants morale to remain high among one's caregivers." Vlerion withdrew four jars of honey, the handwritten labels in Grandpa's writing.

"Oh." Kaylina had forgotten to grab those from the pantry when she'd been rescuing the mead from the root cellar. Perhaps because a broken bottle had forced her to rescue some of that mead into her stomach, which had left her mind fuzzy that night. "Thank you."

"You are welcome." It might have been the first time he'd said that.

Kaylina resisted the urge to dance around the desk to kiss him, but he appeared pleased by her beaming smile. The four jars weren't enough to make mead, but she could whip up numerous batches of honey-drop candies for people—and taybarri.

When she cleared her name and could return her focus to opening a meadery, she would have to send for more honey from her grandparents. Since they hadn't approved of this venture—or even known about it, except belatedly, thanks to the letter Frayvar had left—they might not be willing to support it. Still, she hoped they would forgive her, maybe even want to see her succeed. Since Grandpa's bees feasted on the pollen of altered plants, their honey was far superior to anything she could buy locally.

"Are you hungry?" Vlerion asked.

"Starving," Kaylina admitted.

He delved into the cabinet again and pulled out a tin of crackers along with a salami and a knife. "I can get you a real meal after this."

"That would be nice. We haven't eaten since before the guard chased us into the preserve and the Kar'ruk chased us into the river."

Vlerion dropped the salami. "The what?"

Right, she should have brought up the Kar'ruk before the newspaper. She might be more concerned about *his* wellbeing, but he would worry about the city and the kingdom first and foremost.

As she explained the night's adventures, Vlerion's mask remained in place, but his eyes grew grimmer and grimmer.

"I can't remember a time the Kar'ruk have successfully sneaked past our border patrols and watchtowers. There aren't that many ways through the mountains. They must have slipped past on the day of the assassination attempt." Vlerion shook his head, as if he couldn't believe it, but he added, "The outposts and watchtowers *were* lightly manned since we needed more people in the city." He pushed his hands through his short hair. "We'll have to figure out how many Kar'ruk got through and deal with them. I need to tell Targon." He headed for the door.

"What about the newspaper?"

Vlerion waved dismissively. "I'll read it in a minute."

Kaylina watched his back as he left, hoping he returned and took the newspaper seriously. While she didn't doubt the Kar'ruk were a threat to the city, if the real link between the rangers and the beast—between *him* and the beast—became common knowledge, it could mean his death.

5

THE MINOR DANGER WE FLIRT WITH DAILY IS FAR MORE A THREAT THAN the greater danger that is distant.

~ King Voromnar

The noises coming from Captain Targon's room had ended before Vlerion went over there, so Kaylina hoped he hadn't been forced to walk in on his boss having the good time that the curse wouldn't allow him to have. While waiting for him to return, she alternated between pacing and eating crackers. She hoped her brother had also gotten some food. Now and then, she yawned, a reminder of how little sleep she'd gotten the last few days. How little she'd gotten since they'd arrived in Port Jirador.

Exhaustion prompted her to creep into the other room and lie on Vlerion's bed, hoping he wouldn't mind. His appealing masculine scent clung to the pillow and sheets, and her mind drifted back to when she'd been in his arms. How she wished their embrace could have lasted—and turned into more.

If only she could find a way to lift his curse, they could be together without fear of repercussions. Later, she would visit Still-guard Castle and check on the plant. She couldn't help but feel the two curses were linked and that if she could solve the one in the castle, she might learn how to lift his. Then they could share his bed and do whatever they wished.

At that moment, what she *wished* must have been to fall asleep, because she dozed off snuggled under a blanket. How much time passed before quiet voices woke her, she didn't know, but the lanterns were dimmed, and she was warm for the first time in days, so she was reluctant to lift her head.

"I can't believe you have *her* in here," came Targon's voice from the office.

"I didn't realize you had *her* in there," Vlerion replied. "Had you apprised me of your scandalous intentions, I would have taken Kaylina elsewhere."

"They're not scandalous," Targon snapped.

"Uh-huh. I'll expect an article about your liaison to appear in the new underground newspaper tomorrow."

Kaylina let her eyelids droop back shut, wondering if she might reclaim sleep. She didn't want to hear about Targon's scandalous conquest.

"She left her guards outside the compound, and nobody saw under her hood," Targon said. "Not even Lenark. Had *you* not knocked on my door, you'd also have no idea she was in my room."

"The whole compound knows there was a woman in there with you."

Targon's tone turned smug when he said, "I can't help it that she was an enthusiastic lover. Far more so than you'd expect from an older woman, but she's an *experienced* older woman."

"One assumes the king chose her for a reason."

Kaylina's eyes opened. What? Were they talking about... the queen?

No, it had to be some mistress. But Targon had spoken of guards. Would a mistress have guards?

"Without a doubt." Targon still sounded smug.

Vlerion sighed.

"Forgive me. I forget that you find such matters tedious and have no interest in them."

"A lack of *interest* isn't the problem."

The men fell silent. Even though Kaylina couldn't see them from the bed, something told her they were both looking in her direction. Warmth crept into her cheeks as she began to feel she was doing something wrong by eavesdropping. Not that it was her fault they hadn't shut the door to the office.

"To have her in your bed and do nothing about it," Targon said, "you really are cursed."

"Yes. Did you finish reading this?" The newspaper rustled.

"I got the gist. It's like the others that have come out since this dubious press started publishing daily instead of weekly."

"Since the castle invasion and the assassination attempt," Vlerion said.

"Yes. Whoever's running the paper clearly wasn't pleased that their side was defeated. There are enough details that are correct in the stories about the beast that I assume some of the Virts who saw you got away to talk about it."

"Yes."

"What happened down in that dungeon? While I'm not sad that you lost it and decimated their forces—*more* than decimated them—it's unfortunate that there were witnesses. Witnesses who are now linking the beast to the rangers for the public."

"I don't remember exactly." Vlerion paused.

Was Targon giving him a skeptical look? Vlerion had said his memories of when he was a beast were fuzzy, but did that hold true for the moments before he changed? When he was still fully human?

"Kaylina was in trouble," Vlerion admitted.

"That's what I figured. Were the rebels going to maul her?"

"No. One of the guards was trying, or had at least tried, to rape her."

"Your mother is right. She's a problem for you."

Targon's tone held not a hint of empathy for Kaylina's experience, and she bared her teeth at him through the wall.

"Seeing *any* woman in that predicament would have made me lose it," Vlerion said stiffly.

"Yeah, but she makes you extra crazy. For lots of reasons."

"You're not helping."

"*You* didn't rape her after dealing with the guard, did you? As the beast? How come so many of those men got away? The beast usually kills everyone in its path."

"Of *course* I didn't do that."

"Don't give me that look. I've seen your mother's scars."

Kaylina curled her fist in the silence that followed. She was tempted to leap to her feet and rush in to defend Vlerion.

"I've done more research into your curse than you might suspect," Targon added, his voice gentler. "I know what happens when you change isn't your fault, but that doesn't keep it from being horrific."

"She's fine," Vlerion said, his tone clipped. "The men got away because there were fifty of them, and they had the common sense to run from a beast."

"I guess she wouldn't be sleeping in your bed if you'd given her a reason to be afraid of you."

"No." After a long pause, Vlerion said, "She does have reasons to be afraid, unfortunately, but not that one. Not that time."

"What about next time?"

Footsteps sounded. Vlerion pacing? "I don't know. Is that what you want me to say? I'm doing my best to make sure that the situation, the possibility, doesn't arise. I'm..." He exhaled a long breath. "I wouldn't forgive myself for that."

"What about for beheading rebels?"

"I don't like that I'm capable of *that* either, but, if you refer to the events in the castle, given what they were there for, I don't regret that."

A long moment passed, and Kaylina wished she could see their faces.

"*Are* you referring to the events in the castle?" Vlerion finally asked.

The newspaper rustled again. "You tell me."

"I didn't kill the rebels that have been found in the last couple of days if that's what you're asking."

"Are you sure? You've said you don't remember everything when you're the beast."

"I'm sure because I haven't *been* the beast. I don't forget when that happens." Vlerion's tone turned dry. "Neither does my wardrobe."

"All right. I'd just like to know. *Something* with claws is killing people in the city, and we're being blamed. Us and our beast."

"I'm aware, but I would tell you if I turned."

"Would you? In the catacombs, you didn't mention it until *after* I noticed one of the Virt bodies was missing his head. Gorily."

"Is there a non-gory way to lose one's head?"

"You know what I mean."

"I didn't deny it when you asked."

"But you didn't volunteer the information ahead of time. I got the feeling you were hoping I wouldn't notice."

Vlerion sighed. "What do you want from me, Targon?"

"Not to be blindsided. And to have your loyalty."

"You've always had it."

"You seem a little divided when it comes to her. And lately you're more... secretive."

"Targon."

"All I'm saying is that your mother has a point. Maybe you should stay away from her."

"Don't tell me you care about Kaylina."

"I care about *you,* you obtuse bastard. But I don't want to lose my *anrokk* either. Did you see her firing her sling while riding that taybarri like she'd been practicing it for years?"

The praise might have pleased Kaylina, but she well remembered how poor her aim from Levitke's back had been. She'd struggled to compensate for the taybarri's unpredictable movement.

"I *want* her as a ranger," Targon continued. "She could be one of our leaders one day. If we can get her to focus on training and not making booze. Though I did get a taste of that mead. It's damn good. Even if I hadn't believed you when you shared that wild story about the innkeeper being motivated to frame her out of fear of competition, I might have changed my mind after tasting it. I want her alive and working for the kingdom—for *us*—not dead in a river somewhere."

"I want her alive as well." Vlerion didn't comment on the rest.

"Then you should stay away from her. Help her clear her name, but don't invite her into your room. That's too much of a temptation, even for you. I'm *positive.*"

"I didn't invite her. In fact, I ordered her to stay away."

"That worked real well. You need to flog her until she brings her mouth and actions in line with what's proper for a commoner and a ranger trainee."

"Yes, I'm certain *beating* her is the way to win her allegiance."

"It's called discipline, Vlerion. Young rangers are supposed to obey their superiors."

"If I weren't being watched, I wouldn't have ordered her to stay away. After standing with us, she deserves our help in getting rid of that accusation. I don't suppose your interlude tonight changed anything about me having a watcher?"

"I'm doing my best to cement a relationship with the queen, especially since I think she may be one of her husband's puppet masters. Even as often as I report to the royal castle, it's been hard to pin down who's running the kingdom right now. He can barely remember the way to the dining hall, and the prince doesn't care about anything other than gambling, booze, and women."

"Just warn me next time there'll be *cementing* going on next door."

"The queen doesn't send me a calendar of dates and times she'll feel randy for a ranger."

"Disgusting, Targon."

"I assure you it's not, but I'm not deluded enough to think I'm the only one she visits at night."

"I can't believe she's poisoned—murdered—other women for sleeping with her husband when she does the same."

"That was years ago. *Decades* ago. Though I understand the king does still try to flirt."

"Enough. Do you want me to take a team into the preserve? If Kaylina *did* see Kar'ruk..."

"Do you doubt that she did? It's hard for me to believe they've gotten that close, especially when a sighting hasn't been reported from the watchtowers in months. You know how assiduously we guard all the access points through the mountains."

"I do, but it's hard to mistake a Kar'ruk."

"It could have been Virts in masks. I don't believe for a moment that the failed assassination attempt has stopped their scheming."

Kaylina sat up, deciding she had better join the conversation. It sounded like Targon wanted to deem her an unreliable witness and dismiss the threat.

Both men were looking at the doorway before she stepped into it, neither surprised, and she wondered if they suspected she'd been listening for a while. Vlerion had caught her eavesdropping more than once. Not that this time had been her fault.

"They spoke in a language I hadn't heard before," she said. "My brother, who's read about them and their language in books, said it was Kar'ruk before we saw them."

Skepticism narrowed Targon's eyes.

"Do you remember anything they said?" Vlerion nodded with encouragement, and she thought he wanted to believe her.

"Not… really. Something like *clak druk* when they first saw us."

"Over there," Vlerion translated, giving Targon a meaningful look.

"Huh."

"I can take Kaylina out there, find the spot where she was attacked, and look for tracks."

"The druid preserve isn't a healthy place for rangers," Targon said. "I suppose the Kar'ruk know that, and that's why they chose to lurk there."

"It's not as bad as the castle. Vines hardly ever try to kill our people out there."

"Hardly ever." Targon snorted. "It *has* happened. There's a reason we usually send the Kingdom Guard to patrol that area."

"Something that's apparently not being effective."

"I guess not."

"Horses aren't taybarri, and the guards don't have the wilderness training that we do."

"Something the Kar'ruk might have finally figured out." Targon lifted the newspaper. "You don't think *they're* behind this new press, do you?"

"Doubtful. In the past, they've been disinclined to learn even a word of our language. After all, humans are beneath them."

Targon snorted. "Must be hard getting through life being superior to everything."

Kaylina resisted the urge to roll her eyes at an aristocrat saying that. Besides, she reminded herself that Targon was a bastard and probably hadn't grown up in the same world as most of the pampered nobles.

"I'm positive the Virts are responsible for the newspaper," Vlerion said.

"It's being printed outside the city. I don't know if a press would be in the preserve, but..." Kaylina explained the wagon—and the guard who'd lied to the ranger and helped the incendiary cargo through the gate.

"Interesting," Vlerion said.

"And irritating," Targon said. "I'll go talk with that guard myself. Middle east gate, you said?"

Kaylina nodded.

"You're pretty useful, girl. I'm glad I saw your worth and decided to support you." The smugness had returned to Targon's tone, and he wore a self-congratulatory expression.

Again, Kaylina struggled to restrain an eye roll. She didn't want Targon to suggest flogging her again.

"Escort her out there to look," he told Vlerion, "but make sure to take a couple of other rangers with you."

"Because I can't be alone with her without a chaperone?" Vlerion asked.

"Because you don't want to be alone with only her sling for backup if you run into a pack of Kar'ruk. Then, after you've verified whether or not they're there, I want you to stow Korbian somewhere. *Not* your barracks room." Targon's expression turned sour as he eyed Kaylina. "Until we figure out where these clawed-up bodies are coming from, we don't need more beast sightings taking place."

Vlerion's jaw tightened, and he looked like he might object. Kaylina wanted to object to being *stowed*. But Vlerion ended up sighing and looking sadly at Kaylina before saying, "Agreed," to Targon.

"What will happen if the rebels figure out..." Kaylina extended a hand toward Vlerion and then Targon to indicate their link—the secret the ranger captain knew.

Vlerion had already said it would be problematic if his enemies learned about his curse, implying the Virts would demand he be killed for the crimes the beast had committed over the years—maybe the crimes *all* the beasts in his lineage had committed—but if people learned the rangers had been protecting his secret, the ramifications could be even greater. Not that Kaylina cared that much about the rangers. She cared about Vlerion. Still, she didn't want to see utter chaos sweep over the capital, especially if the Kar'ruk were plotting to take advantage of it. If the city and the royal castle fell, what would happen to the rest of the kingdom? Even her family far to the south could be negatively impacted.

Targon was the one to answer. "Nothing good, so keep your mouth shut about it, girl."

Kaylina bristled.

Vlerion frowned at him.

Maybe Targon decided he shouldn't be obnoxious to his *anrokk* protégé, because he softened his voice to say, "If you keep his secret, I'll make sure Levitke becomes *your* taybarri when your training has progressed far enough to earn a mount."

Kaylina almost snorted at the blatant manipulation, but she couldn't help but feel wistful as well. She was starting to love the taybarri, and riding Levitke into battle had been amazing.

"Levitke is the one who can make sure of that," Vlerion said. "Kaylina could have any mount she wants."

Targon flicked his fingers at him. "You're interfering with my bribe, a bribe I'm making for *your* sake."

"Our sakes, perhaps," Vlerion murmured.

That prompted another finger flick.

"You don't have to bribe me," Kaylina said. "I have no intention of spreading his secret around."

"Good," Targon said, as Vlerion nodded, as if he'd already known. Maybe he had. Maybe he was starting to trust her. "But you'll take a taybarri mount anyway, right?"

"Gladly," Kaylina said.

"I thought so." Targon nodded as he walked out, smug again.

"I'm sad I've never had the opportunity to hit him in the head with a sling round," Kaylina said.

"He has mentioned wanting to witness your skill with that weapon." Vlerion's eyes gleamed with rare humor as his hand drifted to the back of his head where she'd once struck him.

"He wouldn't mind if I targeted him?"

"I don't think he implied that, but it would be a way to demonstrate your ability."

"It might lead to flogging."

"Oh, most assuredly, but some punishments are worth receiving."

"Maybe *you* should crack him on the head."

"Maybe so. I'd like to let you sleep more, but it will be easier to get you out of the city without being seen if we leave before dawn." Vlerion opened his palm and raised his eyebrows. "Are you willing to go look for sign of the Kar'ruk now?"

Though Kaylina was weary and doubted she'd slept more than twenty minutes, she didn't feel she could say no. "Yes, but I might leave Frayvar here and ask him to poke around and try to figure out who's behind that newspaper. Your people don't know, right?"

Her gaze drifted to the story open on the desk, the promise that someone was trying to blame the beast—blame *Vlerion*—for murders.

"We do not," Vlerion said. "I agree that it would be better not to take the boy into what might turn into a battle."

"But you're okay taking me?"

"*You* have proven yourself."

Kaylina didn't think hitting a couple of guards using her sling counted as proving oneself, but the pleased smile Vlerion gave her filled her with warmth, maybe even pride. Even though her family was supportive in their own overly critical way, she couldn't remember many people ever telling her that she had worth. She liked it. A part of her even appreciated that Targon believed she had value, even if it was only because he wanted to use her.

Vlerion stepped forward, giving her a one-armed hug and resting his face against her hair. "One day, I would like to take a ride in the woods alone with you, but I'd best do as Targon suggests and round up a couple more rangers."

Her heart ached because she would also enjoy a private ride in the woods with him. She kept herself from leaning into him and made her tone light as she asked, "To help against the Kar'ruk or to be chaperones for us?"

Vlerion sighed. "Both."

6

The beauty of the flower, so oft protected by thorns.

~ Dainbridge III, the playwright

Kaylina kept smiling under her hood as she stroked the fur on Levitke's back, delighted to ride the spunky female taybarri again. She refused to think it was a result of Targon's bribe. When she and Vlerion had walked out of the barracks, Levitke and Crenoch had been waiting at the door, certain they would be needed tonight.

"Thank you for taking me to Stillguard Castle first, Vlerion."

Kaylina had requested that they stop by on the way out of the city. She'd almost gone earlier, but she hadn't wanted to delay getting the information about the newspapers and the Kar'ruk to the rangers. The desire to see the tower and the glowing plant hadn't been far from her mind, though, not since its strange magical light had shifted from red to purple.

Vlerion also had his hood up as they rode side by side over the bridge not far downriver from the castle, so she couldn't tell if he nodded. When he said, "There's something there you should see," he sounded grim.

That concerned her. Did it mean he would have taken her to the castle on the way whether she'd requested it or not?

"There hasn't been another fire, has there?"

"No." Vlerion glanced back.

Another taybarri with a rider was trotting to catch up with them. As they moved from the bridge to the river trail, the new arrival urged his mount to come alongside theirs.

"When Targon knocked on my door and told me to get ready and join you on a quest," Jankarr said, his hood back, "he didn't suggest you wouldn't wait for me."

"Odd," Vlerion replied.

"All these adventures you're going on without me, Vlerion. If I weren't self-assured and secure in my worth, I'd think you didn't want me around."

"You are always welcome to come along and watch my back."

"And an honor that is." Jankarr might have winked. The streetlamps only burned alongside the main roads, not the trail, so Kaylina couldn't tell. He looked toward her and bowed. "It's good to see you, person riding anonymously with Vlerion. I trust he's offered to let you watch some of his body parts, as well?"

"Body parts haven't come up," Kaylina said.

"No? I'd expect there's at least one that's up regularly around you."

Heat flushed Kaylina's cheeks as she remembered Vlerion answering the door naked.

"Did you come along to be crude, Jankarr?" Vlerion asked.

"Every chance I get." That time he *definitely* winked; Kaylina didn't need light to see it. "As a future ranger, Ms. Korbian needs to get used to the ribaldry of men. I'm helping her assimilate."

"Your kindness may make her swoon."

"Are you swooning now, Ms. Korbian?" Jankarr asked.

"Yes, I can barely contain it."

"I suspected."

They reached the back of the castle, the gate closed and the thick wall keeping the courtyard in shadows. Vlerion gave Kaylina a long look that she couldn't interpret and nudged Crenoch to lead them around to the front.

When they reached the corner tower, Kaylina peered up, wanting to see—

"What?" she blurted with disappointment. "No."

The red glow seeping through the narrow tower window had returned. After she'd poured a liquid honey-based fertilizer into the great plant's pot, its eerie red had turned to a still-mysterious but less ominous purple. She'd thought… Well, she'd *hoped* she'd found an answer to the curse.

"I rode by yesterday morning," Vlerion said. "That's when I noticed the glow had changed back."

"Was it still purple when you went inside to get my jars of honey?"

"It was."

"Maybe the change only lasts as long as the fertilizer is moist on its dirt and the plant is drawing nutrients from it."

Kaylina touched a new pack that Vlerion had given her, one carrying fresh supplies and a jar of honey. She'd left the other three in his cabinet, since they would have been heavy to tote on a journey. Vlerion had promised nobody would disturb them. Since his rooms were on the second floor, she trusted taybarri snouts couldn't reach through the window on a honey-acquisition quest.

He'd found another copy of *The Ranger's Guide to Honor, Duty, and Tenets* and inserted it into the pack along with the supplies. The book was also heavy, but he hadn't appeared amused when she'd suggested she might leave *it* undisturbed in his cabinet.

"If we have a few minutes, we can fertilize the plant again. I want to see if we can make it happy. It has to be linked to the curse on the castle." Her evidence for that was scant, but Kaylina *believed* it in her heart.

"Hm," Vlerion said noncommittally.

"It'll only take a moment." She dug in the pack and held the jar aloft.

"What is that?" Jankarr asked.

"Honey imported all the way from the Vamorka Islands."

"Are you hoping the Kar'ruk have tongues for sweets?" Jankarr asked.

"I don't usually share with people trying to shoot me full of holes, but it could come in useful on the journey."

As soon as Kaylina slid off Levitke's back, three large taybarri snouts swung toward her—toward the jar. Copious sniffing ensued.

"Useful to taybarri," Vlerion murmured.

Kaylina unscrewed the lid, but she didn't have a spoon. Since the sniffing snouts moved straight toward the jar, she put her finger in it and stuck it out for their large tongues to lick. Not long ago, she would have been terrified of having those fang-filled maws so close, but she trusted the taybarri wouldn't accidentally bite off her finger.

"That is supposed to make the *plant* happy?" Vlerion asked.

"Well, I didn't get a chance to make honey drops." Kaylina stood patiently as the taybarri slurped her finger, washing the back of her hand and halfway to her elbow in the process, but she couldn't help shifting her weight, longing to make another batch of fertilizer to try on the plant.

"Did that answer your question?" Jankarr asked Vlerion.

"I don't know."

"I'll be right back." Kaylina withdrew her hand, wiped it on her trousers, and headed for the courtyard.

"Hold." Vlerion lit a lantern and handed it to her. "Call if you need help."

"We're letting her go in there alone?" Jankarr rested his hand on the hilt of his sword.

"She's been in there alone often. The castle hasn't hurt her."

"Has it hurt *you*?"

"Ask Targon how it feels about rangers," Vlerion said.

The taybarri tried to follow Kaylina into the keep, but they couldn't fit through the doorway. She paused in the vestibule to look back at Vlerion, noting that he hadn't answered the question. *Had* the cursed castle tried to hurt him before?

Even if it hadn't, it might not be pleased that he'd helped Targon escape by cutting vines from the plant. Of course, *she'd* also helped the ranger captain escape. Would the castle remember that? And hold a grudge?

By now, whatever intelligence possessed it might have figured out that she was working with the rangers. And it didn't like people who worked with the rangers.

All she could hope was that the fertilizer had appeased it.

"The taybarri want to follow her," Jankarr noted as his mount, tongue washing blue lips, thrust his head through the doorway. Crenoch and Levitke stood right beside it.

"They like her honey," Vlerion said.

"Yes, I remember. The mead too, as I recall."

"*That* makes them pass out. They won't be dumb enough to try it again." Vlerion looked at the back of Crenoch's head.

He whuffed and sniffed indignantly.

"I'll be right back," Kaylina repeated and headed toward the kitchen.

The smell of soot from the fire lingered, and she had to step over burned debris. Once she cleared her name and could return to trying to open a meadery, she and Frayvar would have a lot of work to make the place serviceable. Again.

Bleakness crept into her at the thought of starting from scratch, especially when they'd been so close to their launch before, but it was her dream. They had to make it work. She tried not to think about how she was now helping the rangers and doing nothing toward proving her innocence.

An ominous moan came from the rooftop, something she'd once dismissed as wind blowing over the crenellations but now knew had to do with the curse. A rattling of glass followed, one of the chandeliers shaking as if in an earthquake. Kaylina hurried out from under it, reminded that one of the huge fixtures had fallen during their first night there.

She couldn't help but feel the castle was as agitated as it had ever been. Because the fertilizer had worn off? Or because she'd returned with rangers?

In the kitchen, she grabbed the same pot she'd used before. Aware of the rangers waiting, she didn't start a fire, instead doing her best to mix the honey into cold water from the well. It didn't work effectively, but she headed upstairs with the pot, a ladle, and the lantern, hoping it wouldn't matter, that the plant could take sustenance even from gloppy honey water.

"When there's more time, I'll make a proper batch," Kaylina promised the dark walls.

Another moan wafted down from above. Again, the feeling that the castle was irked with her came to mind. Hoping it was her imagination, she pressed on.

When she neared the tower, she paused to eye the section of wall that vines had erupted from to attack Targon. Nothing stuck out of the stone and mortar now, but a few shriveled husks lay on the floorboards, the pieces that Targon and Vlerion had cut.

The hole remained in the floor of the tower room, the boards Kaylina had torn free leaning against the wall. The red glow that seeped down was stronger than ever.

Belatedly, she realized she didn't have anyone to hand the pot up to her after she climbed through the opening.

As she debated calling up the rangers and putting them at risk, a thick vine slithered out of the hole to dangle not two feet from her face. She jumped back, water sloshing in the pot. The tip curled as if offering itself as a hook.

"You want the pot?" Kaylina hadn't determined if the plant fully understood her, but it had shown her not only visions of its past but some of her own memories. She had no doubt it had intelligence. "It's heavy," she warned but crept forward, lifting the handle.

The vine didn't move. She hung the pot from the end, releasing it slowly to let the plant gauge its weight. The vine proved strong enough to hold it.

She didn't know why she was surprised. The rangers had struck these vines multiple times with their swords, and only their greatest of blows had been enough to cut the dense plant matter. The *magical* plant matter, she corrected herself.

After she let go, the vine drew the pot up through the hole.

"Very magical," she murmured.

A soft clunk sounded as the plant set the pot on the floor. The vine lowered down again, its tip twitching a couple of times. In invitation?

"Guess you can't fertilize yourself, huh?" Kaylina wouldn't have minded skipping the climb up the wall, the only handholds the bent and rusty bits of iron left behind after the removal of the stairs.

The vine flicked its tip again, beckoning for her.

"Right." She set the lantern down, climbed the wall, and lunged to grip the edge of the hole. As she'd done before, she swung herself like a pendulum until she could throw her leg up and lever herself into the room.

A few dead star-shaped leaves that littered the floor fell through the hole. Nobody had been up there to disturb the plant since Kaylina's last visit, but it had grown more vines and branches. And did the leaves on those branches appear larger and more robust than before?

It hadn't been her imagination that the red glow was stronger. She could see the details of the room clearly. Already, a number of vines draped over the pot, absorbing the liquid inside.

Careful not to touch anything—the soil had zapped her before—she took the ladle and spooned the mixture over the dirt in the large pot. A soft sigh came from the plant. One of the branches shifted, a leaf brushing her cheek, its surface velvety.

"I'm glad you approve," she murmured, determined not to find it creepy that a plant was caressing her. "I don't suppose you'd like to give me a hint about how to permanently remove the..." She paused, not certain the plant *wanted* the curse removed, not if it had been left long ago by the druids to punish the rangers. "How to permanently make you happy?"

The plant didn't answer, so she ladled more liquid onto the soil, thoroughly moistening it.

"I can leave the pot here in case you want more, but the honey will settle on the bottom since I didn't get it mixed in very well. After I'm no longer a wanted criminal and can live here again, I'll make a proper fertilizer, okay?"

Kaylina returned the ladle to the pot. No sooner had she released it than a vine wrapped around her wrist, trapping her.

Alarm coursed through her veins. "Uhm, do you want more fertilizer?"

A leaf pressed against the top of her hand.

"I can give you more. There's plenty for—"

Searing pain erupted in her hand, as if someone had jammed a hot iron against her skin. Kaylina couldn't keep from screaming as she stumbled back, trying to fling herself through the hole and away from the plant.

The vine tightened around her wrist, keeping her in place. The pain intensified.

She screamed again and cried, "Vlerion!"

The vine released her so abruptly that she fell through the hole.

Cursing, she tried to twist so that she could land on her feet, but there wasn't time. She smashed to the floorboards on her side, shoulder ramming into the unyielding wood, and cried out again.

Confusion, betrayal, and anger gave her the strength to push herself to her knees. She almost knocked over the lantern. Frustrated, she was tempted to throw it through the hole at the plant, but her hand hurt too much to contemplate grabbing anything.

Footsteps thundered toward her, Vlerion with Jankarr right behind him, their swords out.

With her hand cradled to her chest, she opened her mouth to explain what had happened, but they didn't stop to ask. Vlerion swept her into his arms.

Two thick vines lowered through the hole like vipers. One of them even seemed to hiss.

Jankarr sprang at them, sword slashing as Vlerion backed away.

"Don't stay to fight," he ordered.

A vine whipped toward Jankarr's face. He ducked as he struck it, barely gouging its green flesh. "Tell that to… What *is* this thing?"

"A plant."

"There's no way it's just a *plant*. Plants don't attack people, Vlerion."

"Just back away."

The rangers retreated down the hallway, Vlerion carrying Kaylina and Jankarr swinging defensively at vines that lashed out, trying to impede them.

Kaylina lowered her hand to look at the spot where the leaf

had plastered her. It still burned, and she gaped at her darkened skin, smoke wafting from it.

Envisioning a hot iron had been appropriate. The plant had marked her with a smaller version of one of its star-shaped leaves, the tiny stem pointing between her middle knuckles.

"What happened?" Vlerion asked as he jogged down the stairs, Jankarr right behind.

"It branded me," Kaylina said numbly.

7

Threats to the herd are threats to all.

~ Elder Taybarri Seerathi

"Do you want to go back to headquarters and see the doctor?" Vlerion asked as he gently wrapped a bandage around Kaylina's hand.

It had stopped steaming, but the burn mark continued to ache. Gingerly, she flexed her fingers, grimacing as that small movement hurt.

"It'll be dawn soon, right?" Kaylina looked toward the eastern sky, Jankarr's dark outline more visible in the shadows of the courtyard than it had been a few minutes ago. They had shut the front doors—hard—and he stood guard with his sword out while the taybarri milled.

"Yes," Vlerion said.

"I'll be all right. Let's continue on to the preserve." Not only was Kaylina more at risk of being spotted under the light of day, but if the Kar'ruk were plotting something, every hour moved them closer to whatever it was. "The sooner I can show you the Kar'ruk footprints, the sooner you can hunt them down and make sure the city is safe."

Vlerion lifted his gaze to her eyes, though he still clasped her hand gently. "I understand why Targon wants you to become a ranger."

"Because he's a dick who will use anyone to further his goals?"

Vlerion snorted softly. "That's not untrue, but I meant... you have a noble heart."

"Not that noble. It's hard to open a meadery in a city being besieged by horrible horned enemies."

"Ah, of course." He kissed her on the cheek, his lips warm in the cool morning air, before releasing her.

Even though Kaylina was drawn to powerful and aloof Vlerion, gentle and encouraging Vlerion made her insides melt, especially since he didn't seem to be that way with many people. He could never risk letting his guard down—letting himself care. Maybe it would have been better if he didn't care for her either, but she couldn't wish that.

"Thank you for risking the plant's ire to come get me," she said.

"Any time." Vlerion helped her onto Levitke's back.

Jankarr mounted his taybarri and pointed to Kaylina's hand. "What does it mean?"

He'd glimpsed the brand before Vlerion bandaged it.

"I have no idea," Kaylina said as they rode out of the courtyard, her hood up again. "I *thought* the plant was pleased with me."

"It might not appreciate the company you keep," Vlerion said grimly, looking back at the tower.

It continued to glow red as they rode away. Last time, it had taken hours before the color changed, so Kaylina wouldn't yet consider this a failure, but being attacked by the plant—*marked* by the plant—filled her with doubt. She struggled not to feel this was a step backward, a step farther from lifting the curse. *Both* curses.

"What are you talking about?" Jankarr touched his chest. "*My* company is a delight."

"That vine hissed at you," Vlerion said.

"It hissed at you too."

They passed a few merchants heading to the markets with wagons of goods and fell silent. Two city guardsmen on patrol were even more cause for concern, but they nodded at the trio, murmuring, "My lords," to them, and continued on. With the cloak and hood—and *taybarri*—Kaylina must have passed as one of the rangers.

That would be harder to pull off once it got light. She was relieved when their mounts picked up speed, and one of the eastern gates came into view.

"Good hunting," one of the guards called to the rangers as they rode out.

"Do they already know about the Kar'ruk?" Kaylina asked.

"Not unless the news came from another source. That's a common farewell to rangers." Vlerion looked at her, then pointed to her pack. "It's in the book."

"I haven't read it all yet."

"Hm."

"I've been a little busy."

"Quit harassing her, Vlerion," Jankarr said. "Half the rangers haven't read that book."

"Young recruits are frequently drilled on the information within."

"Oh, I know it. I used to hide behind the vegetable cart in the dining hall whenever Sergeant Vimrok came through. He liked to pull us out of line and quiz us."

"It's remarkable that Targon believes you're an exemplary model of a commoner rising in the ranger ranks."

"I know how to suck up to him and stroke his ego."

"I'd think it would be easier to read the book," Vlerion murmured.

Kaylina agreed and vowed to continue on with the text, however dry it was, when she had time. After all, reading aloud from it had helped her calm Vlerion when he'd turned into the beast. At the least, he hadn't attacked her in any way as she'd spouted passages about good behavior for rangers.

When the city disappeared from view behind them, Kaylina let herself relax. She even dozed as the taybarri loped across the miles, their gaits more similar to wolves than horses. Vlerion and Jankarr continued to banter, occasionally including her. Whatever danger the kingdom faced, the rangers' normalcy was comforting, as if it meant *they* weren't concerned. This was work as usual for those in their profession. Given what Vlerion had to worry about every day, she was amazed he *could* manage a semblance of normalcy, though Jankarr had an easygoing manner that made people around him comfortable.

As the highway followed the river past farms and into the foothills where sheep and goats grazed, Kaylina spotted the beaver dam. She slowed Levitke and pointed out the place where she and Frayvar had climbed out of the water.

"We need to see where you fell in," Vlerion said.

"Frayvar fell in. I dove. And it's in the preserve." Kaylina pointed to the dark forest visible in the distance, the dense leaves making a verdant rug that stretched up into the mountains.

"Didn't you say the Kar'ruk were shooting at you?"

"That's why I dove in, yes. And because I didn't want to lose my brother."

"Yes, I understand." Vlerion nodded, reminding her that he *had* lost a brother, and also that he understood she had to protect hers. He'd been the one to point out that Frayvar was a motivation for her, that she found it much harder to stand up for herself than those she cared about.

They stopped talking as lands that had long ago been cleared by men gave way to the first trees of the preserve, thick oaks, pines, cedars, and other species Kaylina couldn't name. Because of the promise the druids had once extracted from humans, this forest had never been tamed by axes and plows, nor did men hunt the animals within.

Though the highway had veered away from the river to avoid the preserve, and trails were few, the sure-footed taybarri sprang over ferns, nurse logs, and boulders with ease. The waterway came in and out of view, but they never lost their way. Within the borders of the preserve, birds sang and squawked while animals called to each other, some roaring and others yipping. They didn't fall silent with the rangers' passing, not the way everything had grown quiet when the Kar'ruk had tramped through the forest.

"I think that's the log we were crossing when they opened fire." Kaylina pointed, and her eyes widened when she spotted a waterfall not far beyond it, the frothy flow plunging down a mossy cliff. Only then did she realize how lucky she and Frayvar had been after dropping into the river. Had they gone over falls along the way downstream, they might not have survived.

The taybarri slowed down, nostrils twitching, and the men looking around before dismounting. *Their* nostrils flexed too as they inhaled.

Kaylina breathed in the loamy scent of the forest and was about to ask what they smelled when she caught a musky odor. It had been in the air the night before too. She'd forgotten.

"I don't think the Kar'ruk are here now," Vlerion said, "but they *were* here."

Jankarr nodded. "I smell their trace too."

"Targon thought you saw men in masks." Vlerion looked at Kaylina and scoffed. "I knew you would not be fooled by such."

"I appreciate your faith in me." That was especially true since she felt like an idiot for letting that plant brand her. She would likely have the mark for life. Had it been a tattoo, she might not have minded carrying a touch of nature, admittedly *unnatural* nature, but the burn mark would be ugly, even after it healed.

"You two were more entertaining when you sniped at each other." Jankarr examined the ground for tracks.

"She hasn't called me *pirate* in days," Vlerion said. "I've not been moved to snipe."

"You sure it's not because she spent the night in your room last night?"

"Lenark has a big mouth."

Jankarr grinned, pointed out a broken branch, and headed into the brush.

Vlerion gave Kaylina a long-suffering look.

"I'm amazed Targon has kept *his* bedroom visitor a secret," he murmured. "The barracks have a lot of ears."

"I'm positive it wasn't a secret that he *had* a visitor."

"I'm also positive of that. It's surprising that she came to the barracks." Vlerion shook his head and joined Jankarr.

Kaylina had some experience tracking game for the Spitting Gull's menu, but she trusted the rangers were more experienced when it came to finding Kar'ruk, so she gazed around at the trees and plants as the men searched. The night before, it hadn't been light enough to get a good look at the preserve. Now, she looked for signs of... unusualness. Magic the druids had long ago embedded in some of the plants.

It didn't take long to find those signs. Here and there, vines hanging from branches twitched. There was no wind.

Whenever those vines moved, the rangers glanced warily at them. Their swords were out as they examined the ground, gradually moving away from the river and back the way the Kar'ruk had come. The taybarri also searched, sniffing at leaves and the ground.

Kaylina trailed the rangers on foot, keeping an eye on the vines whenever one was close to Vlerion or Jankarr. The preserve flora reminded her far too much of the plant in the castle, though she didn't see anything identical growing in the wild, nothing with branches and vines and star-shaped leaves.

A pitiful moan came from somewhere ahead.

Vlerion's head snapped up.

"That sounded human." Jankarr squinted into the forest, but the trees kept them from seeing far.

Like a woman, Kaylina thought. A wounded woman.

"Take us to her," Vlerion told Crenoch.

He let the taybarri lead while remaining on foot. Swords in hand, the rangers followed Crenoch and Jankarr's mount. Levitke remained with Kaylina. She gave the taybarri an appreciative pat on the shoulder as they followed the men.

More than once, Vlerion glanced back to make sure Kaylina hadn't fallen behind, but another moan sounded, pulling him in that direction.

"That woman is in pain." Jankarr broke into a run and took the lead.

"Watch for traps," Vlerion warned.

Jankarr kept running.

Also worried about traps, Kaylina drew her sling. Had that musky scent grown stronger, or was it her imagination?

Ahead of them, Jankarr halted abruptly and swore. Another moan sounded, weaker than the first.

"Hold on," Vlerion called softly. "Are there any—"

Branches rattled, and an inhuman yell—almost a roar—erupted as something big sprang out of the brush toward Jankarr.

Vlerion and Crenoch sprinted forward.

Between the tree trunks and branches in the way, Kaylina couldn't see how many enemies attacked the rangers, but Levitke and Jankarr's mount also charged into the fray.

She crept forward at a more reasonable pace, afraid to get in the way. One of the horned Kar'ruk came into view, looming two feet taller than the rangers. He swung an axe fearlessly at them, ducking between trees to avoid the snapping jaws of the taybarri. A soft blue powder coated that axe, and did it glow slightly?

Almost blurring, the blade swept toward Jankarr's head with alarming speed. He barely managed to duck and avoid it. Vlerion sprang to his side to help.

Kaylina eased closer, but she couldn't aim effectively through all the branches. And with the taybarri joining the battle, it was soon too chaotic to follow.

"I hate their damn axes," Jankarr snarled, his words the only ones among the grunts and growls of the Kar'ruk and the taybarri.

As usual, Vlerion remained silent, his face a cool mask of focus as he deflected powerful blows that could have beheaded him. That blurring axe cut a six-inch tree in half as if it were a reed. Vlerion barely reacted, even when another Kar'ruk appeared.

Beyond the battle, Kaylina glimpsed a pond in an open area, the remnants of a campfire smoldering beside the water. Behind it, three humans—two men and a woman—had been stripped of their clothing, tied to trees, and tortured. Or... killed? Someone had moaned, but none of the bound figures were moving, and at least one of the men was dead, his throat slashed open.

Kaylina shuddered. That had almost been the fate of her and Frayvar.

She lifted her sling in the hope of helping bring down the Kar'ruk, but the rangers and taybarri had the two horned warriors surrounded. That didn't mean victory was assured. With those deadly axes, the Kar'ruk kept them at bay. Crenoch roared in pain as a blade clipped his shoulder.

A vine flicked at the corner of Kaylina's vision. She whirled, realizing the forest might attack the rangers and tilt the odds in favor of the Kar'ruk.

But all that vine did was twitch a couple of times. Something *else* moved to Kaylina's left, something she wouldn't have seen if the vine hadn't drawn her eye. Half-hidden by the foliage, another Kar'ruk stood, this one raising a bow. It was the same archer who'd fired at her the night before.

Afraid the rangers hadn't seen him, Kaylina loosed a lead round before her self-preservation instincts pointed out that drawing the attention of an archer was a bad idea. Especially when her round slammed into the side of his head and... did absolutely nothing.

The Kar'ruk looked at her, giving no indication that the blow had hurt, and shifted his aim between her eyes. The dark iron arrowhead came into sharp focus across the distance.

"Archer!" Kaylina called to warn the others, then threw herself to the ground.

The arrow thudded into a tree behind her.

Branches snapped as someone charged past. Humming floated to her ears.

Vlerion. Trying not to turn into the beast at the threat to her.

"Stay down," he whispered, then returned to humming and hurled a knife, following it toward his target.

On the ground, with undergrowth all around, Kaylina lost view of him. She could only hear the archer's roar-yell as he engaged with Vlerion.

Before rising to her feet, she crawled behind a tree for cover. Somewhat protected, she risked leaning out, intending to help the rangers if she could.

One of the Kar'ruk near the camp was down, and the taybarri had a second surrounded. They'd forced him hip-deep into the pond. Jankarr had drawn a bow of his own, his arrow pointed at the enemy.

Since that portion of the battle was under control, Kaylina stepped away from the tree as thrashes and clangs came from Vlerion's skirmish. He and the Kar'ruk were within melee range now, the bow cast aside in favor of an axe. Like the other, it glowed a faint blue, leaving a trail in the air as it swept toward Vlerion's head.

He ducked, then charged in, his sword blurring as he stabbed and slashed at the Kar'ruk. His foe swung his axe down like a logger splitting wood. But Vlerion anticipated the attack and darted out of the way, lunging past the Kar'ruk and around to his back. Vlerion slipped his blade between his enemy's ribs, then launched a kick. The heavy Kar'ruk didn't fly as far as a man might, but he did stumble forward, fumbling the axe.

Vlerion sprang onto the warrior's back, legs wrapping around his torso as he gripped a horn and pulled the Kar'ruk's head back. His long sword should have been too unwieldy for throat slashing, at least from that position, but he whipped it in as if it were a dagger. As the Kar'ruk tried to buck him off, Vlerion twisted the warrior's head and sliced the blade into his thick throat, cutting deep into arteries.

"No!" Jankarr called as Vlerion's foe sank to his knees, gripping his bleeding throat.

Worried the other half of the battle wasn't as in control as she'd thought, Kaylina stepped in that direction as she raised her sling. The Kar'ruk in the pond was wobbling, not attacking. His axe slipped from his hands, and he tottered sideways, splashing into the water.

The taybarri that had surrounded the warrior whuffed uncertainly. Crenoch stepped forward and nudged the Kar'ruk with his snout. The warrior didn't react. He'd tilted onto his back and floated face up. His eyes were frozen open. In death?

"What happened?" Vlerion asked Jankarr as he came up beside Kaylina, his sword in hand, dripping blood. He looked her up and down.

"I'm fine," she said.

"Do not shoot enemies far more powerful than you."

He was right—her round hadn't done anything but draw the Kar'ruk's arrow—but she bristled at the order. "I'll *shoot* whomever I please, whenever I please, thank you very much."

Vlerion looked toward the wounded woman, then turned grave eyes toward Kaylina again as he rested a hand on her arm. The touch was light, his voice calm, if irritatingly pompous. "Not the Kar'ruk."

"You think I should stick to rangers?"

He managed a tight smile. "Targon awaits proof of your accuracy with ranged weapons."

"I can't wait to give it to him," Kaylina muttered as he walked toward Jankarr.

"I'm not sure how..." Jankarr pushed a hand through his sweaty blond hair. "But I think the Kar'ruk took his own life."

"A pill or a tooth capsule," Vlerion said. "Their scouts often carry poison into battle at the orders of their chieftains, who would rather have them die than betray secrets under torture."

"Meaning there *are* secrets to be discovered?"

"Their reason for being in our land, at the least. And how they slipped past our watchtowers."

"We need to question one." Jankarr looked toward the Kar'ruk that Vlerion had battled, but the throat cutting had been fatal.

"That's exactly what they didn't want. But maybe the woman learned something."

Kaylina joined them in the camp as they turned their attention toward the tied woman, her lip puffy, her face bruised, and blood dripping from her broken nose. The two men strung up to nearby trees were both dead. Only she had survived.

The woman turned glassy eyes toward the rangers. When Jankarr touched her shoulder and asked if she was all right, she barely stirred.

"She's in shock," he said, reaching for her bindings.

"Understandable." Vlerion checked the men for pulses before

cutting them down but shook his head. "These two were killed after being tortured."

"Or they died *because* of the torture," Jankarr said grimly.

Kaylina hung her sling on her belt and flexed her hands, feeling like she should be doing something. Being useful. But she didn't know how.

Reminded of Crenoch's wound, she went over to check on him. Blood matted his fur under the axe gouge, but he whuffed, as if to say it was nothing.

Kaylina didn't agree, but she also didn't know how to treat it. A doctor—or was there a ranger veterinarian who handled the taybarri?—would have to stitch it.

When Jankarr removed the wounded woman's bindings, her knees gave out. He caught her and held her in his arms.

"She needs a doctor," Vlerion said. "She'll have to be treated and recover before she can tell us anything."

"Are we heading back, then?" Jankarr lifted the woman to carry her to his taybarri.

"Take her to see Penderbrock." Vlerion pointed at tracks on the ground, some heading east from the camp—deeper into the preserve and toward the mountains. "There were a lot more than these Kar'ruk in the area at one point." He looked toward Kaylina.

She nodded. "We saw several last night, and there could have been a lot more."

"We should *all* go back," Jankarr said. "As delightful as Ms. Korbian smacking Kar'ruk with rocks is, she's not yet a ranger and can't help you."

Kaylina winced, disappointed by how ineffective her sling had been. Kar'ruk skulls had to be harder than human skulls.

"You need experienced men with you in case you run into more," Jankarr said when Vlerion continued to look east, his jaw set. He wanted to go after the rest of the Kar'ruk.

"You are correct that it would be smarter for Kaylina to return with you," he said, ignoring the rest of Jankarr's objection, "but you must be careful that she's not seen in the city."

"That sounds like a reason for me to stay out here with you," Kaylina told Vlerion, though she didn't truly want to remain in the preserve. She'd helped them find the tracks. Her duty was done.

Maybe she could ask Jankarr to help her locate an unguarded catacombs entrance so she could return unnoticed and start gathering evidence to prove her innocence. But he needed to get the injured woman to a doctor, not take side trips with Kaylina.

"You will return with Jankarr," Vlerion told her.

"Maybe stop giving me orders, *my lord.*" Kaylina didn't mean the honorific to sound sarcastic, but she was still bristling from his earlier command.

"You are a ranger trainee. It is your honor to dutifully obey orders from your superiors."

"Oh, bite a snake, pirate."

His tone always remained calm and detached, but his eyes narrowed at this last. He really hated that appellation, didn't he?

"Look." Kaylina lifted an apologetic hand. She didn't *want* to irk Vlerion. He was just being a stick. "I'm sorry. You're a noble ranger, not a pirate, but I didn't sign up to be your *trainee.* You were there when Targon foisted that on me, so you shouldn't have trouble remembering that. I'm a mead maker."

"Targon—"

"Can bite an even *bigger* snake," she snapped.

The woman groaned again.

Kaylina closed her mouth, regretting starting an argument while someone was injured and needed medical attention. Struggling for a reasonable tone, she said, "Jankarr needs to take her straight back. He *doesn't* need to be distracted, worrying about guards spotting me."

Vlerion clenched his jaw, a muscle ticking in his cheek. It made the scars that ran down from his eye more noticeable.

He glanced at the woman, then back at Kaylina. Annoyed with her for being difficult? Maybe, but he looked more like he was worried and wanted to get her out of danger. Maybe it had also crossed his mind that Kaylina could easily have suffered the same fate as this woman.

Jankarr cleared his throat diffidently and surprised Kaylina by suggesting, "She might be safer out here with you, Vlerion."

"Doubtful."

"Who better to protect her? You're a beast in battle." Jankarr smiled, clearly intending it as a compliment.

Vlerion looked sharply at him.

Confusion creased Jankarr's brow. Kaylina had to remind herself that Jankarr wasn't in on Vlerion's family secret and hadn't meant his comment to be literal.

"There would be many better," Vlerion said softly.

Jankarr tilted his head, further confused.

Vlerion sighed and waved in the direction of the city. "Go. Take the woman to Penderbrock, and tell Targon to round up more men and send them out to join us in the hunt. Someone will also need to collect the dead and find out who they were." He pointed at the two fallen men. "Probably people caught in the wrong place at the wrong time, but it's possible there was some significance to the Kar'ruk choosing them."

Kaylina shivered, again thinking how she and Frayvar had nearly been in the wrong place at the wrong time too. Maybe she was a fool to want to stay out here with Vlerion, but she'd helped him, damn it. He hadn't seen that archer taking aim at the back of his head. She was sure of it.

Admittedly, she wouldn't have seen the archer, either, if that vine hadn't twitched. It had been dumb luck. Even so, with enemies possibly lurking around every tree, two sets of eyes had to be better than one.

"Go," Vlerion repeated softly since Jankarr was hesitating. His tone left no room for argument.

"All right. But don't you dare get yourself killed while I'm gone."

"You'd prefer to be present to witness my death?" Vlerion helped lift the woman onto Jankarr's taybarri.

"You *know* what I mean." Jankarr climbed on behind the woman. "You're a horrible partner. You're *always* going off without me."

"After my death, you can tell Targon I requested you be assigned a more amenable soul as your next partner."

"You're a bastard."

"Yes." Vlerion swatted Jankarr's mount on the rump and waved for them to head to the city.

The taybarri blew hot air at Vlerion and swatted *him* with his tail before trotting off.

"They're not quite as domesticated as horses, are they?" Kaylina asked, hoping to stave off a return of Vlerion's ire.

Levitke waded out of the pond, leaving the dead Kar'ruk floating face up.

"The taybarri? Not in the least." Vlerion eyed Kaylina, as if he knew exactly what she was doing, but he didn't comment on it. "It's only because their elders made an alliance with humans long ago that they permit themselves to be ridden."

Levitke stopped beside Kaylina and sniffed her pack before gazing at her with imploring eyes.

"Maybe not the *only* reason." Kaylina removed the honey jar she'd opened earlier. The taybarri had helped in the battle. They deserved a reward, didn't they?

Crenoch also came over, tongue lolling out. Vlerion snorted and pulled a first-aid kit out of his pack. While Crenoch was distracted by the honey, he washed the taybarri's wound and spread some medicinal goo on it, followed by a bandage.

The taybarri licked honey from Kaylina's fingers while swishing their tails contentedly.

Vlerion walked about, checking tracks. "It looks like there's a whole war party roaming around in the preserve. The majority went that way." He pointed toward the east again. "Two went that way." His finger shifted toward the south. "And three went the way we came, toward the river. It's hard to tell how many hours ago. They may be the ones who chased you."

"Which way will *we* go? If you want Kar'ruk to question, it might be wiser to go after the smallest group." *Safer*, she added to herself.

Vlerion gazed with determination in the direction the larger group had gone, and she could tell he wanted to take out the greater threat, to protect the city and make sure whatever plot they were enacting didn't work. But he also looked at her with consideration.

She felt a twinge of guilt, certain she was ruining his plans. But he didn't need to head off alone on a suicide mission, damn it. If her being here made him choose the safer course... *good*.

"Yes. We'll wait until more rangers arrive to go after the large group." Vlerion pointed south. "Two will be easier to capture and subdue."

Easier than a whole pack, maybe, but even one Kar'ruk warrior was a handful. It was a good thing the taybarri were happy to jump into the fray to help.

If Kaylina had to continue her training—the thought of obeying every ranger who had seniority over her made her desire that like a thorn in the foot—she vowed to ask someone to teach her to use deadlier weapons. With the way her life was going, she would need them.

8

That affront we feel for another dwarfs that which we experience on our own behalf.

~ Dionadra, Essays on the Motivations of Men

The taybarri, energized by their honey sampling, had noses as good as Grandpa's hounds and followed the Kar'ruk trail without trouble while Kaylina and Vlerion rode. The axe wound didn't slow Crenoch at all, and he issued a defiant *whuff* when Vlerion asked if Crenoch wanted him to walk.

Kaylina was glad for the taybarri and their keen noses because she rarely saw tracks, even though she did keep her eyes toward the ground and the branches. Surprising for such large beings, the Kar'ruk had moved through the forest without disturbing much.

At a creek crossing, the taybarri whuffed several times and turned their long necks to look back at their riders.

"Do you know what that means?" Kaylina asked.

"They want a moment to drink and rest." Vlerion slid off Crenoch's back and checked his bandage. "They're also pointing out that we left before dawn, and they haven't had anything to eat for hours, aside from the small bit of honey they licked off your fingers."

"You got all that from three whuffs?" Trusting his interpretation, Kaylina also slid to the ground.

"I did."

The taybarri leaped into the creek, tails splashing the water with enthusiasm as they lapped up the cool water. Refreshed, they nipped playfully at each other, and Levitke rolled onto her back in a deeper pool.

"I guess your interpretation is correct," Kaylina said.

"I've had plenty of experience with taybarri." Vlerion kept an eye on their surroundings as he removed his pack and pulled out some of the protein pellets the rangers fed their mounts.

The musky scent had faded from the air. Kaylina hoped that meant there weren't any Kar'ruk lurking, waiting to spring a trap.

"You've mentioned that there's a treaty between the taybarri and the rangers from way back," she said. "How was that created when they mostly whuff and growl?"

"The elders understand Zaldorian, and they have a language of their own as well. The whuffs and growls have meaning, but the taybarri also speak directly into each other's minds. And *our* minds when they're so inclined."

Kaylina touched her temple with wonder. "How is that possible? Magic?"

"They are inherently magical beings. Scholars debate whether the druids altered their kind to grant them that or if they existed in the world before the druids ever arrived."

"Have you had one speak to you before? In your head?"

"Yes. It can be disconcerting because they also can hear your replies whether you say them aloud or not, which implies they can read minds."

Kaylina remembered the plant plucking memories from her head. That had been more than disconcerting. It had been creepy.

"It's possible the young ones can to some extent too," Vlerion added. "I've never been certain."

"Do the Kar'ruk have magic too? Those axes... There was something on them, right? Or can they make special metal?" Kaylina thought she recalled reading about magical Kar'ruk weapons before—or maybe Frayvar had shared that tidbit from one of his books.

"Your first guess is correct. From axes and tools that we've collected from fallen Kar'ruk, we know there's a powder they apply to them, presumably from an altered plant. They apply it wet, and when it dries, it sticks and is hard to scrape off. We know the powder gives the weapons greater strength and a keener edge, but it's possible there are other attributes as well. What we don't know is what plant it comes from. That's a secret the Kar'ruk hold close. We've tried to learn it for a long time."

"Maybe if I could coat my lead rounds in magical powder, they'd hurt more when they hit Kar'ruk skulls."

"Maybe if you continued your ranger training, we could give you a bow or crossbow and teach you to use it."

"My schedule has been full lately. You'd be amazed how much time running for your life occupies."

She'd meant it as a joke, but he didn't smile.

"I should have sent you back with Jankarr. And your brother should be seeking evidence to remove suspicion from you, not researching newspaper proprietors."

"You're not my keeper. And you know why I stayed."

Vlerion arched an eyebrow. "My allure?"

"Your allure is the reason I *shouldn't* have stayed. I was thinking of all the people in the city who want to capture or kill me."

"Hm."

"Don't worry; if I know my brother, he's researching a *lot* of things. He'll probably have written a journal on it all by the time we get back." Kaylina held her thumb and forefinger up to indicate the thickness of the hypothetical journal.

When the taybarri stepped out of the creek, water dripping from their blue fur, Vlerion poured a pile of protein pellets for each of them.

Crenoch eyed his, eyed Levitke's, then sniffed Vlerion's pockets, searching for something more interesting.

"*I* don't have any honey treats." He tapped what was presumably an empty pocket. "Sweets are bad for your teeth."

Crenoch bared his fangs and flapped his tongue at Vlerion. Kaylina decided having the taybarri read her mind might not be as creepy as the plant doing it. Thus far, the *taybarri* hadn't tried to kill any rangers.

"I do have this. I'd forgotten." Vlerion withdrew a small item from his pocket and came to Kaylina's side. He opened his palm to reveal an empty glass vial with a stopper.

She recognized it. For a confused moment, she thought she'd lost the vial of poison Jana had left in the dungeon and that Vlerion had somehow found it. But when she patted her pocket, she felt the tiny bulge and extracted it. *Hers* was full of purple liquid. Kaylina hadn't removed the stopper at any point, not wanting to risk sniffing the poison.

"Where did you get that?" Vlerion asked.

"Jana thoughtfully brought it to my dungeon and suggested I kill myself with it so you wouldn't do something foolish on my behalf that would ruin your career."

Vlerion's face froze, his jaw clenching. Kaylina hadn't shared that information with him before—perhaps with good reason.

"I should have *killed* her instead of snooping in her inn." The dangerous glint appeared in his blue eyes, the promise that the beast lurked near the surface.

Under other circumstances, Kaylina would have been touched

that he cared enough to feel affronted on her behalf, but they were alone in the forest, with only the taybarri around if he turned into the beast.

"Do you want me to hum to you?" She rested a hand on his shoulder, hoping to help calm him, but maybe touching wasn't a good idea since that tended to rouse *other* emotions in him. "I'll have to get you to teach me your song. I doubt I could replicate it based on the snatches of humming I've heard."

Vlerion closed his eyes and took several long slow breaths. "I don't know if that would work, but I'll play it for you one day on my violin. There are lyrics too, though I don't have the voice that my brother had."

"Is yours more pompous and gruff?" Kaylina didn't know if teasing him was a good way to calm his riled emotions, but it had to be less incendiary than him mulling over murdering Jana.

Vlerion opened his eyes but only so he could squint at her. "As a mead maker and gatherer of honey, you of all people ought to know better than to poke a wasp's nest."

"I avoid wasp nests, generally. Some species can make honey but not very much. They don't store it as food for the winter. They mostly nosh on other insects to stave off hunger." Kaylina pointed at the empty vial in his hand. "You searched Nakeron Inn?"

"The office, yes. I thought I might find evidence that could help you clear your name. I didn't know you already had a vial of her poison." The coolness returned to his gaze as he regarded it. At least the dangerous glint had faded. "There's a maker's mark on the bottom of this." He rotated the empty vial to show her. "Does that one have the same?"

Kaylina turned hers toward the dappled sunlight creeping through the leaves overhead. "Yes."

"When we finish here, you or your brother can seek out the glassmaker. He or she might be able to point you to whomever buys the vials. Poison makers don't hang out signs, so they're hard to find.

They're usually alchemists and apothecaries, doing that at night while practicing their more respectable trades during the day."

"Thank you." Kaylina took the empty vial and tucked it in another pocket.

"It crossed my mind to grab Jana Bloomlong by the neck while I was there and threaten her life if she didn't go to the queen and tell the truth, but the ranger handbook forbids dishonorable conduct like coercion, blackmail, and extortion."

"And wringing old ladies' necks?"

"That's not mentioned specifically, but it falls under the other categories."

"Good. Books should imply a need for respectable behavior."

"Yes." Vlerion sighed. "I suggested she be brought to ranger headquarters and questioned under kafdari root, but Targon balked at the idea. The queen absolutely would have. Even though Bloomlong isn't a noble, she's run her inn and served her mead to the royal family for years, if not decades. As Targon pointed out, it's not acceptable to force respected citizens to chew kafdari root."

"But it's okay to stuff wads of it into the mouths of visitors from another part of the kingdom?"

"You did consent to that."

"As if I had a choice when I was going to otherwise be a prisoner in jail indefinitely."

Vlerion tilted his palm toward the canopy and didn't deny that.

"Either way, I can't break any laws or even customs right now. I'm suspect in the queen's eyes, and that could get even worse. So far, that newspaper has been vague about the origins of *the beast* supposedly working with the rangers, but I can't assume the Virts don't know my secret. I need to tread lightly."

"I understand, and I'm sorry that you're... suspect, as you said, because of me. I didn't mean to get in trouble like this and certainly not to drag you into it with me."

"You don't deserve to be in trouble for wanting to open a meadery." Vlerion managed a faint smile. "Perhaps for calling aristocrats pirates, but that's another matter."

"I only call *you* that."

"Such an honor you bestow on me."

"Yes." She kissed him on the cheek, ignoring his sarcasm. "I'm glad you realize that."

Vlerion drew her into a hug. "You've an amazing knack for irritating a man while simultaneously driving him to reckless actions out of a desire to protect you."

"I'd say I've practiced a lot, but there haven't been that many men. Until I met you, only those who were related to me and obligated by blood would have gotten reckless on my behalf."

"Not the man you spoke of who asked why you weren't normal?" Vlerion leaned back, looking at her as he raised his eyebrows.

"I don't think so. For a while, I thought I was happier with him, that I needed to be in a relationship like all my other female friends, but, in hindsight, I think he just wanted to have sex with me." Kaylina wrinkled her nose.

"I suspect *many* men have wanted that."

"That's not as appealing as guys seem to think."

"No? What *is* appealing?"

"Having men respect you and not order you around."

"It is easier to have sex with women."

"I'm sure."

But it wasn't for him. Not with the possible repercussions.

Maybe that thought came to his mind, because Vlerion sighed, released her, and stepped back.

Crenoch whuffed. The taybarri had finished their piles of pellets, and both their snouts pointed toward the trail.

"We're ready to continue on." Vlerion waved for Kaylina to

follow Crenoch and Levitke, and he walked behind her, keeping her protectively between the strong taybarri and his sword arm.

She didn't mind him wanting to keep her safe, but she *did* worry that seeing her in danger would bring out the beast. She supposed it wouldn't be the worst thing if he was surrounded by Kar'ruk when it happened and could use all that deadly strength against enemies of the kingdom. But if he attacked her or the innocent taybarri... that would be horrific—if not fatal. She knew he wouldn't forgive himself for either crime.

9

A MYSTERY ENTICES LIKE THE KNOWN NEVER CAN.
~ Lord General Menok

Hours passed, and the day grew warmer as Kaylina and Vlerion clambered through the preserve on the trail of the Kar'ruk. The taybarri, faithfully tracking their enemies across the miles, picked up their pace.

Kaylina, who'd alternated walking behind and riding on Levitke, looked around, realizing she'd been daydreaming, if not dozing. The scant minutes of sleep she'd gotten in Vlerion's bed the night before hadn't been refreshing, and her eyes were gritty with fatigue.

Earlier, he'd sung to her, his voice far more appealing than he'd implied, so she could learn the lyrics of his song of soothing. Unfortunately, its pleasant notes and his rich voice had turned it into a lullaby, prompting her to doze, and she didn't remember the words.

As the taybarri loped through the trees, Vlerion sniffed the air. Trying to detect the telltale musky scent of the Kar'ruk?

Throughout the day, they hadn't caught any glimpses of the two warriors they'd been following. More than once, Kaylina had seen Vlerion look back, as if wishing he'd gone after the main group. It was possible these two were deliberately leading them away from their comrades, from the core of whatever plot the Kar'ruk were enacting.

"With luck, the rangers have reached that camp by now and are on the trail of the larger group," Vlerion mused.

Crenoch and Levitke whuffed and increased their pace again. Vlerion turned his focus forward.

Kaylina touched her sling, but she didn't smell anything other than growing vegetation and a few early spring flowers blooming. Ahead, the forest thinned, and she wondered if they were coming out of the preserve.

No, they had reached a lake that spread along the floor of a valley, the banks thick with trees aside from a couple of pebbly beaches allowing access. At the far end, a waterfall flowed into the clear blue lake. At the closer end, reeds rose up around lily pads. Beyond the walls of the valley, the snow-smothered Evardor peaks were visible. Geese and other waterfowl Kaylina couldn't name floated near the lilies, dipping their beaks in for food.

The view was beautiful, and, for some reason, it was also familiar.

"Huh," Vlerion said from Crenoch's back as the two taybarri headed for one of the beaches.

"Have you been here before?" Kaylina peered around for threats, but it looked like the taybarri had momentarily forgotten their tracking mission and wanted a drink and a swim, much as they had at the creek. Indeed, they padded straight into the lake, stout tails swishing across the surface.

"Not personally, but the artist who did my brother's painting must have been here." Vlerion looked around, his gaze lingering on the waterfall.

Yes, Kaylina realized with a jolt. *That* was where she'd seen this lake before. On a wall in the hallway of Vlerion's estate. His mother had said the painting had been created to honor her fallen son, Vlarek.

"The real Lake of Sorrow and Triumph, that which inspired my brother's song and is loosely tied to historical events, is in the Southern Evardor mountains, near the Pass of Tears, hundreds of miles from here. Halfway to your islands, in fact."

"That's the name of the song you're teaching me, right? That you hum."

"Teaching you? You fell asleep every time I sang it."

"Because your voice is soothing. You should be honored that it lulled me so."

"There was snoring."

"A gentleman doesn't point out if a woman makes noise in her sleep."

"Once, there was drooling."

Kaylina stuck her tongue out at him.

"To answer your question, yes, it's one of several songs that I hum. The others are more calming—one is a lullaby. My brother's tale is haunting, though parts are up-lifting. As you might have caught in between snores, it speaks of what the lake saw over the millennia of its existence, especially witnessing the history of man. The triumph part tells of when men first banded together to carve out a place for themselves against the Kar'ruk and the great predators that dominated the fertile coastal lands." Vlerion turned slow circles, peering into the distant banks and surrounding forests for enemies as he spoke. "Our ancestors overcame great odds by merging their tribes and learning from each other. But later, once their enemies were at bay, they turned on each other. As you may know from your history books, the kingdom has risen and fallen numerous times. When men squabbled among men, all that they'd achieved disintegrated into chaos until outside threats imposed themselves, forcing humans to work together again. The song speaks of the cycles and of how it seems impossible for our kind to ever be content and achieve lasting peace among ourselves."

Kaylina nodded, having gotten the gist from the lyrics. She hadn't been *entirely* asleep.

"It is haunting," she agreed. Or maybe depressing was the word. "I'm surprised it brings you calm when the beast encroaches."

"It's not so much because of the history or the lyrics but because my brother wrote it, and it has meaning to me. And it's a lesson. On many topics. I'll play it on the violin for you when we return to ranger headquarters so you can get more of a feel for the beauty of it." Vlerion hesitated. "When it's *safe* for you to return with me."

Kaylina smiled at the thought of him playing, but, in a moment of fatigue-induced defeat, she wondered if it would ever be safe for her to return to the barracks with him. Even if she cleared her name, the beast remained a threat. Her failure to change the plant at the castle filled her with anxiety about lifting his curse. She'd been naive to think she could do what all the men in his family, generations of his ancestors, had researched and failed to do.

"I suppose if I'd thought about it," Vlerion mused, looking toward the lake again, "I would have known the vegetation and mountains in the painting were local, not from a lake a thousand miles to the south, but I didn't contemplate it deeply. I assumed it was a fictional depiction of the real Lake of Sorrow and Triumph."

Movement at the corner of Kaylina's eye made her spin, her hand dropping to her sling. No breeze stirred, but a vine twitched farther inland, dangling not from a branch but a large rectangular rock. There were *numerous* slabs of rock jumbled about the area, barely discernible due to moss and vines smothering them.

"Are those natural?" she wondered.

Vlerion followed her gaze. "There are Daygarii ruins in the preserve. Those might be some of them."

"Did any of your ancestors ever visit them?"

The vine twitched again.

Vlerion squinted at it. "I cannot know all of my ancestors' actions, but, as I said before, the rangers are not welcome in the preserve, so I've never come here. I doubt my brother did either."

"Maybe there are clues in the ruins. Information the druids left behind that might share how to lift curses." The thought pushed aside Kaylina's earlier feeling of defeat and rekindled hope. "Did they have a written language?"

"I don't know. A lot of humanity's previous knowledge about the Daygarii has been forgotten. Some say the druids, before leaving our world, destroyed our records pertaining to their kind. The taybarri elders would be the ones to ask, as their people have long lives and genetic memories that can't be destroyed except in death. The elders, however, only appear and communicate with men when they wish to do so. People who seek them out usually only find vacated tunnels and lairs."

Kaylina wished she'd brought Frayvar instead of asking him to research newspapers in the city. Maybe if she found hieroglyphs or something else the druids had left behind, she could draw pictures to show him later. Except she hadn't brought any paper.

"I'm going to take a look." If she found something, they could come back later.

She'd only taken two steps before Vlerion gripped her shoulder to stop her.

"Even those who aren't cursed are wise to avoid druid ruins. They did not like humanity." He pointed toward the still-twitching vine.

"Don't you think it's worth the risk of looking if it could help you?" Kaylina admitted it was unlikely anything applicable to his curse could be found in a jumble of rocks, but if she could learn more in general about the ancient druids, might it not help her discover a solution for him?

"No," Vlerion stated.

"No?"

"No."

"But imagine..." Kaylina spread her arms, brushing off Vlerion's grip, as if she were about to describe one of her visions about the success of her meadery. Instead of goblets of honey wine, she saw the druids. Oh, they were nebulous since she didn't know what they'd looked like, but they moved about on the banks in a time when these ruins had been a seat of civilization for them, a place where they lived near and interacted with the wildness. "If this was a home for them, they might have kept records of what they saw and did, and who they were as a people. Some could remain. There could be libraries hidden here, libraries full of knowledge, and maybe ancient books all about curses—and how to lift them."

"In that jumble of mossy rocks, a library."

"Sure, why not?"

One of the taybarri whuffed and stepped out of the water, nose turning into a breeze. Vlerion also sniffed the air.

Kaylina didn't smell the musky odor of the Kar'ruk but trusted the taybarri had better senses and might have caught something. What she *did* smell was intense floral scents that reminded her of the islands back home where the bees foraged on wildflowers. *Altered* wildflowers that grew vigorously despite the surrounding saltwater and the hurricanes that swept through.

A hint of a glow by the ruins drew her in that direction. In the shadow of one of the stone slabs, a flower reminiscent of lavender emitted a soft violet light. Beautiful. She longed to touch it.

"Kaylina," Vlerion said, a warning in his tone.

"Kar'ruk?" She turned toward him.

Vlerion was watching her, not their surroundings. "Possibly. *Likely*. But you need to stay away from those ruins. If there *was* a library, it wasn't meant for human eyes, and that flower is glowing."

"Yes, isn't it beautiful?"

Kaylina did stop walking toward it, as she didn't recall deciding to do so, and that made her uneasy. Most of the altered flowers back home had medicinal or culinary uses. Having magic that was dangerous was rare. She had, however, heard of altered plants elsewhere that would defend themselves from perceived threats, animal, human, or otherwise.

"It could be poisonous." Vlerion beckoned for her to return to the beach.

The tip of the vine that had been twitching earlier rose up and flicked in his direction.

Yeah, he was right. This place wasn't safe. Yet...

As Kaylina headed toward the beach with him, she couldn't help but look wistfully at the ruins, believing they held answers.

Before she'd taken more than a few steps, the back of her hand warmed. She halted and stared down at the bandage. It didn't hurt the way it had when the plant branded her, but that mark was doing *something*. It itched a little, like it was healing, but the warmth was strange. It couldn't have gotten infected, could it?

"Are you all right?" Vlerion stepped in front of her, and she jumped.

Distracted by her hand, she hadn't noticed him returning to her. She shook her head at her inattentiveness—a Kar'ruk could have sprung out and lopped her head off. "Yes. But my hand is being weird."

Kaylina was tempted to remove the bandage and look.

"*Only* your hand?" He cocked an eyebrow.

She squinted at him. "You're not going to ask me why I can't be more *normal*, are you?"

His other eyebrow went up. "No. If you were normal, you wouldn't want anything to do with me."

"That can't be true. I've seen women throw themselves at you." Maybe she'd only seen Lady Ghara do that, but she trusted there had been others. Even his mother had said the beast gave a man an inexplicable allure.

"None who know what I am and all that it entails." Vlerion took her hand gently. "How is it being weird?"

"It's warm. Intensely so. And it just started." For some reason, Kaylina felt compelled to look at the vine again.

Its tip turned toward them, as if it was *watching* them. A week ago, she would have called herself crazy for thinking something like that, but after her encounters with the plant in the castle, she wasn't quick to dismiss anything.

"Let's see." Vlerion carefully unwrapped the bandage.

Kaylina held her breath, thoughts that it might have grown infected returning. That didn't usually happen so quickly, but who knew what the rules were when dealing with magical cursed plants? The fear that her hand might have to be amputated made her close her eyes and look away as the bandage loosened.

"It's healed quickly," Vlerion said.

"What?" She turned back, hoping that meant the mark had disappeared. It hadn't. The star-shaped leaf brand remained, but it now looked like a scar she'd had for years instead of hours. That was better than an infection that could spread and kill her, but... She slumped against Vlerion. "Am I going to have this forever? Because I poured honey on a plant that I thought *liked* it?"

He wrapped his arms around her. "It does look permanent, but it may fade over time."

"What is *wrong* with the north, Vlerion? Innocent people get accused of crimes left and right, and glowing sentient *plants* attack when you least expect it." Kaylina reminded herself that Targon had almost been killed by that plant, so she shouldn't whine, but she struggled not to feel sorry for herself. To feel exhausted and defeated. If not for Vlerion and a desire to help him, she might have grabbed Frayvar days ago and stowed away on a ship heading south, even if it meant returning to her family a failure. She regretted all the times she'd snapped at them, and she missed their camaraderie and predictability. These days, her life was far from predictable.

"The north is not an easy place," Vlerion said.

He *could* have pointed out that she'd brought at least some of her trouble on herself by insisting on leasing that awful cursed castle, but he didn't. He merely held her and offered his support. It touched her so much that she teared up and had to wipe her eyes surreptitiously on his leather armor.

"You're a good man, Vlerion. Even if your boss is an ass. And you're sometimes uptight and haughty."

"You've an interesting way of complimenting people."

"It's my island charm." Her hand warmed again, and she scowled at it.

The vine she felt was watching them made another flicking motion at Vlerion. When it shifted toward her, the motion changed.

"Is it my imagination or is that vine beckoning to me?" she asked.

Vlerion glared dourly at it. "If it's beckoning, it wants you to step into a trap."

Kaylina bit her lip, less certain. "Let me try something."

His eyes closed to slits, but he released her. She took a few steps toward the ruins. Her hand cooled. She moved toward him again. It heated up.

"Something's going on," she said.

"Yes. We're tracking the Kar'ruk." Vlerion turned toward the taybarri, who were watching them instead of sniffing the air. "Which way, Crenoch? There are prints all along the shoreline."

Kaylina gazed into the ruins, longing to investigate, but she had no idea if her hand would lead her to something useful or to her death.

Crenoch and Levitke ambled over. They sniffed Kaylina's pockets, and Crenoch licked her hand. The brand. A coincidence? Or did the taybarri know something?

"Does that mean you're on strike until she gives you more honey?" Vlerion asked them.

Levitke sashayed toward the ruins.

"The Kar'ruk did *not* go in there." Vlerion shot an exasperated look at Kaylina, as if the actions of their wayward mounts were her fault.

Crenoch placed a paw next to a faint indention in a patch of bare earth.

"Is that a footprint?" Vlerion asked. "Moon craters, maybe the Kar'ruk did go in there."

"I'll check," Kaylina said.

Vlerion drew his sword and raised a hand, indicating he would go first.

She pointed at the animated vine. It hadn't reacted to the taybarri ambling past, but that didn't mean it would appreciate Vlerion entering the ruins.

"It might attack you," she said.

"Then I'll lop it in half," he growled.

"Let me investigate, and I'll call out if I get in trouble. Then you can spring in and nobly save me from the Kar'ruk or the ruins or the vines—whatever turns dastardly."

Vlerion sighed. "I'll check the bank more thoroughly. With as many prints as there are, I think other Kar'ruk joined the ones we were tracking. Either that, or they danced up and down the shoreline like drunken nobles at a festival." Back stiff, he walked toward the lake.

Kaylina looked at Crenoch. "I'm not sure if he agreed with my plan or not."

The taybarri licked her face with his large tongue.

"You'd agree with anything that might get you some honey."

He whuffed.

Since Levitke was already wandering among the ruins and nothing had happened, Kaylina headed after her. She would only poke around for a few minutes, and she would be careful in case the Kar'ruk had set traps.

Of course, if they had wanted to deter pursuers, they would have laid traps along the shoreline, where thirsty rangers might stop to fill their canteens. If the Kar'ruk knew how the druids had felt about humans, they would have assumed rangers wouldn't go anywhere near the ruins. If anything, a former druid village would be a place the Kar'ruk might camp, believing humans wouldn't disturb them in there.

The thought made Kaylina halt and eye the moss-covered slabs of rock warily. But she didn't smell any musky odors, and Levitke was ambling about without concern. Kaylina didn't think any Kar'ruk were there, at least not now. Her hand remained cool, almost soothingly so, as she headed deeper into the ruins.

Ahead, stone benches rose up a slope in a semi-circle that overlooked the lake and a flat, cleared area among the ruins. An amphitheater of sorts?

In the cleared area, Kaylina spotted large footprints. Levitke sniffed them, then swished her tail as she gazed about.

"Do you think there's anything useful in here that could help me learn how to remove curses?" Kaylina didn't expect her to respond in any way, but the taybarri brushed her tail over the ground, wiping out a couple of footprints. What did that mean?

Next, Levitke ambled past the benches and toward rectangular stone formations that reminded Kaylina of raised garden beds. Flowers heady with unfamiliar scents grew inside and outside of their borders. The taybarri's tail brushed some plants, and orange pollen wafted into the air.

Levitke stopped in one formation and placed her foot on something. She wiped it side to side, her claws scraping on stone or metal as she brushed away dirt.

Kaylina joined her. It was a plaque. Though it was as weathered and pitted as the stone slabs, runes were visible on it, the first sign of writing.

"Did you know this was here? Have you been here before?"

Levitke whuffed, then wandered into the flowers and squatted to pee on them.

"I have no idea how to interpret that response."

Levitke whuffed again, tail batting more pollen into the air. It tickled Kaylina's nostrils, and she sneezed. The cloying stuff lingered in her nose and made her skin tingle.

"Tingly nostrils. Just what one wants." Kaylina knelt and brushed more dirt off the plaque. "If I had paper and some charcoal, I could make a rubbing. But all I've got is the ranger book." She glanced toward the lake, but enough ruins blocked the view that she couldn't see Vlerion. She did glimpse the tip of Crenoch's blue tail swishing about and trusted his rider wasn't far. "If Vlerion is looking at tracks, he might not notice a touch of book blasphemy, right?"

As she eased off her pack, Levitke moved into a different patch of flowers and rolled on her back like a hound. She swished from side to side, this time sending yellow pollen into the air.

"You like this place, huh?" Kaylina pulled out the ranger book and checked for blank pages. "The title page might do, but I don't have charcoal for a rubbing." She eyed the pollen dusting the area —thanks to Levitke's rolling it was all over the nearby stones. "I don't know if that'll be waxy enough, but let's try."

After making sure Vlerion couldn't see her, and wouldn't notice her destroying his book, Kaylina carefully tore out the title page and laid it over the raised runes. She swept pollen from the rocks into her palm, then spread it over the paper. She used the binding of the book to rub over the page, pressing and trying to get the pollen to stick to the paper. It worked better than she expected.

"It's sticking to my nostrils, so why not," she murmured and raised the page, blowing off loose pollen.

Levitke padded over.

"What do you think?"

The taybarri snorted, her hot breath blowing across the page.

"Yeah, it probably won't help Frayvar or whoever knows how to read this language, but you never know." Kaylina tucked the page back into the book to protect her rubbing and returned it to her pack. Someone else had probably done this long ago with professional rubbing materials. For all she knew, every library in Port Jirador had copies of the plaque with translations. Even though it felt like they were out in the middle of nowhere, it couldn't be more than ten or fifteen miles back to the city.

One of the plants that Levitke had rolled in straightened its stalk, its bulbous flower rising up and rotating toward the lake. Several others did the same. They looked like a herd of animals lifting their heads because they'd detected a predator approaching.

Levitke whined and pawed at her ears with one limb while her other three carried her away from the flowers. She hid behind a stone slab.

"Vlerion?" Kaylina couldn't hear anything, but maybe the taybarri could. Something that bothered her ears? "Are you doing something… offensive?"

"I'm looking at refuse the Kar'ruk left behind and searching for clues about their plans," he called back.

"Offensively?"

"I don't think so. Why?"

A shriek came from the heart of the flowers.

It startled Kaylina so much that she fell over, grasping for her sling. The petals of several flowers undulated as another shriek sounded. An alarm?

Levitke roared and ran away, shaking her head, her tail smacking the ruins.

"Kaylina?" Vlerion yelled, concern in his voice.

"I'm fine." Another shriek sounded, battering her eardrums. "I think," she muttered.

She started to stand but was lightheaded and wobbled. Was that pollen affecting her somehow? Her foot bumped against the corner of the plaque, and she fell back to her butt.

Taybarri footfalls sounded on the shoreline—Crenoch also running?

As more shrieks echoed from the ruins, Vlerion charged into view. His eyes grew round when he spotted Kaylina on the ground, and he sprinted toward her.

"No, no," Kaylina called, lifting a hand, but the shrieks of the plants drowned her out.

Face set with determination, Vlerion leaped over a mossy stone and ran toward her as he glanced at the flowers and into dark nooks for threats.

Alert as always, he saw a vine uncoil like a snake and lash out at him. He twisted, swinging his sword as it reached for his throat. The blade sliced into the rubbery tip, but, as with the vines in the castle, it was sturdy and doubtless magical. He barely deflected it.

As he sprang away from the area, another vine detached from an upright slab behind him. It whipped toward his waist.

"Look out!" Kaylina surged to her feet, but she was still lightheaded and almost pitched over again. She caught herself on a boulder and managed to stay upright.

Vlerion had heard her warning and dove away from the grasping vine, but four others snaked out. One snagged him, wrapping around his waist.

Face remaining a calm mask, he slashed at it with his sword. But another caught his wrist as yet another slithered in from the opposite direction. It also wrapped around his waist. A new vine erupted from the ground under his feet and clasped his ankle. Two more descended from a thick tree branch and stretched for his neck.

"No!" Kaylina staggered toward him, cursing the lightheadedness that affected her balance. As soon as she moved away from the boulder she'd gripped for support, she pitched to her knees.

What in all the altered orchards was happening to her?

Vlerion twisted to avoid the vines grasping for his neck, but they slid under his armpits instead, wrapped over his shoulders, and pulled his feet off the ground. He retained his sword, but with another vine ensnaring his wrist, he couldn't use it.

On hands and knees, Kaylina crawled toward him, determined to reach his side, but she had no idea how she could help. The way the magical vines gripped him from all directions ensured he was trapped.

10

Vestiges of the past can haunt the future.
~ Lord Professor Varhesson, Port Jirador University

Even after the vines had Vlerion ensnared, the flowers continued to shriek. Kaylina had no idea where the taybarri had gone, but they needed to return. *Soon.* She wasn't strong enough to hack Vlerion free on her own. He and Targon, with their swords and powerful swings, had barely cut into the vines in Stillguard Castle.

Hanging off the ground, Vlerion pulled and twisted. His muscles bulged under his sleeves as he tried to break free, but since his wrists were restrained, he couldn't swing his sword. He didn't have a chance. The vines shifted only a little with his movements.

Once more, Kaylina tried to stand, but, again, the lightheadedness affected her balance. She couldn't stay upright without grabbing a rock for support. Frustration and fear made her spit curses.

Vlerion called to her, but she couldn't understand him over the continued shrieks.

"Will you stop that damn noise?" Kaylina screamed, so furious that she didn't care if Kar'ruk warriors all over the preserve heard her.

No, that wasn't true. If the Kar'ruk showed up, she and Vlerion would have even *more* of a problem. She clamped her mouth shut and leaned on a stone slab to help her move closer to Vlerion.

Her progress was painstakingly slow. The frustration of the situation boiled over, making her curse more, denouncing every moon god and the king on his throne. A final snarl of, "*Sywretha!*" came out of her mouth.

The shrieks halted so abruptly that Kaylina almost fell over again.

Sywretha? Where had that come from? She had no idea what it meant.

As soon as the noise stopped, her lightheadedness disappeared. She released the slab and took a wary step. Her balance had returned. Maybe it hadn't been the pollen coating her nose but the shrieks affecting her ears.

After the noise, the silence was so profound that it was almost eerie. Wanting nothing more to do with the druid ruins, Kaylina rushed toward Vlerion.

One of the vines flickered, and she halted a few feet away. But it only adjusted to wrap more firmly around him. The aggressive vines didn't react to her approach at all.

Vlerion had stopped struggling. His eyes were closed, and he was humming.

Kaylina almost swore again, realizing the beast threatened to rise, to overcome him. In that form, he could be strong enough to break free, but as soon as he did, with no other enemies present, he might turn on her.

"Are you okay?" she whispered. "Other than being completely immobilized by ranger-hating vines?"

Vlerion finished the refrain of his song and took a long breath before lifting his lids to meet her gaze. His face was calm, and she didn't catch the telltale dangerous glint in his eyes.

"I've been better." He looked her up and down. "They didn't attack you."

"The vines? No."

Not yet, anyway…

"I thought you were in danger." He shook his head ruefully.

"Well, I might be. If you weren't doing anything over there, you shouldn't be what set the flowers off. I'm assuming they're an alarm." An alarm that battered friends and their furry companions as badly as whatever they were meant to stave off…

"The Kar'ruk could be returning." Vlerion's face turned grim again as his head turned, his gaze sliding toward the lake. "Just before the noise started, I saw a glint on the far side of the lake. Like armor or a sword reflecting sunlight."

Oh, great. As if this situation wasn't bad enough.

"Let's get you down then. I need to borrow your sword." Kaylina risked stepping closer and stretching upward, but a vine held Vlerion's arm over his head, and she couldn't reach the hilt.

"Please, my lord," he murmured.

"Really? You're going to be haughty, right now? I don't know if you noticed, but you're not in a great position to, as Targon suggested, beat respect into me."

Vlerion managed a smile. "I knew you were awake during that conversation."

"You should have shut your office door if you wanted privacy."

"I'll remember that in the future. Stand back."

She did, and he moved his hand as much as he could and tossed the sword so the blade didn't clip him as it fell. The vine tightened around his wrist. He curled his lip at it.

Kaylina picked up the weapon, wrapping both hands around the hilt and debating which vines were most responsible for immobilizing him. Unfortunately, it was a *lot* of them.

Aiming for one wrapped around his waist, she lifted the blade overhead like a logger chopping kindling. With that image in mind, she threw all her weight behind the blow, but the sword lacked the heft of an axe. Not only did it fail to sink in deeply, but it flexed as it hit and sent a wobbly jolt up her arm.

"If the Kar'ruk do show up, I'll ask if I can use one of their magical axes," she said.

"That *would* be the ideal weapon for the task."

She took more experimental swings, trying to find a weak spot. With each blow, she glanced at the vines, afraid her actions would make them decide she was an enemy too.

"Is this all because you're a ranger?" she wondered. "Do all your people get attacked when they come in the preserve?"

"There's a reason we usually avoid the area, but I've not heard of rangers being outright attacked. It's more that they find their way blocked and paths disappearing behind them. Some other eerie things that the plants do to let our kind know they're not welcome." Vlerion sighed again. "From what I've heard and read, it wasn't always like that. Before the years of famine when the king ordered my predecessors to hunt in the preserve and bring back game to feed the starving populace, rangers were welcome. They found the forest peaceful and loved to spend time here. It was only after the druids returned and put the curse on the castle and my ancestors that the preserve changed toward them."

"How does it know if a person is a ranger? If you came without a taybarri or your black leather armor, could the plants tell?"

"I don't know, but I suspect this…" Vlerion grimaced and flexed an arm, again trying to pull free. He only managed to move an inch before the vine tightened. "This is because they can tell I'm one of the cursed. An enemy, someone not to be trusted." Frustration twisted his lips, but he caught himself and closed his eyes again, forcing his breathing to calm.

"It's not fair that you're being punished for something your ancestor decided to do two hundred years ago."

Kaylina had barely gouged a divot in the vine. She switched her focus to a narrower tendril, even though it wasn't as instrumental in restraining Vlerion. Still, it gripped his arm. If she could cut it away, maybe he could swing his own sword. His stronger blows would be more effective.

"When I was a boy and said exactly that, my father told me that it was good that only our family had been cursed instead of the entire populace. As horrible as it's been, especially since beasts throughout the years have killed innocent people, it could have been worse. Imagine if a population of, oh, at least thirty or forty thousand lived in the capital back then, had *all* been cursed with this. They not only would have killed each other, but the beasts might have spread throughout the kingdom. It could have been the end of all humanity."

"If the druids had the power to curse that many, they probably would have done it, since they supposedly hate humans. You got a shitty deal."

Vlerion opened his eyes and managed a smile. "I think you would have been more sympathetic to my tantrums than my father was."

"I'm sympathetic to you because..." Kaylina hacked several more times at the vine while groping for words to finish that sentence. "You've saved my life, and you've been supportive of me, more than you should have, considering all the trouble that keeps finding me."

"The *trouble* finding you also isn't fair."

"Oh, I *know* that."

Hack, hack, hack.

Kaylina stepped back, needing to catch her breath. She was halfway through the thinner vine, so maybe there was hope, but more than a dozen others secured Vlerion. It was hard not to feel daunted.

"What did you say that caused the flowers—they were making the noise, right?—to stop screeching like stuck pigs?" he asked.

"I've never heard of screaming flowers before, but I'm positive they were responsible for the noise. And... I don't know that I had anything to do with them stopping."

"You said something."

"I said a *lot* of things. I was cursing."

"The last word was something like *shyrecka*."

"*Sywretha,*" she pulled from her memory.

"Yes. What language is that?"

"I have no idea. As far as I know, I made it up."

Vlerion gazed thoughtfully at her. "Is your hand still... being weird?"

She'd forgotten all about it. "It's neutral. I'm surprised it's not objecting to me hacking at these vines. It seems tied to this place somehow."

She supposed that made sense. If the plant in the castle had been placed by the druids—its job to monitor the curse or maybe even enact the curse?—it could be related to the trees, bushes, and flowers growing around their former home. They'd likely cultivated a lot of the plants here and surely all the altered ones.

"*This place*, as you call it, may not object to you at all."

"Because of my inherent charisma and natural inclination to snark at rangers?"

"Because of whatever in your blood caused you to be born an *anrokk*."

"I don't think that was anything in my blood. I have the same blood as my brother, and Grandpa's hounds never slept in *his* bed."

"Do you?" Vlerion tilted his head, considering her from a new angle. "Are you sure?"

"Of course. I'm the middle kid of three. There's Frayvar, me, and an older sister. And cousins. My whole family lives on the same island and works at the Spitting Gull. There aren't any mysteries about our heritage."

"You're quite beautiful."

Kaylina blinked at the random compliment. "Uh, thanks, but what's your point? I'll assume that, given your current situation, you're not being moved to ardor."

Before she could catch herself, she glanced down, the memory of Vlerion nearly naked in the barracks popping into her mind. She blushed and jerked her gaze away.

"I am not currently experiencing ardor, no." He had to have noticed the glance but didn't comment on it, though a hint of a smug smile *did* touch his face. "What I meant is your brother is gangly and homely. Awkward."

"Boys are different." Kaylina shrugged. It wasn't as if she was the epitome of grace either.

"Your older sister is also beautiful?"

She shrugged again. "She's fine."

"Fine," Vlerion mouthed, his eyebrows rising.

"She's married and has kids. Her *husband* is into her. Her beauty must have appeal." Kaylina returned to hacking at the vine, not comfortable with what he was implying. "We all like books and mead." She glared at him as she hacked.

"Is that supposed to be evidence of a hereditary link?"

"You don't think mead-adoration is in the blood?"

His eyebrows remained up. Skeptical.

"Look, I'm not adopted, or whatever you're trying to imply, okay? I look a lot like my mother." Kaylina had the same dark hair and brown skin anyway. Just as Frayvar and Silana did. And all their cousins. She scowled.

"It is not my intention to offend you. Nor am I certain that being an *anrokk* is something passed along by one's parents. It's rare enough that I haven't seen many people who qualify, but Sergeant Jastadar's parents are adored by the taybarri as well."

"I'd like to meet him and see someone else constantly get their face licked."

"I'll introduce you when we get back. When I've escaped." With his own energy perhaps renewed, Vlerion returned to shifting and trying to twist his way free of the vines, but they gave no more than before.

Kaylina backed away and called, "Crenoch!" into the bushes in the direction the taybarri had gone. "Levitke!"

"Their bites might be able to break through these vines," Vlerion said, guessing her reason for wanting them to return. "But I don't blame them for running. Their ears are much more sensitive to noises, especially high-pitched noises, than ours, and those flowers were dreadful."

"Yeah, but they're quiet now."

Kaylina opened her mouth to call again, but Vlerion's nostrils twitched, and he whispered a quick, "Ssh."

She sniffed the air and caught what he'd caught. A faint musky scent blowing in from the lake.

"The Kar'ruk are returning," Vlerion said.

11

After error, verity a rarity.
~ Ganizbar, the poet

"I did determine that there were more than two sets of tracks by the lake." Vlerion flexed his shoulders, wrestling with the vines suspending him several inches above the ground. Like this, he was defenseless. If the Kar'ruk charged into the ruins, they would be able to kill him easily. "I'm still flummoxed as to how so many Kar'ruk could have slipped past the rangers in the watchtowers. The city may be in grave danger."

Kaylina was far more concerned about *Vlerion* than the city. As the breeze carried the Kar'ruk's musky odor toward them, panic surged through her. It renewed her strength, and she hacked at the vines with fresh vigor, chopping tiny gouges into their rubbery flesh. But it wasn't enough. She wanted to call again for the taybarri, but if the Kar'ruk were close, they would hear her and know she and Vlerion were in trouble. That might bring them more quickly. Even the noise from her blows worried her.

"Stop," Vlerion whispered. "I appreciate your effort, but it's not working."

"I know." Sweat stung her eyes, and Kaylina dragged her sleeve across her forehead. "But I don't know what else to do."

"Hide."

"*You* can't hide. You're out in the open."

"If you get away, you can find the other rangers and bring help. I should have sent you to look for them right away."

Kaylina glared at him in exasperation. "Even if Targon gathered men and came as soon as Jankarr got back to the city, they'd have to be hours behind us. Besides, I can't leave you here alone."

She looked around, hoping to spot blue taybarri fur.

"You need to get away," Vlerion said firmly.

The musky odor was growing stronger, and was that a clipped voice speaking in the distance?

"Go and hide." It was an order.

"Not without you."

If the two taybarri returned to help, the three of them could make a stand and protect Vlerion. Her sling rounds might not do much, but their claws and fangs did genuine damage. But where *were* they?

"Leave, Kaylina. Please. If they hurt you..." Vlerion closed his eyes. "I wouldn't forgive myself for not forcing you to return to the city with Jankarr."

"I wouldn't have forgiven you if you *had* forced me to do something."

"I would accept your anger if it came with your safety."

"*Vlerion.*" Kaylina glared at him, but his eyes were closed, so he missed it.

He was trying to keep his emotions under control. Maybe he shouldn't...

Nervous at the idea that came to mind, she licked her lips. "If you turned into the beast, would you be strong enough to break free?"

She'd seen him throw two-hundred-pound men twenty feet in that form.

"I don't know." His eyes opened but only so he could look warily at her.

"I bet you could," she whispered.

"This isn't the time for experimentation."

The voices were drawing closer. The Kar'ruk had to be along the lake, not far from the ruins. Their words were unintelligible to her, but they sounded excited. Like they knew they were on the trail of their enemies...

A war horn blew, the musical blast traveling over the lake—and probably for miles in all directions. A call for more Kar'ruk to come? It had to be.

"No, it's the time for *desperation.*" Kaylina stepped close to Vlerion and rested her hands on his chest.

Even on tiptoes, she couldn't reach his mouth to kiss him, but his forbidding expression didn't suggest he was amenable to that anyway. She loosened his armor—the bindings would break when he turned anyway—and slid her hands under his shirt, scraping her nails over the taut muscles of his abdomen.

"Go hide," he whispered, more tension than arousal in his eyes. "I can speak a few of their words. I'll attempt to bargain with them, get them to release me in exchange for... something."

"That's not going to work. Even I know that. They hate humans. They hate *you.*" Remembering his words about her beauty, she stepped back and unbuttoned her shirt. She didn't want to disrobe with enemies about to charge in, but she showed the skin of her stomach and touched her breasts, hoping to draw his eye. If there was a chance he could, as the beast, free himself and defend himself...

"Stop," Vlerion whispered harshly. "I'm not going to get

aroused like this, and the beast is too dangerous to deliberately call forth." Despite the words, his eyes tracked her movements. "Hide," he repeated. "If I do turn… I could go after you as readily as them."

"You could have killed me in the dungeon, and you didn't."

"You don't know what I *wanted* to do." Vlerion squinted his eyes shut, his face aggrieved. "I don't always remember much of what happens afterward, but sometimes there are snatches of memories, and I recall…" His eyes opened. "Hide. Please."

Kaylina paused, remembering the beast rasping, "*My female.*"

His mother had hinted of encounters with her husband in beast form. And she had those scars on her neck. Kaylina might survive the beast taking her, but would Vlerion forgive himself afterward? And would she… still want to be with him? It sounded like his mother hadn't had a choice about marrying his father. Would she have stayed if she had?

The Kar'ruk voices sounded again, closer, and she shook away the worries. If she trusted that he would change as soon as his life was in danger, she could stand back and let the inevitable occur, but Vlerion didn't lose his equanimity when he fought on his own behalf, not that she'd ever seen. She couldn't be sure.

"Bring out the beast," she whispered. "To save yourself."

Before he could object, she stepped closer again, pushing his shirt up and his armor aside to kiss his stomach. She ran her hands over his hard muscles, scraping her nails over his flesh, trying to make her touches as enticing as possible. As *erotic* as possible. She didn't dare loosen his belt and lower his trousers when enemies approached, but she held him, stroking him through his clothing.

"Kaylina," Vlerion rasped. Was that desire in his voice? Lust? "Go, damn it. If they hurt you…"

Yes, that was what had made him change in the past. Fear for her. The need to protect her.

She should have realized that would motivate him more than the need to save himself. And it would be more likely to prompt him to change than this. She shouldn't have disrespected his wishes and touched him when he didn't want it.

She bit her lip with regret, afraid she'd made a mistake, one he would resent her for. Wary, she looked up and met his eyes.

That dangerous glint was there, a full gleam, the promise of change imminent. It sent a fresh shiver of fear through her, not fear of the Kar'ruk this time. Fear of him. Of what he could become, what she was trying to *cause* him to become.

His gaze dipped to her bared abdomen and the swell of her breasts above her bra. She saw the spark that flared in his eyes, the instant when the change was initiated.

He threw his head back and roared, an inhuman beast of a roar.

Kaylina sprang back as he changed, the same as he had in the dungeon under the royal castle. His muscles grew larger, tearing his clothing, as sleek auburn fur sprouted from his flesh.

When he roared again, his human teeth had changed into fangs. Claws extended from hands that transformed into something closer to paws. His feet bulged in his boots, and he kicked them off.

Kaylina wanted to stay and make sure Vlerion could break away, but when his head lowered, the savage animalistic rage in the fiery depths of his eyes terrified her. There was no sign of Vlerion in that gaze, not anymore, and when it swept over her body, the fear of what he might do to her scared her every bit as much as the Kar'ruk.

She turned, grabbed her pack, and sprinted away. She wouldn't go far, but she wanted to make sure she was out of the beast's view so he would focus on the approaching threat, not on her.

Snaps came from behind her, and she paused, not certain

what that was. Had the Kar'ruk reached him and started firing a weapon?

Ahead, a jumble of fallen stone slabs caught her eye. She dropped her pack at the base and scrambled up the mound as a Kar'ruk call of surprise echoed through the camp.

From the top, careful to keep her head low, she peered back. The height gave her a view over the ruins, and she was in time to see the beast snap the last of the vines in half. He dropped to the ground, free and able to defend himself.

That was a relief, but would it be enough?

The beast spun toward four Kar'ruk who were approaching him with their axes raised. They didn't appear alarmed.

The beast roared, the thunderous noise echoing from the ruins. Vlerion's sword lay at his feet, but he ignored it. He ran toward the Kar'ruk like an animal—a *predator*—and sprang to the top of a six-foot-tall slab overlooking his prey.

This was what Kaylina had hoped for, but she couldn't help but fear for his life. Especially when she saw the Kar'ruk calmly ready themselves to face him as a team.

Afraid their powerful axes would outmatch the beast, Kaylina readied her sling. Her fingers shook, and she worried she was too far away to hit the Kar'ruk, but she had to try.

Fearless, the beast sprang from the slab toward the warriors. Axes swung toward him. He twisted in the air, defying gravity to dodge the attacks as he slashed with his claws. The blades glowed blue from their powder coating, but even magic wasn't enough to allow the Kar'ruk to strike the equally magical beast.

By the time he landed in their midst, he'd drawn blood from two enemies. Before they could recover and surround him, he sprang at one, landing on him and sinking fangs into the warrior's neck.

As he tore his enemy's throat out, the beast spun the Kar'ruk about so that his back was to another warrior—another warrior swinging an axe. Instead of hitting the beast, the Kar'ruk struck his own comrade in the shoulder, burying the blade deep. The doubly wounded warrior crumpled to the ground.

One of the Kar'ruk carried a bow. He swung it off his shoulder and stepped back, making room to aim at the beast.

On the slab pile, Kaylina rose, standing straight, and aimed her sling. While the Kar'ruk waited to get a good shot at the beast, not wanting to hit his own comrades, Kaylina hurled a round over the ruins and toward the fray. The archer was about to loose his arrow when it struck.

Distance affected her aim, and the round hit his bowstring instead of him. She was lucky she hadn't missed completely. He fumbled his arrow in surprise and whirled to see where the round had come from.

Kaylina squatted down but was too late to avoid notice. When the archer nocked his arrow again, he aimed it at her.

Before he could fire, the beast escaped the skirmish and sprang, landing on the archer's chest and knocking him to the ground.

In that form, Vlerion had as much muscle and mass as the eight-foot Kar'ruk. Maybe he had more, because his foe couldn't shove him aside to rise, couldn't escape. The beast clawed into the Kar'ruk's abdomen as his fanged maw bit down into the warrior's neck.

Horrified by the blood that spattered everywhere, Kaylina looked to the other warriors, afraid they would take advantage of the beast's distraction. She loaded another round, ready to shoot.

But they were already down—*dead*—with their throats torn out, the same as the one the beast was finishing off. A snap sounded, the breaking of a neck, and silence fell upon the preserve.

The beast whirled, blood matting his fur and dripping from

his fangs. When those wild blue eyes met Kaylina's, a jolt of utter fear shook her.

She backed away to escape his view, but he sprang onto one of the slabs, powerful muscles rippling under sleek fur, and looked right at her. She couldn't tell if his savage eyes were full of lust or the desire to kill, but she knew without a doubt that she didn't want him to catch her.

As he leaped from the slab, loping through the ruins toward her, she scrambled down from the rock pile. She grabbed her pack but had no idea where to run. Belatedly, she realized it hadn't been a good idea to turn *off* the druid's alarm system, if she'd truly had anything to do with that.

As she ran around the rubble pile, she spotted a gap between two broken slabs that leaned against each other. She peered into a dark nook that they made. Could she fit? It would be close. Too close a fit for the beast. But what if he tore the stone slabs away with that great strength?

The sound of heavy footfalls drew closer, promising she didn't have time to run anywhere else. Dropping to hands and knees, she squeezed into the gap. Rock scraped at her shoulders, and as she pushed deeper, a jagged corner caught her shirt. The fabric ripped as she squeezed in tighter, then turned, wanting to face the beast instead of being dragged out by her ankle.

Something thudded above her. Him. He'd landed atop the rubble pile.

Realizing she'd left the pack outside, she risked squeezing partially back out so she could grab it. She yanked it inside with her.

Two furred feet landed inches away from it. A shriek of pure fear escaped her lips, and she cracked her head on the rock as she scrambled back from the entrance, dragging the pack after her.

The beast bent low and peered into her dark nook.

In the tight, quiet spot, Kaylina could hear her heartbeat

throbbing in her ears. Throbbing so rapidly that she might have been sprinting up a mountain.

"If only," she whispered as those paws shifted.

Claws wrapped around the edge of one of the tipped stones, pulling. Dust wafted down over the entrance, but the tons of weight from the rest of the stones in the pile kept the beast from tugging the slab free.

Kaylina started to open her pack, thinking to read to him, but it was too dark in the nook to see words, especially when his body blocked the light from the entrance.

"What'd you do with your boots, Vlerion?" Kaylina called softly, struggling for a reasonable tone, a friendly tone. "It says in your book that rangers are supposed to keep their gear, clothing, and weapons in good condition at all times."

The beast dropped to all fours, shifting so he could look in at her. Most of his clothing was missing too. Whether the change had shredded it or he'd torn it off, she didn't know, but only the leather torso piece remained on him, flopping about since the fasteners had broken.

He sniffed, nostrils more like a wolf's than a man's. Then he growled, a very animalistic growl, then rasped, "*Female.*"

"Yes, I am."

"*My female.*" He clawed at the stone, again trying to pull it free. When that didn't work, he reached a long muscled arm in.

Kaylina drew back as far as she could, her back and butt jammed against rock. "Yes, I'd like to be with you but the *Vlerion* side of you. Please change back."

He snarled, clawing at the ground. Digging, she realized with another jolt of fear. Yes, that might work. If he made a hole large enough, he would be able to reach her.

Though she couldn't remember the lyrics of his song, she attempted to hum it for him, willing it to soothe him.

He snarled and dug faster. "*My female.*"

Kaylina trembled, knowing that if he got her, she would have no one to blame but herself. She'd wanted to help him fight off the Kar'ruk, and she couldn't regret that she'd roused the beast, but…

A roar came from the forest.

The beast paused and whirled, crouching with his back to her as he faced the threat.

"That was a taybarri." At first, Kaylina was relieved that one of them had come back, but she remembered Vlerion saying that Crenoch didn't respond to him as well as others because Crenoch sensed the danger in him, knew about the beast. And knew the beast was a threat to taybarri. Vlerion wouldn't forgive himself for killing Crenoch. "*Your* taybarri, Vlerion. He loves you and is loyal to you. You can't hurt him. Just as you can't hurt me."

Another roar sounded. Was Crenoch, or maybe that was Levitke, trying to distract the beast? To save Kaylina?

The beast snarled and shifted his weight back and forth. Kaylina caught a glimpse of genitalia that suggested *killing* her wasn't what he'd had in mind.

"He's a friend, Vlerion," she said, hoping that repeating his name would remind him of who he was. "He won't hurt you, and neither will I. You dealt with the Kar'ruk, which we're very grateful for, and now you can change back into a man." She crept closer as she spoke, trying to make her voice soothing, hoping he would pass out, as he had in her dungeon cell under the royal castle. If the beast believed the threat was gone…

Though it felt like sticking her hand in a cobra's nest, she reached out and touched the side of his furred calf. His muscles quivered, but he didn't jerk away, nor did he turn back toward her. He sniffed again. Tracking the location of the taybarri by scent? She hoped he hadn't caught a whiff of more Kar'ruk in the area.

"It's all right, Vlerion." Kaylina stroked the side of his leg, the fur soft and supple over the taut muscles. "You can relax. It's all right."

A low growl sounded in his chest.

"I apologize for not listening to you earlier, for trying to make you change when you wanted me to be safe. I couldn't leave you, but... that wasn't a good way to handle things. It was all I could think of at the time, but I'm sorry, okay?"

Surprisingly, he went down to one knee. One paw-like hand curled into a fist to support him as he leaned forward.

"We can talk about it later," she murmured, suspecting the curse was winding down.

With a soft moan, the beast collapsed.

12

When the stomach orders, the body obeys.
~ Elder Taybarri Seerathi

Kaylina waited until the unconscious beast transformed back into Vlerion before crawling out of the nook. Dirt and pebbles fell out of her hair, and her body ached from scraping against the stone slabs. Further, blisters were rising on her palms from her many futile hacks of the vines with Vlerion's sword.

He'd collapsed on his back, and she rested a hand on his chest, the leather torso armor slumped halfway off. He was naked from the waist down, with his shirt in tatters, the seams ripped. She hoped he had spare clothing in his pack and looked around, thinking of searching for it—and the taybarri—but she wouldn't leave him alone when he was vulnerable.

"Did you get all the Kar'ruk, I wonder?" she murmured, remembering how fast and powerful he'd been in the battle, too much for even the powerful warriors to handle. "If more show up while you're napping, we'll be in trouble." She smiled and patted him, hoping his eyelids would flutter.

As magnificent as the beast was, she wanted the man for company. She glanced at the torn earth, its scent lingering in the air, and attempted to forget about the beast digging, trying to reach her, to pull her out and mate with her. She had little doubt that he'd wanted that, and she shivered as she recalled Vlerion's mother warning her that women didn't always survive such encounters.

Uneasy, Kaylina drew her hand back, as if her simple touch might make the beast return. "Vlerion, I don't suppose you know where your underwear is."

A bird chirped at the edge of the ruins, and a frog in the lake answered. Hopefully, that meant the Kar'ruk in the area were all dead.

Kaylina rose to her feet and flexed her battered body. A few tentative whuffs came from the ruins.

Crenoch and Levitke padded into view, their heads held lower than their long bodies as they slinked forward. They eyed Vlerion warily before looking at Kaylina.

"I don't think he's dangerous anymore," she told them. "Thank you for your help and for coming back."

They looked at each other, heads still low as they continued toward her. For the first time since she'd met the taybarri, their whuffs sounded apologetic.

"It's not your fault," she assured them.

They would have been helpful against the Kar'ruk, but she couldn't blame them for not wanting to fight at the beast's side. In that form, Vlerion could have turned on them. No, he *would* have turned on them. She was positive. When he was the beast, he saw everyone as an enemy. Everyone except... his female. She swallowed, not relieved by having that designation.

Using his snout, Crenoch nudged Vlerion's shoulder.

"He'll be all right," Kaylina told them, glad Crenoch didn't seem to hold a grudge. He had to understand that Vlerion wasn't a threat in his normal form.

Crenoch stepped around him, then pointed his nose past the ruins and toward the lake. He swayed his tail, looked at Kaylina, and pointed his nose toward the lake again.

"Is there danger in that direction? More Kar'ruk?"

Crenoch shook his big head, then lifted one clawed forelimb as he pointed his snout toward the lake again. He reminded Kaylina of her Grandpa's hounds. A few of them also lifted one forelimb as they pointed into the brush at birds. Levitke watched Crenoch but didn't offer any indications of her own that she wanted to go that way. Maybe when they'd been scared by the shrieking flowers, they'd fled in different directions.

"Do you want me to see something in the lake? Or on the other side of it?"

Whuff.

"All right, uhm." Kaylina considered Vlerion. He hadn't yet stirred. He probably would soon if they waited, but she wouldn't mind getting out of the strange ruins, the strange ruins that more Kar'ruk might visit. She recalled the blowing of that war horn. The warriors might have been summoning allies. "Will you help me get him on your back, Crenoch?"

The taybarri returned to Vlerion's side and lay down, stretching his long body out. His back was still a few feet off the ground, but that was as low as he could get.

Kaylina grabbed Vlerion's wrist and lifted him enough to drape his arm over Crenoch's back, but the rest of him was heavier. Grunting and straining, she struggled to pull him up. She shifted to his leg and got *that* over, though the muscled limb wasn't light. Levitke stepped forward and used a paw to pin the leg in place so it wouldn't slip down again. She used her snout to anchor his arm over Crenoch's back.

"Thank you." Kaylina trotted to Vlerion's other side so she could shove, straining to heft him up. "I was... admiring your... nice muscles before... I realized how *heavy* they are." With a final shove, she pushed his body onto Crenoch's back. The taybarri waited patiently through the manhandling of his rider. "You're a good boy, Crenoch."

The responding whuff sounded like the equivalent of *obviously*.

Levitke issued a querying whuff.

"Yes, you're a good girl. Very helpful, thank you. Both of you."

The next whuffs sounded smug.

Kaylina no longer doubted that the intelligent taybarri understood everything humans said.

Once she had Vlerion's legs and arms astraddle, his chest and face smashed into blue fur, she climbed up behind him.

"I'll hold him up here," she told Levitke, lest she be upset that her rider was cheating on her with another taybarri.

Levitke trotted off into the ruins while Crenoch headed straight for the lake. As Kaylina gripped Vlerion's bare legs to hold him in place, she glanced at his pack strapped between Crenoch's shoulders, thinking of delving in for spare clothes. But it would be almost as hard to dress him as it was to lift him. Once he woke, he could handle that himself.

It concerned her that he *hadn't* woken yet. In the dungeon, it had taken several minutes, but more time than that had passed now. And she didn't think the battle against the Kar'ruk had lasted as long as the fight under the castle. Nor did he appear to have been injured as badly. A few shallow axe gouges bled here and there, but he'd been peppered with crossbow quarrels when he'd fought the Virts.

"If you're not conscious by the time Crenoch gets us wherever, I'll try waking you with a kiss." Kaylina patted Vlerion's thigh. "After I wash your face and mouth. You're nasty right now, *my lord.*" She smiled, half-expecting him to wake to tell her that her honorific had been sarcastic rather than properly respectful. He did not.

Levitke caught up to them, carrying Vlerion's sword, boots, and were those his torn clothes in her mouth?

"Thank you," Kaylina said. "I forgot. And he would have been crabby if we left his sword behind."

She was less certain he would want to put his underwear on after they'd been covered in saliva in a taybarri's mouth, but maybe she wouldn't mention that to him.

Crenoch padded through trees as they followed the shoreline of the lake, heading to the other side. More birds, insects, and other wildlife made noise, a sign that the forest had returned to normal.

Here and there, a few vines flicked, making Kaylina feel that she was being monitored, as if the altered plants had a sentience and the druids had left them to guard the preserve. Maybe they had. After all, the druids must have been alerted somehow during the famine when rangers had hunted within its borders. Were they still in the world somewhere, and would they be drawn to return if poaching happened again?

Kaylina eyed the brand on her skin. She wasn't eager to meet the people who'd animated the murdering vines in the castle.

When the taybarri reached a stream trickling into the lake, Crenoch turned to follow it inland. Through breaks in the trees, the mountains were visible, white peaks stretching toward the blue sky.

The forest thinned further as they entered a valley carpeted with lush green grass that rose a foot or two, spreading outward from either side of the stream. Numerous plants grew amid the grass, leaves and buds stretching above the blades, a few flowers starting to open. They dotted the verdant valley with blues, purples, oranges, and yellows and made the area vibrate with electricity. Or… with magic?

Kaylina picked up buzzes among the humming. Were those bees? Yes, she spotted a couple of plump black-and-yellow honeybees flitting among the flowers. Who could blame them for living in such a place? With the mountains visible in the backdrop, the valley was breathtakingly beautiful. As with the lake, it would be a wonderful scene to paint.

"You should wake up, Vlerion." Kaylina trusted that anyone who played an instrument and hummed to calm himself would appreciate the beauty of nature.

Levitke issued a questioning whuff, her tail swishing with interest. Kaylina sniffed but didn't catch the musky odor of the Kar'ruk. Crenoch looked toward one of several stone or maybe ceramic domes that dotted the verdant valley and headed toward it.

He shifted from walking to trotting. Eager to reach it?

Kaylina pressed her hands down on Vlerion's back to keep him from slipping sideways.

More bees buzzed around the ceramic dome, numerous slit openings all around its sides. The holes, as well as the structure itself, were time-worn, as if the dome had been there for centuries, but no moss or mildew grew on it.

"Are these… hives?" Kaylina wondered. "Built by the druids?"

Crenoch and Levitke slowed down, but their nostrils twitched with interest.

"Is there honey inside?" she guessed.

It was early in the season for there to be much, but the taybarri must have caught the scent. A bee buzzed toward Crenoch's face, and he backed away with a mournful clucking sound and looked over his shoulder at Kaylina.

"Did you get stung when you were here earlier?"

He whuffed and shook his head, gazing with longing at the hive but not moving closer.

Since the taybarri had thick fur, she was surprised Crenoch would have noticed a sting, but maybe a bee had targeted his nose or eyes. The druids might also have embedded magic in the nearby plants or the hives themselves that helped the bees defend their territory.

As if to demonstrate, Crenoch lifted a paw, reached toward the hive, then jerked it back.

"Did the dome zap you?" Kaylina remembered touching the soil of the plant in the castle tower and receiving a shock that had knocked her on her ass.

Crenoch gave an affirmative whuff.

"I can share some of my honey if we can't get in, but… I wonder if that plant would enjoy this even more than my honey from back home."

Her family's honey was delicious, the best she'd ever tasted, but if these bees were taking pollen from altered flowers, what they stored here might be its equivalent. Further, it might be exactly what the plant would have received from the druids who'd placed it there, assuming they'd also made a fertilizer from honey.

"What are the odds that I could get a sample without being zapped, stung, or mutilated in any way?"

The taybarri looked at her intently, both swishing their tails and rustling the grass.

"You guys want honey. I don't trust you as good resources on the odds of my mutilation." Thinking of the castle curse, Kaylina slid off Crenoch's back anyway. "It's too bad I don't have one of my grandpa's smokers with me."

Levitke tilted her head.

"Smoke puts bees to sleep. Well, not to *sleep* exactly, but it masks the alarm pheromones that they put out to warn the hive, so you're less likely to get stung. But, as my brother recently pointed out, I've had good luck taking honey from hives without smoking them. He was trying to tell me that's evidence that I'm an *anrokk*."

The taybarri swished their tails encouragingly.

Kaylina crept forward, hands out and open, and attempted to stay calm and do nothing to alarm the bees. As she approached the hive, the hum of magic she'd felt since entering the valley grew stronger. She probably had to worry more about alarming *it* than the bees.

Not sure how to open the lid—did it even *have* a lid?—she circled the dome. Then she halted and stared, for there was a mark on the weathered ceramic. Though faint, it was distinct. A star-shaped leaf had been carved into one side. She looked at her hand, but she already knew it matched.

"If that isn't a sign that I should get some honey to try on that plant, I don't know what would be."

The comment received a chorus of whuffs.

"It's so great to have spectators."

Bees buzzed past her head on the way in and out of the hive but didn't react to her presence. Kaylina slowly stretched her fingers toward the dome but shifted before touching it, instead turning her hand over to press the brand against the larger leaf on the side.

Warmth flowed from her skin as it touched, followed by a soothing coolness.

A faint click reverberated through the dome, and the top opened, revealing slats partially full of honeycomb and covered in bees.

"I don't have any tools or empty jars with me for collecting this stuff." She had the jar of honey in her pack but was hesitant to mix the two substances. She wanted to isolate this to try on the plant.

The taybarri whuffed and lolled their tongues out.

Kaylina snorted. "Yeah, we're not *collecting* anything with those."

Carefully, she removed one of the slats. The bees flew off in a huff, but none stung her. It was almost eerie how easy it was to take their prized honey, and she wondered if the plant in the castle had somehow orchestrated this, marking her so that she could gain access and get honey for it. But how could it have known she would go to the preserve and find this place? She believed its magic instilled it with intelligence, but this much?

Levitke made a distressed noise and backed farther away. A few bees had been circling her head, buzzing aggressively. The hum from the dome intensified.

With the slat in hand, Kaylina backed slowly away. She hoped none of the flowers in the valley would start shrieking.

She patted Levitke and removed her pack, poking inside for something she could use to collect some of the comb. Other than food and a change of clothes, there wasn't much. She was on the verge of using the half-empty jar of honey when her knuckles bumped the ranger handbook.

"You can be useful again," she murmured to it and tore a page out of the back.

As she wiped some comb into it, Vlerion spoke.

"That is the most blasphemous thing I've seen you do, ranger trainee."

13

Magic tantalizes before it destroys.

~ Kar'ruk proverb

Kaylina spun at the sound of Vlerion's voice, almost dropping the honeycomb.

He sat upright on Crenoch's back, looking sternly at her.

"If you weren't unconscious so often, you'd see me doing even *more* blasphemous things." She tried a smile, hoping he wasn't *that* annoyed that she'd ripped pages out of his book. After all, she'd lost the first one he'd given her, and he hadn't seemed that distressed.

"Such as?" Vlerion looked her up and down, his gaze lingering on a rip in her shirt. His eyes shifted from stern to grim. Maybe even haunted.

"Earlier, I was fondling an unconscious ranger," she said, though her chest pats probably hadn't counted as that. Heaving him onto Crenoch's back *definitely* hadn't. "That must be against the rules."

Vlerion managed a slight smile, but it didn't reach his eyes. They were focused on the rip. Did he think he'd done it?

"Fondling isn't against the rules, nor mentioned at all in the handbook, but rangers do prefer to be conscious for it."

"I'll keep that in mind."

He slid gingerly off Crenoch, probably sore after his battle, and pulled off his lopsided leather armor, the straps broken.

Kaylina wrapped most of the honeycomb in the page and tucked it away, reserving a couple of pieces for the taybarri. They lapped it down with such gratitude in their eyes that she suspected she was right about the honey, that it tasted amazing.

She touched a piece to her tongue. Oh yes, it was divine. Maybe better than her grandpa's honey.

What kind of mead could she make from it? Would the druids —the *brand*—allow her to return for more? Or was this a one-time chance to collect honey for that plant?

After licking their blue lips numerous times, the taybarri rolled on their backs in the grass. Vlerion, who'd been about to delve into his pack, presumably for clothes, stepped back with his hand dangling in the air.

"I'm glad Crenoch waited until I dismounted to do that," he murmured.

"I hope there's nothing breakable in your pack." Kaylina waved toward Crenoch, the straps making sure it stayed attached, however flattened it now was.

"Clothes and food."

"I wondered if there's fresh underwear in there." She glanced at him, blushed, then pointed toward where Levitke had left his sword and boots. "We brought your other stuff."

"Thank you." Vlerion stepped closer and pointed toward the rip in her shirt. His voice softened as he asked, "Did I do that?"

"No. I did it to myself when I was fleeing from, uhm." Kaylina realized he might feel equally bad if he learned he'd *caused* her to rip her clothes. "Those who pursued me," she finished.

Vlerion wasn't fooled. Eyes grimmer than ever, he said, "Me."

"The beast."

"As you well know, I *am* the beast."

"It'll be all right, Vlerion. I'm working on a way to lift your curse." A piece of comb remained, and she offered it to him on her finger. "The plant was happy when I poured honey fertilizer on it, the first time at least. I'll try again with this stuff." Hopefully, she could avoid being branded again. "And if it works..."

"You'll pour honey on *me*?"

"Sure, but we'll have to do it when taybarri aren't present or they'll lick it off."

His eyelids drooped. "I'd rather have *you* lick it off."

She flushed with warmth as a vision of doing exactly that came easily to mind. She blamed it on his nudity. "If we could ensure certain things wouldn't happen, I might be interested in that."

Vlerion sighed and looked at the torn fabric again. "I can't ensure that, but that you care enough to try to lift my curse... means much. I never would have expected someone I so recently met to be that invested in me." He gazed into her eyes. "And to stand fearlessly in front of me right after I..." He waved vaguely in the direction of the lake and the ruins.

She almost said she'd been far from fearless—she'd been terrified—but if he knew that, it would distress him further. Besides, she didn't want him to think he needed to stay away from her. Maybe it was what they both should have wanted, but the idea was so unappealing that she caught herself stepping closer to him. Drawn to him, as always.

Attempting a bright smile, Kaylina held her finger to his mouth, the honey on the tip. "Taste?"

With his gaze still locked onto hers, she didn't miss the spark of interest in his eyes. Only when he opened his lips and sucked gently on her finger, a tingle of pleasure delighting her nerves, did she realize it might be sexual interest instead of a desire for honey.

His tongue *did* slide over the honey, tasting it as he watched her for her reaction. She didn't consciously move or notice she had shifted closer until her chest brushed his.

"Fearless," he whispered, lifting his lips from her finger and gazing at her with appreciation.

The look heated her body almost as much as his lips had.

"Unwisely so," she whispered.

"Undoubtedly."

Resisting the urge to grip his shoulders and kiss him, Kaylina stepped back and turned around. She knelt to tuck the honeycomb away.

"You probably didn't hear me before, but I want to apologize for..." She poked in the pack, struggling to voice the words that had come more easily when he'd been the beast and couldn't understand. "I'm sorry I kept trying to make you change when you didn't want... when you told me not to." She flushed at the memory of running her lips over his bare abdomen, of letting her hand drift lower to stroke him. In another situation, they both would have enjoyed it, but it had been a move of desperation. An ill thought out one.

"It's disheartening to know I can be so easily manipulated by a woman—by *anyone*—but I understand why you did it. And it did work."

"I should have thought of something less..."

"Arousing?" He'd stepped closer, and he brushed the back of her head, fingers pushing through her hair, rubbing her scalp.

"Maybe." Kaylina leaned back into his touch, relieved he wasn't angry with her. The taybarri had moved away, sniffing at the grass and flowers as they explored the valley. For the moment, there didn't seem to be any danger around. "I could have picked an argument with you and called you a pirate over and over until you were so irked that the beast came out."

"For future reference, I'd much rather have you kiss me than curse me." His fingers drifted lower, massaging the back of her neck, and she slumped back against him before remembering he wasn't wearing any clothes. A glance to the side made her aware that he was aroused again.

Her heart pounded. She'd been foolish to think there was no danger about, when *he* was with her.

Afraid the beast would return, she lurched to her feet. She started to step away, but Vlerion caught her and pulled her back against him. Her mind told her to spring away while her body wanted nothing more than to bask in his embrace, to turn toward him and wrap her arms around him.

"At the time, I might not have appreciated it," he murmured softly, lips brushing her ear, "but the memory will come to me often in my dreams."

Physical pleasure shot through her even as she delighted in knowing she affected him that much, that he found her desirable.

His lips lowered to her neck, and he kissed her.

A tremble went through her. Fear? Desire? *Both?*

"Vlerion," she whispered, hardly believing he was willing to flirt with this danger.

"I've never changed into the beast again a short time after a turning," he said as if he could guess her thoughts.

Her breath caught. She remembered him saying that before. He'd also said he wasn't *certain* it couldn't happen, only that it hadn't.

"There's no reason you should have any loyalty to me." His lips traced her throat as he inhaled her scent, one hand wrapped around her waist, the other drifting, stroking her. "We are not of the same class, and I arrested you when we met."

"I remember." Kaylina caught herself tilting her head so he

could reach more of her neck, so he could touch whatever he wished. He smiled against her skin, then gave her a soft nip that made her ache with need. "You were an ass," she added.

He laughed softly, his breath warm against her skin. "Yes."

One of his hands slid under her shirt, fingers trailing over the bare skin of her abdomen, and another tremble went through her. It drifted higher, cupping her breast and sliding her bra down so his thumb could brush her taut nipple. She arched into him, the touch so arousing she instantly craved more.

"Loyalty should be rewarded," he murmured, watching her avidly. Enjoying her reactions to him?

"Even when the rewardee isn't properly respectful?"

"In the event of extenuating circumstances, small infractions might be overlooked." His fingers trailed over to explore her other breast as his lips shifted to her earlobe, sucking, then nipping, making pleasure ricochet through her from multiple locations.

She stifled a gasp out of some notion that she shouldn't let him know how hot he could make her, how easily he could arouse her.

Striving for a casual tone, she asked, "Are you quoting from your book?"

The hitch in her breath might have betrayed his effect on her.

"The paragraph on rewards and rank, yes." His fingers slid lower, nails grazing sensitive skin.

"There's only one paragraph on that? I bet there are pages on punishment."

He smiled as he nipped her ear again. "An entire chapter."

That should have been repulsive, not erotic, but she struggled to find it so. With his hands so expertly stroking her body, it wouldn't have mattered *what* he said. And she couldn't help but imagine scenarios in which Vlerion might reward and punish her… in bed.

She turned her head, wanting to see him, wanting to kiss him.

He gazed back at her with unwavering intensity. Was there a

dangerous glint in his eyes? The one that promised he was on the verge of turning into the beast? She didn't think so, but passion gleamed in their blue depths, passion and lust as he bent, bringing his lips to hers.

She couldn't keep from kissing him—didn't *want* to keep from it. He tasted of honey and heat and desire. He unfastened her trousers, sending his fingers lower. His touch tantalized, promising the reward he'd spoken of.

She trembled, her body eager for more, even as she acknowledged this was playing with fire. If he was wrong about his ability to turn again, and she roused the beast, there was nowhere to hide in the open valley. Nowhere to run. She would be his—the *beast's*—to do with whatever he wished.

As he touched her intimately, she struggled to retain logical thoughts, to make practical decisions. She squirmed in his arms, pushing against his hand as he rubbed her. If they had sex, would he lie her in the grass and come down atop her? Or would he take her from behind? Like an animal. Like the beast.

Her body throbbed as fantasies of both scenarios shot through her, and she gripped the back of his head, kissing him recklessly. He growled with desire of his own as she writhed, intense need like nothing she'd known scattering thoughts, making her forget all threats of danger. Never had she wanted a man's *reward* so badly.

One of the taybarri roared.

Vlerion broke the kiss before she did—she didn't *want* to break it—and his hands stilled. She groaned a protest as her rational mind tried to reengage. Enemies, she reminded herself. There could be enemies.

But she didn't *want* enemies. She wanted Vlerion's fingers to finish bringing her to a climax and then, if the beast stayed away, she could reward *him*.

A rumble of irritation emanated from his chest as he looked past her shoulder. "Where were they an hour ago?"

She turned her head and stared in horror. Not Kar'ruk but eight rangers mounted on taybarri stared across the grass at them from the valley entrance. Jankarr was with them, and he smiled when he met their eyes, but Targon was also with them. His gaze was frosty and forbidding as he looked at them. Because *he* knew the danger.

Vlerion hadn't let Kaylina go. His grip tightened, as if he would refuse to. Maybe he was thinking of ordering the rangers to leave? She doubted that would work with his captain among the men. She hoped Vlerion wasn't thinking of carrying on with them watching.

"I'm not having sex in front of anyone," she whispered to him.

"You didn't mind the taybarri."

"They're *furry*. And didn't seem to care." Kaylina caught a couple of the rangers gazing avidly at her and realized her trousers were drooping off her hips, her shirt was open, and her breasts were hanging out of her bra.

Cheeks fiery with embarrassment, she stepped out of Vlerion's arms and hurried to fix her clothing.

She hoped his mother succeeded in getting her out of the ranger training, as she'd promised to do, because it would be awkward and even *more* embarrassing if she ended up in classes or weapons practice with these men.

Even though Targon was mostly glaring at Vlerion, she caught the captain checking her out and remembered comments he'd made in the past. The night they'd met, Targon had asked Vlerion if he'd enjoyed having her squirm in his arms. If Vlerion hadn't then, he had this time. She'd been able to tell that without glancing down.

When she finished fixing her clothes, she realized Vlerion had stepped in front of her to block the rangers' view of her. *He* was utterly naked with his arms folded across his chest, but he probably didn't care if they saw him. Unless their preferences ran toward men, they wouldn't be that interested in him. *She* was and lamented that they hadn't gotten further.

Vlerion turned, putting his back to the men as they rode into the valley. His eyes were still heated, and Kaylina had a feeling he *had* been thinking of finishing, of bringing her to a climax even after the men had arrived. Maybe he'd even been thinking of taking her afterward, of finding his own reward. If the beast hadn't been encroaching, that was understandable. How long had it been since he'd been with a woman, one he could take fully without worry?

"I'll find you later," he whispered softly, stepping forward and resting his hand on her hip while pressing his face into her hair. "If not for my pleasure, then yours."

"We both know that's not a good idea."

Later, the beast would have the ability to return.

"One day, we'll find a way," he said and kissed her.

"By all the warring gods," Targon snapped from scant feet behind them, "put your cock away, Vlerion."

Vlerion broke the kiss but didn't move away from Kaylina, only turning his head to level a cold, defiant look at his captain.

His mother's words came to mind, that the beast in him was drawn to the *anrokk* in Kaylina. Isla had been worried Vlerion might not be able to control himself around her. Maybe she'd been right. Kaylina wasn't even positive *she* could control herself fully.

"There are Kar'ruk all over this forest," Targon added, glaring back as defiantly.

"I know," Vlerion said. "I killed many of them."

Some of the men who'd ridden up behind Targon exchanged confused looks with each other.

Had they been to the ruins? Had they seen that claws and fangs, not a sword, had killed those Kar'ruk?

Afraid he would get in a fight with his captain or give away his secret—or both—Kaylina stepped away from Vlerion.

"I'll find your clothes for you while you men talk," she said, trying to sound bright and normal.

But as she took a few more steps away and looked for the taybarri, Vlerion stalked off, apparently not interested in talking with his captain. He'd spotted Crenoch at the edge of the valley and headed to hopefully grab his clothes out of his pack.

Targon turned his focus on Kaylina, giving her a baleful you-know-what's-at-stake glare. Or maybe it was a how-could-you-be-so-stupid-and-you're-horrible-for-him glare. Just because Targon had looked at her bared skin earlier and had admitted he had uses for her didn't mean he liked her.

Maybe it *hadn't* been wise to kiss Vlerion, but she hated the reproof in Targon's eyes and lifted her chin. If other men hadn't been within earshot, men who didn't know Vlerion's secret, she would have told Targon that the threat had been low because Vlerion had shifted earlier. If she'd seen that dangerous glint in his eyes, she would have stepped away.

Targon looked like he might say something to her, but he had to be aware of the men too—and that he'd also sworn to keep Vlerion's secret.

His eyes narrowed with speculation, the way they had when he'd been contemplating using her to further his goals. Maybe this time, he was contemplating her death and how it would make things less dangerous for his ranger subordinate.

Vlerion returned, clothed and with his sword in hand. He stood shoulder to shoulder with Kaylina and went back to glaring at Targon. This time, it seemed less about irritation that the rangers had interrupted and more about protection. Maybe he'd also seen something unsettling in his captain's eyes.

Targon shook his head. "Jankarr, take the girl someplace the guards and the queen won't stumble upon her."

Annoyance flashed in Jankarr's eyes, but he covered it quickly. He had to be tired of being sent back to the city instead of allowed to fight. Even if he seemed like a nice guy, he couldn't be pleased with a babysitting duty.

"Vlerion and everyone else," Targon continued, "we have more Kar'ruk to hunt down. I gather from that bloodbath by the lake that none have been captured for questioning?"

"No," Vlerion said curtly.

"We've got to capture at least one. I want to know how many are in the preserve, what they're planning, and how in all the altered orchards they sneaked this many Kar'ruk over the mountains and into our lands."

"Whatever they're planning, it's nothing good for the city," one of the rangers said. "That's for sure."

Targon waved for his men to follow him and rode out of the valley without another word for Jankarr.

"Later," Vlerion told Kaylina, "I'll find you and help you clear your name. And with anything else you wish."

The significant look he gave her, his eyes raking down her body, turned her on all over again. By the gods, she wanted to be with him.

But with his words delivered, he mounted his taybarri and took off with the other rangers. He had a duty, and she… she had a mission. She needed to prove her innocence, and she also had honey to try on that plant if she could sneak into the castle again without being spotted.

14

Your destiny may seem a mystery, but clues lie in the shadows along your path.

~ Winter Moon Priest Dazibaru

The overgrown trail Jankarr found through the preserve was too narrow for the taybarri to ride side by side, but that didn't keep him from sending curious glances over his shoulder at Kaylina. Frequently.

Exhausted, she didn't ask him what was on his mind. As soon as they escaped the Kar'ruk-filled preserve, she planned to flop her face into Levitke's fur and sleep until they reached… whatever safe place Jankarr intended to store her. But with towering trees all about, vines flicking now and then, and the threat of invaders remaining, she didn't dare doze off. So she noticed Jankarr's glances.

When they reached a wider section of the trail, he slowed his taybarri to walk beside Levitke.

"I have *so* many questions," Jankarr said. "Will you answer them if I ask?"

"My favorite color is lavender, I'm sworn to Elsavi, the Forest Goddess, and I cheated twice on tests in school, but only because my grandmother had high expectations and let us know—sternly—if we didn't perform to her standards."

Jankarr's mouth drooped open.

"Those weren't the questions you were wondering about?" Kaylina didn't want to answer anything about Vlerion or those clawed and bitten Kar'ruk, and she was positive that was what Jankarr was pondering. She worried about accidentally giving away Vlerion's secret.

"No, but why your grandmother instead of your parents?"

"My father was long gone by the time I was in school, and my mother was... *is* more focused on herself these days." Kaylina didn't want to talk about her family or her mother's addiction to tarmav weed either. "Grandma is the founder of the Spitting Gull and the matriarch of the family."

"Huh." Jankarr glanced into the forest ahead. The birds were chirping, and there weren't any musky scents, so hopefully that meant all the Kar'ruk were in a different part of the preserve, being chased down by Vlerion, Targon, and the other rangers. "My first question is why was Vlerion naked in that valley?"

She blinked. "Based on what we were doing when you all showed up, you can't guess?"

"Well, I don't know why *he* would be naked and you'd still be dressed. Sort of dressed." He glanced toward her chest but quickly looked away. "I could see both naked or both with rumpled clothes, but, uhm."

"Is this *really* the burning question that has had you glancing back at me for the last half hour?" Kaylina asked to buy herself time to think of a reason since the *real* reason was tied up in the beast change.

"One of them. It's not like Vlerion to let himself be caught with his pants down when enemies might be in the area. And that was a lot more than his pants down." Jankarr arched his eyebrows. "*Your* pants were almost down."

"Yes, thank you for the recap."

"Sorry." He shrugged and smiled sheepishly.

As she'd noticed before, he was handsome, and she suspected that sheepish smile had gotten him out of a lot of trouble with women in his life.

"He was tense after the battle," Kaylina said. "I offered to relax him. I gave him a massage, which he appreciated."

"Oh, yeah, we all saw how appreciative he was." Jankarr smirked, then waggled his eyebrows. "I'm kind of tense. It's been a long day."

"Are you going to hop off your taybarri and strip if I offer a massage?"

"I might. Did you see the battle with the Kar'ruk? Were you there?"

"I was... hiding in the ruins. I did mess up an archer's shot with a sling round, but you may have seen in our earlier battle that my lead shots don't faze them in the least. I cracked one guy in the head, and all he did was look at me."

"Yeah, even swords aren't great weapons on them. I'd like to get my hands on one of their magical axes, though I've heard the berry juice, or whatever it is they coat them with, wears off and has to be reapplied. Supposedly, the ingredient only grows in their frigid land to the north. Our people have tried to find it, trade for it, and bribe Kar'ruk for information on it, but their people keep the secret close." Jankarr glanced at her again. "Did the taybarri join in the battle?"

Kaylina started to shake her head but realized he wondered about the claw and fang marks. "Yes. I believe they were crucial in Vlerion's victory."

She lay an apologetic hand on Levitke's shoulder, not wanting to lie about the taybarri involvement, but... if it kept the rangers from figuring out what had truly killed the Kar'ruk, that would be ideal.

Levitke looked back at her without whuffing or giving any indication that she minded. If anything, her soulful brown eyes seemed to hold regret, like maybe she wished she *had* been there in the battle instead of running.

No. Kaylina patted her. Better that the taybarri hadn't been where they could have been accidental victims of the beast.

"The Kar'ruk bodies were more, ah, ravaged than is typical for enemies the taybarri take down." Jankarr watched her.

"Were they? It was a chaotic battle. Vlerion was outnumbered. Like I said, I wasn't much help, unfortunately."

"It didn't look like any died to sword wounds."

Kaylina shrugged. "You said slender blades don't do a lot against them."

"Vlerion usually manages."

She gave him another shrug. "I don't know. Like I said, I was hiding. And I'm tired. Could we just ride?"

She willed the trail to grow narrow again. Or for a vine to swing down and cover Jankarr's mouth. No, she had better not wish for that.

"Sure. I was curious, that's all. A lot of people have been mauled by claws and fangs lately." He kept watching her.

Why did she have a feeling he wouldn't be content to *just ride*? She was starting to wish she'd asked to stay with the rangers, but Targon hadn't been in the mood to do her any favors.

"You haven't been reading those newspapers, have you?" she asked.

This time, *Jankarr* shrugged. "I've seen them. All the rangers are talking about them. We're being implicated, and none of us know why."

"The Kar'ruk don't have claws, do they?" Kaylina tried to remember the hands of the archer who'd shot at her, hopeful the deaths in the city might be blamed on the invaders. But, no, she was fairly certain the Kar'ruk had dark nails but not claws.

"No," Jankarr said.

The beast wasn't the only being around with claws, but there weren't that many predators that wandered through Port Jirador. There were taybarri, of course, but they weren't that bloodthirsty. Thus far, she'd only seen them leap into battle against threats to the kingdom.

A vine dangling from a branch flicked, drawing Kaylina's eye to a few stone slabs set back from the trail. Moss, leaves, and more vines almost hid the ruins. She wanted to urge Levitke to move past the area as quickly as possible but spotted what might have been a boot sticking out of undergrowth near one of the slabs.

"Stop, my friend." Jankarr patted his taybarri. "I smell..."

Levitke and his mount whuffed uncertainly and looked around. Kaylina caught the odor too, the musky Kar'ruk odor.

She pointed toward the ruins—toward the boot. "There's something over there."

Or *someone*. A Kar'ruk?

A faint breeze blew toward the ruins instead of away, else they might have caught the scent sooner.

"Stay on the trail." Jankarr slid off his taybarri and drew his sword. "I'll check."

Since Kaylina wanted nothing more than to leave the preserve, she didn't mind obeying the order, but she did load her sling. Thus far, the vines hadn't drawn her into trouble, but this could be a Kar'ruk trap, the boot placed as bait to lure them to investigate.

Jankarr stepped off the trail, looking at drag marks on the ground and broken branches. The vine flicked again.

Kaylina pointed at it. "Watch out for that. The vines here can come to life and entrap you. It happened to Vlerion in the ruins by the lake."

"I've heard stories about them." Jankarr skirted the vine as he approached the boot. "Rangers respect the wilderness and the animals and plants within. It's a shame that this place hates us."

Kaylina didn't ask if he knew the full story of the curse. He probably did, just not the part about Vlerion and his family.

Using his sword, Jankarr gingerly lifted a leaf-laden branch next to the boot. That revealed the leg and the Kar'ruk body attached to it, attached but smothered in vines.

The thick green tendrils were wrapped numerous times around the warrior's midsection, and one had snaked around his neck too. The haft of his axe was visible in the dirt, a vine also securing it.

Kaylina assumed the Kar'ruk was dead, but the boot twitched, and the warrior's eyes popped open.

Swearing, Jankarr jumped back and raised his sword to strike.

The Kar'ruk growled weakly at him and shifted, but he couldn't move more than an inch, thanks to the vines that pinned his torso and limbs to the ground. That didn't keep hatred from burning in his eyes as he glared at Jankarr.

"Targon wanted a Kar'ruk brought in alive to question." Jankarr didn't lower his sword, but he looked thoughtfully toward his taybarri. "If we could keep this guy wrapped up and subdued, he would do. Assuming he doesn't have any poison in his mouth to kill himself with."

"And assuming you can break him free of the vines. It's not easy."

"How did Vlerion escape?"

Kaylina hesitated. How indeed. "I feebly whacked at the vines with his sword." True. "But the taybarri were the ones with the strength to break them." Possibly true, even if they hadn't been around to do it.

"Ours can help then. Or maybe this would do the job." Only a thin tendril wrapped around the axe haft, so Jankarr was able to cut it free. Despite a coating of dirt and pieces of cut vegetation, the sharp head glowed a soft blue. "Beautiful craftsmanship, and it tingles in my hand."

The Kar'ruk snarled, fingers twitching toward Jankarr. No doubt the warrior wanted to throttle him for presuming to touch the weapon.

"Sorry, my enemy." Jankarr shifted the axe to aim at one of the thick vines binding the Kar'ruk's torso. "I'd feel dishonorable for using your weapon and taking advantage of your predicament, but you *are* trespassing on kingdom land and doing who knows what out here. No." Jankarr's jaw clenched. "I know *exactly* what you've done."

He had to be thinking of the injured woman and dead men.

"Do you want me to help?" Kaylina asked when the tip of the thick vine twitched. "So far, the plants in here haven't bothered me. I assume because I'm not a ranger."

She glanced at the brand on the back of her hand and almost added, *Possibly for other reasons*, but worried she'd already shared too much with Jankarr. He was rubbing his mental sticks together to make fire too quickly for the safety of Vlerion's secret.

"Nope." Jankarr hefted the axe overhead but paused to wink back at her. "I'll take a massage afterward, though, if you're inclined."

"I don't think you want to get naked out here." Kaylina watched the twitchy vine, worried the Kar'ruk wasn't the only one who would end up entrapped.

"Vlerion seemed to think it was the thing to do."

"He's a unique soul."

"I've noticed that." Jankarr chopped the axe into the vine. It cut halfway through on the first blow. "Given how much prettier than him I am, you'd think the ladies we ride past would proposition *me*, but they're oddly drawn to him." After he cleaved the vine in half, he gave her another look, one more curious and puzzled than his wink.

"Scars intrigue girls. And I'm sure you do fine too."

"When I'm not beside him, yes. Do you think I should let myself get hit in the face more often? You know, for scars?"

"You could go to one of the playhouses and have a makeup artist paint one on. It would be less painful."

"I suppose that's true." Jankarr shifted to target another vine, but, as he raised the axe, several more shot out of the undergrowth.

Kaylina cursed and rushed forward. She'd been afraid of that.

Jankarr leaped back, almost evading the viper-like vines, but they were too fast. One caught him by the ankle, yanking him off balance. He kept hold of the axe but landed hard on his back, unable to soften the fall with the vine pulling at him. It drew him across the earth, rucking his clothing, until he was side by side with the Kar'ruk. The horned warrior roared with satisfaction, even though his predicament hadn't improved.

Jankarr sat up, aiming the axe for the vine around his ankle, but two more swept out of the undergrowth, and one slithered across an overhead branch and descended. Toward his neck?

"Look out!" Kaylina stopped a few feet away, afraid to get too close while he swung the axe around.

The blade struck vines, splitting them, but more appeared. One lashed out, smacking him in the eye and stunning him for a second. It was long enough for the vines to plaster him flat to the ground, the same as the Kar'ruk. One pinned his wrist so he couldn't use the axe.

All around them, the foliage buzzed with the magical energy Kaylina had felt earlier. It seemed angry, like a disturbed hornet's nest.

She crept closer and risked resting a hand on Jankarr's shoulder. The vines rippled and undulated without letting him go. They didn't lash out at her, but she didn't know what to do.

"It's not going to eat us, is it?" Jankarr asked plaintively.

"If the plants were carnivorous, they would have eaten the Kar'ruk," Kaylina said.

"Maybe their kind don't taste good. All hate and gristle."

"*Kluk ka borgluk,*" the Kar'ruk snarled.

"Let go of the axe, and I'll try to cut you free." Kaylina debated if the vines would capture her if she did that. They hadn't attacked Jankarr until he'd damaged them.

"I don't think I can." Jankarr moved his head as much as he could to glance at his wrist. Not only was a vine wrapped around it, pinning his arm to the ground, but one had snaked around the haft of the axe, pinning *it*.

"I… could go get the others." Maybe. Kaylina didn't have any idea where the rest of the rangers had gone after leaving the valley. Even if she did, enough time had passed that they would be miles away.

Jankarr groaned. "I'd rather die than let them see that I got myself into this predicament."

"If it helps, the Kar'ruk did too."

"It does *not* help."

Leaves rustled behind Kaylina, and she spun. But it was only Levitke and Jankarr's mount.

"Can you two bite me free?" Jankarr asked the taybarri hopefully.

"Yes." Kaylina nodded, stepping aside for them. Thanks to their fangs and claws, they had weapons the vines couldn't steal from them.

But as soon as the taybarri approached, their maws opening, several new vines slithered into view, rearing up to strike like the cobras she kept comparing them to.

The taybarri hesitated, issuing uncertain whuffs. One snapped toward Levitke like a whip cracking.

"*No!*" Kaylina snarled, furious that a plant would attack her friendly taybarri mount.

Maybe it wasn't smart, but she lunged forward and grabbed the vine, willing it to leave the animals alone. To leave Jankarr alone too.

The tip flicked in irritation. What was that word she'd blurted before?

"*Sywretha!*"

The vine went limp. They *all* went limp, and the hum of power faded.

Though surprised, Jankarr reacted before the Kar'ruk. He sat up, hefting the axe, then lunged to his knee and one foot as he slammed the flat of the blade down on the warrior's head. The Kar'ruk had been entangled longer and half unconscious when they'd found him, so he didn't get his arms up in time to block. Jankarr struck him again and again. It took several mighty blows with the flat of the blade before the warrior slumped back, falling unconscious.

"Wish I had some of that knock-out powder the apothecaries make." Jankarr made sure the Kar'ruk was truly unconscious and not feigning before turning to look at Kaylina. His eyes were round as he asked, "What did you do?"

"Nothing." Realizing she gripped the now-limp vine, Kaylina dropped it.

"That was not nothing."

Kaylina shrugged. "I said that word before in the other ruins, and it helped."

"What does it mean?"

"I have no idea. I'm not even sure where I heard it. Or read it."

Jankarr stared at her for a long silent moment as if she were the strangest thing he'd ever seen. The words of her past lover,

Domas, floated to mind again: *What is* wrong *with you? You look so normal.*

"Something tells me that if I'd yelled that," Jankarr said, "nothing would have happened."

"Probably not." Kaylina eyed the back of her hand. "You haven't fed honey to any plants lately."

After checking the Kar'ruk one more time, Jankarr said, "Let's tie up our prisoner—with *ropes*, not vines—and head back. Maybe if Captain Targon gets some answers from questioning this guy, he'll be in a better mood."

"Okay."

"I'll have to report to him that you... can do whatever it is you did."

"I wouldn't mind if he *didn't* learn about this." Kaylina had saved Jankarr's life, however atypically. Couldn't he keep a secret for her?

Jankarr smiled sadly. "I am, sometimes unfortunately, honor bound to report everything that's a matter of kingdom security or safety for the rangers."

"I don't have anything to do with either of those things."

"We'll see," he said grimly.

15

For those who don't know where to look, there is no water in the desert.

~ Sandsteader proverb

It was dark and drizzling by the time Kaylina, Jankarr—and the Kar'ruk prisoner bound and draped over his taybarri—rode toward one of the eastern city gates. Kaylina had her cloak on again, her hood pulled low to hide her face, but she considered slipping off Levitke and running into the countryside. She didn't want to endure an interrogation at ranger headquarters any more than she wanted to be arrested for the poisoning attempt of the queen. Even if she wasn't bound, she felt as much a prisoner as the Kar'ruk.

"Halt, ranger." A city guard and a man in ranger blacks stepped out of the gatehouse. "What is your— Is that a *Kar'ruk*?"

"A prisoner I'm taking for questioning, yes," Jankarr said.

Both the guard and ranger swore in surprise.

Kaylina assumed Targon hadn't yet put the word out that

Kar'ruk had crossed the border and infiltrated the preserve. Maybe he hoped to *never* do that since it meant the invaders had gotten past the rangers in the watchtowers.

"What about him?" The ranger pointed at Kaylina, the wan light from the lanterns not enough to illuminate the lack of beard stubble on her jaw.

"That's the person who assisted me in capturing the Kar'ruk."

"Jankarr, you know we need the identities of everyone entering the gate after dark. And during daylight right now, as well." The ranger waved in the direction of the royal castle on its cliff overlooking the harbor and the city.

"Come, then." Jankarr crooked a finger to beckon him closer, then bent and whispered in the ranger's ear.

The guard folded his arms over his chest while glowering suspiciously.

"Ah. Go ahead through, Jankarr." The ranger looked at the guard. "That is a trainee who has not yet earned the right to be called a ranger, but my colleague vouches for him."

"The rangers are vouching for a lot lately," the guard grumbled, but he stepped back.

What did that mean? Something to do with the murders? The stories in the newspaper?

Not responding to that, Jankarr led the way toward headquarters. The paces of both taybarri picked up. Maybe they knew they would get food once they arrived.

Though their route took them down the far side of the river from Stillguard Castle, Kaylina glimpsed the dark towers as they passed over an arched bridge. She sucked in a breath. A purple glow emanated from the plant's window.

"It changed back," she whispered. "It *does* like the honey water."

Jankarr looked at the tower, then at her, again giving her the you-have-turned-into-something-strange look.

He probably wouldn't ask her again for a massage. Which was fine. She hadn't even massaged *Vlerion*, but she worried about what Jankarr would tell Targon, Targon who already had far too much of an interest in her.

When they entered ranger headquarters, men in the courtyard spotted the Kar'ruk and rushed over to help Jankarr haul him off. Kaylina dismounted at the stable, thanking Levitke for the ride.

Momentarily left alone, she was tempted to sneak out through the still-open gate before Targon returned. And before anyone thought to lock her in a room—or a cell.

Then her brother poked his head out a window in the stone infirmary building where Doctor Penderbrock worked.

"Fray?" Kaylina gave Levitke a final pat and jogged across the courtyard toward the window. "Are you all right? Did you get hurt again?"

"No, but researching in dusty basement archives made me wheezy. The doctor stirred up a concoction that I've been faithfully breathing while I read. He's been letting me work in the office of his infirmary. I'll show you what I have so far."

"That's good of him to let you loiter." Kaylina noticed Levitke trailing her across the courtyard, despite the parting pat. Was she supposed to feed the taybarri? She made a shooing motion and whispered, "Tell Jankarr I said you should get extra food."

"I haven't been loitering. I've been working assiduously on the requested research. I also helped him organize the medicines in his cabinets. They weren't alphabetized or filed by category or *anything*. They were all shoved haphazardly in there. Some were upside down. Two were *leaking*. An apothecary shop struck by a meteor couldn't have been in more disarray." Frayvar clasped an aggrieved hand to his chest. "I don't know how he found anything."

"Sometimes, you seem closer to eighty than eighteen."

"A need for organization has nothing to do with one's age."

"Oh, I'm not sure about that." As Kaylina opened the door to join him inside, she added, "Did the doctor *want* you to help tidy his medicines?"

"Not at first, but he's seen the benefits of having them grouped by treatment category and, within each grouping, alphabetized. Once we've cleared your name, I'm planning to make a ledger for him so he can keep a record of everything and know when to re-order. It'll also help him track medicines that go missing a lot. He's had a problem with that. Apparently, rangers slip in and help themselves to painkillers, mood enhancers, and a stimulant they take to keep them awake on long patrols."

Kaylina yawned and wished she had some of that. On the way back, she'd dozed, but napping while riding a taybarri wasn't the same as sleeping in a comfortable—and stationary—bed.

The doctor wasn't inside, but Frayvar led her to a small office beyond the cots, as if he'd made the infirmary his second home. Since the cabinet doors were closed, Kaylina couldn't see evidence of her brother's organizing, but the whole place had been dusted and cleaned since she'd last visited. Frayvar might have been responsible for that.

"I was only gone a day," she murmured.

"I like to earn my keep and pay people back for favors." Frayvar touched his side, indicating the ribs that had been broken in the fire. They didn't seem to be slowing him down—he could wheeze even without a chest injury. "But don't worry. I've prioritized doing the research Targon requested as well as working on our problem."

"My problem."

"Considering the latest wanted poster also has my face on it and lists me as an accomplice, it's *our* problem. Trust me."

Kaylina winced. "That's awful."

"The drawing was, yes. It made me look like a frail, spindly hunchback." Frayvar stopped in front of the office desk.

"You don't hunch that much unless you're organizing spices on the bottom shelves of the pantry."

"I'll refrain from observing that you didn't object to the two adjectives preceding that noun."

"Smart. Is that a map?" Kaylina pointed at a large parchment on the desk, the corners pinned down by books, an inkwell, and forceps—a natural paperweight found in a doctor's office.

"Of the city, yes. Here's Nakeron Inn, Jana Bloomlong's establishment. I was tempted to visit today until a ranger showed me that wanted poster. What do you think about going by tonight to take a look?"

"We could." If Kaylina was allowed to leave... "Vlerion already visited Jana's inn and searched the drawers there though."

"Oh? Well, I've also marked the various apothecaries in town." Frayvar pointed to pebbles on the map—no, those were taybarri protein pellets. No wonder Levitke was lurking nearby. "And a ranger mentioned someone who makes and sells paint by day and is known to dabble in poisons by night. Apparently, the paint business isn't very lucrative."

"But making poisons is?"

"You can sell them by the ounce—or less—for a much higher amount than paint. It's not illegal to make them, the ranger said, just to use them on people. He also said Lord Vlerion already visited the paint shop, but the owner wasn't there."

Kaylina touched the pocket holding the vials, including the one Vlerion had given her, touched by how much he'd poked around to try to help her. She withdrew them and set them on the map, pointing to the tiny maker's marks on the bottoms.

"Vlerion thought the glassmaker who made these might know who bought his vials," she said.

"Probably a lot of people." Frayvar sounded dismissive, like he didn't think that would turn into a lead, but he did look at the empty vial, then pointed at a market square on the map. "All the glassworkers have shops in this area. We can check during their open hours tomorrow."

"All right. I need to visit Stillguard Castle too and look at the plant again." Kaylina eyed the brand on her hand, wondering if she was crazy to go back, but its magic had helped her in the preserve. "I have a new type of honey that I want to fertilize it with."

"Plant fertilization should be low on our priority list. Besides, the Kingdom Guard might be watching the castle in case we return there."

"I know, but I want to solve the problem of the curse, both for our future and for... other reasons."

"Let's solve the problem of you being wanted dead as a criminal first. The curse doesn't matter until we're free to walk around town and open our business without being thrown in jail—or worse."

Not wanting to argue with him—she never won arguments with her oh-so-logical brother, anyway—Kaylina nodded. "Okay."

After visiting poison makers and glassworkers, she would sneak into the castle.

A roar that didn't sound human or animal came from one of the buildings across the courtyard. Was that the Kar'ruk? The noise had come from the direction Jankarr and the other rangers had taken their prisoner.

Kaylina suspected the questioning would be violent, unless the rangers could force kafdari root down the Kar'ruk's throat, but she wished she could hear his answers. Even though she had her own problems, it was hard not to worry about how many horned invaders might be about. Especially since Vlerion was out there hunting them.

Another roar wafted out, followed by a defiant string of clipped Kar'ruk words. The questioning might not be going well.

"Did you get a chance to research the newspaper?" Kaylina

opened a window to peer across the courtyard, but the interrogation was taking place indoors. A few taybarri near the stable looked at each other and swished their tails, perhaps in agitation. They might be uneasy about the roars or the presence of a Kar'ruk in general.

"I read all the issues that have been printed and asked around, but nobody knows where they're coming from."

"Do they know to search *outside* the city for their origins?" she asked.

"Probably not. Maybe we should have climbed out the back of that wagon and subdued and questioned the person driving."

"Have you subdued anyone in your life?" Kaylina didn't bring up his spindly frailness.

"No, but you could have pummeled him with sling rounds until he answered our questions."

"Or drew a sword and kicked our asses. I'm not any more of a fighter than you are."

"Not even with your ranger training?"

"The *one* day of training I had didn't teach me that much." Kaylina scratched her jaw. "What if we lie in wait in the dark of night on the highway near the river to see if another wagon carrying newspapers comes through? I think Vlerion said it's been delivered daily lately."

"We? Kay, *we* have a more important mission." Frayvar pointed at her chest, then his. "We need to focus on that. *Tonight*."

The courtyard gate opened, several rangers on taybarri riding in, and she didn't respond. Was that the party that Targon had led into the preserve?

Yes, she spotted the captain in the lead, but where was Vlerion? Sent off on another mission? Not injured, she hoped.

A ranger ran up to Targon, reporting something to him. About the Kar'ruk prisoner? Yes, he pointed at the building that held him.

After ordering a subordinate to care for the taybarri, Targon dismounted and jogged inside with the ranger.

"Kaylina." Frayvar poked her.

"Sorry. I heard you. I know our mission is important, and I do want to clear my name. Trust me." Maybe it was foolish, but she worried *more* about Vlerion. As long as she could avoid the Kingdom Guard, she ought to be okay, but he would be in grave trouble if the Virts spread the word about his link to the beast—and roused the entire populace against him. There wouldn't be anywhere for him to hide to escape the ire of an entire city.

"I wonder," Frayvar muttered.

"I'm just tired. Did you get any sleep today?"

"You're so tired that your brain is scheming on a different topic every two minutes." He waved at one of the cots. "I napped in between organizing, researching, and worrying about you."

"So, no sleep."

"No *long* sleep."

"We should both rest."

"And then we'll visit Nakeron Inn and the paint shop?" Frayvar waved at the map while holding her gaze intently.

"Like I said, Vlerion already checked the inn. That's where he got the vial. I don't know what else we'd find."

"I'm an expert researcher. I might find things a simple pugilist missed. Such as drawers full of incriminating evidence."

"I doubt Jana is keeping *drawers* of her written plans for my demise, and Vlerion is a lot more than a pugilist."

Frayvar waved dismissively at that, saying only, "We might find *something* he missed."

"All right." Kaylina yawned and rubbed her gritty eyes, too tired to anticipate a search, especially one her brother wanted to start that night. "Tomorrow, we'll—"

The door to the infirmary opened, and Targon walked in,

looking straight toward the office. One of his men must have told him Kaylina and Frayvar were inside.

Targon ignored him and squinted at her. Suspiciously?

Kaylina hadn't done anything that should irk him. She'd even helped Jankarr. Of course, Targon might still be irked that she'd been entwined with Vlerion when he and his rangers had shown up in the preserve...

"Is everything okay, Captain?" Kaylina wanted to ask if *Vlerion* was okay, especially since he hadn't come back with the rangers, but she didn't bring him up in case their relationship was the reason for Targon's squinty eyes. She would prefer to distract the captain from whatever dark thoughts he was having about them together.

"Little has been *okay* of late." Targon looked at Frayvar, then back to her. "Come to my office, Korbian. We need to talk."

"All right."

His squint deepened.

"My lord," Kaylina made herself add.

He grunted and walked out.

"Does this mean we're not visiting the inn tonight?" Frayvar asked.

Kaylina only shook her head. As she followed the dour Captain Targon across the courtyard, she worried she was about to lose any semblance of freedom she'd had.

16

Prove yourself useful, and you'll never want for a place in the world.

~ "Foundations III" Scribe Menalow

Because Vlerion's office had been attached to his bedroom, Kaylina worried Targon would take her to the barracks. She didn't want to see the room—or bed—where he'd entertained the queen and who knew how many more women.

But, after she grabbed her pack, he led her into a building that held an armory on the first floor, the air smelling of metal and weapons-cleaning oil. They climbed wooden stairs to a hall lined with offices, name plaques stating they belonged to various high-ranking rangers. Most of the doors were closed, the occupants gone for the night. Targon opened one at the end and stepped inside to multiple chairs, a desk, a conference table, and a bookcase full of thick texts, atlases, and old scrolls, as well as a few dented helmets and daggers. A huge fossilized skull leered from the top. Prizes he'd won over the years?

A lamp burned low on the desk, and Targon turned it up and used the flame to light others. The placement of some emphasized the daggers, helmets, and skull.

"I don't know what to do with you, Korbian. You're turning out to be much more than I expected."

Much more what? Of a delight?

Kaylina doubted it. She suspected Jankarr had told his captain about her new ability to convince vines not to kill rangers.

"Vlerion is helping me find evidence to clear my name," she offered. "If you would like to do the same, I would be most grateful."

"*Vlerion* is obsessed with you."

"I don't think that's true. He's helping me because..."

Because why? He'd admitted that he had come to care for her, but Kaylina didn't know if that was because she was appealing to him as a person or if the beast in him was drawn to the *anrokk* in her.

Targon finished lighting lamps and raised his eyebrows, waiting for her to complete the sentence.

"He's a nice guy," Kaylina finished lamely.

"Uh-huh. I would have said he's helping because he's into your tits, but I've never seen him fall for a beautiful woman. Up until he met you, he was almost preternaturally restrained when it came to that. His mother has a hypothesis about it."

Yes, Kaylina had been thinking about that hypothesis. She grimaced at the thought that Isla of Havartaft might have come to the city to talk to Targon about her.

Oh, Isla had specifically said she would do that, but she'd implied it would be about her destiny as a mead maker. She'd said she would try to get Targon to release her from the ranger training. The thought that they might also have been discussing her and Vlerion's sexual attraction mortified her.

"I'm aware of the, uhm, hypothesis, my lord." Kaylina selected her words carefully, not sure what Targon wanted. Was he thinking about making her disappear?

"She thinks *you're* drawn to him too. That I've seen before, so it's not that surprising. Women somehow sense what he is." Targon waved, not mentioning the beast specifically, maybe because he'd also sworn to keep that secret. "The way the taybarri do, maybe. Except women aren't as smart as taybarri. *They* know to be wary of Vlerion."

Kaylina clenched her jaw to keep from blurting an indignation about being compared to big furry animals, even if the taybarri were more than that. They weren't animals at all if their elders were as intelligent as humans.

"I suppose if I forbade you from getting close to him, it wouldn't do anything," Targon added.

"Captain, I'm aware of the danger. I'm not *trying* to get close to him. I'm just appreciative that he's helping me."

"So appreciative that you can't keep from rubbing up against him and shoving your tongue in his mouth."

"That *hasn't* happened." Her cheeks heated with embarrassment as well as her ongoing indignation over the whole situation. Kaylina hated that Targon had seen them together, but tongues hadn't been in mouths. There had only been… Well, maybe there had been a little rubbing.

"What would have happened if we hadn't shown up?"

"I don't know, but Vlerion said that after he's already changed, it's less likely to happen again. I think— I'm sure if he had believed there was a threat, he wouldn't have hugged me."

"*Hugging* isn't what was about to happen."

Kaylina sighed.

"And he shouldn't have *changed* in the first place." Targon pulled a newspaper off a shelf and smacked it down on the desk, the article she'd already seen on top. "That's the last thing we need right now. Between the mangled bodies showing up in the city, the Virts having spotted him furry in the castle dungeon, and this anonymous journalist trying to link him to the rangers... Vlerion is lucky his name hasn't specifically been printed in this gossip rag yet. Once that happens, it's going to be hard to protect him."

"I understand, Captain, but it was out in the preserve, and it was because the vines had him and the Kar'ruk were coming, not because I was rubbing anything of his." Her cheeks grew hotter as she lied. Shame filled her because she felt the need, but it wasn't her fault the situation had forced her to try to rouse the beast.

"Vlerion also said he changed because of the Kar'ruk." The frank look Targon leveled at Kaylina made her think he knew the truth. Somehow. "*Usually,* he's honorable and honest with me and the men. He's not a great liar, so when it happens, I can tell."

"I wanted to save his life," Kaylina whispered. Tears threatened, and she blinked to stave them off. She didn't want to cry in front of this man. "He was trapped, and I thought the beast could break the vines. He wasn't able to as a man, you see, and I wasn't strong enough, not even with his sword."

"How come you could get the vines off Jankarr but not Vlerion?" Targon walked around the desk and closer to her, studying her intently.

Trying to tell if *she* was lying?

"I didn't know I could then. And I have no idea if I could do it again. It surprised me. I'm still not sure what I did." Kaylina resisted the urge to back away from Targon. She hated that he was taller than she—taller and bigger and stronger—and could loom over her. "I think it has to do with this." She lifted her hand, turning the back toward him. "The plant in Stillguard Castle branded me. Did Vlerion tell you? It seemed to convey some... I'm not sure what. Out in the preserve, it was kind of guiding me. I think it's what let me free Jankarr."

"I've never heard of anyone being branded by a plant." Targon gazed at the mark, then took her hand and rubbed his thumb across the raised scar.

Kaylina gritted her teeth, bristling at the presumptuousness. If Vlerion had rubbed her hand, she wouldn't have minded, but she didn't like Targon, Targon who wanted to use her. And what did his statement mean? That he thought she was lying?

"Strange." He let go of her hand.

She wanted to stuff it into her pocket. "I've been told before that I'm not normal."

Targon snorted and walked around to the other side of the desk, glancing out the window on the way. "*That* I believe."

His glance became a second look, then a longer one back at her as he pointed out the window.

Kaylina crept closer until she could see four taybarri, including Levitke, gazing up at her through the panes.

"I didn't feed and groom her when we returned, like the ranger book says," she admitted, backing away from Targon again. "I wasn't sure it was my place to or where their food is stored."

"Book?"

"The something guide to honor and things."

"*The Ranger's Guide to Honor, Duty, and Tenets.* You've been reading it?"

"Vlerion keeps giving me copies." Kaylina didn't mention the pages she'd ripped out of the latest one. Thinking of it reminded her to give the rubbing she'd made to Frayvar. Later, when he wasn't peeved because she was interested in things besides digging up evidence to prove her innocence.

"Hm." Targon waved her to a chair, then sat in the large one behind the desk. "Listen, Korbian. You've got some power I don't understand, and apparently it's more than being appealing to animals."

"I don't understand it either."

"I'd rather you work with us, for the good of the kingdom, than have to worry about you becoming an enemy. No." Targon held up a hand as she started to protest. "Enemy isn't the right word. I saw you fight with Vlerion to save the king and queen—though I suspect that was more for *him* than for them—and you've helped the rangers." He pointed to his own chest, and she hoped he remembered that she'd tried to keep the vine in Stillguard Castle from killing him, even if she hadn't been effective. "What I should say is that I'd like to be able to use you, for the good of the kingdom, and I'd prefer you weren't a *liability*."

Kaylina didn't have a protest for that. The word stung as true. At the least, she was a liability to Vlerion. If his desire for her caused him to turn into the beast in the city with innocent people around...

"Is that why you didn't bring him back?" she asked. "So he wouldn't be around me?"

"He's with a few other rangers, spending more time looking for Kar'ruk in the preserve and also seeing if any have been spotted on estates in the countryside. That's important work that needs to be done."

"That will also keep him away from me." The thought saddened Kaylina, but could she blame the captain? She ought to appreciate that he wanted to protect Vlerion and keep his secret.

"A bonus perk. I don't know what to do with you, Korbian. If you weren't wanted by the Kingdom Guard, I'd see if I could get a couple of scholars and scientists to come study you. You and that brand."

"Wouldn't that be appealing."

"I suppose Vlerion would get huffy and object to us poking and prodding you and looking at skin and blood samples under a microscope."

"*I'd* get huffy."

"I'm less worried about your ire, though I suppose that's

foolish of me. If you're left free without a keeper, you could go to the Virts and tell them everything you've learned."

"I wouldn't betray Vlerion. But it *is* foolish of you to dismiss me." Kaylina lifted her chin. "You've seen my marksmanship ability with the sling."

Targon smiled faintly. "Yes, I have. As I've said, I'd far rather have you working with us than against us." He gazed thoughtfully at her. "I understand honey clumps are more appealing to the taybarri than protein pellets."

She blinked at the topic change but managed to murmur, "Honey *drops*, my lord."

"What manner of honey drop would appeal to *you*?"

"I enjoy many of the candies and sweets and, of course, the mead made from my family's honey." Only as Kaylina finished the statement and noticed his intent gaze upon her did she realize he was asking what reward he could offer to ensure her cooperation. Her *loyalty*. More a bribe than a reward, probably. "Oh."

"For obvious reasons, I can't offer you Vlerion."

"Because he's not *yours* to offer."

Targon grunted. "He's loyal to the crown, the rangers, *and* to me—he's sworn oaths that bind him. That means I could offer his services, but that would result in exactly what we must avoid. Especially now." He waved at the newspaper again.

"You don't have to bribe me, Captain. I just want some help… no, I don't even want *help*. All I want is the freedom to open a meadery and compete fairly against the other eating houses, wineries, and breweries in the city. I want a chance to prove that my family's mead is delicious and worth being sampled by all."

"And you don't want to become a ranger."

Kaylina opened her mouth to state an emphatic *no*, but if all she ever did was make mead, she wouldn't have an opportunity to ride one of the taybarri again. And, with the way trouble kept finding her, wouldn't it be smart to get some weapons training? With more than a sling?

Yes, it would. But if the rangers trained her, they would expect her to then work for them. Probably to swear the oaths Targon had spoken of and to dedicate her *life* to the duty.

With his expectant gaze on her, she felt compelled to say something. "I want to start a meadery."

"What if you could do both? If your ranger duties, assuming you complete the training without turning into a plant—" Targon glanced at her hand as if that were a possibility, "—didn't demand all of your time, would you consider it?"

Would she? If Frayvar was willing to remain in the north long enough to get the business off the ground, she might be able to hire staff and work at the castle only part time. Maybe.

Kaylina couldn't help but think about Targon's question about honey drops for her. About *bribes*. "Is that something you offer to other people becoming rangers?"

"No."

"Other *anrokk*?"

"The only one we have, Sergeant Jastadar, was never interested in starting a meadery on the side."

"Can I meet him?" Maybe Kaylina should have asked that when the rangers had first started throwing the word *anrokk* around. As she recalled, Jastadar was almost to retirement age. Targon and Vlerion had implied it was rare for rangers to survive all their years of fighting to be *able* to retire.

"Yes." Targon shrugged. "If you stuck with the training, you'd meet all the rangers in this province sooner or later."

"I'd like to think about it." Kaylina admitted that *because I want to ride a taybarri* wasn't a great reason to become a ranger, to constantly have to put her life in danger. As noble as the profession was, she doubted it would suit her. She hated following orders, even from her own family members, people who loved her. She might end up flogged if she kept training with the rangers. The way things were going, she might end up flogged *often*.

"Of course." Targon's tone was perfectly reasonable. Because he thought she would inevitably agree and he had won?

"Obviously, I'd need to figure out how to clear my name first."

"Yes, obviously."

"And I'm on a quest to lift Vlerion's curse."

Targon blinked, looking surprised for the first time during their meeting. Maybe for the first time since she'd met him. "What?"

"It has to be possible."

"I don't think that's true. Some of his ancestors dedicated their lives to researching ways to end the curse, and none of them ever figured it out."

"Yeah, but I'm special." Kaylina showed him her brand. "You said so yourself."

"I believe I said you're *strange*."

"I chose to hear a less offensive word, thus to be able to continue having this conversation without thinking of you as an odious villain."

"How thoughtful of you."

"Yes. You're aware that the glow of the plant in the tower at Stillguard Castle changed color after I fertilized it with honey water?"

"I heard it turned purple for a couple of days."

"I have more honey to try on it, *druid* honey. I'm going to lift the curse from the castle, and then I'm going to use what I learn there to lift Vlerion's curse."

Targon started to scoff but looked at her hand again and didn't. "I'd never pondered it before, but it does make sense that the two curses might be related."

"Based on the story I heard, they're absolutely related. Whatever lifts the curse from the castle might lift the curse of the beast."

"Are you going to pour honey water on Vlerion?"

"I don't know if that's how the curse can be lifted, just that it affected the plant. If people weren't trying to arrest me, I could have spent time studying it."

"A team of scientists might be needed after all," Targon muttered.

"I doubt the plant would permit them to poke and prod it. Even I got zapped when I touched its soil."

Targon walked to the window and gazed out. "I would like to see Vlerion be able to live a normal life and not have to worry about the beast."

"Yes. So would I." Kaylina might not like Targon, but she was encouraged that he cared for Vlerion.

"If he weren't cursed, maybe he could even..." Targon's gaze shifted toward the plateau that held the royal castle, but he didn't finish that sentence. Instead, he looked over his shoulder at her and changed the topic. "I don't know if I should or shouldn't point out that if the curse were lifted and his beast element disappeared, he might be indifferent to you."

Kaylina froze. She'd envisioned that if the curse were lifted, she and Vlerion could be together without concern for safety.

He had denied that the beast had anything to do with his attraction to her—to her *anrokk* side—but could he truly know that? His mother believed it was the reason, and didn't mothers know best? Queen Henova, who'd written that famous book on rearing children who became great leaders, had said that.

Without the supernatural link, what if Vlerion no longer found himself so strongly attracted to Kaylina? Or attracted to her at all? Lady Ghara, with her striking blonde locks, might bestir him far more than she.

"I would hope he's not indifferent, but I would be happy to see the curse lifted regardless of how he felt about me afterward." Kaylina barely kept from frowning. It wasn't an untrue statement, but she would be disappointed if he lost interest in her. Devastatingly disappointed. How had she grown to care for him—and want to be with him—so quickly? Would *her* feelings change if he no longer had the beast within him? What if they both lost interest in each other? She shook her head, not wanting to believe that would happen. "He's saved my life," she added, uncomfortable under Targon's all-too-knowing gaze. "No matter what else might happen, I owe him."

Targon grunted, not appearing moved by her dedication, and flicked a glance down her body. "You're hot enough that he'd probably want you, beast-*anrokk* regardless."

Kaylina gritted her teeth. The captain might care for Vlerion, but she was positive he saw her as nothing more than a tool.

Something outside the window drew Targon's gaze, and he frowned.

"Who's bringing carriages to ranger headquarters this late at night?"

Kaylina wanted to look, but it was the only window on that wall, and she didn't want to stand that close to Targon, not after his comments proving he'd noticed her body. More than once. She didn't trust him one iota and might be a fool for wanting anything to do with the rangers. It was the *taybarri* that she wanted to be around. And Vlerion.

"Shit." Targon backed away and scowled at her. "It's the Castle Guard with a squadron from the Kingdom Guard. This *has* to be about you. Someone must have seen you riding through the city with Jankarr and reported it."

Kaylina forgot her aversion to the captain and lunged close to the window to look out. Two carriages painted in the royal colors had stopped in the courtyard, and two wagons full of armored men were entering after them.

Targon gripped her arm and pulled her away from the window.

"If I were smart," he said, not letting her go, "I would tie you up and say we'd captured you and were about to take you to the royal castle."

Kaylina tried to pull away, but his grip might as well have been an iron shackle. It didn't budge.

She searched his eyes by the lamplight and refrained from sharing an opinion on his intelligence. Long seconds passed. He had to be contemplating her fate—or maybe risks to his career if she was found unfettered here.

"Is that what you're going to do?" Kaylina finally asked.

"After you saved Jankarr and fought at Vlerion's side to save the king and queen? No. But I need you to get out of here before your presence condemns me."

Men called out in the courtyard, orders to search the compound wafting through the window.

"I don't suppose you have a secret exit?" she asked.

"Of course I have a secret exit." Targon pulled her behind the desk, pushed the bookcase sideways—it slid easily on well-oiled hinges—and revealed a dark cubby. "Take the stairs down two levels, follow the hall at the bottom to a dead end, and there's a switch on the eighth brick from the ground on the left side. Head out into the sewers until you find an access point up into the city. From there, you'd better work on clearing your name. You're not going to have the luxury of lifting any curses until you can walk freely about the city."

Targon pushed her toward the secret exit, but Kaylina planted her hands on the doorframe to stop herself. "I need Frayvar. He's in the infirmary."

"There aren't any secret exits from there, and you can't get over there without going through the courtyard." Targon put a hand on her back.

"I can't leave him here alone to be caught."

Footfalls sounded in the hallway. "Captain Targon?" someone hollered.

"That's not one of my men." He pushed her into the dark nook.

Kaylina's foot almost slipped off the top of the landing. The stairs were too dim to see.

She spun back toward him. "I can't—"

"I'll try to keep them from finding him and taking him." Targon held his palm up, as if she were a dog he was commanding to stay.

Kaylina wanted to spring out of the nook, to find a way to her brother.

"If you're caught, it'll make Vlerion crazy." Targon gave her a significant look. "*More* than crazy."

Damn it, he was right.

Her shoulders slumped, and she didn't stop Targon when he slid the bookcase shut, plunging her into darkness.

17

Nothing is so fascinating as listening to others ponder your fate.

~ Grandma Korbian

Kaylina should have carefully descended the dark stairs, finding her way out of ranger headquarters while she remembered Targon's instructions on how to do so, but a fist pounded on his door scant seconds after he closed her in. She couldn't help but lean her ear against the bookcase.

Not a true wall, it wasn't soundproof. She could hear Targon grumbling to himself and then the fist pounding again. Without respect. Maybe the owner didn't know Targon was a noble—or half-noble—and insisted on *my lords* and proper reverence.

Footsteps sounded—Targon walking to the door.

"Spymaster Sabor," he stated. "You're not who I expected."

Spymaster? Kaylina remembered Vlerion teasing Targon about fancying himself a spymaster, but she hadn't realized it was an actual position in the kingdom.

"Were the queen here to sate her needs," a man with a low wry voice said, "she would have gone to your quarters instead of your office. Or so I presume. Your desk looks sturdy enough, I suppose, but royalty generally prefers mattresses."

"I had no idea you spent time musing on the queen's sex life."

"I'm letting you know I'm aware of the role you recently played in it."

"As the spymaster, aren't you paid to be aware of everything?"

"Yes, and you'd best not forget it. Where's the girl?"

A chill went through Kaylina. As much as she would like for there to be some *other* girl, she had little doubt that the man meant her. She might have been foolish not to dart immediately down the stairs and leave. If the spymaster knew about the secret door, he would check it. But, aside from their conversation, it was quiet in the building, and she worried that if she left now, the stairs would creak, and they would hear her.

"Not here," Targon said.

"No? A recent report says otherwise. As you can see, I've got men checking the compound—they started with your barracks room."

Targon's grunt didn't sound that concerned. If nothing else, he knew Kaylina wasn't there. "Nice to know I've got spies among my rangers who report to you."

"I wouldn't be much of a spymaster if I didn't have eyes all over the capital, as well as in the kingdom at large."

"We're on the same side, Sabor. You don't need to *spy* on the rangers."

"One would hope. The girl?"

"The *girl* helped save the king and queen. She didn't poison anyone."

Kaylina hadn't expected Targon to stand up for her. She refused to reassess her opinion of him—he was still a dick—but she was relieved he had believed Vlerion. Targon might have seen her help out at the castle, but he couldn't have directly witnessed anything to make him certain she hadn't delivered poisoned mead.

"That's what you believe?" the spymaster asked after a pause.

"I was there and saw the role she played with my own eyes. She hit the suborned guard who was feigning the castle gate wouldn't open—pounded him with a lead round between the eyes—so my men could get in."

"You have taybarri. They couldn't flash through the gate?"

"They can't pass through solid objects. You ought to be aware of that, all-knowing spymaster."

"My knowledge is in the political sphere, not animal husbandry."

"Go call one of the taybarri an animal, and we'll see how the rest of your search goes."

"No need to be testy, Captain. But as to the poisoning and the girl *helping* the royals… you know she's allied with the Virts, right?"

Kaylina scowled at the bookcase. Why did the guy think that?

"What makes you believe so?" Targon asked.

"They're claiming it. Oh, they haven't printed it in that subversive rag yet, nor have they spoken the words aloud to any of our people, but they're praising her attempt to poison the queen. A girl named Mitzy says they have a deal with Korbian and that they'll retaliate if she's struck down. My spies have seen the Virts out looking for her, to take her in and protect her."

Kaylina shook her head. Why were the Virts trying to claim her? Or make her look worse? She couldn't guess their motivations.

"They tried to burn her castle down and almost killed her brother," Targon said. "I don't know what their angle is, unless they've figured out she's an *anrokk* and think they can use that, but she's not working for them."

That was true, though Kaylina was surprised Targon was that confident about it.

"Is that the brother you've been sheltering since before the assassination attempt? My men are looking for him in your compound too."

"Not in my quarters, I hope. My tastes don't run toward boys."

"Mine trend that way more often than yours, but he's on the scrawny side. I prefer your fit young rangers."

"You're welcome to proposition them. Just be prepared for a no."

"Is my lack of height the problem? Or my bastard heritage? I wouldn't think you or they would condemn me for that."

"This conversation is giving me a headache. Take your men and go, Sabor."

"Not until the search is complete. If you'd like to produce the girl so I can deliver her to the queen, I'll be pleased to leave straight afterward."

"I don't have her, and she's more than the queen could handle anyway."

"*I* can handle her for the queen."

"We questioned her with kafdari when she first arrived in the city. She's not a Virt sympathizer. She's a tourist starting a meadery."

"Oh, of course. In the middle of a civil war in which the first arrows have already been loosed."

"You know what versions of the newspapers they get across the provinces. You've a hand in it. If it's anyone's fault that ignorant tourists think it's a good time to sail up here, it's yours."

"I do what I do for the security of the kingdom."

"Why don't you squelch that illegal newspaper then?"

The spymaster snorted. "Are you upset that it's printing truths about the rangers?"

"It hasn't printed a truth yet."

"No? Vlerion screwed up in the dungeon."

Kaylina stopped breathing. The spymaster knew Vlerion's secret.

Had he always? Or had he learned about it because of the dungeon? Vlerion had said the king and maybe the prince knew as well as some rangers, but…

"Even if finding all those clawed-up, mauled bodies hadn't set the staff to talking," Sabor continued, "he changed into a beast right in front of a bunch of Virts. Dozens of witnesses. Oh, he killed a lot of them, and you and the rangers helped the guards kill or round up more, but not all of them died that day. And the living have tongues. I'm surprised his name hasn't come out in that paper yet. Maybe they're waiting until they have a bigger readership."

"Maybe you should put them out of business before that happens," Targon growled.

"I've got men scouring the city for their press. Its location won't remain secret for long."

Except the Virts weren't printing the newspapers *in* the city. Kaylina wished she'd thought to peek out of the back of that wagon and get a look at the guard who'd lied to the ranger, ensuring nobody reported the arrival of the cargo.

"I'm more concerned about the Kar'ruk I've just heard about," Sabor said. "Through my *spies*, mind you. *You* haven't sent a report over to the castle."

"I was waiting to hear what my sergeant learns from questioning the one we captured. Who are your spies among my men, Sabor?"

"If I told you, you would punish them. Relax, Targon. We're all on the same side here."

"Uh-huh. If the Kar'ruk have got you concerned, why are you here for a clueless tourist? Even if Korbian *were* guilty, the poison didn't hurt anyone. She can't be a priority for you."

"Except that she's more than a tourist, isn't she?" Sabor asked softly. "I'm sure her looks aren't the only reason you're interested in her."

"She's an *anrokk.* You know how rare they are."

"She's more than that." The words were so soft now that Kaylina strained to hear them. Further, the men seemed to have their backs to her. Were they standing side by side and looking out the window?

"Like what?" Targon asked.

Kaylina caught herself pressing her hand against the bookcase. It moved slightly but fortunately soundlessly. A tiny vertical gap of light entered her hidden nook.

"What more than that *is* there?" Targon added.

She pressed her eye to the gap. The narrow view allowed her to see Targon's shoulder and the side of a shorter graying man with a mustache and a lean build.

"You tell me," Sabor said. "She used druid magic to save the life of one of your men."

Kaylina drew back. How could he know that? Only Jankarr knew that. Was *Jankarr* his spy?

But, no. Jankarr might have been the only one there besides the Kar'ruk warrior, but he would have reported everything that happened to his superiors and however many rangers had been around to hear it. Kaylina rubbed the back of her neck, wishing she and Jankarr had never noticed the Kar'ruk trapped in the undergrowth, that they'd gone right past those ruins.

"Jankarr isn't sure *what* she did," Targon said after a long moment. He probably hadn't expected the spymaster to gather that information so quickly.

Kaylina didn't appreciate that the whole city seemed to know about her now.

"I'm sure she doesn't have any access to *magic*," Targon added. "She's human, like you and me."

"She's not like you and me, and you know that."

"Have you met her? She's mouthy and disrespectful. She's not anything special."

Had she not been so disturbed to be the subject of their conversation, Kaylina would have stuck her tongue out at the bookcase. At *them*.

"You don't believe that," Sabor said, "or you wouldn't be protecting her. You want to use her power."

"She doesn't have any power beyond getting herds of taybarri to show up at her door."

"And that's not a power? Where is she, Targon? I won't ask again."

"Are you trying to find her because you believe she poisoned that mead? Or because you want her for your own plans?"

"If she *does* have access to druid power, she could be useful. Just as Vlerion has been useful, however accidentally. It's not wise to cast aside valuable tools, especially in uncertain times. If there are a handful of Kar'ruk near our city, there could be thousands more poised on the border, ready to take advantage of our distraction with the Virts."

"Then why don't you get out of my compound and leave me to do my job?"

A knock sounded at the door, and the men moved out of Kaylina's view.

"My lord Spymaster? We've searched the compound and didn't find the brother or the sister. We questioned a few rangers, but they were tightlipped. One started to talk—one who's friendly to you, I think—but a taybarri stepped on his boot, and he changed his mind."

"Those furry mounts are smarter than they look, aren't they?" Sabor grumbled.

"They're *very* smart, yes," Targon said.

"When you see her next, send the girl to me, Targon," Sabor

said. "I won't let her be put to death. We'll find a use for her. Better us than the Virts."

"I won't argue that."

"But you don't believe she's loyal to them?"

"No," Targon said. "She's loyal to Vlerion."

A long silence followed, making Kaylina wonder if they'd stepped out of the office to finish the conversation.

Then the spymaster snorted. "Does it go both ways? Is *that* why the beast has been seen so much lately?"

"He's only been *seen* in the dungeon. Whatever is happening to dead Virts that the newspapers are reporting on doesn't have anything to do with Vlerion."

"Are you sure? Have you seen the bodies? They're not that dissimilarly mauled to the ones in the dungeon."

"Lots of big animals with claws could have been responsible. The Virts threw a yekizar at us a few weeks ago."

Yes, Kaylina had witnessed that battle. Vlerion had prevailed, but it had been a ferocious creature. Few other lone humans would have come out on top in a fight with it.

"I understand that he's your subordinate and probably your friend, Targon, but defending him if he's been killing citizens..."

"He hasn't been. Had the beast come out in the city, it wouldn't be a single body found here or there. When he changes... You know what happens when he changes."

"I've not seen what Vlerion has done, other than in that dungeon—I'll admit that was terrifying in and of itself—but I remember the aftermath of some of his father's meltdowns. It's a shame we can't harness that power, call on it to defend the kingdom while ensuring Vlerion doesn't hurt anyone on his own side."

"That's not how the druids wanted the curse to work. They wanted the kingdom punished."

"I'm aware of the lore." Sabor paused, rapping his knuckles

thoughtfully against something wooden. "Do you think *she* can control him?"

"Korbian?" Targon grunted. "So far, she mostly pisses him off when she isn't getting him hard."

Kaylina's fingers fisted at the crude words used to describe her relationship with Vlerion.

"That answers my question less than you'd think," Sabor said dryly.

"She's not controlling him in any way. Trust me. Vlerion isn't dumb or easily manipulated."

"Ah, but it's not *Vlerion* that I meant. Can the girl control the *beast*?"

Targon hesitated, not as quick to dismiss that thought.

Kaylina shook her head again, memories of crawling under those rocks to escape the beast springing to mind. There was no way she controlled Vlerion in that form. In any form. So far, all she'd managed was to keep him from killing her. Or… mating with her. She admitted that seemed more where the beast's interests lay when it came to her.

"You mean because she's an *anrokk*," Targon said.

"That's exactly what I mean. She may be the only one who has a shot at controlling him."

"Don't forget my ranger, Jastadar."

"Your bald sergeant? I doubt *he's* going to win the beast's loyalty."

"If it's about drawing the affection of animals, he might."

"Uh-huh. I want the girl, Targon."

"A lot of people do."

"Send her my way. Send Vlerion too. We'll do some experiments."

"People do love being experimented on."

"For the good of the kingdom, Targon. I know that matters to you, the same as me. Good night."

18

On a frosty morn, a track without ice crystals is freshly made.

~ Ranger Founder Saruk

Kaylina waited in the dark until the door thudded shut with Spymaster Sabor's departure. Since she assumed the search would continue, she was about to start down the stairs when the bookcase slid open. The intrusion of the lamplight wasn't bright enough to make her squint, but Targon's glowering face did cause her to grimace.

"I had a hunch," he said.

"There wasn't enough time for me to climb down—I was worried about making noise." Kaylina looked past his shoulder to make sure he was alone in the office.

"Sure you were. You're a practiced eavesdropper."

"If that were true, I wouldn't get caught all the time."

Targon grunted, pointed at the floor, and said, "Stay there," before sliding the bookcase closed again.

Though the order without any explanation rankled, Kaylina waited for him to return. She wanted to know when the guards left and make sure Frayvar had continued to elude them. If they found her brother, they might think to use him—to *threaten* him—to get her to turn herself in.

The thought chagrined her. Already, he'd been hurt numerous times, all because he was a loyal sibling who'd followed her north, believing she needed his assistance. And she *did* need it, at least when it came to starting a business.

Long minutes passed, and she didn't hear any triumphant shouts to suggest the guards had found Frayvar. She didn't hear anything else either, not until footsteps sounded in the office again.

Once more, the bookcase slid aside. This time, Frayvar stood in the light, a pack and books gathered in his arms. Targon stood behind him.

"I want both of you out of here, and don't come back unless you've cleared your name." Targon gave Frayvar a shove, but not a hard one, only enough to send him into the dark nook with Kaylina. "Maybe not even then. Apparently, the Virts are claiming you're one of them, and with Spymaster Sabor now interested in you..." He curled his lip and closed the bookcase without finishing the thought.

Kaylina found her brother's arm in the dark, gripped it, and patted him on the back.

"Hugging." Frayvar said it as a warning to forestall the unpleasant activity, and she didn't need light to know he was wincing in anticipation.

"I wasn't going to, but that's something you should allow from a sibling when you've narrowly escaped being captured by the Kingdom Guard, if not the Castle Guard. How did you avoid their notice? Targon said there weren't secret doors in the infirmary."

"There was a somewhat hidden cabinet large enough to hold

me. Barely. I have some fresh dents in my side. Penderbrock locked me in there before I knew what was happening. I think he saved me because he was grateful that I organized his medicine cabinets."

"As demonstrated by him locking you in? What would he have done if he *hadn't* been grateful?"

"Handed me to the guards, I suppose. I have the maps and my plans for researching Bloomlong and clearing your name. Do you want to—"

"Go to the castle to test my honey on that plant before dawn? Yes."

"That's… not going to clear your name."

"I know, but there's more going on. We may need—"

A thump sounded on the bookcase.

"Have your meeting elsewhere," Targon grumbled from the other side.

"Right. Thank you." Kaylina released her brother's arm, found the stairs with her foot, and whispered, "Follow me as we talk. And watch your step."

"I thought I'd dance, leap, and spring my way down."

"I've seen you dance. I wouldn't recommend it even when there *is* good lighting."

"Ha ha."

Hands on dusty wooden walls, Kaylina led the way slowly down the stairs while relaying the conversation she'd overheard, as much as she could. Since she couldn't say anything that would lead her brother to guess Vlerion's secret, she couldn't be as complete as she wished.

"Because the Virts are claiming we're aligned," she finished, "we may need to help the authorities find their press to stop the printing of their secret newspaper. Maybe that would prove we're not involved with them."

"Before the authorities will *let* us help them, we'll need the testimony of the poisoner who sold vials to Jana Bloomlong, or that of the messenger who delivered the tainted mead."

"We can work on getting those things. After visiting the plant."

"How is messing with that *plant* going to help anything?" Frayvar grunted as he lost his balance. The steps weren't even.

"I want to see if the druid honey makes it... happy." What she wanted was to see if it lifted the curse on the castle so she would be closer to figuring out how to lift Vlerion's curse. Those words she couldn't speak aloud.

"*It's* not going to give its testimony."

"You never know."

"Be logical, Kay."

"You know that's not my strength."

Frayvar harrumphed like Grandpa.

Even feeling her way carefully through the dark passage, Kaylina cracked her knuckles against the hard wall that marked the dead end Targon had mentioned. After cursing sufficiently, she slid her fingers over the rough bricks and aged mortar, counting from the bottom to locate the secret switch. Nothing obvious stuck out, but when she found the right brick and pushed, a hidden door ground open.

It sounded like the heavy stone lid of an ancient sarcophagus shifting aside, reminding Kaylina unpleasantly of her time in the catacombs. But, as Targon had promised, his passageway opened into the sewers, not the catacombs.

As soon as the pungent aroma of effluent struck her, making her nostrils sting, she decided the catacombs might have been preferable, even with Kar'ruk statues that spat poison.

"Do you have a lantern handy?" Kaylina could hear water flowing, but no grates let in light from the city above, at least not in this area.

"Of course. Give me a moment." His voice sounded odd. He was probably doing his best to breathe through his mouth, possibly while pinching his nostrils shut. "I might try to find a gag too. Or a bag to put over my entire head."

"This is better than if guards had charged into the infirmary and captured you," Kaylina said, though she also didn't want to linger in the sewers.

"Are you sure? They might have been interested by my organization methods, which could have led to a lively and stimulating conversation."

"I can't believe you accuse *me* of having hallucinations."

"You've admitted to seeing things before."

"Only when I'm absorbed by my visions for the future."

"By your schemes." After striking a match, Frayvar lit two small lanterns.

"I should have left you in ranger headquarters."

Unfazed, he handed her a lantern.

"Thank you."

With the wan light to lead them, they followed a stone ledge along a murky channel. Sludge and slime covered the walkway, making the footing treacherous. It coated the nearest wall as well, and Kaylina was loath to touch it for balance—or for any reason at all. That was hard when they had to duck under periodic chutes in the wall with more effluent flowing out, splashing down into the main channel.

"This might be Targon's revenge for my irreverence." Kaylina wiped her watering eyes, the potent air affecting her ten times more than cutting onions. "Or he wants to make *sure* Vlerion isn't attracted to me."

"Why would the ranger captain care if Lord Vlerion is attracted to you?"

"Because..." She realized she shouldn't have made the joke. "I'm a commoner, and he doesn't approve of his rangers getting horizontal with such riffraff."

"He said that? The rangers tend to gossip, and I've heard he's been with a lot of women, nobles and commoners."

"Double standards." Kaylina hurried around a corner. It was getting harder and harder to avoid saying anything that might give him clues about Vlerion's secret.

Intersections forced them to make more turns than she wanted, and she worried they would come up in front of ranger headquarters. Or a pair of kingdom guards. Not that she'd yet seen any ladders or ways out. Maybe there *weren't* any. Since Targon wanted her to disappear, he might have decided having her get lost for weeks in the city sewers would be a good way to accomplish that.

"There's a grate." Frayvar pointed toward bars across a narrow rectangular opening in the ceiling, a few drops of rainwater trickling down. Though night was deep, a hint of light from a nearby streetlamp brightened the area under the grate. "Have we gone far enough? We might be able to get out there."

"There isn't a ladder, and I don't see a manhole or a way through those bars."

"Let's look closer. My nose is ready to escape this miasma of stenches. Another minute, and it'll be permanently damaged, and I'll lose all my ability to be an effective chef."

"You'll still have your tastebuds."

"A good chef uses *all* of his senses to cook."

"Really? I haven't seen you stir a pot with your ears."

"I've used my lips when my hands were full."

"A skill Lady Ghara would swoon over." Kaylina stopped a few steps from the opening, listening for horses, wagons, or anything else that might be above. They didn't need witnesses spotting them climbing out of the sewer. She touched the variegated and slick growth on the wall, doubting she could climb it. "Are you going to boost me up?"

"You know how great my strength is."

"So, you want me to boost *you* up."

"Probably. I—" Frayvar stopped as a shadow blocked the grate.

Kaylina hadn't heard whatever it was approach, but she stood still, hoping it would move on. It didn't. Snuffling sounds came from above.

"Is that... a taybarri?" she whispered, though it was too dark to make out fur or the shape of a head. "Or a stray dog?"

An indignant *whuff* floated down.

"Not a dog," Frayvar said.

"Crenoch? Or Levitke?" Kaylina couldn't recognize any of the taybarri from a whuff alone and was guessing.

The answering whuff sounded like one of agreement.

"How did they find us?" Frayvar whispered, though they couldn't tell if there was more than one.

"I don't know. You can't tell me the scent of my honey is detectable with the other odors down here overpowering it."

"It might be. Animals have better noses than we do."

A clink came from above as taybarri fangs wrapped around two bars of the grate.

"Uhm," Frayvar said.

A great wrenching of metal sounded, and pieces of brick and mortar trickled down as the taybarri tore the grate out.

"Whoa," Frayvar said. "I didn't know their jaws were that strong."

"A reason not to piss them off."

"Oh, I already had a list of reasons not to do that."

The shadow—the head—disappeared from view as the taybarri flung the grate away. Kaylina winced when it clattered on the cobblestone street. She hoped it was as late as she believed and that nobody was around to hear or see that.

"I'll take that boost up now." She stepped under the opening.

"I thought you were boosting *me*," Frayvar grumbled but came forward. "Please tell me you don't want me to get on hands and knees to be a stool. The ground here is disgusting."

"We're going to need a bath after this anyway."

"Yeah, but will we get the opportunity for one?"

"You could always fall in the river again."

"I adore being your brother." Frayvar sighed and lowered himself to all fours.

"Thank you." Kaylina carefully stepped on his back as she braced herself against the wall. It was as disgusting as the ground. "You're a good brother."

"I'm an *amazing* brother."

"I'm not arguing."

With him boosting her, Kaylina gripped the ragged edge left by the grate removal. Pieces of mortar and brick crumbled under her grip, and she hesitated to hang her weight from her fingers.

"I don't suppose you taybarri brought a rope," she called softly.

The shadows stirred but not because of a head this time. A thick taybarri tail drooped through the opening.

"You want me to grab that?" Kaylina asked. "Won't that hurt?"

She wasn't sure she could get a good grip since the tail was a lot thicker than a rope. Despite the fur, they always reminded her more of lizard tails than those of mammals.

The two whuffs that floated down sounded amused. Kaylina reminded herself that she'd seen enemies swing axes at the taybarri. They were tough creatures.

"All right." She ended up hugging the tail more than gripping it like a rope, then risked shifting her weight from Frayvar's back to it.

The taybarri took a couple of steps, pulling her up. Her shoulder bashed against the side of the opening, knocking more debris free, and Frayvar groaned as pieces pelted him.

"Sorry," she whispered, rolling away from the opening as soon as she could.

In the street, Kaylina pushed herself to her knees, intending to turn and lower a hand down for her brother. But her taybarri helper had already backed close and lowered his tail again. *Her* tail. By the streetlamp, there was enough to see Levitke's familiar snout and warm brown eyes in her blue-furred face.

A male taybarri stood nearby, but that wasn't Crenoch. He was probably still with Vlerion in the preserve. Maybe Levitke had batted her lashes and lured this one away from headquarters to help. The male had his nostrils in the air, his floppy ears twitching as he sampled the city scents—and whatever wafted up from the sewer opening.

"Uhm?" Frayvar's voice wafted up.

"That tail is for you. Grab on." Kaylina refrained from using the word *hug* since he had an aversion to that.

"Do I... jump?"

"Do chefs not do that?"

"I'm not sure how much weight a tail can handle."

Levitke looked over her shoulder, then backed closer to the hole so it would lower further. The bend in her tail did not appear natural. It usually stuck out horizontally, swishing back and forth low to the ground as the taybarri walked.

"That's as low as it's going to get." Kaylina crouched near the hole so she could help.

"Give me a second. I'll try to get a running start. Without falling."

Having seen her brother attempt athletic feats, Kaylina winced. She also hoped he wouldn't hurt Levitke.

"Is it easy to kink your tail like that?" Kaylina asked the taybarri as she looked around, not recognizing the street where they'd come up. Brick row houses lined either side, with a fountain at a well-lit intersection a half a block away. She hadn't spent much time exploring residential areas since they'd arrived. "Or are you doing us a huge favor?"

Levitke curved her body so that she could lick Kaylina's face.

"Favor. Got it. Hurry up, Frayvar."

A scrape and thump came from below, followed by a grunt. "I'm on."

Levitke walked forward, the weight on her tail not noticeably bothering her. As soon as Frayvar's head came into view, Kaylina grabbed him under the armpits and helped him into the street.

He let go of the tail and wiped his hands on his clothes several times before standing—and several times after. Kaylina couldn't blame him. A bath sounded appealing, but she doubted they would have an opportunity for that any time soon.

The two taybarri started walking away. At first, Kaylina thought they'd done what they came to do, somehow knowing she and Frayvar needed assistance, and were leaving. But Levitke paused and looked expectantly back.

"Do we follow? Are you leading us somewhere helpful? Like Stillguard Castle?"

The affirmative whuff was promising.

Kaylina and Frayvar followed the taybarri. Surprisingly, they didn't stop and offer themselves as mounts. Instead, the creatures' big heads kept swinging toward each other as they strode ahead, walking side by side over the rain-dampened cobblestones. It was as if they were exchanging meaningful looks. Did taybarri do that the way humans did?

After passing the fountain, the taybarri led them several more blocks, turning at a stone building that seemed familiar. It wasn't until Kaylina saw the river and a bridge in the midst of being repaired that she identified it. The last time she'd visited the city jail, they'd entered through a back entrance.

The taybarri stopped in front of the area where Vlerion and Targon had battled Virts who'd been buying time for a jailbreak.

Tonight, there wasn't anyone in view—not anyone upright anyway. Levitke stopped in front of a cloaked figure lying prone on the ground. Lying… *dead* on the ground?

Frayvar sucked in a breath as he spotted the person, and he and Kaylina were the ones to exchange long looks.

The nearby jail made Kaylina hesitate to get close. What if guards walked out and spotted the body, and her and Frayvar standing next to it, and believed they'd been responsible? Kaylina's entire episode with the rangers had begun because she'd been caught in proximity to a murdered noble.

"Let's leave that for the authorities to find," Kaylina whispered when Levitke looked expectantly back at her again. She pointed down the river in the direction of the castle. "I've got some honey I can share once we get to Stillguard."

Levitke's tail swished, but she didn't leave the body. The male sniffed the air again, his long furry form tense, his tail not moving. If he'd heard and understood the honey offer, he gave no indication of it.

"Is something dangerous about?" Kaylina asked. "The person who did this?"

Against her better judgment, she crept toward the body. After a quick look, they could leave. If the taybarri wanted, they could stay until some rangers found them.

A dark damp puddle had formed on the cobblestones under the man. Blood. This couldn't have happened that long ago, or the earlier rain would have washed it away.

Even before she got close, Kaylina suspected he hadn't been run through with a sword. And she was right. Something with claws had torn out his throat—it had torn his head half off.

The male taybarri moaned. Kaylina hadn't heard that noise from one of them before and didn't know what to make of it until she realized the fallen man wore black leather armor. *Ranger* armor.

"Is this one of your people?" Kaylina peered more closely at the face and realized it was one of the men who'd accompanied Targon into the preserve. He must have returned and been sent out on a patrol of the city. "Or," she guessed, her intuition striking, "your rider?"

The male taybarri moaned again.

Levitke looked at Kaylina.

"I'm sorry, but I can't do anything." She didn't understand why the taybarri had brought her here. Why didn't they go to ranger headquarters for Targon and some of his men?

Levitke stepped closer, facing Kaylina fully and gazing into her eyes as if she longed to convey a message. Or... a warning?

"Do you know who killed him?" Kaylina wished she could read the taybarri's thoughts.

The male sniffed the air again, then lowered his large snout toward the dead ranger. With their keen noses, they might know exactly who'd killed the man.

"An animal, right?" Kaylina asked.

It had to be. Though the body and the claw marks reminded her uncomfortably of the dead Virts from the dungeon under the royal castle—men the *beast* had killed. She didn't believe Vlerion could have had anything to do with this murder though. He wasn't even in the city.

The two taybarri exchanged long looks again. She almost wondered if they could read *her* thoughts.

"Or maybe one of the Kar'ruk sneaked into the city?" Kaylina suggested. "Do they by chance tame wild animals and train them to fight?"

Levitke whuffed, but Kaylina couldn't tell if it was a negative, an affirmative, or an acknowledgment of the possibility. Maybe the taybarri wasn't answering at all and was simply unsettled by the situation.

"It wasn't anything to do with Vlerion, right?"

The taybarri looked at each other and shifted their weight on their large paws. The male's tail swished in agitation.

"I know he wouldn't hurt one of his own people," Kaylina said, but she *didn't* know that. As a man, he wouldn't, but as a beast, would he recognize friend from foe? Not based on what he'd admitted.

The clip-clop of horse hooves sounded on the road across the river. Numerous horse hooves.

"Kaylina," Frayvar whispered. "We need to get out of here."

"I know." She backed away, though Levitke's sad eyes made her want to stay and help the taybarri get to the bottom of this. "We'll find out who's responsible, all right?"

Levitke whuffed, but the male had turned toward the bridge. He trotted in the direction of the approaching riders.

When Frayvar gripped Kaylina's arm, she let him guide her into the shadows. They rounded the corner of the jail and slipped into an alley but not before she glimpsed horses *and* taybarri riding into view, rangers and guards on their backs.

She picked up the pace, passing her brother and urging him into a jog. As soon as the authorities spotted the dead ranger, they would start searching for the responsible party. Since Kaylina and Frayvar didn't have claws, they shouldn't be considered suspects, but she had other reasons to avoid being found.

"Why did you ask the taybarri if Vlerion had something to do with that man's death?" Frayvar whispered as they jogged down a street toward Stillguard Castle.

Kaylina winced. Since her brother had been quiet while Levitke showed her the body, she'd forgotten about keeping Vlerion's secret from him.

"He was with that ranger in the preserve," she said.

"They ought to be friends, then, right? Why'd you tell the taybarri that he wouldn't hurt his own people. Of course he wouldn't." Frayvar hesitated. "Right?"

"Right," she said firmly. Feeling his eyes upon her, she added, "Just forget I said anything, Fray. Please."

He hesitated. "Okay."

Despite his agreement, she imagined the cogs and gears in his mind turning, and she sighed, afraid Vlerion's secret would be harder to keep than she'd guessed.

19

If you don't have a purpose in life, someone will use you toward their purpose.

~ Lord Professor Varhesson, Port Jirador University

The tower at Stillguard Castle was glowing purple, its window visible over the courtyard wall.

Kaylina bit her lip. She and Frayvar had come through an alley a couple of buildings down the block and stood in the shadows, peering toward it from across the street. She longed to charge straight in to investigate—and to see if the druid honey would affect the plant even more than Grandpa's had—but her instincts told her to be wary. Between the guards looking for her and the mauled corpses appearing in the city, she dared not assume it was safe to enter the castle.

"Interesting." Frayvar gazed at the tower.

"Yes. It must take some time before the honey fertilizer affects its glow."

"But it didn't take any time for the plant to attack and brand you." He glanced at her hand.

Even though he hadn't been there, she'd shared the details.

"The first time, it didn't do that. Last time, it was... perkier."

"Perky like a hungry viper?"

"A hungry viper with a branding iron, yes."

Kaylina looked up and down the street, peering into the dark shadows. As usual, there weren't any streetlamps lit near the castle, as if the city workers responsible for the duty didn't want to encourage anyone to visit this particular block at night. Or ever.

It was on her second perusal of the area that Kaylina spotted a human-sized shadow against the wall a few buildings away. It was on the same side of the street as they were, opposite the castle. The man wore a cloak with the hood pulled low while watching the front gate. Was his job to alert someone in case Kaylina returned? Since it was well past midnight, the watcher had no other reason to loiter there, facing in that direction. Someone else might be keeping an eye on the back gatehouse.

Kaylina pointed the person out to Frayvar.

He pulled her back into the alley. "It's too dangerous for you to go in. They're probably *expecting* us to visit."

"Because the inherent appeal of a cursed castle naturally draws people."

"It's drawing *you*," he grumped. "Let's go visit the glassmaker. Or paint-poison maker. And then we can find someplace to sleep. I'm exhausted."

"I am too."

"Are you sure? Two days ago, you were in a funk deeper than Braleor Bog. Now, you're perkier than that plant."

"I'm... on a mission."

"The *wrong* mission."

"Just help me with it. I'll explain everything later." Kaylina paused. "I'll explain *most* things later."

She peered out again, catching movement in the street near the castle, and didn't hear her brother's reply, other than to note its sarcastic tone.

The person watching the gate had disappeared, but four people with lanterns were heading toward the gatehouse. They also wore cloaks and hoods, but Kaylina glimpsed a braid of long brown hair hanging down one person's curved chest. A woman.

Her first thought was that Jana Bloomlong was visiting the castle for some reason, but she had gray hair. This woman moved like a younger person, almost skipping as she led the group. The others were hesitant, warily eyeing the gate and courtyard wall—and especially the glowing tower window.

Given how rare visitors were, Kaylina was surprised when they all entered the courtyard. Before disappearing through the gate, the woman glanced down the street, and Kaylina glimpsed her face.

"Mitzy," she whispered.

Frayvar peered out. "The Virt girl?"

"The Virt girl who tried to get me to agree to help the rebels the day of the assassination attempt. Well, not exactly. She told me their people would be making their move that night instead of during the day, so it was a test. Like the fire. They were trying to see whose side we're on."

"By lighting me on fire? That doesn't make me inclined to join their cause."

"Me either."

"Why are they going into our cursed castle at night? They're not going to light it on fire *again,* are they?"

"I wouldn't think so. They have to be looking for me."

"Uh, why?"

"I heard Spymaster Sabor—the guy who ordered those guards to search ranger headquarters—say the Virts are claiming I'm on their side. Apparently, they heard I tried to poison the queen and liked that."

"But you didn't do that. And why would they care that much about you, anyway?"

"I'm not sure," Kaylina said, though she had a feeling this had to do with the brand and her helping Jankarr. Somehow, word about her supposedly having magical power was spreading fast through the city.

"Maybe they're heading into the castle because it's an access point into the catacombs," Frayvar suggested. "The Virts could be starting a new plan to try to get what they want."

"That is possible."

Lantern light grew visible through a second-floor window, one high enough to be seen over the courtyard wall.

"But there isn't a catacombs entrance up there," she added.

"Weird."

"Are they going to see the plant?" Kaylina wondered as the lantern moved away from the window. "Or searching for me?"

"I don't know, but why don't we avoid them? And the castle? Let's get some rest, then go see—"

"The glassmaker and the poison-maker, I know, I know. I'm willing to do that, but let's see what the Virts are up to first. I'd like to hear what they're saying about me."

"Nothing flattering, I'm sure."

"You don't think they've noticed and are admiring my sling abilities?"

Kaylina leaned out again, making sure the watcher hadn't returned. The man was still gone, or had backed off the street, at least. Maybe he'd left to alert his boss about the castle visitors. If he was working for the guard, a bunch of armed men might show up soon. If Kaylina wanted to eavesdrop, she needed to do it now.

"I'm going in the back way," she whispered, making sure her hood hid her face.

"Kay..."

"Wait here. If I get myself in trouble, you can save me."

"With what? I don't have a weapon."

"You can leap out and challenge the Virts to math problems."

"Hilarious."

Kaylina patted him on the shoulder, then strode across the street. Though she wanted to run, she made herself walk. If the watcher remained in the area, she didn't want to draw attention, but she supposed anyone wandering about this late at night would.

Staying outside the courtyard wall, she kept to the shadows and followed it to the gatehouse in the back. A barge floated down the river, a couple of lanterns burning on its deck, but there wasn't anyone on the path or watching from across the waterway, at least that she could see.

Someone had closed the gate since she'd last visited. She eased it open, careful not to let it creak, then padded cautiously toward the door leading to the kitchen. She didn't see any lanterns through the windows on this side of the castle and hoped she wouldn't run into the trespassers.

The kitchen door opened without trouble, remnants of soot from the fire wafting out into the night air. It was dark inside, but Kaylina knew the layout well enough to find her way. Voices floated down from upstairs.

Though worried about being caught, Kaylina felt anticipation too. Even excitement. Maybe she could learn something useful here, such as why the Virts were *really* looking for her.

But she had to make sure they didn't find her, so she hesitated to climb the steps. The long halls upstairs didn't offer many hiding spots unless one slipped into the rooms, and some of *those* had skeletons inside.

"I don't think she's here," a male voice wafted down, the words clear.

Footsteps sounded in the upstairs hallway.

"I wasn't sure she would be—she has to know the guards are looking for her—but that plant was red a few hours ago," came Mitzy's voice in reply. It sounded like they were heading toward the stairs, so Kaylina backed into the kitchen. "I think she's the one changing it. That's why I thought she might be here."

"You don't know she's causing it to change."

"No, but it was always red before she showed up. Who else could be responsible?"

"Maybe the druid magic is feeling feisty this spring."

The footsteps reached the stairs, clumping softly as the speakers came down.

Kaylina eased farther away, angling toward the pantry. There weren't many other hiding spots in the kitchen, and she'd eavesdropped on Vlerion once from there. She tried not to think about how she'd been *caught* eavesdropping on Vlerion.

"Of course it's the magic," Mitzy said, "but *she's* the one stirring it up. We need to get her before the guard shoots her or who knows what they want to do."

Kaylina's heel bumped something unexpected on the floor, and she halted. The huge wrought-iron pot rack. She'd forgotten it had fallen during the fire.

Lantern light swung in the stairwell.

"Did you hear something?" the male asked.

Kaylina swore to herself and glanced back. She was almost to the pantry door.

"Rats probably," Mitzy said.

"Or the curse," a second man muttered.

"Relax." Mitzy sounded like she was in charge even though she was Frayvar's age. Maybe they were following her orders because she was the only one who'd been inside before. "The castle isn't moaning and groaning tonight. I bet the purple light means something has changed."

"I wouldn't take that bet," the man said. "We don't need that girl. Besides, she's friendly with the rangers. She fought with them against us in the royal castle. That's what Hokkens said. If anything, it would be better to kill her before the rangers can use her against us."

Kaylina eased the pantry door open and stepped inside, slow to put her weight fully on each foot, remembering broken glass and other debris on the floor. With someone talking about killing her, she especially didn't want to be caught.

"They say she's an *anrokk* and has druid powers," Mitzy said. "She could help us against the rangers if we could win her to our side."

"It's not worth taking the risk. Besides, druid magic is creepy. That makes *her* creepy."

"Someone had better deal with her before she becomes a problem," another man said, his voice right outside the kitchen. "*More* of a problem. We don't need to fight someone with druid magic."

Kaylina closed the pantry door most of the way, leaving only a peep hole. The speakers hadn't yet entered the kitchen, but she could see the light from their lanterns.

"Druid magic." The third man scoffed. "The only magic in the world that really exists is from altered plants."

"The only magic that we know about that's left in the world, but the druids had all kinds of powers. And don't forget taybarri magic."

"All they can do is move really fast."

"According to Cougar," Mitzy said, "our man inside the rangers believes Korbian *does* have some druid magic. Or it was given to her somehow."

Our man *inside* the rangers? Targon had been right to assume there was a spy. Or were there *two* spies? One for the Virts and one for Spymaster Sabor?

Kaylina hoped Jankarr wasn't either of them. She liked him. She liked the doctor too. The rest of the rangers… Well, she didn't know many of the rest of them, but she was inclined to dislike the ones who'd ogled her chest during her training day. *They* could be spies.

"Humans don't get druid magic," one of the men said after a pause.

"Maybe she's not fully human."

Kaylina had to bite her lip to keep herself from scoffing, the same as the Virts. Of *course* she was human. What else could she be?

Since the druids had disappeared, the Kar'ruk and the taybarri elders were the only intelligent species besides humans left wandering the world. Legends spoke of Kar'ruk-human mixed bloods who'd once existed, but modern science said that wasn't possible. The two species couldn't produce offspring, even if they deigned to have sex with each other.

"Whatever she is," Mitzy said, "it would be better to get her on our side than to let her help the rangers. They're all rich and noble. They don't *need* any more help. And we need advantages."

"We've got an advantage happening right now."

Kaylina pressed her ear to the door. What advantage?

"We just need to make sure things don't get screwed up again," the man added.

"Based on who we made that deal with, the odds are in favor of screw-ups," Mitzy said. "That was a desperate move. I'm surprised Cougar reached out to them. There's no way those guys are going to keep doing what we ask without demanding something much more than access to the catacombs. I'd much rather deal with Korbian."

"*Korbian* hasn't proven amenable to joining us."

"She hasn't said no to it. She's new."

"She's just a girl. Our new allies—"

"*Aren't* allies," Mitzy interrupted. "They're using us, the same as we're using them, and that's only going to last until they don't need us anymore."

The man sighed. "If you insist on finding the girl, physical coercion might help get a *yes* out of her."

Kaylina shuddered. Having them want to use her might be better than them wanting to kill her, but she already had Targon bribing her. She didn't need anyone else *coercing* her to help. What could she even do for the Virts? Use her *anrokk* power to round up stray cats to add to their army of rebels?

"We're the good guys, Dendron," Mitzy said. "We're not killing or coercing anyone."

"The ends justify the means."

"It would be safer to get rid of her," another man said. "If she's got magical powers, we don't want her helping the enemy."

"We need allies," Mitzy said firmly. "Commoners, like us, who understand what we want to do. And we don't *get rid of* people. We want a world that's fair and safe for all, not one where inconvenient people disappear."

A door thumped. Were they still searching the castle? Mitzy sounded like she was standing in one spot, but the men might have been moving around.

If they *were* searching, the pantry would be an obvious place to look. Kaylina stepped back and crouched, finding the crease in the flagstone floor that indicated the trapdoor leading to the root cellar—and the catacombs. She didn't want to miss anything, but she couldn't let the Virts find her.

"She might come to us naturally when she learns the truth about the rangers," Mitzy said. "About what they're protecting."

Kaylina froze with her hand on the cold stone of the trapdoor.

"Not what," the man said. "*Who.*"

"It's both, really, isn't it? If Hokkens can be believed."

"I didn't believe him at first, but...."

"He survived the massacre at the castle," Mitzy said, and Kaylina scowled, certain of where the conversation was going. They knew about Vlerion. "He said—"

"I know what Hokkens said, girl, but men don't turn into animals. There's no magic that can do that."

"No magic that we know about and remember, but the druids had a lot, and there have been stories about a beast ravaging this part of the kingdom for generations."

"Vlerion isn't that old."

Kaylina closed her eyes. Yes, they knew. It was exactly as Vlerion had feared.

"He doesn't *seem* that old. But if Hokkens is right, he's been turning into that... *thing* and killing people for centuries."

Kaylina shook her head. They had *part* of the story but not all of it. They didn't know the curse was linked to the entire Havartaft family, that Vlerion's ancestors had been to blame for previous atrocities.

"When is our paper going to print up the story? Put the blame where it belongs and demand the rangers out him—if they're not in collusion with him? After that, those on the fence about joining our cause should turn. Altered orchards, even the nobility might turn on *that*."

"Soon," Mitzy said. "According to Cougar, anyway. They've been laying the groundwork. It's a big accusation to make, but if more bodies show up..."

"Oh, I'm sure they will. The rangers don't care enough to stop it."

"We've searched the entire castle," another speaker said, footsteps accompanying the words. "Except that creepy-as-the-catacombs tower. I'm not going up there. The vines hanging down are twitching."

"I hate this place."

"Check the kitchen, and then we'll go."

Kaylina cursed to herself and lifted the trapdoor as quietly as she could. Footsteps sounded in the kitchen, and a shadow moved in front of the cracked pantry door. Hurrying to climb down, she almost missed a ladder rung and fell. She caught herself, pulling the trap door closed and wincing at the *thump* it made.

She stepped back, worried she would have to flee into the catacombs, but bumped into something. No, *someone*. She gasped, barely keeping from making it a cry of alarm.

An arm wrapped around her, pulling her against a hard male chest, and a hand flattened over her mouth to keep her from screaming.

20

You want to wear that uniform, you put the good of the kingdom ahead of your personal desires.

~ Ranger Captain Targon

Kaylina didn't try to scream or bite the hand across her mouth, and it soon loosened. Even in the dark, she recognized the hard body behind her, the way the muscled arms gripped her, and the aura of her captor.

"You're not a Virt," Vlerion whispered in her ear as he lowered his hand.

"Nope," she whispered back. "I'm still an independent."

"With a leaning toward helping rangers, I hope."

"Helping *one* ranger whom I happen to like. I'm less enamored with the others."

"Even Doc Penderbrock? He's healed you and your brother. I thought you might be favorably inclined toward him." Vlerion took her hand and guided her to the back half of the root cellar.

"He's the one ranger I like."

Vlerion snorted softly as he un-shuttered a lantern, letting its yellow flame appear, the soft light warming his face from below. He glanced toward the pantry trapdoor as a footfall thudded on it and released Kaylina to grip the hilt of the sword belted at his waist.

"I don't know if I got the door fully shut," Kaylina admitted.

"We'll find out."

More boots thudded across the flagstone as the Virts searched the pantry and the rest of the kitchen. At least some of their people were aware that Stillguard Castle had an access point to the catacombs, but maybe Mitzy's bunch didn't know where.

"Did you hear their conversation?" Kaylina whispered.

"No. I was coming to see if you, with half the city looking for you, were unwisely visiting the castle everyone knows you leased."

"I haven't been unwisely visiting anything," she said, even if that was a lie.

"Are you certain? You've an atypical aroma about you."

Maybe that was the polite way an aristocrat told a person they stank.

"Targon's secret way out of ranger headquarters involved a trek through the sewers."

"It's hard to keep your route a secret for long when such a stench is wafting from you."

"No wonder you didn't greet me with a kiss." Kaylina was surprised he'd grabbed her at all. Maybe her *anrokk* blood really *did* magically compel him to be close to her. "I spotted Virts wandering around in my castle and was compelled by each and every god to sneak in and eavesdrop on them. I thought they might say something important."

"How did you know they were inside if you weren't here, unwisely visiting?"

"I happened to be walking past the castle on my way to see the poisoner my brother hopes will link Jana Bloomlong to the tainted mead. Really, Vlerion. I can't believe you suspect me of foolishness."

"Uh-huh. If you mean that paint maker, he lives two miles away. I also looked him up."

"We were taking the scenic route to avoid guards."

"There are castle *and* kingdom guards watching this place, and I think the boy across the river may be one of the spymaster's kids."

Kaylina hadn't spotted the second guard or anyone across the river, but she refused to admit she'd been foolish. Not when she'd learned information from eavesdropping.

"That's why I came through the catacombs," Vlerion added. "That and the fact that Targon ordered a number of us to search them. He thinks the preserve might not be the only place the Kar'ruk have infiltrated. I came here first." He pointed toward the ceiling—the castle above. "I had a hunch the purple glow would draw you."

"The possibility that I can lift the castle's curse—and get clues about how to lift *your* curse—is what drew me. Not some glowing plant."

"I appreciate you wanting to do that." Vlerion shifted the lantern to his sword hand so he could wrap an arm around her shoulders. "But your mission is to clear your name."

"So my brother keeps telling me." Kaylina hoped Frayvar was staying out of sight up there. She hadn't realized there were that many people watching the castle. "But, Vlerion..." She gripped his forearm, the muscles tense under his sleeve—he still had an eye toward the trapdoor, as if he expected an army to storm down at any second. "The Virts know about you. About the beast."

"After the incident in the castle dungeon, I'm not surprised."

"They're calling it a massacre."

He winced. "Perhaps not inaccurate."

"You saved the king and the queen." Kaylina hoped he forgave himself for the killing. Those people had been intruders, though she knew it wouldn't have mattered if they hadn't been. The beast would have killed them regardless. But that wasn't his fault, and she hoped he wouldn't come to believe it was *her* fault. But if she hadn't been in danger, would he have turned into the beast? Likely not.

"This time." Vlerion touched her hand on his arm and nodded to her. "And with your help."

"Yes, my tide-turning sling."

"Your sling was useful."

"Thank you. Let me tell you the rest." Kaylina glanced toward the root-cellar ladder, but no more footsteps came from the flagstones in the pantry, and silence wrapped around them. Hoping that meant the Virts had left the castle, she summed up what she'd learned from eavesdropping, including that the rangers had a spy or *spies* within their organization. She finished with, "We have to clear your name even more than mine. There's a lot more at stake if your secret comes out, right? You've said as much. And the Virts believe the rangers have been protecting you. It could start a war." She flexed her hand in the air, acknowledging there was *already* a war, even if nothing had officially been declared. But this could escalate matters.

"It touches me that you've come to care, but it's not possible to clear my name. The beast... is guilty of some of the crimes of which it—" Vlerion touched his chest, not distancing himself fully from that part of him, "—has been accused."

"But not the dead Virts that have been found these last few nights, right? The ones mauled by claws and left in the street by the canals."

"No."

"Oh, and there was a ranger. Just tonight. Did you know?" Kaylina wondered if he'd been back to his headquarters or if Targon had ordered him earlier to search the catacombs after finishing in the preserve. He might have recently returned to the city and come to check on her first.

Vlerion's eyes widened. "No. Who? Where?"

Kaylina didn't know the man's name but described him and the male taybarri that had been with Levitke.

"Cursed craters." Vlerion bent forward and gripped his knee, barely noticing when the lantern clinked on the ground. "That sounds like Ravcliff. He is—*was* a good man. He didn't deserve that." He shook his head slowly. "I was talking to him not two hours ago."

Kaylina rested her hand on his back. "I'm sorry." After a pause to let him process his grief, as much as one could in a short time, she added, "This is another reason to clear your name, though, right? We don't want any of the rangers to read that newspaper and start to believe..." She spread her hand. He'd told her that only Targon and a couple of the rangers knew his secret. To the rest, it would be shocking news. They might turn their backs on him. That might sting him nearly as much as the death of a comrade.

"As I said, my name can't be cleared. Not when I *have* killed."

"If not clear your name, then we can find out who's behind the murders. It's someone—or something—with claws a *lot* like the beast's. I saw the body, the marks." Kaylina curled her fingers and slashed them in the air in front of her neck.

"Yes, I've seen the dead as well."

"We need to keep the guy who saw you change—Hokkens, is his name—from telling more people about it. Definitely from printing it in that paper." Kaylina didn't know how to accomplish that. Find the Virt and bribe him? The way Targon was trying to bribe her? The Virt probably didn't need help opening a meadery...

"Rebel or not, I can't hunt him down and kill him to keep him silent," Vlerion said.

Kaylina was glad he didn't consider that an option even if it would have made the task easier. The Virts were humans—and kingdom subjects.

"No, I wasn't going to suggest that, but he *was* part of the assassination attempt." Kaylina waved her hand. "Can't you arrest him? And put him in a cell far removed from other people? And then lose the key?"

"I suppose if we can find him, arrest is a possibility, but if he's already told the other Virts..."

"He might be the only witness. And the others are skeptical. If you can silence him and make that newspaper disappear, then your secret won't come out."

Too bad Kaylina didn't know how to find Hokkens *or* the press. She regretted not bringing her brother into the castle with her. She might be a natural schemer, but he was smart, organized, and liked to do research like this.

"Thank you for wanting to help," Vlerion said quietly and pulled her into a hug, his arms shifting from her shoulders to her waist. He patted her gently, making her again long to solve his problems for him, to change the world—or at least his life—so he could find peace.

"You're welcome."

"I still want you to focus on clearing your own name."

"I'm not *un*focused on it." Except that was exactly what she was, as her brother would be quick to point out.

Vlerion leaned back to give her a frank look, but his hands lingered on her waist, so he couldn't have been too perturbed. "Once you're safe, you can help me all you wish. I'll keep an eye out and try to help you as well. As soon as the rangers deal with the Kar'ruk problem."

"And you stop the Virts from blathering about you."

He managed a smile, but it was far from a firm nod of agreement. "After checking the catacombs, I'll talk to Targon and see if he's made progress on finding the press. I also want to see what the rangers learned by questioning the Kar'ruk. As much as I would prefer my secret remain buried, the safety of the kingdom is my priority."

"And yet, you came here to fondle my waist first."

"I couldn't resist. I feared you would be here, drawn by the mystery of the plant and the curse. I came to warn you of the spies keeping an eye on the castle—and to chastise you for not prioritizing yourself." His rueful expression suggested he knew he was being hypocritical; he wasn't prioritizing *himself* either.

"To chastise me while waist fondling?"

"It's a more appealing way to do it than with whips and harsh words."

"I don't disagree."

A clank sounded, not from the direction of the root cellar or the castle above but from the tunnel that led into the catacombs.

Vlerion released Kaylina and drew his sword.

"Stay here." He left her the lantern and advanced into the darkness.

"You might need help." Kaylina bristled at the order, especially since she had her sling and could assist him, if only in a small way. She refrained from adding something tart, reminding herself that she would need to obey superior officers if she became a ranger, even a *part-time* ranger.

When Vlerion gave her a long look over his shoulder, she realized he'd given the order more because he didn't want her to be in danger—something that would rouse strong emotions in him—than because he thought she couldn't help.

She nodded back and stayed where she was, but she did set down the lantern and step away from it so she wouldn't be an easy target if someone made it past him. She also drew her sling.

Vlerion padded into the chamber that held a hidden cubby that had been used by the Virts to stash weapons. The darkness swallowed him, so she didn't know if he continued deeper into the catacombs or stepped to the side to wait for someone's approach.

Less than a minute after she lost sight of him, the sounds of a scuffle floated back to her. It was close—in that chamber.

A roar echoed from the stone walls. A *Kar'ruk* roar.

Kaylina readied her sling, poised to run forward to help if Vlerion called out.

Something clattered as it landed on the stone floor at the edge of the lamplight, then skidded into the shadows of a wall. A gauntlet? She couldn't tell, but it had almost startled her into slinging a round at it.

Thumps and grunts continued, then the sound of a blade clinking off stone. Or armor?

Kaylina couldn't help but creep forward, leaving the lantern on the floor and following the wall. The next grunt belonged to Vlerion and carried a hint of pain.

She hurried to the chamber's doorway but she couldn't see the fight in the gloom. How had Vlerion and the Kar'ruk even found each other? And did Vlerion have more than one enemy? She couldn't tell.

A moist thud sounded, and she paused. The sounds of the scuffle stopped.

Ahead, the shadows stirred, and Kaylina raised her weapon, not certain who had come out the victor.

"It's me," Vlerion said softly, walking into view with a fresh rip in his sleeve and parallel gouges in his leather armor. Claw marks? Fortunately for his ribs—and organs—they hadn't pierced the armor fully.

"Was it a Kar'ruk? Or an animal?" Kaylina remembered her earlier thought. "Or a Kar'ruk with a trained animal?"

"Just the Kar'ruk, but..." Vlerion frowned at the gouges in his armor, then looked around the chamber.

Kaylina lowered her sling. "Why would a Kar'ruk be coming to Stillguard Castle?"

"Maybe he's a mead enthusiast. Ah." Vlerion pointed toward the shadows, the gauntlet on the floor. "He was fighting with that instead of an axe. I managed to knock it off his hand."

Kaylina crouched to pick up the item that had clattered down and carried it closer to the lantern, almost dropping it when she saw it better. The word gauntlet *might* apply, but blades extended from above the knuckles, each several inches long. And *sharp*. Further, they were painted with that same blue concoction that marked the Kar'ruk axes. The blades didn't glow, or she would have noticed them before, but she was glad she hadn't touched one.

"Careful. Those are sharp." Vlerion pointed, then waved to his armor.

"I see. Wet too." With blood, Kaylina thought at first, but it was water.

"So was he. He might have fallen into that underground lake."

Kaylina blushed, remembering doing the same because the ledge had been so slick.

"It happens," she murmured, then thought back to the body the taybarri had shown her. "Could this weapon be what was used to murder people these last few days? That guy might have just killed your ranger friend."

"That thought crossed my mind. It would mean that at least one Kar'ruk has been here longer than we suspected. I suppose the group in the preserve could have been in the kingdom for a while too. Observing." Vlerion's jaw clenched.

"My brother and I probably weren't supposed to stumble across them. Maybe they would have gone on observing until..." Until what? She had no idea what they planned. "Oh, wait," she blurted. "Mitzy implied the Virts are working with some new ally. No, *not* an ally. Someone they're using who's using them right back. Could the Virts have hooked up with the Kar'ruk? Talked them into helping make the rangers look bad for the newspaper? And to further their cause overall?"

"It's hard to imagine the two groups joining forces or even seeking each other out for a discussion. There haven't been many instances of humans and Kar'ruk conspiring over the centuries. Usually, the Kar'ruk will, given the opportunity, kill our people on sight." Vlerion shook his head. "I'm more inclined to believe the Kar'ruk are up to something on their own and that the Virts are capitalizing on it."

"Why would the Kar'ruk be killing one person at a time and trying to make it look like an animal—or a beast—did it?"

"I don't know yet."

Kaylina held up the gauntlet. "Could this at least be used to prove someone is masquerading as the beast? A Kar'ruk?"

"It could be used as evidence to lend credence to that idea, especially if the blades match the wounds on the dead." Vlerion took it from her. "I don't know how closely the civilian bodies were examined, but Ravcliff's would have gone to headquarters for storage before being returned to his family for a funeral. I need to talk to Targon and show him this."

"Okay."

"Do you want to come with me?"

"Targon forbade me from returning until I've proven my innocence." Kaylina also hadn't yet gotten to try the new honey on the plant.

Vlerion's eyes slitted. "He won't forbid you from anything with me at your side." His voice came out as a menacing growl.

Kaylina patted his arm. "Go report to him. I need to find Frayvar, make sure the Virts are out of the castle, and..." She still wanted to help him with *his* problem, and she gazed thoughtfully at the gauntlet.

"Clear your name," Vlerion finished for her, his tone gruff. It sounded more like an order than a suggestion.

"Naturally, but..." Kaylina plucked the gauntlet from his grip, careful to avoid the blades. "I have an idea."

"Not one that involves getting caught with that, I hope." His fingers lifted, as if he might take it back from her, but he waited for her to explain.

"Hopefully not. If I can show this weapon to the right person, we can clear the beast of suspicion, at least when it comes to the recent murders. Look, it's got Kar'ruk blue gunk on the blades. That's a giveaway, right?"

Vlerion's grunt didn't convey as much agreement as she would have liked. Instead, he asked, "What *right person* do you have in mind?"

"The journalist writing those articles," Kaylina said. "He might be convinced to print a retraction."

"You just suggested the Kar'ruk and the Virts could be aligned. If that *were* true, the journalist would already know the truth and would be a part of the lie."

"I didn't say the convincing would be with words." She held the gauntlet up and made a swiping motion.

"Are *you* going to threaten him?" Vlerion arched his eyebrows.

"The Virts seem to know all about my supposedly magical powers now. I might be exactly the right person to intimidate a journalist." Kaylina showed him her brand and wiggled her fingers.

That earned her another noncommittal grunt. But he relented with, "Wait for me before looking for the journalist. If it makes sense, *I'll* do the intimidating."

"The Virts don't like you much. And don't you need to report to Targon?"

"That won't take long." Vlerion squinted at her. "Do you know where the press is located? Did your eavesdropping unearth that?"

"No, but we think it's outside the city. Maybe Frayvar and I can figure it out. We were already talking about hiding alongside the highway in the middle of the night and waiting for another newspaper-filled wagon to pass."

"That isn't your mission, Kaylina. And you shouldn't assume the Virts aren't dangerous to you."

"Oh, I'm not." She remembered the men casually discussing killing her. Mitzy hadn't wanted her dead, but she was only one person in the organization. "But, as a future ranger, I need to learn to court danger, don't I?"

"You only need to obey your superior officers when they order you to face it."

"So… no courting is involved?"

"No." Vlerion reached for the gauntlet. "I need to show this to Targon."

Kaylina resisted his attempt to take it away. "*I* need to show it to the Virts—specifically their journalist. If they're *not* aligned, it might convince him to retract the story without the need for intimidation."

"I'll return it after we compare the prongs to those found on the body. And I will assist you in searching for the press and journalist, though I suggest you prioritize—"

"Clearing my name. Yeah, yeah, I know."

"You know, but you're not striving to do it."

"I will. Trust me. I want to open my meadery—I'm aching to make a batch using honey from the preserve—and I need people to stop trying to arrest, imprison, and execute me to achieve that goal. But first…" Kaylina tilted her thumb over her shoulder toward the root cellar. "Assuming the Virts got tired of looking for me and left, I'm going to have a chat with the plant while drizzling honey over its roots."

"You shouldn't *chat* with that plant alone."

"Frayvar is waiting for me outside. And the castle doesn't hate him the way it does rangers, so he can pull me out of harm's way if it attacks again."

"That boy would be hard-pressed to pull a carrot out of a garden."

"Carrots can have long roots and be tough. I'm *much* easier to deal with."

"Really." Vlerion looked pointedly at the gauntlet she hadn't yet released.

Kaylina made herself let it go and clasped her hands behind her back. "Really. I won't even court danger while I'm in the castle."

Vlerion grumbled under his breath—she caught the words *vexing woman*—but followed her when she headed toward the root cellar. Only after they climbed the ladder, entered the kitchen, and didn't see or hear anyone did he let her push him out the door.

"Don't forget to bring that back to me." Kaylina waved at the bladed gauntlet.

"The ranger trainee is giving the experienced ranger orders now? Targon will not be pleased by my lack of progress with instilling reverence in you."

"He's not pleased by much that I've noticed." She made a shooing motion toward the gate.

In truth, she wouldn't have minded Vlerion's company—and his sword arm. The plant's presumptuous *branding* had scared her. Even though the mark had helped her in the preserve, she had no confidence that it was for her benefit. The plant might be using her to some end that only it knew. By now, she couldn't dismiss the idea that it was intelligent and could be enacting a plan for its ancient masters.

But having Vlerion at her side, when the plant loathed rangers, was more of a risk than visiting it alone. For both of them. She would go out and find Frayvar before climbing to the tower. If something happened, he could run for help.

Despite her attempts to shoo Vlerion away, it wasn't until a moan drifted through the castle and a ceiling beam creaked that he stepped into the courtyard.

"Be careful," he murmured, giving her a long look over his shoulder as he walked toward the gate.

"Same to you. Watch out for Kar'ruk springing out of the sewers with fake claws."

"It was the catacombs." His eyes glinted with humor. "Civilized people don't traipse about in sewers."

"Listen, pirate." Kaylina pointed at the gauntlet. "Don't make me hope you fall and prong yourself on that."

"Such irreverence." He lifted a hand before passing through the gatehouse and disappearing into the night.

Even though she'd urged him to leave, Kaylina felt a pang of emptiness at his departure.

"It's for his own good," she told herself.

Lantern in hand, she headed through the bottom level of the keep, wanting to make sure the Virts had left before she looked for Frayvar. She'd no sooner stepped into the dining hall than a creak and bump came from the front of the keep. It sounded like the door blowing against the wall in the wind. The Virts must have gone out that way and left it open.

She crept into the great hall and reached the vestibule, spotting the open door at the same time as a dark lump on the floor. A person.

Someone dead? Fist tightening on her lantern handle, she stared at the inert figure and feared she'd made a mistake in sending Vlerion away.

21

The wilderness is not malevolent but can kill you nonetheless.
~ Ranger Founder Saruk

Though she was tempted to run the other way, Kaylina made herself creep toward the body. Another moan emanated from somewhere above. A chandelier, one of the ones that *hadn't* fallen already, shivered, glass clinking.

She'd thought the purple light meant something had changed about the curse, but maybe that had been a naive belief.

The person had died face down, so Kaylina had to set down her lantern and roll him over to identify him. It was one of the Virts who had been with Mitzy, fingernail marks now on his throat. He'd clawed at himself before dying. In addition, there was a red welt where one of those vines must have wrapped around his neck and choked him.

Kaylina eyed the nearby walls. There was no sign of a vine or anything else, but she'd seen them appear and disappear before, so she had no trouble imagining one sprouting from the mortar and attacking.

But why this guy? He hadn't been a ranger. As one of the party plotting insurrections and assassinations, he'd been an *enemy* of the rangers. The plant ought to have loved him.

She wondered if it was the man who'd commented that killing her would be a good idea. Was it possible the plant had attacked him to *protect* her? If so, that was a chilling thought. She didn't want a magical botanical bodyguard that murdered people.

"Kaylina?" came Frayvar's soft voice from the kitchen. "Are you in here?"

"Yes, by the body," she called back, glancing at the open front door and suspecting they were alone.

The Virts must have been scared off by the attack. Kaylina didn't think much of them if they'd abandoned an ally in need, but maybe they'd tried and failed to save him. When she'd attempted to free Targon from one of those vines, she'd been useless until Vlerion had arrived with his sword and powerful muscles.

"You keep strange company these days." Frayvar approached warily, a lantern in hand.

"Trust me. I'd rather be back home with Grandpa's hounds. I'd even take a lecture on hard work and propriety from Silana over this."

"Would you?" Frayvar stopped well away from the body and looked at her. "I wonder."

"What, you think I'm enjoying my new life of being a wanted felon branded by sentient plants?"

"Well, aside from our time huddled in the rain on various estates, you've fallen into fewer funks since we got up here. Remember the Grouper Gala last year when you didn't leave your bedroom for a week?"

"I've been busy trying to stay alive."

"So, if there had been more attempts to kill you back home, you would have been perkier."

"Absolutely. Terror and fear are energizing." Kaylina eyed the body, not able to smile to make the words a joke. They were all too true. "I don't know what to do with him. He looks heavy, but we can't leave him in the vestibule."

"Maybe his buddies will come back for him. They would presumably have more of an idea about his funeral preferences than we do."

Kaylina had a feeling the scared Virts wouldn't risk returning. Mitzy might have been brave before, but seeing the curse in action made bravery evaporate.

"We could try to push him outside." The way Frayvar clasped his hands behind his back suggested he meant *she* could do that.

"Vlerion is supposed to bring me something later. He can make arrangements." Kaylina closed the door, stepped around the body, and headed for the kitchen.

"What if it draws rats?"

"There are some traps in one of the closets upstairs. You can set them out and catch a few for a stew."

"Oh yes, rat tartare is a dish that's sure to bring aristocrats and proletariats alike to our door." Frayvar glanced back numerous times as they departed. "Do you know why… I assume a vine got him, right? What did he do?"

"I'm not sure."

"He doesn't look like a friend of the rangers."

"He wasn't." As Kaylina removed the honeycomb from her pack, she spotted a newspaper article clipped out and lying on the counter. "Did you put that there?"

"Not me."

"It had to be the Virts." Kaylina picked it up. It was the article about the beast that they'd already read. Had Mitzy left it for her as a message?

She growled, tempted to use it to start a fire, but she folded it and put it in her pocket instead. If she chanced upon more druidic beehives, she could wrap the comb in the paper instead of having to tear pages out of the ranger handbook.

That done, she located a pot to make her fertilizer. This time, she would heat it so the honey dissolved properly. "Bribery Attempt Number Two coming up."

The back of her hand itched. She frowned at it, then knelt to start a fire in the hearth.

"Maybe you should call it a gift." Frayvar looked toward the walls and the ceiling, as if the castle—the *plant*—might be listening. Maybe it was. "Or an offering."

"I'm not particular about what we call it. I just want it to lift the curse."

"You think the honey from the preserve will do more than Grandpa's honey? They were both made from bees foraging on altered plants, right?" Frayvar looked wistfully in the direction of the mountains. "I would have liked to see the valley you described."

"We can visit the preserve again when there aren't axe-toting Kar'ruk lurking around every tree." Not wanting him to worry more about the castle than he already did, Kaylina didn't mention the Kar'ruk that Vlerion had killed in the catacombs, fifty yards from their root cellar.

"And with sturdy rangers beside us?"

"Possibly."

Once the fire was burning, Kaylina hung the pot of water to boil. Her hand itched again, then warmed. The desire to go upstairs and see the plant swept over her.

She didn't think it came fully from her, which made her wonder if it had been entirely *her* will that had prompted her to return to the castle. Was there a reason she kept prioritizing this over solving her own problem? What if the brand could control her on some level?

"Not at all creepy," she murmured.

Frayvar yawned loudly. "Are we sleeping here tonight? Or maybe I should ask if we're *sleeping* tonight."

"I do miss it."

His yawn made Kaylina do the same. Tears sprang to her eyes, and three more yawns followed the first.

"We'll have to find somewhere safe to do it," she added. "Not in the castle. It's a risk even starting a fire here. Vlerion mentioned spies, more than the one person we saw. It's only that so few people are willing to come in here that I'm not more worried. Also, we could, if we had to, escape into the catacombs."

"Maybe one of the passageways down there leads to the poison-maker's home." Frayvar looked at her, but he didn't repeat his desire to prioritize that mission.

Kaylina sighed. She couldn't blame him for wanting the charges removed and again wondered if an outside influence—she glanced at the brand—might be the reason she kept putting it off. It might just be that she didn't see how finding the maker of the poison would lead to Jana admitting she'd been responsible and that Kaylina was innocent. The poisoner might be a good friend of hers or at least value her as a client. Why would he rat her out to the authorities to protect a newcomer from the far end of the kingdom?

The water boiled, and Kaylina removed the pot to stir in honey. Realizing she hadn't answered her brother's question about whether it was superior, she gave him a piece of the comb to taste.

"It's even better than Grandpa's," Kaylina said. "You've got the chef's palate, but tell me I'm wrong."

Frayvar swept a finger through the comb and touched it to his tongue, then let it linger for a thoughtful moment while she finished making the fertilizer.

"It *is* good," he said. "It's got a zing to it."

"That's probably the magic."

He snorted but didn't deny the possibility. "I wonder if it conveys any health benefits. Remember when Aplar Dunefar did those scientific experiments on Grandpa's honey?"

"I remember him cadging a lot of free samples under the premise that he was studying it."

"He published his findings in some university journals," Frayvar said, indignation in his tone. "There were charts and columns of data."

"Oh, well if there were charts, I'm sure it was legitimate."

"You're such a skeptic."

"We don't need the druid honey to have health benefits for anyone except the plant. I want it to feel so vibrant and chuffed about life that it lifts the curse."

"You think a plant has that power?"

"I'm hoping *that* plant does." Kaylina held the back of her hand toward him to remind him how much power it had.

"All right."

She grabbed her ladle and hefted the pot. "Come with me, please, to hand this up to me, then stand back in case I need help."

"Shouldn't I stand *forward* in case you need help?"

"No, because I don't want you to get cracked in the head by a vine, zapped by branding magic, or otherwise maimed. If you think it's necessary, I want you to run for help."

"Run to whom?"

Kaylina hesitated, reluctant to bring any of the rangers into the castle when the curse wanted them dead, but who else did she know who would help her? No one.

"Vlerion. Or the ranger doctor. Or both."

Frayvar looked at her with grave eyes, probably imagining scenarios that would require him to get the doctor. All he said was a soft, "Okay."

More nervous than she'd been on her previous visits to the tower, Kaylina wiped her hands on her trousers a few times as they ascended the stairs and walked down the hall. She tried not to think of the man the castle had killed less than an hour ago, the body still in the vestibule.

"Was the tower glowing red or purple when you came in?" She wondered if it had turned back to red and that was what had made it grumpy enough to kill.

"Purple."

"Hm."

When they passed the window at the end of the hall and turned into the narrow passageway that led to the tower, Kaylina could see the purple glow for herself, seeping through the gap in the boards she'd made days earlier. More vines than before dangled down. One ran along the ceiling and down the wall, the end lying on the floor, the tip twitching slightly.

"I've invigorated it, haven't I?" Kaylina asked.

"Feed it more honey, and it could take over the city." Frayvar stopped well back. The way he eyed the twitching tip suggested he would have whether she'd recommended it or not.

Before committing to climbing up, Kaylina handed him the pot and walked close to the vine, wanting to see how it would react to her. Even though she believed the plant hadn't marked her out of malice, despite the pain it had caused, she didn't want it to hurt her again. Or worse. By now, it might have figured out that she considered Vlerion an ally. *More* than an ally.

The tip of the vine twitched toward her and rose a few inches from the floor. It reminded her of a hound with its nose in the air, sniffing the wind.

"I brought some special honey," she told it.

The tip flicked toward the hole. An invitation?

Kaylina took a deep breath. That might be the most reassurance that she would get.

"My brother will hand it to me once I climb up to you," she added, wanting to make sure the plant understood that he wasn't an enemy either.

Again, the tip flicked toward the hole.

"Right."

While avoiding touching the vines, Kaylina climbed the wall, using the rusty brackets that had once supported stairs. The floorboards creaked when she gripped them, but having made several trips up, she trusted them to support her weight. She swung her leg over the edge, and, with a grunt and straining of muscles, she pulled herself into the room.

The purple glow intensified, bathing her in its light. The plant had sprouted more branches and vines from its ancient soil, and several waved in the air.

Afraid one would grab her again, she kept an eye on them as she pushed herself to her hands and knees.

"Is it safe?" Frayvar called from down the hall.

"What's your definition of safe?"

"Protected from and not exposed to danger or risk. Harmless. Offering safety from danger or difficulty."

"I said *your* definition, not the dictionary definition."

"They're the same. I'm a faithful devotee of dictionaries."

"Yeah, yeah. The plant isn't any of those things. Come to the hole, and hand me the pot anyway."

Since the branches and vines, despite waving in the air, weren't threatening her, Kaylina risked taking her gaze off them to lie beside the hole and lower her hand down.

"I'm not sure why you didn't bring your ra— your new friend for this," Frayvar grumbled as he approached slowly.

"I didn't want him to be killed."

"Naturally, you're saving that fate for your little brother."

"The plant doesn't hate you."

"It's knocked me unconscious before." He glanced from vine to vine, not looking up at her, as he stopped under the hole and held the pot overhead.

"Not hatefully." Glad for his height, Kaylina reached down and gripped the handle.

"*So* comforting."

The water sloshed, the ladle clinking against the lip, as she pulled the pot up. Before she sat back, vines stretched toward it.

"Don't be greedy. Give me a second." Kaylina set the pot down next to the huge planter and grabbed the ladle.

The vines didn't obey and dipped into the water. One brushed her hand, and she jerked back, the memory of the *last* time the plant had touched her springing to mind.

But it only wanted the honey-water and didn't reach for her.

"If it understands our language," Frayvar said, backing down the hall, "it might not appreciate you giving it orders. The same way you don't appreciate certain lords giving you orders."

"It's a wise plant." Kaylina plucked out the ladle. "I'm sure it knows they're only suggestions."

"Maybe you should bow and add *my lord* when you speak to it."

"You think it's an aristocratic plant?"

"It's *something*. It might appreciate your obeisance."

Kaylina eased closer to ladle her fertilizer over the soil around the inches-thick stem of the plant. The *trunk*, she amended. It didn't look anything like a tree, but that was a very stout stem.

The purple glow intensified. She hoped that meant the plant liked the honey.

A vine lifted from the pot, water dripping from the tip, and drifted toward her face.

Kaylina skittered back, almost dropping the ladle. "You're welcome. No need for touching. Thanks."

The vine paused, as if considering her words.

"My lord," she added in case her brother was right. "Or lady. Or high plantness."

A snort drifted up from Frayvar, but he didn't suggest another title.

The tip of the vine eased closer to her face, stretching toward her temple.

Heart hammering against her ribcage, Kaylina lifted the ladle to use as a shield and backed away as far as she could. When she bumped into the stone wall, she had to stop. Either that, or she had to dive past the vine, out the hole, and tumble to the floor below, possibly breaking her neck.

The vine paused again, the tip only a few inches from her eyes.

It wasn't *aggressively* reaching for her—when the plant had branded her, its movement had been abrupt, too quick for her to escape—but she found even this mild interest alarming. Yet it paused, hanging there. Silently asking if it could touch her? She didn't know why it needed to. Before, it had shared visions with her without any contact. No, not visions. It had taken her memories and shown them to her, shown her it could read minds.

But now it seemed to be asking permission.

Kaylina lowered the ladle. "Go ahead."

The vine drifted closer, the cool green tip touching her temple. In the still quiet of the tower, she could feel every rapid thump of her heart. She closed her eyes, hoping she wouldn't regret this.

22

Ask not for the Creator to grant you clairvoyance, for the future inevitably holds your death.

~ Talivaria, Daygarii wise woman

Kaylina's eyesight darkened, awareness of the tower around her fading, and a vision swept over her.

This time, it wasn't a memory. She was riding through a deep forest on a taybarri with nobody else around. Was it Levitke? She believed so, but she couldn't see her mount's face in the vision. She could see her *own* face, which was odd. She seemed to be flying along, watching herself from above.

The taybarri came out of the trees and into the valley with the druid beehives. Instead of stopping, Levitke passed through it and out the other end, climbing into the mountains.

The afternoon sun beat on their backs, meaning they were traveling east, farther and farther from Port Jirador. The ground sloped upward, growing rocky and treacherous, but the taybarri was sure-footed. They passed goats and rams but didn't slow, only climbing higher and higher until they reached a mountain valley with snowy peaks all around and patches of snow in the shade on the ground. Here and there, huge tunnel openings dotted the earth, as if giant gophers lived there. But no gophers could have dug such large holes.

The taybarri evolved as diggers and tunnel dwellers, a dry voice spoke into her mind, *to escape the great prehistoric winged predators of the time, predators that swept down from the sky and preyed upon the young and old and infirm. Only later did taybarri venture forth more freely, when the winged predators became extinct. Some traveled down from the mountains and adopted residence in the temperate blue-grass plains, where they encountered humans more frequently, but many remain in the mountains in their original homeland.*

Kaylina didn't know who was speaking but guessed it was the plant. Or someone sharing the vision *through* the plant? She had no idea, but it had never spoken to her before.

As Levitke carried her into the valley, numerous taybarri came into view. *Silver* taybarri. Elders?

Vlerion had once explained that the taybarri turned from blue to gray as they matured. That was when they supposedly gained the ability to communicate with humans. Maybe a *taybarri* rather than the plant was somehow monitoring her thoughts and communicating with her. But this was a vision or a dream, right? A real taybarri off in the mountains somewhere couldn't know about it.

Four blue-furred youths bounded out of a tunnel as the large silver creatures calmly watched Levitke approach. She stopped, and the Kaylina in the vision slid off her back.

Levitke bounded over and romped with the young taybarri, wrestling and racing about, as if their long journey hadn't tired her in the least. Or maybe it was a reunion, and she was seeing family and friends she hadn't visited with since joining the rangers.

The Kaylina in the vision approached the elders and spoke

and gestured. Whatever she said wasn't relayed to Kaylina in the tower. Frequently, she pointed back in the direction of the city. She also touched her head with the index fingers of each hand, making horns. That had to indicate the Kar'ruk.

The silver-furred taybarri ambled away and conferred with each other. Levitke finished playing with the others and returned so that Kaylina could climb onto her back again. One of the elders joined them, and they rode the way Levitke and Kaylina had come, down out of the mountains and toward Port Jirador.

As an anrokk, *you may use your kinship with the taybarri to assist with your problems and with those of your people,* the same voice said.

The elders can help with the Kar'ruk? Kaylina asked. *And to clear my name?*

Was that what the voice was implying?

The speaker didn't respond, and the vision faded before showing Kaylina and the taybarri arriving at Port Jirador, but she had a lingering sense that the elder going to the city was a good thing. She questioned how one lone taybarri could stop the Kar'ruk or help her with her problems, but a spark of hope lingered. Maybe the plant had given her a solution.

Before Kaylina could contemplate it further, another vision swept over her, a more alarming one.

Again, she was in the mountains, a camp set up around a pond in another valley, but, this time, Kar'ruk approached her with their axes raised. She was alone with no taybarri to ride, no way to escape, and the horned warriors surrounded her. She used her sling on them, but the lead rounds didn't deter them. The Kar'ruk charged at her with their blades swinging.

Before they struck, Vlerion rushed into view, turning into the beast as he ran. He sprang into the Kar'ruk warriors, his power enough to match theirs. To *more* than match theirs. Ruthless, he killed them all. Before Kaylina could express her gratitude, the beast sprang upon her.

There was nowhere to run, no caves or rock piles to crawl into for safety. With no hint of recognition in his eyes, only the murderous frenzy of a rabid predator, the beast bore her to the ground.

You haven't enough blood of the ancients in your veins to control him, the same voice as before said, grave instead of dry. *He will slay you as he has slain many others. To kill is embedded in the curse, in* him. *It is the punishment for his line, for all humans in the area. Even the taybarri know not to disobey the mandates of the druids. The desperation of the humans made them foolish.*

As the beast's claws ripped into her torso, such pain blasted Kaylina that she woke screaming.

Utter confusion scattered her thoughts as she stared up at a wooden ceiling bathed in purple light. She lay on her back, her chest heaving, and touched her abdomen, expecting to find it bloody with the deep gashes made by the beast.

"Kaylina." A hand shook her shoulder.

It took her a moment to recognize Frayvar kneeling over her, alternately staring down at her with worry and glancing at a vine hovering in the air near her head. The same vine that had touched her temple? It withdrew without bothering her further, but the visions it had delivered would disturb her for a long time.

"Here. Smell this again." Frayvar waved a vial of something pungent under her nose.

Its odor was almost as offensive as that of the sewer, and Kaylina jerked her head away. "What is that?"

"Doc Penderbrock's smelling salts. He said they can wake up rangers who pass out drunk."

"I'm not drunk." Kaylina *did* feel hung over. When she pushed herself into a sitting position, she realized daylight mingled with the purple glow. "How long was I out?"

"*Hours*. I went to ranger headquarters and got the doctor, but it took me a while since I had to dodge guards that were out searching for you—or searching for trouble in general. Either way, I didn't want them to see me. Doc Penderbrock came back with me but wouldn't come in. He said Targon forbade any rangers from entering Stillguard Castle. I think the doctor was tempted to disobey that order, but I told him it would be a bad idea. He gave me this." Frayvar squinted at her before corking the vial.

"Well, at least I got that night's sleep I've been needing."

If only Kaylina felt refreshed. She rubbed her gritty eyes, weariness making her wish for her bed back home. Her bed where curses and troubling visions rarely disturbed her.

Lately, her life had been so harrowing that she couldn't help but feel she'd made a mistake in running off to the north. Oh, there wasn't anything wrong with having a quest or a desire to prove herself, but she'd let her emotions and grievances with family members motivate her. *That* had been foolish. In comparison to everything that was happening here in the capital—even here in this castle—a few arguments with family were such minor concerns.

Of course, if she hadn't left home, she wouldn't have met Vlerion. And he was...

Memories of him kissing her, wrapping his arms around her, and protecting her from threats filled her with warmth. But the emotion was fleeting as the plant's vision reared up in her mind, bringing the horrifying memory of the beast tearing her to pieces.

"I didn't," Frayvar grumbled, oblivious to her thoughts.

"Sorry. You got to sleep the last time the curse knocked you unconscious though."

"Oh, yes, how could I forget about that delightful evening?" Frayvar bared his teeth. "Can we get out of here? You fed the plant, right?" He waved at the honey-water pot, which had almost disappeared under vines, branches, and leaves. "It's feeding *itself*."

"I see that. I guess we can leave the pot up here."

"I would." Frayvar shuddered. "Did your, ah, *gift* result in anything useful?" He waved at the pot.

"I... maybe?"

"You can't answer a question with a question."

"The plant gave me a vision. *Two* visions. I don't know if they were foretelling the future or were a warning of what might come to pass if I..."

If she what? Went off into the mountains with Vlerion? If she went *anywhere* with him?

The thought of avoiding him completely depressed her, and she tried to focus on the first vision. It had conveyed that the taybarri would help if she could find the elders.

"If you what?"

"If I can't avoid certain situations," she finished. "At least *one* of them."

Frayvar looked at her as if she were being illogical. Or might have hit her head when she fell. At least he'd stopped waving the foul vial under her nose.

"Yes, we can leave. I just need one more moment." Kaylina shifted to face the plant. "You must know by now that we want to start a meadery here."

"And eating house," Frayvar said with a wistful look in the direction of the kitchen.

"Yes. But we can't do that if you, or, uhm, the curse, kill our potential customers." Kaylina didn't mention that the queen and the city's entire guard regiment wanting her dead was also an impediment. "Is there any way we can lift the curse? Or that you'll at least work with us to allow the business, the visitors? Without..." She waved downward to indicate the vestibule but didn't know if the plant could interpret her gestures. She didn't even know for certain that it understood her words, but it had seemed to before. "Without killing people. At least not people coming to enjoy our food and drink."

That one sought your death.

It was the same voice as before, but it startled her since it came outside of a vision. Had feeding the plant the honey fertilizer given it more power to communicate?

Descendants of the Daygarii must be protected, the voice added.

Kaylina touched her chest. Did that mean *her*? Was this confirmation that she somehow had a hint of the ancient druid blood in her veins?

The plant didn't respond to her gesture.

Aloud, she asked her more pressing question. "Does that mean you'll allow visitors if they don't want to kill me?"

Those who are not a threat to you may enter your abode as long as you reside here and care for the sentinel.

"The sentinel? Is that you?"

Frayvar's eyebrows arched as he presumably only heard one side of the conversation.

Those who are not a threat to you may enter, the plant repeated.

No vines stretched toward Kaylina, but another vision crept over her. Shorter and simpler than the others, it showed Vlerion on the cobblestone street outside of Stillguard Castle with a knife thrust into his chest. His dead blue eyes were open to the sky as snow fell, dusting his body.

Kaylina drew back in horror. Before the vision faded, she recognized the hilt of the blade embedded in his chest—piercing his heart. It was *her* knife, the one she used for peeling fruit and cutting meat at the dinner table. It wasn't for *killing* people, especially not friends.

You must slay that one before he slays you.

"That won't happen. He's *not* a threat to me."

But he was. She knew it, and the plant knew it.

It repeated the vision of Vlerion lying dead, then showed her dozens and dozens of people sitting at the tables inside the castle and in the courtyard, drinking heartily and laughing and enjoying themselves.

"Is that a bribe?" Kaylina demanded. "If I kill him, you'll help me be successful with my meadery? Look, I don't care what blood I might have. I would never—"

Frayvar touched her arm, and she stopped.

He held a finger to his lips as he tilted his head toward the plant. Had he also received that vision?

"If that's the deal it's offering us—*you*," Frayvar said, "then we must consider it."

Kaylina realized his words were for the sake of the plant—it clearly *could* understand them—but she couldn't keep from scowling. No dream would be worth killing someone over. Especially not Vlerion.

Had she believed for a second that Frayvar would consider that idea, she would have knocked him on his ass. But it was moot anyway. It wasn't as if either of them had the fighting prowess to kill a ranger. And Vlerion was far more than a ranger.

"Let's discuss it further outside," Frayvar added.

"Fine."

Leaving the pot of honey water behind, Kaylina swung down through the hole to the floor. She almost landed on a chair that Frayvar had dragged down the hall to help him up. He dropped down, using it for a stool, before joining her.

She strode out of the keep without saying another word to him. It wasn't his fault the plant had offered that awful suggestion—or *deal*, as her brother had said—but frustration and anger made it hard for her to be reasonable.

Frayvar followed her into the courtyard, then out the gatehouse to the river trail. Even there, Kaylina wasn't sure it was safe to talk, that the plant wouldn't be able to hear them, but her frustration boiled over and she whirled on him.

"Did you get that vision? And see what that awful plant wants?"

"I saw," Frayvar said. "I don't understand why it would single out Lord Vlerion specifically though. Why him over the other rangers?"

Frayvar must not have heard the words, the plant's promise that Vlerion was a threat to her.

"It hates him," was all she could say without explaining the beast. "He hacked up one of its vines to help Targon." That wasn't the true reason it wanted him dead. She knew that, but she couldn't help but clench her fists with frustration. "We're not plotting to kill Vlerion," she snapped, even though Frayvar hadn't argued for that.

"*Vlerion* appreciates that," came a dry voice from the courtyard wall. *His* dry voice.

Startled, Kaylina looked over to find Vlerion and Doctor Penderbrock leaning against the wall, their hoods pulled up. Since the gatehouse extended outward, it had blocked her view of them.

A whuff came from farther up the trail. Crenoch and another taybarri had found a spot where they could drink from the river.

"You didn't say Vlerion came with the doctor," Kaylina muttered to Frayvar.

"He didn't." Frayvar shrugged.

Kaylina told herself she hadn't said anything that would condemn her, and Vlerion looked more amused than concerned by her outburst, but the fact that the plant had been encouraging her to murder him flustered her. It made her feel guilty of a crime. A betrayal.

"Someone new wants to have you killed?" Penderbrock asked, also without concern, as he walked over to look Kaylina up and down. Frayvar handed the corked vial to him, and he tucked it into his bag. "Perhaps you should stop irking people, Vlerion."

"My job as a ranger," Vlerion said, "ensures I irk everyone from the Kar'ruk to human rebels to criminals to large predators in the mountains."

"It was the curse this time. The *plant*." Kaylina pointed toward the tower, though they couldn't see its window or purple glow from the trail.

"Well, that's nothing new." Vlerion shrugged. "The curse has been killing rangers for generations. Knowing that—and seeing it try to strangle Targon—is the only reason I didn't charge in to find you as soon as I got here. Are you all right, Kaylina?"

"*I'm* the reason you didn't charge in." Penderbrock peered into Kaylina's eyes, maybe checking her pupils to see if they were abnormal after she'd been knocked out.

"You have a startlingly strong left hook for a doctor, and you aren't afraid to punch a man when he isn't looking—" Vlerion touched his jaw, "—but I *could* have gotten past you. I was allowing my wisdom to guide me and waiting patiently for Frayvar to return with an update."

"Waiting patiently under Crenoch's large furry backside," Penderbrock muttered. "The *taybarri* are the only ones around here with much wisdom or patience."

The flat expression Vlerion gave him suggested he might not have wanted Kaylina to learn about that.

She stepped forward and gripped his arm, more concerned about what the plant had shown her than what it had done to her. "It may still hate rangers, but it wants you dead specifically."

After taking a deep breath, she explained the vision and the deal it was trying to make with her.

"That may be a first in ranger history." Penderbrock still sounded more amused than concerned. Maybe the rangers' lives were so fraught with danger that it didn't bother them. Or maybe he didn't think anyone would carry out murder based on what a *plant* wanted.

Kaylina hoped that was true, but she couldn't help but be disturbed by the vision.

Less amusement lurked in Vlerion's grave blue eyes, so maybe he found it unsettling as well. She hoped he trusted that she wouldn't consider the plant's offer.

But when he looked into her eyes and said, "Walk with me," she worried he *did* believe that.

She made herself respond in a light tone. "The correct way to request a woman accompany you for a stroll along the river is to say, *Won't you please walk with me, gentle companion whom I respect and admire?*"

Vlerion's eyebrows rose, and he looked at Penderbrock.

"I've been married almost forty years, and I've never said anything like that to my wife."

"Oh, I assumed that," Vlerion said. "I've seen the way she looks at you."

"With adoration," Penderbrock said.

"Like you're a particularly vexing new recruit who must be shown everything five times before grasping it."

"She only looks at me like that *some* of the time."

Vlerion waved dismissively. "What I was wondering is if you agreed with Ms. Korbian's assessment of herself as *gentle*."

Penderbrock considered her. "She hasn't struck *me* in the back of the head with a sling round."

"So her gentleness depends on the company she keeps."

"It's possible you're the problem, Vlerion."

"Huh." Vlerion extended a hand toward the river trail and raised his eyebrows again, this time for Kaylina.

She didn't know what he wanted to talk about, and that made her nervous, but she headed down the trail with him.

A flare of purple at the edge of her vision made her glance back as she walked. For a moment, the glow from the tower was bright enough to see even though the window wasn't visible from their position.

It soon faded, but she didn't miss the warning. The plant knew she was walking off with Vlerion and didn't like it. Or maybe that intense glow had been a command, an order to take her knife out and attack him.

Vlerion looked over at her and also back toward the castle. Since he didn't miss much, Kaylina had little doubt he'd noticed the glow intensifying.

His gaze dropped to the brand on the back of her hand, and his face grew grimmer. Maybe, despite his levity with the doctor, Vlerion *was* concerned.

23

It is easy to be virtuous until temptation appears.
~ *Assai, Priestess of Luvana*

With the sun peeking through the clouds, numerous people were walking along the river trail, and bicycles and wagons rolled along the streets that crossed it, so Vlerion and Kaylina kept their hoods up. Even with her face hidden, it was foolish to stroll through the city by daylight, but she wanted to ease Vlerion's mind about the plant's vision before leaving to look for the press. The press and... should she try to find an elder taybarri? She had less of an idea about how to do that.

As they walked, they didn't see any guards along the trail or in the streets. Vlerion's gaze roved, and Kaylina knew he was keeping an eye out for her sake.

Though she believed he wanted to speak with her in private about the curse—*his* curse as well as the castle's—he started their walk by returning the pronged gauntlet to her.

"The blades match the gashes on our dead ranger's throat," he said.

"Does your captain believe you that the Kar'ruk were responsible for all the murders?"

"Yes. I also told him where to find the Kar'ruk I killed. As for everyone else in the city..." Vlerion rocked his open hand in the air. "I don't know if that'll be enough evidence. Unfortunately, the warrior that you and Jankarr captured has been an unreliable source. The kafdari root doesn't work well on their kind, and his answers while under the duress his guards have put him through—"

"The torture," Kaylina interrupted, looking for a way to hang the gauntlet from her belt without cutting herself.

"Physical duress, yes." Vlerion nodded to acknowledge her statement. "It is not a method of acquiring information that I prefer, but the safety of the city, if not the entire kingdom, is at stake. It is not, however, always effective. Especially on their kind. The Kar'ruk train from an early age to endure pain. Based on the answers he's given us, we think he's lying. He said his people have merely come for a pilgrimage to their holy catacombs. We also believe he doesn't know much, else his superiors would have given him poison and instructed him to take his own life before allowing himself to be captured."

Kaylina nodded, remembering the warrior they'd seen do that.

"The Kar'ruk denied that any of his allies were in the catacombs yet—he didn't know about the one we ran into. Of course, he also emphasized that the catacombs belong to their people. He said this whole area does and that we stole it from them centuries ago."

"There's some truth to that, isn't there?" Kaylina hadn't studied history the way her brother had but assumed the Kar'ruk wouldn't have built catacombs under enemy territory. They must have occupied all this land at one point.

"There is, but it's been almost eight centuries. Also, they've been trying to kill our people and take the land back all this time. This is not a new grievance for them. What *is* new is that an unknown number have slipped past our rangers patrolling the mountain border." Vlerion gazed toward the jagged peaks. The slightly warmer spring weather hadn't yet melted any gaps in the snow blanketing them. "I should be up there. That's a duty I excel at. And up there, I don't have to worry as much about..."

Maybe he remembered who he was speaking with because he looked at Kaylina and fell silent. They had reached a park with people on the far side, and he stopped in the shadows of a few trees and turned to face the river.

"Lovely and gentle but occasionally exasperating women who bestir your emotions?" She stood beside him, looking toward ducks in the water but watching him out of the corner of her eye.

"And whom I struggle to stay away from." Vlerion shifted toward her, his gaze demanding hers. His eyes grew heated as he stepped closer and rested a hand on her arm.

His attention—his *intensity*—never failed to heat her body, to make her want to embrace him. And more.

"Did Crenoch really have to sit on you to keep you from coming into the castle to check on me?" Kaylina whispered.

"Yes. And I almost threw the doctor in the river. I was ready to hack that plant to pieces."

"With your sword or with claws?" Kaylina hoped the danger to her hadn't threatened to make him change but feared it might have, especially when he hesitated to answer.

"I did have to hum to myself to regain control. Knowing your brother was with you helped." Vlerion lifted his hand from her arm to her jaw, his fingers brushing her skin.

Her body heated further, her nerves tingling, tightening with longing. "I'm glad you're not off on the border. Maybe it would be good for you and the kingdom, but I can't regret that I met you.

Even though you're haughty and order me around." She leaned toward him, knowing they dare not kiss but wanting...

"Even though the druid plant wants you to kill me." Vlerion didn't step back, but he did lower his hand, and she sensed the emotional distance he was attempting to put between them.

Distance would be safer for both of them, but Kaylina hated the idea of the plant being responsible for driving them apart. She stepped closer and clasped his hand as she gazed at him, willing him to understand that she cared, that she wasn't tempted by botanical bargains.

"You know I'm not going to do that. I want you to kiss me." Kaylina wanted him to do more than that to her—*with* her. "You can't do that if you're dead." She tried a smile.

"I'm aware of what you want." He curled his fingers around hers and looked down at her chest pressed against his arm.

She hadn't intended to mash herself against him, only to keep him from drawing back, but when she was around him, her body acted of its own accord.

"It's what you want too," she stated with certainty. Or what the beast wanted, the beast within him drawn to the *anrokk* within her.

Targon's words came to mind: *If the curse were lifted and his beast element disappeared, he might be indifferent to you.*

She didn't want to contemplate that. She wanted to be with him. Even the plant's vision of the beast killing her couldn't change that.

"It is," Vlerion agreed.

"Since we're both clear on that, you shouldn't be concerned about manipulative plants. We'll stay away from the castle until I figure out how to lift the curse."

Too bad pouring the druid honey in the pot hadn't been enough for that. She worried that all she was doing was making the plant stronger. It appeared much healthier than when she'd first climbed into that tower room. And what had it said about it being a sentinel? That implied more than a curse. What if it was there to watch over the druids' interest for all time?

"That may not be enough," Vlerion said. "In the preserve, the magic in that brand drew you to the druid ruins."

"It didn't exactly *draw* me. I was curious to begin with, and the sensation from it made me think it was a good idea. That I might find something useful in there."

"What we found were vines capable of ensnaring me."

A flush of indignation rose to her face as, for the first time, Kaylina realized he might blame her for that. "*You* didn't need to come into the ruins. You *shouldn't* have."

"I believed you were in danger."

She opened her mouth to protest, but Vlerion shifted closer, wrapping his arms around her. His face lowered to rest on the top of her head, his breath warm and appealing as it whispered across her cheek.

The warmth of indignation shifted to the heat of desire, her longing to be close to him returning. It was so intense that she struggled not to wrap both arms around him and capture him forever.

"I will always come when you're in danger," Vlerion murmured, his hand sliding around to her back and lower.

He didn't pull her tight against him, but she sensed that he wanted to. She wanted that too, but...

"Don't say that near the castle," she said, "or the plant might set a trap for you."

"It might force you to attack me at any time."

"That's *not* going to happen."

"It marked you," he said softly. "It claimed you. And it's powerful. The druids were extremely powerful."

Even as he spoke of her being claimed by the enemies of the rangers, Vlerion rubbed her back through her shirt, fingers occasionally drifting lower, and she remembered his words about rewarding her. By all the craters in the moon, she wanted that, but it wouldn't be safe now that a full day had passed since he'd shifted. It might not have been safe before, when he'd spoken of it, when he'd been thinking of bringing her the pleasure she longed to experience in his arms.

"The brand would have to do a lot more than tingle and itch for me to spring on you with a knife." Kaylina rested her palm against his chest, but he wore his leather armor over his tunic, so she felt none of his warmth. She moved her hand higher, fingers trailing up his strong neck to push into his short hair and rub his scalp. A rumble almost like an animal growl came from him, and his response to her touch made her want to do more, to make him happy, to reward *him* for the times he'd stood with her. "Even if it somehow could, it's not like it would matter. You'd stop me easily. I'm much better with a sling than a blade."

"I don't doubt that."

"Then what's the problem? Why are we having a private chat? Or did you want an opportunity to rub my butt?"

"I *always* want that." Vlerion squeezed her, and she hoped he would pull her close. Instead, he released her, stepped back, and took a deep breath as he looked toward the water.

As much as she wanted to close the distance again, she lowered her arms to her sides. She couldn't allow herself to make this hard for him. She understood what was at stake. For both of them. The damn vision had made sure of that.

"Do I have to die at your hand for the plant to help you achieve your dream instead of hindering you?" Vlerion didn't look at her as he asked the question.

"I... what?" An inkling of what he was getting at teased her mind, but she didn't want her guess to be correct.

"Is it enough that I die? Or do you have to be the one to drive the dagger through my heart?"

"I don't know. The plant didn't lay out rules. But you're *not* going to die. I'm on a quest to end your curse, not your life."

"Even though it is your own life you should be concerned about right now." Vlerion lifted a hand toward her, but he caught himself and lowered it again without touching her.

Gods, how she wanted him to be able to touch her whenever he wanted. Even if he did it presumptuously and pompously like the haughty aristocrat he was.

"I'm not that bright," she said.

"You are what you choose to be."

"Well, then I don't always make good choices."

Vlerion smiled faintly. "*That*, I'll agree, is true."

"I'm going to find a way to lift your curse, and you're not going to consider… whatever weird thing you were considering when talking about your death." Kaylina frowned at him.

He chuckled. "Not suicide or anything like that. I'm not *that* dedicated to seeing your meadery become a success."

"Good. Right now, it doesn't even exist."

"I was simply musing that the life of a ranger is always dangerous, and with all that's happening right now, *my* life is in an even more precarious state than usual. Should a Kar'ruk blade—or druid vine—take me down, it would be nice to die knowing that plant would allow you to start your business."

"You're in a morbid mood today."

"You might need to have the taybarri drag my body to the courtyard so the plant could see it."

"*Vlerion*."

"I would not be offended, should I be dead already, if you drove a knife into my chest to make the plant believe you'd been responsible."

Exasperated, Kaylina stepped in and gripped his arm again. Not out of a desire to be close to him this time but because she wanted to shake some sense into him.

"I'm not going to stab you or your dead body with a knife, and I insist you do your best *not* to die."

"So you presume to give me orders." Vlerion smiled more genuinely than he had at any point in the conversation. Leave it to a ranger to find talk of his own death amusing.

"Yes, I do. You should be honored that I care and have stopped calling you pirate."

"Perhaps so. I might mention that to Targon as an indication that I'm managing to instill reverence in you."

"If you vow to live and give me time to find a way to lift your curse, I'll call you *my lord* in front of him." Kaylina wished she had a clue about *how* she might lift his curse. The sad smile he issued whenever she spoke of it promised he didn't believe it was possible.

"Such proof of your reverence would doubtless cause him to pin medals on my chest for my superior training abilities."

Kaylina snorted but also smiled, relieved he was off the morbid subject of his death.

"Oh, Kaylina," Vlerion said softly, his gaze snagging on her smile—on her mouth. He swept her into his arms and pressed his lips to her neck.

Though surprised, she responded automatically, wrapping her arms around his shoulders.

"It is difficult to be with you." He kissed her neck, then nuzzled her ear. "And it is difficult to be away."

She swallowed, fighting the urge to completely melt into him, to let him kiss whatever he wished, or to dare to kiss him herself. "Because you're worried I'm getting myself in trouble?" she whispered.

A legitimate concern.

"That, yes. And because I want you."

The raw admission made her heart ache. She wanted him too. As he well knew.

"Never before have I struggled so much to keep my distance from a woman."

"Because of my beauty and wit, I presume, not your weird curse being drawn by my weird blood."

"You *are* beautiful."

"And my wit?" She kept her words light, afraid that if a more serious mood came over her, she would struggle to step back again.

As his hand cupped her, keeping her in his arms, he nipped at her earlobe, sending a jolt of pure arousal through her. "I believe *snark* is the appropriate term for what you possess."

She caught herself arching into him, bringing her lips to *his* ear, slipping her tongue out, tasting his warmth. "I think you like it."

"It bothers me less than it should."

"If I were a noble, would it bother you at all?" She sucked on his earlobe, wanting him to think of her as an equal, even if it was a silly thing to desire. It wasn't the reality in the kingdom, neither the law nor the culture suggesting that commoners and aristocrats stood on the same ground. But she wanted him to admit that she was worthwhile, that she was good enough for him. She grazed his ear with her teeth, then dared to nip, as he had, while her fingers curled into the back of his neck.

"You are more than a noble," he rasped, his grip on her tightening. "You have power I don't understand."

She released his ear, whispering, "Power that draws you." Though her body remained heated in his arms, and she longed for them to remove their clothes and fully explore each other, she couldn't help but feel disappointed at the reminder of why he wanted her.

"*You* draw me." He turned his face to meet her gaze.

She caught the dangerous glint mingling with the lust in his eyes, the promise that the beast lurked under the surface, poised to erupt.

A laugh from somewhere in the park reminded her that they were not alone. Many people could be killed if the beast were freed.

But Vlerion's attention was only for her. He lowered his mouth to hers, claiming her with a kiss filled with desire.

A mistake. She realized she'd made a mistake with her arousing nip. She tried to break the kiss even as her body longed for what he promised to give her. She struggled with her own desire as much as his, but they couldn't allow this to progress.

She planted her hands on his chest. She couldn't— *They* couldn't.

But his grip was too tight to escape, his desire too hard to deny. Any second, the beast would arise.

A scream of alarm came from the other side of the park.

Confused and captured by Vlerion's grip, Kaylina thought he'd already started to change, that people were screaming as they witnessed it.

But when Vlerion broke the kiss, his breathing heavy, his eyes glazed with lust, he was still human. For the moment.

The people on the other side of the park were looking toward the street, not toward Kaylina and Vlerion.

"Something's wrong," he rasped, then swallowed, trying to collect himself. He looked at Kaylina and stepped back, anguish replacing the glint of the beast in his eyes. "I apologize. I was... I have no excuse."

"Yeah, you do," she whispered.

But he shook his head in denial. "I—"

Another scream came from the far side of the park.

"I need to check on that." Vlerion stepped farther away from her.

Kaylina nodded, relieved by the distance now. All along, she should have kept it.

"Kar'ruk!" someone cried.

Alarmed, Kaylina spun toward the call. Trees lining the street on the far side of the park partially blocked the view, and it took her a moment to spot the Kar'ruk. Not one or two but *twenty* of them strode along the cobblestones parallel to the park.

They walked side-by-side in two columns and wore decorative hide tabards instead of the chainmail armor she'd seen on those in the preserve, but deadly axes rode on their shoulders, leaving no doubt that they were warriors. Warriors who didn't like humans. They gazed fiercely at the people in the park. One hefted his axe and pointed it at a man pointing at him, as if declaring he would spring and kill the gawking person.

24

Enemies may approach openly or with stealth. Trust neither.
~ Ranger Captain Targon

Vlerion pushed back his hood and strode across the park toward the twin columns of Kar'ruk striding up the street.

"Ranger," several people blurted in relief, glancing from him to the Kar'ruk.

"That's Lord Vlerion," a boy of nine or ten blurted. "He's savage. He'll pounce on those horned uglies."

Face grim, Vlerion gripped the hilt of his sword as numerous pairs of yellow Kar'ruk eyes shifted toward him.

Keeping her hood up, Kaylina followed at a distance. She had her sling and would help if Vlerion leaped into a fight, but there were a lot of witnesses here, witnesses who could later tell the kingdom guards that they'd seen her.

But why weren't guards already present and rushing to engage the Kar'ruk? Kaylina couldn't believe the warriors were brazenly striding down a main street in the middle of the day. How had they gotten through the city gate?

As she reached the trees, more of the horned figures came into view.

Several steps behind the two columns, four muscular warriors carried a litter on their shoulders, with two female Kar'ruk sitting on pale blue stools atop it. They wore fur-trimmed cloaks open to reveal pale hide dresses embellished with emerald and turquoise beads. Numerous fingerbone and fang necklaces and bracelets added further ornamentation but did nothing to soften their faces. They were as hard as those of the male warriors as they gazed coolly and haughtily at Vlerion and the staring onlookers.

This had to be a diplomatic mission, but, with all those armed fighters, it could easily turn into a war party if they were provoked. Maybe even if they weren't provoked. The appearance of this party at the same time as the Kar'ruk had infiltrated the preserve and catacombs couldn't be a coincidence.

As the procession drew even with Vlerion, who'd stopped on the sidewalk, Kaylina rounded an aspen and spotted a few kingdom guards in gray-and-black uniforms trailing the litter. They carried crossbows and wore swords but weren't pointing their weapons at the visitors. Had the Kar'ruk been invited?

Kaylina halted and stepped back into the shadow of the tree. For her, the guards were as much of a danger as the Kar'ruk.

Vlerion must have been thinking something similar, because he looked at her, a finger twitching, warning her to stay back.

"Oh, I am," she muttered, though he was too far away to hear.

His gaze shifted past her shoulder, and he nodded once. She turned to look for the recipient of the gesture.

Jankarr was riding toward her on his taybarri with Levitke ambling at its side. When he caught her gaze, Jankarr crooked a finger and pointed toward Levitke's back.

Kaylina hesitated. Leaving would be a good idea, but she hated the thought of leaving Vlerion in danger. Especially since he, after his silent exchange with Jankarr, strode out into the street to stop the procession.

What if the Kar'ruk knew he'd killed one of their kind in the catacombs earlier? And others in the preserve?

Kaylina loaded a round into her sling.

"You're to stay out of it," Jankarr said softly, riding into the shadow of the aspen with her.

Levitke bounced around him to stand in front of Kaylina, almost blocking her view of the procession. The Kar'ruk had halted, many of them raising their weapons and glaring at Vlerion.

"Step aside, human," one of the lead Kar'ruk rasped in a deep voice, speaking heavily accented Zaldorian. He was the first Kar'ruk that Kaylina had heard use their language. "Our chieftains come to see your king, not his minions."

"You were not invited," Vlerion said with certainty.

Could he know for sure?

"We are a diplomatic party on a diplomatic mission, and we *will* see him. The treaty of Ansiark Mountain states this is permissible. Leaders from both peoples may enter the enemy's territory without opposition if it is for *diplomatic* purposes."

"The guards might notice you," Jankarr added to Kaylina.

"I know, but Vlerion—"

"Doesn't need your help. The guards are there, and more rangers are on the way and in nearby streets. Our scouts spotted these guys coming from miles away. Besides, Targon wants you out of the city, finding that press."

"*That's* the priority, right now?" Kaylina waved toward the street. There was no way that was a legitimate diplomatic party.

No doubt thinking the same, Vlerion asked, "Is your diplomatic party aware that your kind have been preying on humans of late? Here, in our kingdom?"

"Our kind enjoy *preying* on humans whenever we can, but we know nothing of this happening in your kingdom. We are here in peace to negotiate with your king for access to our sacred catacombs. We have not strayed from your roads and have long been aware of your rangers observing us. Step aside, human." The Kar'ruk leaned closer to Vlerion, and his nostrils twitched. "Or *are* you fully human? You have a unique scent."

Kaylina stared. Could the Kar'ruk *smell* that Vlerion could become a beast?

A few warriors in the column murmured to themselves in their own tongue.

"What will you offer in trade for access to the catacombs?" Vlerion probably sought to divert the speaker's curiosity about him.

"We will speak only with the king, not a minion, but know that your time fornicating and crafting your odious hovels on our holy land is coming to an end. We have brought proof that these valleys and fertile shoreline belong to our people."

"Is that so," Vlerion said in a flat tone.

A few rangers in black leather armor stepped out of side streets to observe, some on foot and others mounted on taybarri.

"It is so, as you will soon see. If you do not accept our proof and leave this land, your kind will be destroyed. We now have the means to eradicate you." The Kar'ruk smiled, revealing a mouthful of fangs. "Step aside, human, or join the escort taking us to your king's domicile. If you do not, we will walk *through* you. Your scent, and what it may indicate, does not concern our strong warriors." Nostrils twitching, the Kar'ruk tested the air again. First, he sniffed toward Vlerion, but he must have caught another scent on the breeze because his head turned.

His yellow eyes locked onto Kaylina.

She froze. Between her hood and cloak, and a taybarri half-blocking the view, the Kar'ruk couldn't have seen much about her

—nothing that should have caught his eye—but his *nose* was what had guided him to look in her direction. No, straight at her.

"I *will* escort you, and if you show any sign of hostility, my rangers and I will put an end to your party." Vlerion followed the Kar'ruk's gaze toward Kaylina and frowned. He flicked his fingers at Jankarr, a why-haven't-you-guided-her-out-of-here-yet gesture.

Jankarr spread his arms, then bent down to grab Kaylina under the armpits.

Startled, she barely kept from squawking when he hefted her onto Levitke's back.

"Time for you to go," Jankarr whispered. "For more reasons than Targon's orders."

Though she worried about Vlerion, Kaylina didn't resist when Jankarr guided his taybarri into the park, making clucking noises to Levitke, convincing her to carry Kaylina away. Vlerion had other rangers nearby to help if trouble broke out. Besides, whatever those Kar'ruk were up to, she had a feeling they wouldn't brawl in the street. If they were trying to enact a plot to take back their land, they wouldn't risk themselves over something insignificant.

"Why does Targon care about the press now?" Kaylina asked when the taybarri veered out of the park toward another street. He wasn't heading back to the castle, where she'd left Frayvar. "I need to check on my brother."

"Your brother went to visit a poison maker with Doc Penderbrock, who apparently knows the man. As for the rest, Targon wants you out of the city so you won't be a distraction for Vlerion."

Kaylina frowned at him, but she struggled to argue with that. It may not have been her intent, but hadn't she almost *distracted* Vlerion to the point of turning into the beast scant minutes earlier? What if the Kar'ruk hadn't shown up? What would have happened?

Jankarr lifted an apologetic hand. "I know. I thought it was a questionable order, or at least a questionable concern, myself. Vlerion has *never* been distracted by a woman, not in the years I've been in the rangers. And with all this Kar'ruk trouble rearing up, I don't know why Targon is worried in the least that it might be a possibility."

Kaylina did, but she didn't say anything about the beast since Jankarr wasn't one of the rangers who knew Vlerion's secret.

"I admit I'm disgruntled to have to leave the city at a time like this too." Jankarr glanced back, though they'd ridden down another street and could no longer see the Kar'ruk or Vlerion. He did spot a pair of guards conferring on a corner. "Make sure your hood is hiding your face," he murmured.

"I am."

Kaylina adjusted it in case it had fallen back. Her elbow brushed the gauntlet hanging from her belt, and she remembered her hope of talking the Virt press operator into printing a retraction. Maybe this wasn't the worst idea. She could help in another way while Vlerion and the rangers kept an eye on the Kar'ruk. With luck, Frayvar would also make progress on their personal problem. *Her* personal problem. She hoped the doctor would keep an eye on him in case any guards spotted him and had the idea of questioning him to learn her whereabouts.

"Excellent," Jankarr said after Kaylina tugged the hood lower over her eyes. "You're a most amenable companion. I don't know why Targon calls you irreverent."

"Because he's an ass."

"Is he? As a ranger, I'm not allowed to say or think such things."

"If I have to be a ranger, I plan to say and think them frequently."

"You might find yourself engaged in a lot of extra onerous duties, such as peeling potatoes in the depths of the night."

"Oh, good. I've been sleeping *way* too much lately."

Jankarr's blond eyebrows arched. "I may possibly be observing some of your fabled irreverence now."

"I've heard rangers have keen eyes."

"A truth, for certain."

Levitke whuffed and swished her tail. Maybe taybarri approved of irreverent riders who spoke their minds.

As Jankarr led the way toward a city gate, Kaylina patted a furry shoulder and thought of the plant's first vision. It occurred to her that the taybarri *youngers* might know where the elders lived.

"Levitke?" she asked softly when they weren't near any guards or pedestrians—and when Jankarr was looking intently toward the gate. "When we get a chance, would you take me to see your family?"

The next whuff had a questioning note to it, and Levitke looked back, one of her floppy ears shifting.

"In the mountains. That's where they live, right? Your elders?"

Depending on how intelligent the young taybarri were, Levitke might be wondering how Kaylina could know anything about her family.

Jankarr's brow furrowed, and he looked over. Maybe he hadn't been as distracted as she'd thought.

"Even if we didn't have another mission, this wouldn't be a good time for a lone woman to venture into the mountains." Jankarr lifted his hand toward the distant peaks. "It's *never* a good time for a lone woman to venture into the mountains."

"Even with a powerful taybarri mount?"

Without a doubt, Levitke understood that because she lifted her head and her tail, then hopped and surged forward to take the lead from Jankarr's taybarri.

A sturdy male named Zavron, he nipped at her shoulder. It didn't break skin or even ruffle fur, but he'd made his point. With a glare, he increased his pace to take the lead back.

"Even with a taybarri, yes, though they can even the odds

against a lot of enemies." Jankarr looked with concern at Kaylina. "Let's focus on locating the press. By the time we complete that duty and return, your brother may have found evidence that will prompt the queen to pull the guards off their hunt for you. The gods know we've got more important things to worry about right now." He glanced back, though the park, Vlerion, and the Kar'ruk had fallen out of view, the intervening buildings hiding even the royal castle on its plateau.

Only the city wall loomed ahead, taller than most of the rooftops. As usual, the gate was open, but two armed graycoats stepped out of a guardhouse and into the street as Jankarr and Kaylina approached on their mounts. In addition to swords belted at their waists, they carried blunderbusses, and they stopped so that they blocked the street. Two more guards stepped out behind them, men with crossbows.

"Let me talk to them," Jankarr murmured, nudging his taybarri to take a greater lead. "Don't say anything."

"Okay." Kaylina rested a hand on Levitke's shoulder, hoping she understood that this wasn't the time to jostle for position with her taybarri herd mate. She resisted the urge to pull her hood lower over her forehead. She'd already done that, and now she had observers.

The cool faces of the guards—and the way they gazed unwaveringly at her approach—made her think they knew who she was. Had some spy glimpsed her and run ahead to alert them?

"Step aside, men," Jankarr said. "We've orders from Captain Targon to ride out."

"You may ride anywhere you wish, Ranger Jankarr," one of the guards said, his voice faintly familiar.

Where had Kaylina heard it before?

"Your companion, however, is not a ranger and is to be detained."

Kaylina rocked back when she recognized the voice. It was the guard who'd pretended not to see that the back of the truck was full of rebel-funded newspapers and had told the ranger nothing important was inside. He had to be a Virt. Did he want to detain Kaylina so the queen's loyal men could drag her to the castle? Or were there Virts around who would take the opportunity to snatch Kaylina?

It didn't matter. She didn't want to be *detained* by either party. She slid her hand into her pocket, using her cloak to hide the withdrawing of her sling.

"She's training to become a ranger and is on the same mission as I, one assigned by Captain Targon himself. Step aside." Jankarr sat tall and imposing on Zavron's back with his hand on his sword.

Even though the guards had blunderbusses, they shifted uneasily, nervous about attacking him. One switched his aim toward Kaylina.

"No," Jankarr barked, moving to block the man's sights.

Kaylina loaded her sling, a puny weapon against firearms, but she couldn't let Jankarr be hurt because of her.

She glanced left and right, but there were no alleys she could veer into, not by the gate. The area was deliberately open.

"Don't make this difficult, Ranger Jankarr," the speaker said. "Step down or—"

Zavron surged forward, Jankarr drawing his sword.

Levitke growled and also surged forward but not to fight. The world blurred as she flashed. Between one blink and the next, she went from inside the gate and in front of the men to the highway outside, charging away from the city.

Kaylina glanced back but also flattened herself, afraid the guards would have a clear shot at her. And a blunderbuss *did* go off, the boom ringing out. But Jankarr had charged into the middle of the guards and knocked the firearm to the side. Its burst of pellets clattered against the stone wall.

He and his taybarri attacked the men to keep them from

aiming at Kaylina. Even though he used the hilt of his sword instead of the deadly blade to strike them, Kaylina worried he would get in trouble for opposing the guard, people obeying the queen's orders to arrest her.

"Get the horses," one guard cried. "Go after her!"

"This has *not* been a good day," Kaylina muttered as Levitke sped away from the city.

25

By day, a strange noise curiosity sparks; by night, a strange noise fright marks.

~ "Fear of the Dark" by the bard Velvenor

Levitke's powerful muscles surged under Kaylina, and the city soon grew distant behind them. She hoped the taybarri could outrun the horseback pursuers the guard had called for. She also hoped Jankarr and Vlerion wouldn't get in trouble for helping her. And that the city and kingdom wouldn't be destroyed by a Kar'ruk plot. By all the craters in the moon, there was a lot to hope for.

"We'd better find that press before visiting your family," Kaylina said, though she didn't know if Levitke had understood her earlier request or planned to take her into the mountains. "Stay on the highway, and I'll watch for the spot where Frayvar and I came out of the river the other night, and then..."

Then *what*? It wasn't as if the wagon carrying the newspapers had left a trail of them that they could follow back to its origins. Unless the taybarri could track the scent somehow.

"Oh, wait." Kaylina dug in her pocket and pulled out the newspaper article the Virts had left in the castle kitchen. "Levitke. Can you smell this, see if you catch the same scent along the trail, and track it to its origins?"

The taybarri slowed from a gallop to a walk as she glanced back. Kaylina explained the load of newspapers and how she and Frayvar had stumbled upon it. After more than a day, and however many horses and wagons had passed along the highway, this would be a long shot, but it couldn't hurt to try.

Levitke stopped in the road, her neck turning, and Kaylina held out the paper. The taybarri sniffed it a few times, then bit it, withdrawing it from Kaylina's hand, and chewed on it.

"Uh, it's not honey."

Maybe Levitke hadn't understood anything and had simply hoped for a treat. Was it Kaylina's imagination, or did the taybarri's expression seem disappointed?

A war horn rang out from the direction of the city, and Kaylina frowned. She wouldn't have thought the guards would prioritize finding one wayward subject when there were Kar'ruk all over the place, but she didn't doubt that the hunt for her had begun. Again.

Maybe Levitke understood too, because she returned to running, following the highway and the river toward the mountains. If they couldn't find the press, Kaylina would ask again if Levitke would take her to see her family. The plant had definitely implied that bringing an elder taybarri back to the city would help with Kaylina's problems. With *everyone's* problems.

Levitke slowed from a run to a walk, snout lowering to the ground. Kaylina recognized the beaver dam in the river. This was the spot where she and Frayvar had managed to climb out of the water.

"You *did* understand me," Kaylina whispered, awed.

This time, the look that Levitke slanted back seemed on the

verge of an eye roll. But, surely, the noble taybarri didn't do such things. *They* weren't irreverent.

Kaylina was tempted to dismount and look for clues, but after a few more sniffs, Levitke continued up the highway. Now and then, she paused to lift her snout in the air for several inhalations. Kaylina took that as a positive sign that she was on the trail, hopefully of the newspaper wagon and not an animal that had crossed that way and might make an appealing meal.

Before entering the preserve, the highway veered away from the river. It traveled between the densely treed area and an estate bordered by a stone wall and intermittent watchtowers that overlooked the ancient druid sanctuary. As they skirted the preserve, Kaylina thought she glimpsed a campfire in the trees. More Kar'ruk warriors lurking, ready to help their so-called diplomats enact their plan?

As Levitke continued past the area, heading farther from Port Jirador, Kaylina tried not to feel like she was abandoning her brother and others who needed help. She wasn't a ranger who could win battles against Kar'ruk. She wouldn't be any assistance in the city. Besides, she was being hunted, as the horns blowing in the distance reminded her.

Levitke climbed into the darkening mountains, eventually detouring from the highway to skirt a watchtower. Near it, fires burned in metal-lined pits, the flames brightening the surrounding area. Thanks to cliffs rising to either side of the highway, it was difficult to pass without being caught by the light.

The faint whuff of a taybarri came from a stable built against the tower's base. One or more rangers had to be stationed inside, keeping an eye on the approach to the valley and the city.

Kaylina tensed, not certain if the men would recognize her and know Targon believed she should be helped instead of arrested.

Levitke answered with a soft grunt.

Another whuff sounded in reply, the agreeable tone seeming to imply, *You may pass.*

They did without anyone in the tower objecting, and Levitke continued uphill, heading deeper into the mountains. The night air grew chillier, and howls sounded in the distance, a reminder that dangerous predators called this wilderness their home. With luck, those animals would find a taybarri an intimidating foe and stay away.

The next time Levitke left the highway, she didn't return to it, instead following a bumpy dirt road that a horse-drawn wagon would have been hard-pressed to maneuver across. Patches of lumpy snow here and there would have been a further impediment.

Kaylina was about to suggest loads of newspapers hadn't likely come this way, but Levitke halted.

Her *whuff* sounded triumphant.

"You think this is the spot?" Kaylina peered dubiously into the dark around them, spruce and pine trees looming up, mostly blocking the night sky. A creek gurgled nearby, but full night had fallen, and Kaylina couldn't see it. She couldn't see much of anything.

The next *whuff* sounded like a confident affirmative.

"If you say so." Kaylina slid off and dug into her pack for her lantern.

When she got it lit, the small flame doing little to stave off the mountain darkness, she spotted Levitke drinking from the creek.

"Are you *sure* this is the spot and not where you want to water yourself and camp for the night?" Kaylina asked.

The taybarri ambled over and licked her with a tongue large enough to wash her entire face.

"Was that an answer to my question?"

After *whuffing* twice more, Levitke wandered to the side of the road and chewed on snow. Kaylina started to sigh in disappointment, but she glimpsed a straight line in the snow. A track left by a wagon wheel.

"Maybe this *is* the spot."

Levitke gave her a flat look that seemed to say, *Obviously*.

Lantern aloft, Kaylina searched further.

Half-buried by snow lay a stone campfire ring, a cast-iron frying pan, and a couple of rusty shovels. By the creek, the wooden remains of a sluice box promised miners had used the area at one time, but it looked like it had been a while since anyone occupied the camp.

Levitke pawed at something on a rocky hillside a dozen yards off the road. Boards had been nailed together to make a semblance of a door that covered a cave entrance. Or maybe an old mine shaft?

The expectant look Levitke turned on Kaylina made her come closer to investigate. A patch of snow held fresh boot prints, some a little larger than hers, some a *lot* larger. Had the Kar'ruk been back here too?

There weren't any hinges on the faux door, and Kaylina had to drag it aside. The shaft she'd been envisioning stretched into darkness.

Levitke growled, and Kaylina jumped back, grabbing her sling before realizing it would be hard to fire while she held the lantern. Instead, she drew her knife.

The taybarri faced into the shaft, lips rippling back from her fangs and her muscles tense. Her nostrils flared as she sampled the earthy air that wafted out. Earthy and *inky* air. It smelled of newspapers inside, but Kaylina doubted that would make Levitke growl.

"Do you go first or do I?" Kaylina whispered. "I haven't finished the ranger handbook yet and am not sure of proper protocol."

In what she had read, the rangers always rode the taybarri into danger so that they faced it together, but the shaft wasn't high enough for that.

Not glancing at her, Levitke growled again. After a few more sniffs, she padded into the shaft, her head almost brushing an earthen ceiling supported by timbers.

Kaylina followed her about ten feet in, thinking the long taybarri would have a hard time turning around if the way grew narrower, but if their species had originated burrowing tunnels, maybe such matters didn't concern them.

Someone had hammered nails into the wooden supports for the shaft, making hooks for lights. Most were empty, but a couple dented lanterns remained. Kaylina opened the cache of one, found that it had kerosene, and used her flame to light it. The next couple of lanterns were empty, but she didn't necessarily want to illuminate the entire shaft anyway. Just enough to help her find… whatever she could down here.

About twenty yards in, she and Levitke reached large alcoves carved out of either side of the shaft, the walls made more from stone than dirt.

To the left, stacks of rusty mining equipment rested, as well as crates that appeared newer. Crates that held newspapers to be transported to the city? Or blank paper for printing them?

Since Levitke had poked her head into the alcove on the right, Kaylina couldn't see much, but something metal reflected the yellow flame of her lantern light.

"Did you find the printing press?"

Levitke shifted around so that she could back up and make room for Kaylina to see into the alcove. Yes, there was a press, as well as a desk with a journal open on top, the page full of writing.

"So… where's the press operator?" Kaylina looked to Levitke, wondering if the taybarri would growl at a Virt or if something more dangerous lurked in the mine.

Levitke wasn't looking at the press. Her snout pointed deeper into the tunnel, nostrils flaring as she tested the air.

The mining shaft sloped downward, disappearing into darkness. An army could have been down there—or a pack of yekizar—and Kaylina wouldn't have known.

After a few more sniffs, Levitke padded deeper into the shaft.

Being left alone made Kaylina nervous, but she wanted to check the journal. She trusted the taybarri would warn her if an enemy approached.

Letters had been set on the press but only a few rows. It was as if someone had started on the next day's newspaper and then been interrupted.

She set her lantern on the press, reading backward to interpret what it would have printed once ink was applied. The first few words sent a chill through her.

Irrefutable evidence has been discovered to affirm that the ranger Lord Vlerion, from the cursed Havartaft line, turns into a beast by night and slays innocent beings in the city. The king and the rangers know of his secret and protect him. Perhaps they even send him to do their bidding, as they did during the Castle Massacre. It's possible the aristocracy has long been using the deadly beast to get rid of the righteous and virtuous, any who oppose their oppressive rule. The king and the rangers must be held accountable, and the evil Lord Vlerion must be hanged before he can take another life. He—

"What?" Kaylina blurted at the unfinished sentence. No further words had been set.

Whirling, she grabbed the journal to see if it held the rest of the story or had the name of the person reporting it. The information wasn't all accurate—*night* wasn't what caused Vlerion to change—but it held enough truth to be dangerous. Very dangerous. Soon, Vlerion might find himself being hunted as assiduously as she.

Her hands shook as she opened the journal and held the last

page with writing to the light. It was the same story. The typesetter had been copying it verbatim. It continued on to promise that only by slaying Vlerion and shining sunlight on the corrupt ranger organization would the murders stop and the Virts be victorious in overthrowing the tyrannical regime.

When she flipped to earlier pages, she found the stories that had already been printed. As with this one, they'd been copied word for word. This story might have shown up as early as the next day, if the press operator hadn't been interrupted.

Where *was* the press operator?

Kaylina looked around, but Levitke hadn't returned. She wondered if a wagon of Virts would arrive in the middle of the night, expecting stacks of newspapers to have been printed.

"If it does, I'll be here waiting for them."

The other wagon had only had one sleepy driver. Maybe she could handle him, questioning him or even forcing him to turn himself in to the ranger in the watchtower.

She flipped back through the journal, looking for a name. Was it that Hokkens that Mitzy and the other Virts had mentioned? The man who'd seen Vlerion change in the dungeon?

The author wasn't named anywhere in the journal, so she had no idea where the journalist had gotten his or her *irrefutable evidence*, but would it matter? There was enough truth to the story that the citizens who read it might believe it all.

"And try to kill Vlerion," she whispered.

She closed the journal and held it to her chest. Maybe it wouldn't do much, since whoever had written on the pages could do so again, but taking it might help delay things a few days. It would give her time to...

"To what?" She couldn't return to the city to help Vlerion without risking herself.

Maybe she could take it to that watchtower and ask the ranger inside to deliver it to Captain Targon. Maybe he could then—

Wood snapped near the mine shaft, and Kaylina almost dropped the journal. She snatched her knife and spun toward the entrance of the alcove.

It had sounded like someone had stepped on that makeshift door. Levitke? Or an approaching enemy who hadn't noticed it in the undergrowth in the dark?

Kaylina didn't think the taybarri had returned from the depths of the shaft. Though she was reluctant to leave the journal, practicality made her set it on the desk so she could grip the lantern and her knife. She listened for footfalls or rustling clothing, evidence of someone walking into the shaft.

Other than a distant owl hooting, the night had returned to silence. As long seconds passed, she bit her lip uncertainly. The *wind* hadn't made that sound.

She was tempted to wait where she was until Levitke came back up the shaft, but her instincts told her that a threat was coming. Even if she couldn't *hear* it, she could sense it. Maybe the press operator had returned. Or maybe a predator was looking for a snack.

Knife leading, Kaylina crept to the alcove entrance and peered around the corner. The shaft was straight enough that she could see the exit, a moon shining silvery light into the forest beyond. She could also see the lantern she'd lit, still hanging on its nail.

Until something moved in front of it.

She twitched, raising the knife, but she couldn't see anyone. Only the dirt walls and wooden supports. But something blocked the light, something that hadn't been there before.

Could the magic of the Kar'ruk axes turn them *invisible*? She'd never heard of such a thing.

Though confused, Kaylina drew back and traded the knife for her sling. When she peeked around the corner again, the lantern had returned to view. Whatever had blocked it had moved.

Guessing it was coming closer, Kaylina licked dry lips and loosed a lead round.

It struck *something* with a clank. As if hitting armor? Chainmail?

The shadows in the shaft blurred, and heavy footsteps thudded toward Kaylina. A deep snarl and clipped words sounded. A Kar'ruk.

Kaylina stepped back, but there was no time for her to fire another round.

26

Nothing troubles a commander more than when one's enemies start working together.

~ Lord General Menok

Kaylina dropped her lantern and skittered behind the press as she traded sling for knife, though neither would help against an eight-foot-tall Kar'ruk warrior. Especially one she couldn't *see*.

"Levitke!" she yelled, hoping the taybarri wasn't so far down the shaft that she couldn't make it back to help.

The shadows stirred at the entrance of the alcove, the only hint that someone was there.

The brand on her hand warmed, and instincts made her duck. A breeze whispered over her hair—no, that was a great Kar'ruk axe being swung. The blue blade grew visible as it slammed into the stone wall behind the press. Magically sharp, it sank in deep, and rock shards flew. They clattered onto the letters and across the alcove, some bouncing off the chest of the warrior wielding the weapon.

Only when Kaylina was scant feet away could she see his shadowy figure. Even then, it wasn't distinct, and his broad gray face was blurry.

While he tugged his axe free from the hole gouged in the wall, Kaylina rushed past, praying she could slip by him before he readied it again. As she ran past what she hoped was the warrior's side, she slashed out with her knife. Chainmail deflected her blade, and something—an elbow?—clubbed her in the back.

The blow sent her tumbling into the dirt wall on the far side of the shaft. She almost cracked her head on a support post.

Fear surging through her veins made Kaylina recover quickly, and she sprang away. None too soon. The axe slammed into the support post, chunks of wood pelting the back of her neck. She sprinted for the exit.

The invisible Kar'ruk roared and rushed after her. But another roar came from deep within the shaft—a taybarri roar.

Kaylina raced outside and toward a copse of trees. If she could survive for a minute or two, Levitke might catch up and even the odds.

But the heavy Kar'ruk footsteps pounded the ground right behind her.

She leaped behind a stout pine, using it for cover, but doubted it would be enough. The trees didn't grow close enough together to hinder even a broad-shouldered Kar'ruk.

Once more, she switched knife for sling and loaded a round, but it was too late. The axe appeared, the shadowy warrior behind it, and the blade whistled toward her head.

Ducking, she scurried back. Luck favored her, and the axe clipped an overhead branch and deflected into the trunk of the pine.

The mark on her hand warmed again. Through it, Kaylina sensed feelings emanating from the tree. Pain, indignation, and fury.

As the Kar'ruk tore his axe out of the pine, she resisted instincts urging her to flee deeper into the forest. Instead, she darted around the thick trunk opposite him and rested a hand on the coarse bark.

Help me defeat him, please, Kaylina thought, not certain if the words were for the brand or the tree or both. Whichever would listen.

Though she doubted she had any power to lend, she willed the tree to take from her whatever it could to obey the plea.

Surprisingly, a wave of weakness washed over her. Her knees threatened to buckle.

Axe free, the Kar'ruk hefted it to swing at her again. This close, she could see him better. He was careful this time not to snag the weapon on the overhead branches.

"Grak toruk!" the warrior yelled.

As Kaylina tried to find the strength to leap away, a thunderous crack sounded twenty feet above.

The Kar'ruk paused, startled yellow eyes looking up. A huge branch crashed down, snapping smaller limbs as it dropped. Needles and wood fell onto the Kar'ruk.

Since he was big and armored, it didn't seriously hurt him, or even knock him down, but he lowered his axe and jumped back. Confusion swam in his eyes when he looked toward Kaylina until, as he backed further, he again blurred, half-fading from her view.

"That's right." Kaylina lifted her sling and aimed it between his eyes. "You mess with me or my tree friends, and you get pummeled." Though she had no idea if she'd caused the pine to do that, she attempted to look fierce and confident—not scared for her life. "Now tell me where the press operator is, and the tree and I will spare your life."

Another roar came from the mine shaft, this time at the entrance. Levitke rushed into the night and toward the copse of trees.

The warrior jumped to the side, turning his axe toward the taybarri, and Kaylina lost sight of him. She ran several steps closer until she could make out his outline again.

Maybe guided by senses other than vision, Levitke didn't have any trouble finding the Kar'ruk. She startled him by flashing, vanishing from the night, then reappearing behind him.

Probably familiar with the taybarri, the Kar'ruk recovered quickly and whirled, swinging his axe toward her. But Levitke was faster. She bowled into him as her jaws snapped together, latching onto the haft of his weapon.

As he braced himself against her weight, he tried to yank it free. Levitke's muscles tensed under her thick fur, and she kept her grip. With one hand, the warrior let go and grabbed a dagger on his belt.

Kaylina stepped closer, making sure of her aim, and fired her sling. The lead round slammed into their foe's head, an inch below one of his horns. As hard as Kar'ruk skulls were, it probably didn't hurt him, but he did flinch in surprise. His grip on the axe loosened slightly, and Levitke tore it free, flinging it into the creek.

A breeze rustled through the trees. Kaylina imagined the needles and leaves were applauding at the loss of the blade.

She loaded her sling and raised it to fire again, but the Kar'ruk lunged at Levitke. With his dagger, he slashed for her shoulder. She spun and whipped her tail at his arm, knocking the blade aside. As fast as a cat, she continued the spin until she faced him again, then sprang. She landed on his chest and bore him to the ground.

With the taybarri atop him, Kaylina couldn't get off a shot without risking hitting Levitke. It didn't matter. He'd lost his weapons, and, as tall and strong as the Kar'ruk were, once he was pinned, he couldn't escape. Levitke bit his arm, tearing it away from his head, then found his thick neck with her fangs. Bone snapped as her jaws crunched down. For the first time, the Kar'ruk cried out in pain.

Lowering her sling, Kaylina looked away.

Levitke finished him off, a reminder that the taybarri were deadly predators as well as honey-loving friends to the rangers.

"Thank you," Kaylina said quietly when the Kar'ruk was dead. She wouldn't get an answer to her question about the press operator, but she hadn't expected him to reply anyway.

Her hands only shook a little as she returned her knife and sling to her belt. Maybe she was getting used to being attacked.

"A depressing thought," she murmured.

Levitke padded over and gazed solemnly into her eyes. Her head shifted from side to side in a semblance of a human *no* shake.

"What's wrong?" Kaylina thought the taybarri should feel triumphant. She'd arrived when Kaylina needed her most. "Were you injured? Are more of them around to worry about?" she added, though Levitke's gesture seemed more regretful than pained or wary.

A soft whuff was her only reply. Kaylina wished she could understand the intelligent taybarri.

Her hand warmed, and a soft voice whispered into her mind.

Fooled I.

Kaylina blinked, glancing from Levitke to the brand and back.

"Did you say that?"

She glanced toward the pine, almost wondering if the voice had come from the tree, but that would be even harder to believe.

Levitke gazed toward the shaft entrance, shook her head again, then flopped onto her back with her legs in the air.

"If you were one of my grandpa's hounds, that would mean you wanted a belly rub."

Levitke collapsed on one side, then lowered her large head toward Kaylina, resting her snout on the ground at her feet.

Fooled I. That *was* Levitke speaking.

Maybe she didn't fully know the human language yet but could use some words. And something had happened so that Kaylina could now hear them.

"Well, you weren't fooled for long." She assumed the taybarri had been following the Kar'ruk's scent when she'd traveled deeper into the shaft. Maybe the warrior had spent time down there earlier and had only left the tunnel when he'd noticed Kaylina and Levitke approaching. He could have waited across the creek for a chance to trap them. But why had he been here to start with? "He was also invisible," Kaylina added and patted Levitke's big head.

Yes. Strange. The taybarri sat up, looked toward the body, and tilted her head. They were far enough away that the Kar'ruk was shadowy again. Even in death, the spell—or whatever it was —remained.

"Maybe they've found an altered plant that grants them the ability to hide themselves." Though Kaylina wanted to grab the journal and get it to Vlerion without delay, she made herself creep closer to the body. "If the rangers don't know about this new ability—maybe it's something the Kar'ruk just figured out?—that could be why so many of these guys have successfully sneaked into the kingdom."

Kaylina remembered Vlerion repeatedly saying that shouldn't have happened. When she crouched right beside the dead Kar'ruk, she could see him well. From this close, she could also see that a faint silvery powder covered his face, neck, and hands. Something made from dried leaves or berries? It even dusted his armor.

When she rubbed a finger over the chainmail, the gritty powder didn't come off. Maybe it had been applied wet and dried?

"It has to come off eventually," she mused. "None of the Kar'ruk we ran into in the preserve were wearing this stuff. Maybe it's rare, and they've only got so much of it. And they reserve it for the Kar'ruk who are doing something vital—or sneaky."

The memory of the Kar'ruk in the catacombs came to mind. He'd been wet, hadn't he? She hadn't thought much of it at the time, but maybe he'd been covered with the powder to commit the murders. Afterward, he could have been running from guards, or someone who'd spotted him, and fallen into that underground lake. *She'd* fallen into it, after all. For a big Kar'ruk, it would have been a tighter fit and the ledge just as treacherous.

Levitke issued a questioning whuff. Words didn't accompany it, but Kaylina could guess at the meaning. What was *this* guy doing that had been vital to his people's plan?

"I don't know."

Kaylina drew her knife and scraped off some of the silvery powder. As she'd done with the honeycomb, she used a page from her book to wipe it on. Had Levitke not *eaten* the newspaper article, she could have used that.

The taybarri padded over, lowering her head over Kaylina's shoulder to watch.

"We need to get this to Vlerion along with the journal. If the rangers don't know about this, they need to." Kaylina frowned at the thought of returning to the city where people were hunting her. "Too bad there's not any powder to hide *me*."

She set down the paper and poked into the dead warrior's pockets and belt pouches, hoping to find more. She didn't, but she did pull out a few small blocks.

"What are..."

She stared. They were letters for the press.

"Did he stumble across this place and plan to take some of these back to show his allies? Or... You don't think *he* was the one setting the type, do you? Copying the journal and making the newspapers?" Kaylina was tempted to dismiss the idea, but the speaker for the diplomatic party had known their tongue. There was no reason some of the Kar'ruk couldn't have studied human languages well enough to read and write. And the powerful warriors would more easily survive alone out here in the wilderness than city-bred rebels. "If that's true, then it implies they *are* working with the Virts. That they made a deal. But for what? Access to the catacombs? When... a new ruler is in power and can allow that? A *Virt* ruler?"

Instead of answering, Levitke sniffed the powder on the paper.

Kaylina shook her head, finding the situation confusing. She would tell everything to Vlerion, and he and the rangers could figure it out.

Levitke drew back from her investigation of the powder and sneezed.

"Not as tasty as honey, huh?"

The terse whuff sounded like firm agreement.

"Does it have a smell? One you could track?" Kaylina lifted the powder to her nose but couldn't detect much. The paper had a more distinct scent.

The next whuff sounded like an affirmative. *Dried cactus.*

"Oh? *Altered* dried cactus?"

Levitke whuffed.

"Maybe some specific variety that grows in Kar'ruk lands? Is it warm enough where they live for cactus?"

The next whuff sounded uncertain.

Kaylina carefully folded the paper with the powder sample so she could tuck it away. "If we can get this to the rangers so the other taybarri can smell it, maybe they can more easily hunt down the Kar'ruk, whether they're invisible or not. How many are out here, do you think? Ready to attack if that so-called negotiating party doesn't get what it wants? And it won't. The Kar'ruk have to know that. After centuries of living here, humans aren't going to give up this land."

Levitke yawned.

"I'm tired too." Kaylina considered the folded paper and the journal. "I don't suppose *you* want to take these items back to the city and find Vlerion and Targon? The gate guards wouldn't object to you walking in alone, riderless, would they? It's either that or give it to the ranger in the watchtower and ask him to take it to them." But could she trust a man she might never have met? One who might be more likely to arrest her than help her?

Levitke gazed thoughtfully at her.

"Am I missing an option?" Kaylina guessed.

A vision floated into her mind, one of Kaylina riding Levitke while blue- and silver-furred taybarri bounded along with them, an entire herd heading along the Stillguard River toward Port Jirador.

"Are you sharing that vision? Can you do that?" Kaylina had her doubts.

It seemed more likely the plant was affecting her from a distance through the brand. But... it wasn't warm now. It wasn't doing anything.

Levitke rested a paw on Kaylina's brand and offered another *whuff*.

"I asked for that, didn't I? To go see your people in case they can help." Kaylina glanced at the brand, not sure how much the plant truly knew—or how much it wanted to assist her. It wanted Vlerion dead. How could she trust it?

Whuff.

"Do you think your people could help? And that they would be willing to if I came and asked? I'm not anybody, especially here. I doubt the taybarri elders have heard of my family's meadery and eating house."

Levitke's solemn gaze turned toward the pine tree, the broken branches on the ground around its roots.

"The tree did that. Not me." Kaylina *had* asked, but she wasn't positive it hadn't been a coincidence. There hadn't, however, been any wind, and tree branches didn't usually spontaneously break. The pine, she felt certain, had been willing to sacrifice a limb to help defeat the axe wielder.

The same vision came to mind, the herd heading to the capital with Kaylina in the middle of it.

"If they can help, I do still want to travel to see them." She couldn't do that without Levitke to guide her, so she couldn't send the taybarri away. But they needed to share their new knowledge with the rangers without delay. "Will you take me back to the watchtower along the highway? We'll tell the ranger there everything and *then* go visit your people."

Assuming the ranger didn't arrest her. Or worse.

The next whuff sounded agreeable. Before grabbing her gear, Kaylina returned to the press and removed the condemning letters on it. Then she tucked the journal safely into her pack and mounted Levitke.

The taybarri headed back toward the highway, but, before turning toward the tower, she gazed deeper into the mountains. Kaylina hoped she wasn't making a mistake in delaying the trip to see the elders.

27

WITHIN THE MOUNTAINS OF EVARDOR, PERIL DOTH PROWL BENEATH every bough.

~ "Spring Cowers" by Erazidar the Poet

Profound yawns sent tears down Kaylina's cheeks as the watchtower came into view.

The fires still burned around it but lower than before, not shedding as much light onto the highway and surrounding land. This time, as they approached, no taybarri greeted Levitke with a *whuff*.

Her neck fur bristled, and her tail swished in agitation. Could she sense that something was wrong?

"More Kar'ruk?" Kaylina whispered, glancing to either side of the highway and toward the looming peaks with trepidation. "If they're invisible, I'm depending on your nose to find them."

Levitke stopped at the base of the tower where the door stood ajar. It hadn't been that way before.

The taybarri sniffed, then pointed her snout into the shadows between fires. A dark lump lay unmoving on the ground.

"A body?" Grim, Kaylina slid to the ground.

After lighting her lantern, she went to investigate, afraid it was the ranger. To her surprise, the body belonged to a horned Kar'ruk male. His throat had been slit by a dagger or sword. Maybe the ranger was alive after all.

"Watch for trouble, please," Kaylina told Levitke, who was sniffing in the middle of the highway.

Trusting the taybarri would, Kaylina eased into the tower. A bedroom and small kitchen occupied the bottom floor. After finding them empty, she climbed stairs that followed the exterior wall, winding upward.

On the top floor, its slitted windows looking out in all directions, Kaylina found another body. The black-clad ranger lay dead beside a desk, a logbook open in which he'd been recording times and conditions in the mountains.

"Damn," she whispered.

The ranger had died with a sword in one hand and a torch in the other. She was surprised it had only charred the wooden floorboards where he'd fallen, not burned down the tower. It looked like he'd been trying to light a premade signal fire in an iron pit by the window facing the city, but he'd run out of time.

"Either you and the dead guy outside dealt each other fatal blows..." Kaylina picked up the torch. "Or there are more Kar'ruk around."

She pushed the torch into the nest of wood shavings and kindling. *She* would light the signal fire.

While she waited for it to catch, she picked up a pen on the desk and wrote a note on a blank page in the logbook. She explained the magical silver powder and the location of the press. She was about to add more about the Kar'ruk she'd battled there, but Levitke roared.

Kaylina dropped the pen.

The screeches of a large feline answered her from the woods nearby. Maybe *several* large felines.

"What now?" Kaylina grumbled.

Though she wanted to check on Levitke, she made herself return to the signal fire, prodding and blowing to ensure the flames caught fully. She had the uneasy feeling that the fate of the city might depend on this.

Levitke roared again, then shared a vision with Kaylina. It showed not only giant crag cougars attacking her—Kaylina had seen illustrations of the thousand-pound animals in the ranger handbook—but shadowy Kar'ruk striding out of the darkness.

Had they trained the powerful cats to obey their commands? Or simply uncaged them and trusted they would attack a taybarri?

The scuffs and growls of a battle engaged wafted up to the tower window. With the kindling burning, Kaylina backed away from the pit, hoping she'd done enough. She looked around for a weapon more deadly than her sling and spotted the ranger's sword.

Though she had no experience with such a blade, she grabbed it. She needed something that could hurt these enemies.

Kar'ruk roars now accompanied the feline screeches. Levitke grunted, then whined with pain.

Intent on helping her, Kaylina charged down the stairs and past the kitchen and bedroom without glancing into them.

A Kar'ruk stepped out of the shadows behind her. Before she could spin toward him, he wrapped a muscular arm around her and hefted her over his shoulder.

Kaylina swung the blade, but it clunked against the wall. She had no leverage in the awkward position, and the Kar'ruk knew it. He strode toward the door without concern.

Twisting and bucking, Kaylina managed to slam an elbow into her captor's ear, but the Kar'ruk might as well have been made from metal for all his kind yielded when struck. Her knee hit the warrior's chest, but his armor ensured that hurt her more than him.

He walked outside with her still captive. The roars and screeches continued, but Levitke had been driven back from the tower. One of the huge crag cougars lay dead in the road, its tan fur matted with blood, but numerous more harried her.

And there were more Kar'ruk as well. Hulking males who weren't camouflaged in any way. Five of them. Six? Far too many to fight, especially with the powerful felines working with them.

But Kaylina couldn't give up. She couldn't let Levitke be killed. Again, she tried to squirm free, thinking that if they could escape, even for a little while, the signal fire would bring help.

Once more, she swung the sword, trying to find an angle that would cut into her captor. Another Kar'ruk stepped forward and caught her wrist, wrenching the blade free.

Kaylina screamed, hoping vainly that potential allies would hear the noise. But she doubted anyone else was within earshot, not in the mountains in the middle of the night.

One of the warriors strode into the tower and thumped up the stairs. She groaned. He would put out the signal fire before it grew large enough to be seen across the miles.

A Kar'ruk with an axe strode up to Kaylina's captor, pointed at her, and shook his blade. That gave her a more immediate problem to worry about. They'd killed everyone else. Surely, they would kill her too.

Levitke roared as she bit and slashed at her feline adversaries. One cougar sprang toward her head, claws extended.

The taybarri flashed to avoid the blow, reappearing on the other side of the highway. She took several running steps, trying to reach Kaylina, but the great cats were too fast. They streaked across the highway to block her again, their long sharp claws slashing for vital targets.

"Save yourself," Kaylina called to her, tears filling her eyes. She didn't want the taybarri to die trying to help her, not when there was no hope.

A defiant roar came in response as Levitke stood her ground.

"Okay, then get Vlerion and Crenoch, and come back to help me," Kaylina called.

Levitke couldn't make it to the city, find them, and return in time to save Kaylina's life. She knew that. But she didn't want them both to die. All she hoped was that the more reasonable plea would prompt Levitke to run instead of dying alongside her.

Levitke didn't roar defiantly this time, but she also didn't turn to run. Instead, she swept her tail at a cougar angling for her back side. The fast animal almost dodged, but the tail clipped it, and it tumbled away. It soon found its feet, however, while another lunged for Levitke's flank. She spun and met the attack with snapping jaws, but there were too many enemies even for her.

"Get help!" Kaylina tried again.

The brand on her hand warmed, reminding her that the plant might be lending her some vague power. She attempted to will her energy into the command, the same as she'd done with the pine tree. She envisioned Vlerion, Targon, Jankarr, and other rangers riding to rescue her. But first, Levitke had to tell them about the trouble. Only then would they know to come help.

If she managed to convey any of that with her mind, Kaylina didn't know, but Levitke flashed again. This time, she appeared farther down the highway and sprinted away from the battle. She glanced back once, meeting Kaylina's eyes, and then she ran full-out away from the tower.

Three of the crag cougars were down, two eviscerated, but four remained on their feet. Without hesitation, they took off after the taybarri.

Kaylina hoped that between Levitke's powerful legs and flash magic, she could evade them. Even if the rangers wouldn't make it here in time to help, the taybarri could at least warn those in Port Jirador about the threat. As if the city didn't have enough threats to deal with from within.

With that upsetting thought in mind, Kaylina turned her head to look at the Kar'ruk party. They were all staring at her, including the axe-wielder, but he hadn't come any closer with his blade. His eyes were closed to slits.

Thoughtful slits?

He regarded her, the direction Levitke had fled, and her again. Kaylina wasn't familiar enough with their people to guess thoughts from their broad gray faces, but the Kar'ruk's narrowed eyes reminded her of the expression Targon got when he was calculating how best to use her for his plans. One of the warriors stepped forward and pointed at her hand. At the star-shaped leaf brand.

They couldn't guess how she'd come by it or what it meant, could they? *She* didn't even know what all it meant. She only had inklings.

Another Kar'ruk grunted, said a few words, then pointed at Kaylina and deeper into the mountains. Others stepped forward to bind her ankles, her wrists, and stuff a gag in her mouth.

She tried to find it encouraging that they would keep her alive, at least for a while. Maybe there was a chance for Vlerion and the rangers to save her. But, as the Kar'ruk carried her away, Kaylina glimpsed the dark windows of the tower and lost hope.

The signal fire was out, Levitke might fall to the fearsome predators chasing her, and whatever these Kar'ruk wanted her for, it couldn't be anything good.

28

IMPRISONED OUR BODIES MAY BE BUT NEVER OUR MINDS.

~ Writings of the Divine Servants

After a time, the Kar'ruk warriors left the highway to trek up an animal trail deeper into the mountains. In the dark and slung over her captor's back, Kaylina struggled to tell which direction they were going. To attack another watchtower? Back to their homeland with her? She had no idea.

Only when dawn lightened the cloudy gray sky did she start to recognize streams, clearings, and rocky cliffs as familiar. Since she'd never been in these mountains, she realized right away *why* they were familiar, and greater and greater dread crept into her.

This was the second vision the plant had given her, the one in which Vlerion changed into the beast, charged into the Kar'ruk gathering, and killed them all, then finished by killing her.

Her gut churned, bile rising into her throat. She didn't want to die. She'd barely found her freedom from her family and begun working on her dream. Further, she didn't want Vlerion to be responsible for her death. When he realized what he—the beast—had done, he might go mad or commit suicide. At the least, he would never forgive himself.

But Kaylina had inadvertently set up the possibility of Vlerion finding her and the plant's vision turning into reality. Because she'd wanted to save Levitke, she'd told the taybarri to locate him, to bring him to help her.

"Fool," she whispered softly.

When full daylight arrived, the Kar'ruk stopped in a valley with goats browsing clumps of tiny flowering plants high on the rocky sides. Dome-shaped tents made from animal skins clustered by a stream-fed pond.

Kar'ruk came outside to greet those returning, several pointing curiously at Kaylina. One grunted and drew a finger across his throat. To suggest human prisoners were all supposed to be killed?

Several of her kidnappers spoke in their tongue while gesturing at Kaylina and also at a few pine trees dotting the slopes. Could they have somehow learned about the Kar'ruk she'd distracted and that Levitke had killed? They couldn't know she'd called to the tree for help, could they?

Her captor lowered her to ground covered with grass and a low creeping plant with small glossy leaves. Red berries grew in clumps among them. It was early in the season for fruit, especially up in the frosty mountains, and Kaylina wondered if it was an altered plant. This encampment was far from the preserve, but the Daygarii had left evidence of their magical touch all over the world.

The discussion about her grew heated, with two more Kar'ruk making throat-cutting gestures. The door flap of a tent pushed open, and a female with a sewn-hide kit strode out. She waved for the males to stop arguing and walked toward Kaylina, opening the kit as she came.

Hopefully not to grab a knife for the suggested throat-slitting.

Kaylina's captor had taken not only the ranger's sword from her but her sling and knife as well. With her ankles and wrists bound, all she could do was watch from her knees as the female approached.

Her eyes were gold instead of yellow, and braided black hair wrapped around her horns before falling behind her head. A magnifying glass and a number of less-familiar tools hung on a leather thong around her neck.

"Hi," Kaylina said. "I don't suppose you or any of your large brethren speak my language and can tell me what you want? I'm a very accommodating soul. I'm trying to open a meadery in town. Do your people like alcoholic beverages? I'll share some with you if you let me return to make another batch."

The female poked in her kit, not indicating if she understood or cared.

One of the Kar'ruk tossed something to the ground a few yards away. Kaylina's pack. He used a knife to slash the cord that held the flap shut.

She scowled. "Yeah, just cut things. That's *much* more civilized than tying and untying knots."

The male looked over at her, waved his knife, and showed her his teeth. Far sharper than a human's, they were suitably intimidating. He dumped the pack upside-down.

At first, she worried about the journal and Vlerion's secret—however bastardized the Virt version of it was—but she doubted that many Kar'ruk would be able to read the pages. The warrior only sniffed the spine of the book before tossing it aside. He fished out dried fruit and jerky and gave them to his comrades.

Kaylina realized he might also find the powder she'd saved and wished she'd thought to tie her pack to Levitke. If Kaylina managed to reunite with the rangers, would they believe her story of invisible Kar'ruk without any evidence?

The female pulled out a small knife. Or was that a scalpel? She held it up triumphantly.

"Uhm." Kaylina might have said more but the pack invader was unwrapping the remains of the honeycomb she'd taken from the druid valley. "That's reserved for a special plant. I'd appreciate it if you didn't take it."

The Kar'ruk not only sniffed it but licked it. Then groaned, his eyes rolling back in his head with unmistakable pleasure.

Kaylina sighed. If she hadn't observed the taybarri sweet tooth in action, she wouldn't have thought beings with so many fangs would be that into honey.

Several other Kar'ruk surrounded the warrior and attempted to snatch some of the treat for themselves. He growled at them and clutched it to his chest.

Maybe they would get in a huge fight involving the entire camp, and Kaylina could escape. If only she could free her wrists and ankles. She eyed the female's scalpel.

"Any chance you want to use that to release me? Since you're a girl, and I'm a girl, we could be secret allies. Sisters from different species. You can't truly enjoy all these brutish—"

The female grabbed her wrist with callused fingers, turning it toward the sky. The scalpel dove for Kaylina's flesh with startling speed.

Kaylina cried out at the sharp pain and jerked back, afraid the horrible female had slit her vein. Blood welled from her skin.

Fury overrode her pain, and she curled her fingers into fists, longing to lash out. The female leaned close to look at the blood.

Kaylina tried to punch her. With her wrists bound, it wasn't effective, and the Kar'ruk didn't bother dodging. She didn't even seem to notice a fist striking her shoulder. She only tightened her grip on Kaylina's wrist and delved into her kit again. This time, she withdrew a vial and took a sample of the blood dribbling from the wound. Not a vein, Kaylina didn't think, but that didn't make the experience much more palatable.

Once the female had a sample, she rose, and stepped back. She lifted the vial overhead and yelled at it. Or... was that singing? Maybe chanting. Kaylina caught rhyming sounds in the language.

A few other voices joined in as the female tapped the tools dangling from her neck and took her kit—and Kaylina's blood—into her tent.

"This is my weirdest kidnapping ever."

The female returned, carrying a flagon and the vial to a campfire. She poured the contents of both into a cauldron and lowered it over the flames. Several males circled the area, and everyone started chanting.

Why did Kaylina have the uneasy feeling they were going to drink a concoction made with her blood? She'd heard before that Kar'ruk didn't mind eating human flesh when their favored prey couldn't be had, but this was chilling.

She glanced down at her wrist as a drop of blood dribbled into the undergrowth. The leaves rustled slightly, and a few rotated toward her.

"You are absolutely an altered plant," she murmured.

The chanting grew louder as more Kar'ruk joined in, circling the fire and waiting for the strange brew to heat.

Kaylina flattened her palms onto the leaves underneath her and silently asked them for help. What two-inch-high berry plants could do, she didn't know. It wasn't as if they could send vines to choke her captors or hurl heavy branches at them. Unfortunately.

The leaves rustled, and an oddly warm breeze swept through the valley. A tingle ran up Kaylina's arms, and a vision filled her mind.

Hundreds if not thousands of Kar'ruk were marching into the area from the end of the valley. Two females, including the one who'd taken her blood, greeted them in a grassy section near the pool. Thick stakes had been driven into the ground around the water, and fire burned in wolf skulls mounted atop them.

As the horde of warriors approached, the females gesticulated and chanted, invoking some ritual. They opened a large cylindrical container on a flat rock near the water. Made from bone and stretched hide, it looked like a drum until the lid came off.

The females wet their hands in the pond, then dipped their fingers into the container and pulled out silver powder. They rubbed it onto the faces, hands, and armor of the new arrivals. Even though the females were brisk and the powder didn't coat the Kar'ruk completely, it caused them to fade from view, the same as the invisible warrior that Kaylina had battled.

The vision blurred, shifting to a nighttime view of Port Jirador. Camouflaged by the magical powder, the Kar'ruk sneaked into the city through the catacombs and flowed up out of entrances, including the one in Stillguard Castle. They charged into the streets with their axes and torches, cutting down humans and setting buildings on fire.

The guards weren't a match for the invaders, and, for some reason, there weren't many rangers and taybarri around to fight them. Soon, Port Jirador burned to the ground, the inhabitants either killed or forced to flee. Afterward, Kar'ruk stomped about in the ashes, celebrating that they'd reclaimed their land.

As the vision faded, Kaylina withdrew her hands, regretting that she'd put them down.

Why all the altered plants liked to share these horrible potential events with her, she didn't know. Nor did she know if that vision was guaranteed to pass or if it was a possible future that might be avoided.

The plant leaves rippled under her knees.

"I don't suppose you could let me go instead of filling my head with visions?" Kaylina whispered, looking toward the pool. The stakes and skulls weren't there yet, but the cylindrical container rested on a rock, the same as the plants had shown her.

Too bad it was a hundred yards away. If she could slip away and reach it, she might slather that powder on herself and disappear.

One of the male Kar'ruk stopped chanting and strode toward Kaylina. Had he been watching her communication with the plants? *Something* contorted his bumpy face into a dyspeptic expression.

He grabbed her and drew a bone knife.

Kaylina twisted, trying to escape while silently asking the plants to help, but they didn't seem capable of more than rustling their leaves.

The Kar'ruk sliced his blade through her wrist bonds but left those tying her ankles. He hoisted her in the air and carried her away from the undergrowth. Some of the plants rustled, but they did nothing more. That didn't keep him from glancing warily at them and toward the female who'd taken Kaylina's blood.

She nodded gravely and pointed to a stout pine, but then shook her head and redirected him toward an eight-foot-stump, the top torn off long ago in a storm, moss covering the rotting remains.

The Kar'ruk pressed Kaylina's back to the stump. When he shifted to move around her, she tried to jump free, envisioning rolling and untying the bonds around her ankles before he could capture her.

But another Kar'ruk rushed forward to keep her pinned while the first yanked her arms behind her back. He tied her wrists again, this time around the stump and behind her. Her shoulder blades ached at the uncomfortable position and pressure.

"This day keeps getting worse." Kaylina looked down, but there were no altered plants beneath her, and the tree had died long ago. She doubted the lingering stump could help her in any way.

With their task accomplished, the Kar'ruk returned to the gathering. The chanting had grown faster and more eager. The female withdrew the cauldron, the concoction inside steaming. Not waiting for it to cool, she passed it around, and each warrior drank from it.

Kaylina tilted her head back against the stump, groping for a way to escape being killed by these people.

A furious roar rang out from the head of the valley. A *familiar* furious roar.

Vlerion. And he'd already turned into the beast.

Kaylina shivered, afraid the plant's vision was about to play out. If the beast prevailed against all the enemies in the camp and turned on her... being killed by him would be even worse than being killed by the Kar'ruk.

29

Throwing a rock in the river of time may alter the downstream flow but never the upstream.

~ Abayar, Founder Sandsteader Press

The Kar'ruk weren't as intimidated by the arrival of the beast as the Virts sneaking into the royal castle had been. They asked questions, perhaps wondering what manner of creature this was, and stepped away from the fire to grab their axes. When they faced him, it was without fear.

Kaylina swallowed, afraid they and their magical blades would be a match for him. Between the party who'd captured her and those who'd been camped here when they arrived, there were twenty Kar'ruk. Twenty that she'd *seen*. What if more lurked, camouflaged from view?

When the warriors spread out to give themselves room to fight, they had the mien of beings who'd practiced often together. Experts in battle. And the beast... His blue eyes were wild, full of unthinking savagery, and Kaylina worried his animal instincts wouldn't be enough to make him victorious.

The beast loped into the valley on his powerful legs, but he stopped before charging into the waiting Kar'ruk. His nostrils twitched as his head lifted into the air.

The Kar'ruk murmured to each other, crouching and waving their weapons, one calling a challenge. Despite their confidence, they didn't rush to greet the beast, instead waiting for the battle to come to them.

Kaylina twisted her wrists, wishing she could free herself. If she ran off, maybe the beast wouldn't feel the need to fight all of them. And, if he won, he wouldn't be able to turn on her.

He charged, and she winced at the bold approach, at all the warriors ready for him. But instead of rushing them, he veered toward the pool.

Kaylina watched in confusion—as did the Kar'ruk. Did he intend to jump into the water to cool off before the fight? Had he overexerted himself in his hurry to get here?

No, the beast sprang for the container of silver powder. His sharp claws tore the lid off.

The female Kar'ruk shouted and pointed. Numerous warriors ran to save their precious magical powder.

Somehow, the beast knew what it was and how to use it. Either Vlerion had encountered it before or he'd seen her message in the logbook, and, as separate as his animalistic side was, it could draw upon his memories.

The beast covered himself and faded from view. And none too soon. Roaring and cursing, the axe-wielders reached the pool.

One must have glimpsed the beast because he chopped his blade down, as if swinging at a foe. It struck the flat rock, shearing it in two. The action upended the container, and the female shouted at him as she pointed in the direction the beast had last been seen.

Get him!

Kaylina didn't have to know the language to understand her words.

But the beast struck before the Kar'ruk could find him. He'd altered his path and circled to the back side of the warriors, leaping onto the shoulders of one. Kaylina couldn't see him but could tell from the way his horned foe reacted.

Even as the Kar'ruk threw his arms back, trying to knock him free, the beast bit down into his skull. The warrior went rigid and screamed in pain. Claws raked into his throat, silencing him.

It all happened quickly, but the nearby Kar'ruk also reacted quickly. They rushed toward their ally as he fell and swung their blades toward the beast.

Most missed as he leaped away, but one must have clipped him. The beast grunted in pain, and Kaylina winced with sympathy. He'd taken one enemy down, but he had so many more...

The Kar'ruk charged at the beast. He ran away, understanding that with distance they would lose sight of him again. And they did. Kaylina could tell because their blades slowed, and they shifted to stand back to back, peering around the valley.

"You're smarter in that form than I would have guessed, Vlerion," she whispered.

The tipped cylinder lifted into the air, and the female shouted again, pointing at it. The beast hurled it into the pool.

The Kar'ruk rushed toward him, but he was faster than the big warriors and managed to get behind them again. This time, they were ready. They spun, fanned out, and swung for him, leaving blue streaks in the air as their magical axes whizzed through it.

Kaylina sucked in a breath, not sure she wished she could see the beast or was glad she couldn't. At least two of the axes met nothing but air. A third seemed to hit something. Him.

Not a fatal blow, she hoped.

Even as the Kar'ruk shouted, one went down, dropping his axe and grabbing for his legs. He spun, half tumbling into the pool, as great gashes appeared. His allies whirled toward him with raised blades, but they couldn't attack or they might hit their wounded ally. The beast eviscerated the Kar'ruk, leaving him in the shallows of the pond, before springing away.

One warrior swung his axe downward like a logger, but it missed the beast, lodging in muddy ground instead. Before he could pull it free, claws sank into his hamstring below his chain-mail tunic. Another Kar'ruk rushed to help him, but, after gouging muscle from his foe, the beast shoved the wounded warrior into the paths of the others, delaying them while he sprinted out of their view.

A part of Kaylina was glad the Kar'ruk were suffering by having their own tactics used against them. A part of her worried that, with this advantage, the beast would be victorious, as he had been in the plant's vision. Then he would turn on her.

She twisted her wrists, desperate now to loosen the bonds, and looked around for anything that might help. If only the Kar'ruk hadn't moved her away from the altered plants. Now and then, one of the warriors stomped through the undergrowth as they rushed about, battling the beast, but she couldn't touch any of the foliage.

Did she need to? Kaylina glanced toward her brand, wishing she knew what she'd done when she'd communicated with the pine tree and the plants. As far as she could recall, she'd only willed her thoughts at them.

Can you help me escape? Kaylina asked silently, focusing on the plants she'd knelt on before. *Not with a vision. Maybe with a knife.* She snorted at herself. As if the undergrowth had a knife. *Maybe some of your berries could be smooshed against my ropes to loosen them,* she suggested instead.

A Kar'ruk went flying, landing among the plants. The leaves rippled, as if displeased, but they didn't respond to Kaylina in any way she could understand.

Only when she looked up did she realize that the Kar'ruk had been the last warrior standing. Using their invisibility powder against them, the beast had been victorious. The bodies of the dead littered the valley, their tents smashed, their magical powder destroyed.

Heavy breathing came from the air near the undergrowth. Heavy breathing and soft snarls that chilled Kaylina.

The beast stepped past the downed Kar'ruk, drawing close enough for her to see. He was staring straight at her with no recognition in his eyes. Blood dripped from numerous axe wounds, but his muscles rippled under his short fur, and he emanated power.

Kaylina tensed. The vision had proven true. He would kill her now.

An uncertain roar came from the forest at the entrance of the valley. Was that a taybarri? Crenoch?

Of course, Vlerion would have been mounted on his taybarri until he turned. But Crenoch might be too afraid to charge in as long as his rider was in this form.

With his blue eyes devoid of humanity, the beast stalked toward Kaylina.

Terrified and trapped against the stump, she couldn't do anything but meet that animalistic gaze. Mouth dry, she hummed the song he'd shared with her, trying to remember some of the lyrics, those detailing the sorrow of the lake as humanity, with its common enemy defeated, turned on each other.

Eyes slitted, the beast looked her up and down. He stopped close enough to touch her, close enough to *kill* her.

A clawed hand—*paw*—reached toward her. Kaylina winced, turning her face away, but made herself sing the snatches of lyrics she remembered. If only she had more of a talent for music. Maybe it would have worked.

A single cold claw traced her cheek to her jaw. It didn't draw blood. It didn't even hurt.

"My... female," the beast rasped.

"Yes," she croaked. Might the plant have been wrong? Maybe Vlerion wouldn't kill her. Maybe he would—

The claw trailed down the side of her neck, to her breast, and she shivered, realizing he might not tear her to pieces, but he could kill her all the same. The scars on his mother's neck came to mind, evidence of the beast's touch, left when Vlerion's father had claimed her. And Isla had said that some women chosen by the various beasts of the Havartaft line *hadn't* survived.

"My *mate*." The beast snarled, gripped her shoulder, and looked back at the dead Kar'ruk. His lips rippled in defiance, showing fangs instead of blunt human teeth.

"Yes," Kaylina said again. Remembering the spymaster's question, asking if she could, with her *anrokk* power, control the beast somehow, she whispered. "Will you free me?"

He leaned closer, inhaled her scent, and licked her throat. With his trousers in shreds, she could see that he was aroused, that he wanted her.

"Vlerion," she whispered, trembling. Afraid. "I *command* you to free me."

He snarled, the grip on her shoulder tightening, and his gaze jerked to her face. Irritated. Defiant. And possessive.

No, ordering him around wasn't a good idea.

"Please," she tried in a far more conciliatory tone. "I won't go anywhere if you free me. I'm your female, okay? Your *mate*." She preferred that term, one that didn't imply that he owned her.

"My mate," he rasped in that inhuman voice.

His paw lowered from her shoulder to cup her breast through her shirt. Another tremble went through her, though she wasn't positive that desire didn't mingle with the fear, raising the question of what it would be like... if she survived.

But she shook her head. With the memory of the plant's vision filling her mind, she doubted she would survive the beast's ministrations. The great power in that body could be unleashed by lust as much as rage.

She didn't try to pull away, but she tried again to get through to him. She had to.

"I know you're in there, Vlerion. I need you to change back. The kingdom needs you too. And your fellow rangers need you. We have to come up with a plan. Do you understand?"

His eyes changed ever so slightly. They became less animal, less savage.

"Once the kingdom is safe, I'll find a way to lift your curse," she promised, vowing that it wouldn't be a lie. "Then we can be together."

Still cupping her, he stroked her, his claw cutting the fabric of her shirt as a hint of defiance entered his eyes again. He wanted to be together *now*.

Though he'd been biting his enemies as much as cutting them with his claws, she made herself lean forward to kiss him, willing whatever power she could command to enter him, to soothe him. To at least make him amenable to her suggestions.

At first, he kissed her back, savage with need. But the brand on her hand tingled, and she imagined magical energy flowing up her arm, through her, and into him.

The beast growled. Or was that a groan? A groan of acceptance?

His lips softened against hers, and he lowered his paw. Some of the tension eased out of his taut muscles, the dangerous edge bleeding away.

Kaylina believed he was on the verge of collapsing and turning back into a man when a blur of blue streaked in from the side.

Captured by her kiss and her power, the beast didn't notice until the last moment. He spun to face the threat, but the taybarri —it *was* Crenoch—flattened him.

A second taybarri charged in right behind him. Levitke.

Together, they pinned the beast's arms and legs to the ground, and Crenoch sat on his chest.

Even their combined power might not have normally been enough to keep him down, but the fight had seeped out of the beast. Trapped under them, he morphed back into a man, his sword and boots lost, his clothes in tatters. In the process, he lost consciousness.

Crenoch and Levitke looked at each other, their floppy ears quirking. Maybe they hadn't expected that to be so easy.

Kaylina almost pointed out that the beast had already been on the verge of collapsing but decided against it. In the future, she might need their help with him again. It would be better if the taybarri weren't as terrified of him.

"Thank you, you two. I don't suppose one of *you* would free me? My shoulders are terribly sore, and there's... a lot to do."

Kaylina hoped Vlerion woke soon, because she wanted to know what was going on in the capital. Had that diplomatic party already enacted some scheme? Were invisible Kar'ruk racing through the city streets with axes and torches, destroying everything and everyone they encountered?

The plant's vision hadn't been entirely accurate about the beast-Kar'ruk confrontation—at least how things ended with her—so she wouldn't assume the new vision would play out exactly as shown. Even so, she had little doubt the Kar'ruk had come to enact a scheme and did want to burn down the city.

"No way are we going to let that happen," she vowed softly. "I have a meadery to open."

After exchanging grave looks that may have hinted of trouble that had already started back in Port Jirador, Levitke and Crenoch moved off Vlerion. Levitke rounded the stump and, using a sharp fang, cut the rope tying Kaylina to it.

A surge of relief came as blood flowed into her arms again. She shook them out, then bent to untie her ankles.

Crenoch whuffed toward Levitke. He remained with Vlerion but must have realized the threat had passed, because he lay on his belly beside him now, only his broad head on Vlerion's chest. It looked more like he was using him for a pillow than trying to keep him in place.

"Long night for you guys too, huh?" Once Kaylina had the rope untied, she kicked it away with passion.

Crenoch whuffed again, then rolled onto his back, jaw opening, and tongue lolling out.

"Yeah, I'd like a nap too, but..." Kaylina picked a path between the dead Kar'ruk, wanting to find her sling, knife, and pick up her maimed pack. Maybe she could locate bandages for Vlerion's wounds too. "A lot more Kar'ruk are coming," she added to the taybarri. "And they can turn invisible. Well, they paint themselves with powder from an altered plant, and *that* makes them hard to see. Did you tell him, Levitke?"

She whuffed an affirmative, then walked toward one of the tents, glancing at the cauldron of Kaylina's blood and who knew what else. She used her tail to knock it over, dousing the fire in the process. Blue-black smoke wafted up.

Ignoring it, Levitke stuck her head in the tent and poked around. She withdrew the kit the female had carried.

Remembering the scalpel, Kaylina shuddered.

Levitke dropped the kit, used a claw to open it, then lowered her fangs to pull out squares of soft hide and strips of braided grass.

"Are those Kar'ruk bandages?" Kaylina asked.

Levitke took them to Vlerion's side and dropped them.

"You guys are really smart, aren't you? I don't know who implied you don't gain intelligence until you become elders... Maybe the rangers aren't as observant as they think."

On his back with his blue-furred belly to the sky, Crenoch

yawned, hunched his spine, and used a hind paw to scratch his armpit.

"Or maybe you're goofy enough that they underestimate you."

Crenoch lolled his tongue out at her.

"Levitke and I need to find your people in case they can help with the Kar'ruk. The plant told me— Uhm, I have a hunch your elders will be able to assist us." Kaylina doubted the taybarri would judge her for taking advice from a sentient plant, but it sounded silly in her own ears. "Crenoch, can you go back to the city and warn the rangers about all these Kar'ruk in the mountains? It's possible more are on the way. You can take Vlerion with you, and he can do the talking." She hoped he would wake up first so she could explain everything to him.

"*Vlerion* will go with you," he spoke from the ground, his head turning to find her with his eyes.

"Someone with a human mouth needs to explain everything to Targon and the king and whoever else will listen." As Kaylina knelt to squeeze his shoulder, relieved he was awake, she summarized what she'd seen with the Kar'ruk. She also found the paper with the silver powder on it to show him. "Did you see my note in the tower? About this stuff?"

"Yes. It explains much." After touching her hand gently, Vlerion groaned and extricated himself from under Crenoch's head. Blood dripped from his wounds, but that didn't keep him from pulling her into a hug and resting his face against the top of her head. "I'm relieved you're all right."

"Me too." Her body leaned into him, relishing his embrace, as it always did.

"I left other rangers back at the tower. They also saw your note and understand the threat. They'll defend the city. You said the taybarri elders can help? I will go with you to find them."

"I have no idea how long it will take. The, uhm, plant didn't say." Kaylina briefly explained the vision, surprised he was willing to go with her and didn't insist they both return immediately to Port Jirador.

"Before this, I'd never heard of magical plants giving people visions, but I can sense your power and believe..." Vlerion leaned back to gaze into her eyes. "Based on what's happened so far, I believe that what the plants are sharing with you is worth heeding."

"Maybe not *all* of it." Kaylina thought of the vision that involved her killing Vlerion, but that had come from the plant in the tower. So far, the vegetation she'd encountered in nature had been more inclined to help her than manipulate her for her own good.

"Whatever they share should not be trusted without question," he said, "but it may be considered."

"That sounds reasonable."

"As I strive to be."

Vlerion leaned his face against her head again and took in a long breath. It was different from the animalistic way the beast had inhaled her scent but did bring that to mind. Vlerion's muscled arms weren't as thick, and definitely weren't furry, but the way he held her conveyed the same interest, a desire to protect her. To claim her.

Maybe she should have objected, but she leaned into him again, wanting his protection. The last couple of days without him had been fraught. How many times had she almost died?

"I'll send a message back with Crenoch. He knows his way home and will find Captain Targon, let him know what we're doing and that we'll return. Once we finish, we'll go back to help the city." His voice grew softer as he added, "I won't be parted from you again."

Kaylina clasped his hand, touched that he cared. "I want you with me too."

"Good."

After Kaylina found her sling and knife, and Vlerion his sword and torn clothing, she used the Kar'ruk bandages to patch him up, at least temporarily. Doctor Penderbrock could do a better job when they returned. Assuming he and the rest of the rangers were still alive by then.

Levitke didn't object when they both climbed on her back. As Crenoch headed back toward the city, she turned to leave the valley and travel deeper and higher into the mountains.

Vlerion rode behind Kaylina with his arms around her. Even as she appreciated it and felt safer traveling with him, she thought of the plant's vision of her and Levitke greeting the taybarri. Vlerion hadn't been in it, and she worried his presence would change their willingness to help. Had he been any other ranger, it probably wouldn't have, but the taybarri could sense the beast within him. That might be a problem.

30

The relief after a storm is great, but new clouds ever lurk on the horizon.

~ Tholegar, captain of the Kingfisher

"I'm relieved that you were alive when I reached you," Vlerion said as they rode, his arms around Kaylina. "After finding the dead ranger—Corporal Oxten—in the tower and all those Kar'ruk prints, not to mention your taybarri coming back terrified and bloody with wounds, I was sure you were already dead." His arms tightened. "I barely refrained from changing right there. If there hadn't been others with me, colleagues I care about, I might have let myself lose control. I managed not to until I was alone, save for poor Crenoch. I know he was alarmed."

"Having someone change into a beast while on my back would alarm me too."

"I did manage to spring free first. He was wise enough to run off before I changed fully. After that... it's a blur in my memory. As it often is. I only knew I had to catch up, had to protect you. The

Kar'ruk aren't known for taking prisoners unless they want to torture and question them."

"They wanted to drink my blood." Kaylina glanced back, not surprised to find a concerned expression on Vlerion's face, and she explained further. Her words did nothing to smooth the furrow in his brow. "I don't understand it either."

"They may sense the power within you. They could have believed that by imbibing a taste of your blood, some of it would convey to them. Or it may have been a superstitious ritual. They have a lot of quirks and believe bad luck will befall those who don't make enough offerings and prayers to their One God."

"Whatever it was, I'm sure my blood didn't *convey* anything. I don't have power; I have a brand." Kaylina held up her hand. "*It* may have power."

"The beast in me is drawn to you, not your hand."

"Actually, he was drawn to my boobs." Kaylina smiled to make it a joke.

Vlerion frowned and looked down at her chest. His eyes fixed on the rip in the fabric the beast's claw had made.

Since it wasn't a long rip, he might not have noticed it before—or, if he had, he might have thought she'd caught her shirt on a thorn while running. Now, the furrow appeared in his brow again. He wore the troubled expression of someone trying to remember something, something unpleasant.

"I did that," he stated with certainty.

"The *beast* did."

"We are not different beings. Unfortunately."

"No. You are. I can tell when I look into your eyes. And into his. There's nothing of you in there."

Vlerion shook his head, refusing to distance himself from the beast—and what the beast did.

Wanting to take his mind from that, Kaylina dug in her pack. "After all the trouble with the Kar'ruk, I almost forgot about this."

Wishing she could distract him with something more pleasant, she hesitated before handing him the journal. But when he saw it, he took it, his expression grim before he opened it. He released her to flip through the pages and read the last entry.

"It is... as I expected," he said.

"We'll keep them from printing that story."

"There are other presses."

"Once the Kar'ruk are dealt with, you can send the rangers on a press-bashing mission to destroy them all." Hoping to ease his concerns, Kaylina smiled and made a punching motion.

"One way or another, the story will come out, and the people will believe it. After all, some of what this person wrote... is not wrong. Only the recent murders can be blamed on the Kar'ruk. In the past... I remember little of the times I've changed in the past, but I've woken up before with blood on my chest. Not mine."

"I understand your concerns about that, and your guilt, but you wouldn't be doing these things if you weren't cursed. Magically cursed. It's not your fault, and the Virts shouldn't be targeting you. From some of the things you've said, I feel like you'd even defend them if they weren't using violent methods. You seem to understand their grievances and why they want what they want." Kaylina checked his face to see if her belief was correct.

"I believe they have a right to protest and argue for better working conditions and opportunities. Were they, as you say, not violent in their methods, I would not take action against them. I know you accuse me of being haughty—" his eyebrow twitched, as if he couldn't believe it, "—but that's only because I'm used to being in charge and accustomed to commanding men. It is sometimes difficult to set aside one's upbringing and accept that a man born into the aristocracy isn't any better than one born a commoner, but... I admit that's likely true. It's the actions that one takes after one's birth that define a man—or woman. It has nothing to do with blood." His expression turned pensive as he regarded her. "Except perhaps in your case."

"My blood is the same as yours. Except less arrogant and uppity."

"It is not. After all that has happened, you must believe that too."

"I'm still struggling to accept that. The rest of my family is..." Kaylina almost said normal, but that wasn't the right word. Other than her perfect older sister, there were quite a few quirky people in her family. "Nobody else has *power*," she decided on.

"It's true that I haven't sensed anything in your brother. I am not *drawn* to him." Vlerion lowered the journal so he could wrap an arm around her again and scoot closer.

"That might have more to do with his sex than blood."

Vlerion shook his head. "I can sense the power in our other *anrokk*, Sergeant Jastadar. Because of *his* sex, his appeal doesn't manifest in me desiring physical relations with him, but I have enjoyed his company more than that of other men. I feel comfortable with him."

"Do you feel comfortable with me? I thought I mostly irritated you."

"You do that less now that you've stopped calling me pirate and suborning my taybarri."

"He stole my honey; I didn't *suborn* him."

"I know." Vlerion kissed her on the neck. "It was childish of me to lose my temper over that."

She leaned her head back against his shoulder, inviting more kisses if he wished.

He eyed her neck but didn't lower his lips again. "I worry that this will end badly," he said softly. "When I'm with you, it's extremely hard for me to resist temptation. When I'm not with you... you're filling my thoughts and making me want nothing more than to find you." His voice lowered, almost a growl as he added, "And take you."

That should have scared her, but it flushed her with heat, making her wish he *could* take her.

Vlerion pulled his gaze from her neck as if it were physically difficult and looked toward the trees they were riding through.

"I don't trust myself with you," he added, "but I can't stay away."

She wished she could make light of the dilemma and promise that nothing would happen, but she was struggling with the same thing. Drawn by their mutual desire—their mutual *lust*—how close had they come to rousing the beast? They'd almost done it in that park with innocent people dangerously close.

"What should I do?" Kaylina asked, though she worried he would say she should stay away from him and he her.

"I don't know. Our fates are intertwined. I'll have to... be stronger than temptation." Doubt lurked in his eyes.

"You can do it. I'll work on it too." She straightened, shifting away from him.

His frown implied he didn't think that would be enough.

Kaylina groped for a way to change the topic. Maybe back to what they'd been discussing before?

"You're a more reasonable and fair man than I originally realized. I wonder... Would the Virts be so set on overthrowing the monarchy if *your* family were still on the throne? I guess you'd be king, since your father and older brother passed."

"That is a duty I'm ill-qualified for and would not want. I prefer the wilderness to the city and protecting my people with my sword and taybarri, not pens and speeches."

"But if your great-great-grandfather hadn't been cursed and abdicated, isn't it a duty that would have fallen to you? That you would have been compelled to accept?"

"My older brother would have been compelled to accept it. If not for the curse, he would be alive." Vlerion stared glumly toward the forest around them. They'd climbed higher in elevation again, and snow lay mounded under the trees. The tireless Levitke was carrying them ever deeper into the mountains, where winter hadn't yet relinquished its grasp. "Vlarek probably *would* have been a good leader, a good king. He was better at keeping his temper than I and had the soul of a poet and a bard. He would have seen the world from both sides and perhaps found a way to appease nobles and commoners alike."

"Your mother said you have some of that temperament as well. You have a violin in your room, after all."

Isla had also said Kaylina should avoid Vlerion and not ask him to play for her. Unfortunately. Kaylina knew she would enjoy the experience. She wagered Vlerion's face would be peaceful and calm as he ran the bow over the strings, soothed by his music.

"A sure sign that I'd be a good ruler," he said dryly.

"Maybe not, but if you were ousted from power, you could dance and play on street corners and make coin."

"Ousted from power." Vlerion snorted. "There will never be any power for me, curse or not. The Virts want a new system of government, one in which commoners run things. They don't want a new king."

"I can't help but think there must be a way that both sides could come together without all this killing. With other threats to the kingdom, it's foolish for people to squabble amongst themselves." Kaylina waved toward the north to indicate the Kar'ruk.

"It is beyond me to solve that problem. All I can do is fight the battles that our leaders assign me."

"Too bad. The current leaders are iffy."

"That's your educated and informed opinion after a month in the capital?" He smiled faintly.

"It's *an* opinion. I won't say it's educated, but I haven't met many people in charge of things here who are... *decent*."

Vlerion sighed. "The last ten years or so have been fraught. It's a challenging time for decency."

"Some people carry it with them in *all* times."

"That is true. You're wise for a mead maker." He patted her thigh, letting his hand settle there, but only for a moment before he pulled it back with a grimace.

"Wrestling with temptation?" she asked.

"Around you? Always." He smiled again, but his eyes were haunted. "I wish you could be..."

"Your mate?" Kaylina raised her eyebrows.

"Is that what the beast said?"

"Yeah. He growled it."

"He's not as conflicted as I am."

She started to smile, sensing he meant it to be a joke, but the words made her pause, remembering her conversation with Targon. "Are you only conflicted because you worry about us being together waking the beast or... do you not want..."

"What?"

"If we weren't— If you weren't *drawn* to me or my blood or whatever it is, would you want to be with me?"

"You're beautiful, Kaylina. *Many* men want to be with you."

"I don't mean just for sex. Would you..." She trailed off. What did she want? For him to say he adored her personality as well as her body and that he wanted to marry her? They hadn't known each other that long, and she didn't want to get married. All she wanted was someone who could care about her, maybe even love her, even though she wasn't normal. "Would you be into me, as a person, if we weren't attracted to each other because of this strange magic?"

Vlerion hesitated.

Kaylina looked away, a lump of disappointment forming in her throat. Before he spoke, she knew what his answer would be.

"I don't know. I believe it's possible, but the draw makes it hard to tell. I do admire your bravery and tenacity."

"Yeah, I hear those are sexy."

He frowned, and she lifted a hand to wave away the discussion. She wasn't being fair by wanting more from him.

"I don't wish to hurt you," Vlerion said, "but I don't want to be dishonest with you either."

"Honesty's good," she mumbled.

And it was. She'd just come to care too much and wanted too much. But could she answer the question any differently if he asked the same of her? She admired him for his bravery and abilities as a ranger, but would she risk rousing the beast if she weren't so intensely attracted to him? To that side of him?

"Sorry." She made herself meet his eyes again. "It was a silly thing to ask."

"It's not silly to wonder that. It's natural. I…" He paused to look around.

Only then did Kaylina realize that Levitke had slowed down and that they weren't alone. Numerous sets of brown taybarri eyes stared out at them from tunnels, clumps of boulders, and the alpine grasses of a valley.

31

No matter how grand the adventure, the yearning to return home always arises.

~ Elder Taybarri Ravarn

Levitke whuffed, then let out a high-pitched noise that Kaylina hadn't heard from a taybarri before, a cross between a goat's bleat and a bird's cheep. Several answering bleat-cheeps came from the tunnels. Levitke rose up on her hind legs, forelimbs swatting at the air, and Kaylina snatched fistfuls of fur to keep from falling off. Vlerion gripped fur and *her*.

As soon as Levitke's paws touched down again, he said, "Get off. Your taybarri is overly excited."

"She's not *my* taybarri," Kaylina said but obeyed the order to slide to the ground. "She's simply been kind enough to give me rides in exchange for honey drops."

Levitke bounced around like a puppy as other blue-furred taybarri ran out of the tunnels. To greet her, Kaylina assumed from Levitke's reaction, but these wild taybarri had the same fangs and powerful muscles of the ranger mounts. Getting in the way of one would not be wise.

Unconcerned, Levitke romped over to meet them. On the way, she bounced and hopped.

Two of the taybarri trotting toward her also rolled across the ground. Pure joy or a part of an official greeting?

"Oh, she's yours," Vlerion said. "She's at least meant for you."

"Because we have the same maturity level?"

"Yes."

"Really, my pirate lord, I hardly ever *bounce* anymore."

His eyebrow twitched at the pirate add-on, but he didn't sound affronted when he replied. "You pace, wiggle, and gesticulate a lot when you scheme."

"When I *dream.* I'll admit I get excited envisioning dreams." Kaylina tried to remember when she'd done that in front of him. It was odd that he'd come to know her so well in the scant weeks she'd been in Port Jirador.

"Schemes," he corrected.

"You sound like Frayvar. Maybe you've spent too much time around him."

"He *does* visit Doc Penderbrock in our headquarters a lot."

"He's frail and easily injured."

"He has his own cot in the infirmary now," Vlerion said. "And I understand he alphabetized and categorized the doctor's medicines."

"He tries to be a helpful houseguest."

Kaylina and Vlerion trailed off as a number of silver-furred taybarri walked into view, their heads high. Unlike the youngsters, they didn't bounce. They didn't even amble, sashay, or swish their tails overmuch. Their steps were graceful but calm and precise, and their eyes, the same silver as their fur, held intelligence and wisdom.

The elders stopped ten paces away and looked at Vlerion instead of Kaylina.

What brings one of the cursed ones to a taybarri community? a female voice spoke into their minds, the words not in the kingdom tongue but somehow understandable. *The cursed ones are dangerous to us—to all.*

Kaylina had worried the taybarri would be wary of Vlerion. She raised a finger. "Actually, it was my idea. Lord Vlerion is kind of… my bodyguard."

"*Really.*" Okay, *that* time he sounded affronted.

"You said you came to protect me."

"Because you're my—" Vlerion glanced at the taybarri and didn't finish.

Too bad. Kaylina would have been curious to hear his label for her. Friend? Responsibility? Mate? Not-normal-girl-that-my-cursed-blood-compels-me-to-guard? She sighed. Probably that one.

He was right. The beast *was* less conflicted.

The taybarri eyes were unwavering as they regarded Vlerion. Only one elder had glanced at Kaylina when she'd spoken.

Resolute, she stepped forward and attempted to command their attention. She turned her hand so they could see the leaf-shaped mark.

"I have been chosen by the plant in Stillguard Castle to seek out your kind in the hope that you can help the people of the kingdom with Kar'ruk invaders." Technically, the plant had only given her a vision, one of many, and she didn't know if it cared a whit about the Kar'ruk, but it wasn't here to naysay her. "A supposed diplomatic party came under the guise of negotiating for access to the catacombs, but they're enacting a plot and hope to kill everyone in the city while burning it down."

Something she only knew because of another vision. Hopefully, the elders wouldn't ask her for proof about the Kar'ruk plans.

This sounds like a human problem, a male taybarri said. *The Kar'ruk have not disturbed us in our mountain valleys or on the plains for many generations.*

"Humans and taybarri have a treaty, wise elders," Vlerion said. "An *alliance.*"

Do not tell us that which we already know, cursed one.

Vlerion's lips rippled at the order, but he didn't get huffy and tell them he was a lord or demand reverence. For all Kaylina knew, these taybarri were royalty. He'd once said Crenoch was a prince.

Our young work with the rangers and will help with the skirmish of which you speak. At least the female elder didn't call Vlerion a cursed one again.

"I think it's going to be a lot more than a skirmish," Kaylina said. "There may be *thousands* of Kar'ruk coming. Your young might be killed right alongside the rangers."

We have not seen or heard of that many in the mountains.

"They're invisible."

The taybarri looked at each other. Skeptically?

"They're not invisible *themselves*, but they're coating their skin and armor with a silver powder from what I assume came from an altered plant that grows in their lands." Kaylina withdrew the scrap of paper with the smudged sample, glad the Kar'ruk who'd poked in her pack hadn't removed it. "Maybe you're familiar with it? Your people have been around a long time and know all about magic, right?"

We have, and we are familiar with much of what the druids did during their time in this realm. The female stepped forward, her head higher than Kaylina's, and trampling came to mind again. All she did was lower her snout to sniff the silver smear on the paper. *This came from a succulent. An altered lithop plant. They are not from the north but from deep in the sandy and rocky deserts to the east and south.* The taybarri telepathically shared an image of flat, round purple, green, and gray succulents growing on stones and in crevices. They looked far more like stones themselves than vegetation. *They camouflage themselves to blend in so that animals won't find them and eat them. As far as I am aware, they are not palatable to humans, Kar'ruk, or taybarri, but some of the sandsteader herbalists cultivate them for medicines. I had not heard that they have the ability to camouflage anyone, but... perhaps it is not surprising, given their native characteristic of blending into the desert. You should have acquired a larger sample so that we could have experimented.*

"Sorry. I was busy trying not to be killed by Kar'ruk."

The female lifted her snout to meet Kaylina's eyes. She didn't *say* anything about irreverence, but her gaze reminded Kaylina a lot of the looks Targon gave her when proclaiming that Vlerion should beat some respect into her.

"If you'd like to come with us, uhm, wise elder—" Kaylina recalled Vlerion had used that to address them, "—to aid our people in repelling the invasion, I can show you where we left a body covered in the stuff. Levitke helped kill—well, she did it all —a Kar'ruk who was trying to kill me, which I found quite rude. She agreed."

You say a druid plant instructed you to make this request of us? The elder's telepathic tone conveyed doubt, and her tail tapped the ground twice as she glanced at her comrades.

"It implied through a vision that you would help, yes."

And it sent this one to protect you? The female pointed her snout at Vlerion. *That is a dubious choice.*

Vlerion clenched his jaw, looking like he would need to hum to calm himself at any moment. As an aristocrat and a proven ranger, he couldn't be used to having his worth questioned.

Kaylina rested a hand on his arm. "The plant didn't recommend him, but we've been working together because..." She looked at Vlerion, groping for a better way to finish the sentence than *our weird blood makes us hot for each other.*

"We both desire to serve the kingdom," Vlerion stated.

"Yes." Kaylina nodded. "I especially hope to serve them mead, but I need invasions, civil wars, and false accusations against me to end so I can focus on my craft and opening my business. Oh, I have a little honey left." Unfortunately, *very* little honey, thanks to the Kar'ruk tongues that had delved into her stash. "Would you like to try some? I'm afraid I don't have any mead along to share, but that's not recommended for taybarri anyway, due to the alcoholic content." She remembered Crenoch snoring on his back in her courtyard as Vlerion worried over him.

Maybe the elder glimpsed the thought in her mind because she snorted. *Our kind cannot ingest fermented products without distress. We do enjoy honey when we can find it in the wild.*

"Here you go." Kaylina beamed a smile as she offered the paper, though it held only smears of honeycomb, and what remained had been contaminated by Kar'ruk tongues. She wouldn't mention that to the taybarri.

"Speaking of dubious," Vlerion murmured, eyeing the treat.

"Ssh. My *anrokk* appeal isn't working on them, so I'm trying gifts. I just wish I had a better gift."

"Your appeal is working on some." Vlerion nodded past her shoulder.

Kaylina hadn't realized Levitke and the other younger taybarri had gathered behind them to watch. She didn't know if it had anything to do with her *anrokk*-ness though. Several sets of nostrils were sniffing the air—and the honey scent now in it.

Kaylina offered it to the female who'd been speaking with her while wishing she had enough for all of them.

A bribe? the elder asked.

"A gift."

The female sniffed it again. *It is from one of the valleys where the Daygarii plants flower.*

"Yes. In the preserve near the city."

We are aware of the place.

Meaning they could get their own honey and didn't need Kaylina's bribe?

The hives and those bees, imbued with and protected by Daygarii magic, do not let us *take samples,* the female continued, as if she'd heard the silent question.

She washed her tongue over the paper, the offering pitifully small in comparison to her size. That didn't keep her from cleaning the paper thoroughly, leaving it—and Kaylina's hand—moist with saliva. She even made the same purr-clucks Crenoch had when he'd enjoyed her mead.

"They didn't seem to mind me taking some. Maybe I can get you more." Since Kaylina had been accused of bribery attempts, she didn't finish with *after you help us save the city.*

Hmm. The female backed up to rejoin the other elders.

Their tails swished slowly back and forth in the grass as they huddled to confer. They made few vocalizations, so Kaylina assumed they communicated with each other telepathically.

When they finished, the female again spoke for the group. *We believe the Daygarii would not have cared if the Kar'ruk and humans killed each other in a great battle. The same would be true of a plant they left behind to watch over their interests.*

"It marked me and gave me that vision for some reason." Kaylina spread her arms.

Indeed. Most curious. Perhaps it has a use for you.

"I believe she carries some druid blood in her veins, wise elders," Vlerion said.

Yes, we can see that is true.

Kaylina rocked back at the taybarri's certainty. Even though Vlerion and the plant itself had suggested that, she remained skeptical, not understanding how that could be. She knew her family and her parents, and nobody else was an *anrokk* or had any strange affinity for flora or fauna.

"I don't know about the plant's motivations, but I care about stopping a war," Kaylina said. "Especially when it's starting in the middle of where I'm trying to open a business."

Maybe she shouldn't have added that. It sounded self-centered, but all the problems in Port Jirador were derailing her quest to prove herself, damn it.

"As do I," Vlerion said. "I also care about Crenoch and the other young taybarri. As Kaylina said, they would be as much in danger as my rangers. If you have a way to stop the Kar'ruk..."

We are aged and beyond the years when we easily sprang into battle, the female said, glancing at her silver-furred comrades, *and the Kar'ruk have ever been willing to kill our kind. That is one of the reasons we allied with humans, to more effectively keep the Kar'ruk out of these lands that we share. We do, however, know a few things about those catacombs and the supposed Kar'ruk rights to the lands humans now inhabit. Perhaps we might speak with their diplomatic party and help with the negotiations.*

"The negotiations are a ruse," Vlerion said. "We believe—"

Kaylina held up a hand. "We'll take any help you can give. Thanks."

Vlerion raised his eyebrows at her interruption, but he didn't say anything further.

We must first have an assurance, the female said. *Before traveling with a cursed one, we must be convinced that he can control himself and refrain from changing into a beast in our presence.* She looked toward Levitke, who lowered her head to study the ground.

Had Levitke relayed that she'd seen Vlerion change earlier that very day?

"I can control myself." Vlerion's words were firm, but he glanced at Kaylina, a hint of uncertainty in his eyes.

The female watched their exchange, her silver eyes more knowing than Kaylina would have liked.

"I'll help you." She smiled at Vlerion. "I know how much my rendition of 'Lake of Sorrow and Triumph' calms you."

"The rendition where you can't remember the lyrics?" he murmured.

"It's not my fault I dozed off while you sang them. I've hardly gotten any sleep lately."

There will be a test, the female said, interrupting them.

She looked toward the group of young taybarri and must have given a command because a perky male loped into a tunnel.

"How will you test my control?" Vlerion asked warily.

In a way that will allow us to escape if need be. If you become a beast, we will not help you, and we will not be here when you return to your human form.

Kaylina watched with concern as the young taybarri reemerged carrying something wrapped in hide. The thought that this long journey might end up being for nothing distressed her. Worse, they could have been back in the city, helping out. The war might already have erupted, with Kar'ruk killing people left and right. Frayvar and the rangers would be in danger.

"I hope this is worth it," Vlerion murmured, his eyes equally concerned.

The taybarri set the hide-wrapped item on a rock.

You may sit there, the female told them. *Do you have rope?*

Kaylina shook her head.

Vlerion nodded. "Yes, why?"

Before we begin, we will tie you to a boulder and to each other so that if you change, we will have time to escape.

"If I *change*, rope won't stop me from attacking anyone nearby."

You will attack the closest being while we leave the valley. The female looked at Kaylina.

"Oh, great. I get to be sacrificed."

Perhaps this will be a test not only for him, the elder said, holding Kaylina's gaze, *but for you.*

32

Students know far in advance which tests will challenge them most.

~ Lady Professora Nila of Yarrowvast, Port Jirador University

For beings without thumbs, the taybarri had no trouble tying Vlerion and Kaylina to a boulder and sitting them close enough to touch each other. Close enough for Vlerion to kill her...

Admittedly, they'd allowed it. Being the noble ranger he was, Vlerion had even helped with the knots. Kaylina hoped that meant he *was* confident that he could resist changing into the beast during whatever this test entailed. She would have felt better about it if he hadn't worn that concerned look when it had first been proposed.

"Are you nervous?" Vlerion must have noticed her expression —or the way she was rubbing her wrist, tempted to dig at the knots to loosen them in case she needed to flee.

Kaylina lowered her hand and looked toward the young male

taybarri using his fangs to gently unwrap the hide-covered whatever. "No."

Vlerion's eyebrows rose. "Are you lying to me?"

"Certainly not, my lord. Mead makers are known to be honest, trustworthy, and stalwart individuals."

"Including Jana Bloomlong?"

"*Southern* mead makers are honest and trustworthy. My grandma never lies. Even if you wish she would. She's blunt and says what's on her mind."

Strange that recalling negative attributes of family members could make Kaylina homesick. She caught herself envying Levitke because she'd been able to visit with her kin. Maybe the homesickness was due to predicament after predicament that Kaylina kept landing herself in. All the danger and chaos made her long for the world she'd found oppressive not two months earlier. Now, she would have basked in the mundanity and predictability of life at the Spitting Gull.

Except, if she hadn't come north, she wouldn't have met Vlerion. And he, even if magic drew him to her and vice versa, was someone she enjoyed knowing. He truly had become her protector. And he didn't even think she should be more normal.

"I am nervous, Vlerion, but as much because of *my* behavior when we're together." Kaylina waved her fingers between them, making vague circles in the air. He knew.

Vlerion eyed the taybarri watching them, the blue-furred youths as well as the elders. "I am hoping this test will involve keeping my equanimity in battle or under physical duress. I'm practiced at that."

Kaylina bit her lip. The way the female elder had looked back and forth between them made her believe she knew exactly what was likely to cause Vlerion to lose his calm and change. Kaylina didn't know how the taybarri would test that, but she worried it wouldn't be pleasant. For either of them.

"I'm also not inclined toward libidinous moods with forty taybarri watching," Vlerion murmured.

"No? You didn't mind when the rangers were watching."

"I minded it."

"But you were tempted to continue anyway."

Vlerion's lips pressed together, but he didn't deny it, other than to mutter, "I think you would have let me."

"Yeah. That's the problem." Kaylina smiled sadly at him.

Vlerion clasped her hand across the boulder. He mustered a reassuring look for her while glowering defiantly at the taybarri.

The test is ready to begin. You will each consume four wazistar berries. The female elder pointed her snout at the flat rock.

After unwrapping the hide, the male taybarri had stepped back to join the others. He'd revealed a few bunches of shriveled berries smaller than but reminiscent of cherries. Desiccated cherries on the verge of turning to dust.

"Are you sure it's safe to eat those?" Kaylina asked. "They look… past their prime."

They are dried to enhance their hallucinogenic potency. You will suffer no harm from consuming them. They are from altered plants harvested by the sandsteaders, and you will find that, in addition to giving vivid dreams, they allow one to see more than human eyes can normally see. A wider spectrum of light. I am uncertain as to this, but you may also find that they, for the time you are influenced by them, will allow you to see through the magic of the altered lithop powder to the Kar'ruk beneath.

Vlerion's eyes sharpened. He removed four for himself and chewed them down. "Do you have more? If there's a remote possibility that these will help us in battle with their kind, I would like to give them to the rest of the rangers."

Let us first see if you pass the test. I'll admit, it was contemplating the lithop and how it might be combatted that prompted me to remember that these exist in our cave of alchemy and herbalism.

"Meaning we brought this test upon ourselves?" Kaylina asked.

The means of enacting it, yes. The female gazed at her. *You must both swallow the berries, then grip each other's hands.*

Kaylina wasn't as quick as Vlerion to snatch up the dried berries, but she doubted the taybarri wanted to kill her, so she gingerly placed them in her mouth. They tasted like chalk more than anything else. She wished she had a cool goblet of cyser to wash the powdery gunk down.

Though she couldn't guess why they needed to hold hands, especially when they were already tied to the same boulder, Kaylina threaded her fingers between Vlerion's. As she waited for the berries to take effect, she did her best not to notice the strength in his callused grip, the strong line of his jaw, and the corded muscles of his arms and shoulders. She *did* let herself admit she took comfort in having him close. Even if, in this case, she shouldn't have.

The female turned her backside toward them and laid the tip of her tail across their clasped hands.

Considering her concerns about Vlerion, her choice to be that close was surprising, but was it possible she could affect their hallucinations that way? With some taybarri magic?

While Kaylina contemplated asking, the lighting shifted, growing brighter. No, that wasn't quite it. It grew more *colorful.*

Where before, Kaylina had interpreted sunlight and shade as little more than bright or dark, she now saw gradations. Pinks, purples, blues, and reds. She was so intent on noticing them that she didn't realize her surroundings were changing. At least, her eyes believed they were.

The valley and the taybarri disappeared, leaving her standing beside a sandy white beach lining a sparkling lake. At the end of the beach, muddy shallows supported reeds and lily pads, their greens so vibrant it almost hurt to look at them. The scenery reminded her of the lake in the preserve—the one that had inspired Vlerion's brother's painting. Thankfully, no druid ruins stood in sight. She'd had enough of those.

A warm breeze whispered past, teasing her bare skin.

Kaylina blinked as she looked down at her *very* bare skin. Her only coverings were snips of white fur that were more for decoration than privacy. They curled around her breasts without hiding their swell or her nipples and dangled to her pubic area.

"What in all the altered orchards is this?"

When she looked around, she expected to see taybarri, but she couldn't remember why she expected that. Her thoughts had grown muzzy, and she couldn't recall where she was or how she'd come to the lake.

Shadows stirred among aspen trees that rose beyond the beach. A naked male human walked into view, the dappled sunlight slipping between the leaves to draw attention to his powerful muscles. *He* wasn't adorned with fur.

His head was almost shaven, auburn hair so short as to be bristly, and scars marred his cheek and drew down the corner of one eye. He shouldn't have been handsome, but Kaylina's body hummed with awareness at his approach.

Vlerion, came a whisper from the back of her mind. She knew him. And she knew she wanted to mate with him.

Mate? A strange word that she wouldn't use. It sounded like something for animals.

She wanted to have *sex* with him.

And from the heated way his gaze traveled over her body, she believed Vlerion wanted to be with her too. His muscles rippling in the sunlight, he strode straight toward her. Lust sparked in his blue eyes.

Wait, there was something besides the lust… something dangerous.

Then she remembered. If Vlerion lost control of his emotions, he would turn into a beast. A deadly beast that could kill her.

Despite the danger, she stood naked before him, decorated in tufts of fur that drew the eye—drew *his* eye—to her female anatomy.

"We can't do this, Vlerion." Kaylina backed down the beach.

The vague memory that someone was controlling the situation came to her. This was a *test*. One they dared not fail. Because if he became a beast in this vision, he might become a beast in reality too. And he would kill her.

"I will have you," Vlerion growled, his gaze roaming her body, lingering on her breasts but also on her hand.

A plant-shaped brand glowed from her skin. Kaylina stared. It had never done that before, not that she'd seen, but a distinct green light emanated from the mark. More, a barely visible glowing tendril stretched from the back of her hand through the air to Vlerion. It ended at his chest and, like a fishing hook on a line, drew him toward her.

"In general, I'd be agreeable to that," Kaylina said, "but not now."

She kept backing up, but Vlerion was gaining on her. Her heel came down on softer ground. She'd reached the end of the beach, and the reeds and mud threatened to bog her down if she continued. Meanwhile, Vlerion prowled closer, like a panther about to spring on his prey.

"We're being manipulated." Kaylina lifted her hands. "Don't you remember? It's a test. The taybarri are testing us. They're testing *you*."

She might be a part of it, but this was about Vlerion. They were using her to test him, to try to make him fail. That irritated her, but she didn't know how to stop it.

Vlerion's brow furrowed, as if she'd reminded him of something, but he couldn't quite remember.

"You'll turn into the beast, and the taybarri won't help us. They'll run away, and you'll have only me, and you might kill me."

"I will not kill you, but I *will* have you," he growled, coming ever closer, his hard body as dangerous as it was appealing.

She couldn't look away. He was mesmerizing, and if he kissed her, if he touched her in any way, she would forget herself and give in to his desire. *Their* desire. Even now, his savage lustful gaze made her body heat and tighten with longing, with the certainty that he would give her greater pleasure than she'd ever known.

"No." Kaylina wrenched her gaze from him, glimpsing her brand again, the tendril drawing Vlerion closer. Was that always there, but this was the only time she'd been able to see it?

Less than five paces away, Vlerion crouched, poised to spring, to take her to the beach under him.

Even as her body reveled at the idea, excitement making her long to rush to meet him, she spun toward the mud. She snatched some up and slathered it over the back of her hand.

At first, her only thought was that if she covered up the brand, the glow might stop, the magical *pull* it had on him would go away. Then it occurred to her that he might not find her as sexy if she were entirely covered in mud.

She waded into it, the cool stuff sucking at her feet, and used both arms to grab handfuls. She slathered it over her breasts and thighs while flinging off the fur decorations. Lastly, she rubbed it in her hair.

Vlerion, still poised to spring, watched. That furrow had returned to his brow.

She smeared more onto her hand, wishing she could rip the brand off. At least she no longer saw the glow or the tendril of power drifting from it.

Wary of his reaction, Kaylina looked into Vlerion's eyes.

"Are you trying to... cover up your allure?" he asked.

The savage glint in his eyes had faded. He seemed more like himself.

"Among other things, yes." She put her hand behind her back.

Then, spotting a few reeds, she snatched them up and thrust them into her muddy hair like bug antennae.

Vlerion smiled, amusement replacing the lust. His taut body suggested it hadn't disappeared entirely, but maybe, with the brand covered, he wasn't so enamored with her—with the druid magic.

His gaze drifted to the reed antennae. "You're a unique soul, Kaylina Korbian."

"Yes, I am."

"And you keep trying to help me." His gaze shifted to her face, a fondness in his eyes that warmed her in a different way than thoughts of being intimate with him.

"I like you, pirate."

He snorted.

"I'm also tied to a boulder with you back in the real world."

"So you've slathered yourself with mud and reeds merely for self-protection purposes."

"Naturally. And because it feels good. I think it's healthy for your skin." She grabbed another handful and held it out to him. "Care to try?"

Only when his gaze narrowed and drifted lower again did she realize inviting him closer wasn't a good idea.

But he took a deep breath and turned his back on her, pointedly looking toward the trees. "For your future edification, slathering your naked body in mud doesn't make it as unappealing as you might think."

"Really?"

"It makes me want to come over there and clean it off." He made rubbing and cupping motions with his hands.

That prompted her to imagine his strong fingers caressing her breasts, and a fresh flush of heat surged into her. She made herself quash it. There was no way *she* would be the one to ruin this for him.

"What about the reeds?" she asked. "You can't find *those* sexy."

"No, they're silly."

"Perfect. And flinging away the tufts of fur had to be the right decision too."

"Most certainly." Vlerion waved toward the trees. "Do you know how we escape this... hallucination?"

Was that truly what it was? Or did the female taybarri have the power to control what they saw? Maybe the elders had more than the flash magic their kind were known for.

"I think we..." Kaylina trailed off because the world shifted, and she could once again see the valley and the observing taybarri. *Some* were observing. The elders. All of the blue-furred youths must have grown bored, because Levitke was the only one who remained, watching with concern.

Kaylina and Vlerion were still holding hands, though the elder had removed her tail and stepped away. Kaylina looked at Vlerion's face, wondering if he'd come out of the hallucination too.

He nodded at her, then smiled slightly. Thinking of reed antennae?

You have passed the test, the female taybarri said.

33

The attack you've prepared to defend against is never the main assault.

~ Lord General Avingatar

On the journey back through the mountains, Kaylina rode Levitke as numerous blue-furred and silver-furred taybarri loped beside and behind them. Surprisingly, the female who'd spoken the most to them—who'd *tested* them—was allowing Vlerion to ride her.

They'd traveled through the night, the taybarri fortunately more rested than Kaylina, and were heading toward the highway as dawn neared, the sky clear. Occasionally, through gaps in the trees, they glimpsed the Strait of Torn Towers in the distance. More than once, they also glimpsed smoke, far more than would have come from fireplaces.

"Do we have a plan for when we reach the city?" Kaylina asked Vlerion. About two dozen taybarri accompanied them, but she didn't know if that would be enough to turn the tides if a full-scale invasion had come to Port Jirador. Though the elders weren't having any trouble keeping up on the journey, they'd said they were past their fighting days. "In case those thousands of Kar'ruk warriors I saw in the vision are already there?"

"You said that horde entered through the valley with the small encampment, right?"

When she'd explained her visions, Vlerion hadn't shown skepticism about whether they would come to pass. He now believed she had the power of the druids in her veins and could access the various magics of altered plants. Kaylina almost wished he *would* doubt the visions. He'd taken that one about the castle wanting him dead too close to heart for her preferences.

"Yes. And the females slathered them with the altered lithop powder to turn them invisible. I'm hoping that what you destroyed will force them to alter their plans, but I wouldn't assume they'd turn around and go home."

"Destroyed?"

"You—the beast—dumped out their vat of invisibility powder."

Vlerion cocked his head.

"You don't remember that?"

"As I've told you—" Vlerion glanced at the surrounding taybarri and lowered his voice, even though they all knew his secret, "—what happens when I'm in that form… is vague to me later. Patchy and fuzzy like a dream."

"Well, the beast had the wherewithal to not only use their powder on himself but to dump their big container of it in a pond."

"Huh."

"The beast is kind of clever."

Vlerion eyed her at this assessment, maybe offended that she'd never called *him* clever. But all he said was, "Let us hope that was a substantial portion of their stash. The diplomatic party wouldn't have been searched, and they may have carried more into the city. It's likely they did."

"Yeah."

"When the army sees the bodies in the valley, they will know they've lost their advantage. They will suspect their plans have been reported to the rangers and the king."

"So they *will* go home?"

"Or they'll try something else." As they crested a ridge providing a view of the farms and estates north of the city, Vlerion pointed toward smoke hanging in the valleys between some of them.

"Someone is setting a lot of fires."

"Yes." His gaze shifted farther north. Toward Havartaft Estate? He had to be wondering if his mother was all right. "Our vineyards and farmlands wouldn't be as crucial for them to claim—or destroy—as the port, the bridges over the river, and the city itself, but the king would send—may already *have* sent—rangers out to defend them."

"Leaving fewer people to defend the city?" Kaylina asked.

"And stop whatever the diplomatic party is really up to, yes."

"Was there any trouble happening yet when you left?"

"No. Let's hope we'll arrive in time to help." Vlerion looked toward the smoke again before the herd descended from the ridge. "The taybarri gave me these to bring." He dipped into a pouch and held up some of the dried berries they'd eaten.

Kaylina curled a lip at the memory of their test.

"You'll recall Seerathi said they may allow one to see those painted with the altered lithop." Vlerion pointed to the back of the female taybarri's head. Was that her name? Seerathi? She hadn't given it to Kaylina. "There aren't many berries," he continued, "but if I can find Targon and get some to the rangers and the best warriors among the Kingdom and Castle Guards, it may help."

"As long as it doesn't make all those expert blade-wielders run around the city, slashing their swords at hallucinations."

"If they have hallucinations similar to the ones *we* had," Vlerion said, "I doubt they'll be *slashing* with their swords. Thrusting, perhaps."

Kaylina wrinkled her nose at his joke. "Nobody wants to see that either, and the Kar'ruk would laugh."

"I assume that *our* hallucination was manipulated by the taybarri." Vlerion waved toward Seerathi again.

We will speak with the diplomatic party and your monarch, she told them without commenting on the rest. With luck, the joke about thrusting swords hadn't registered to her.

"Will that stop the invasion?" Kaylina asked.

We will see. The female glanced at her. *If the threat is eliminated, young Levitke has promised you will serve us a food called honey drops.*

Levitke must have heard the telepathic comment because her gait developed a sashay, and she swished her tail, looking pleased with herself.

"It's not *my* castle, despite the lease, but, yes, I would be happy to make those for you."

"The *real* reason they're helping us." Vlerion smiled at her. "Seerathi must have enjoyed the honey you gave her." He patted the female's shoulder.

The elder didn't sashay, but her tail *might* have swished a few times. Her tongue definitely slipped out to lick her blue lips.

Maybe the druid honey *was* the reason the taybarri had been swayed to help. Kaylina vowed to collect more once the preserve wasn't full of Kar'ruk—and the Kingdom Guard wasn't hunting her.

As the sun crept over the mountains, the tireless taybarri loped along the highway, reaching the watchtower where the ranger had been killed. The dead crag cougars remained, disturbed only by carrion birds, but the Kar'ruk body was gone. Maybe his people had taken it, intending to bury it in the catacombs if they retook them.

"Not going to happen," Kaylina whispered.

The highway descended into the foothills where tree cover was sparser, and they could see Port Jirador for the first time. Even more fires burned within its walls than across the countryside.

In Kaylina's vision, the Kar'ruk had razed the entire city. It didn't look like that had happened yet, but a number of buildings burned, the flames high enough to view over the walls. Billowing smoke hazed the harbor and the royal castle on its plateau, making it hard to see how much had been destroyed.

They couldn't hear the booms of cannons or cracks of firearms, and Kaylina shifted on Levitke's back, worrying they might have arrived too late. What if everyone inside was already dead?

Vlerion leaned forward, as if he might urge the taybarri to run faster, but they'd already traveled all night. The taybarri probably needed a rest, not to sprint the last few miles into a battle.

Even so, they didn't suggest slowing down. Some even roared as they passed the preserve and followed the river toward the gates. They roared *several* times.

At first, Kaylina assumed they were battle cries. Then an uncertain answering roar came from the city, one of the ranger mounts. She realized the taybarri were communicating with each other. A few more roars came from different parts of the city.

"At least somebody is still alive." Vlerion chewed on a couple of the berries, then leaned close enough to hand a few to Kaylina. "Your sling work will be more accurate if you can see your targets."

"I've heard that does help." She made herself chomp down the chalky berries, honored that he'd given her some after he'd spoken of distributing the few handfuls he had to the best rangers and warriors.

The gates to the city stood open—had been *forced* open—with bodies around them, mostly gray-uniformed guards. A Kar'ruk lay among the dead. Had an order from his superiors prompted him to give his life to ensure the gates were open when the Kar'ruk army arrived?

Kaylina looked around for signs of that army as the taybarri took them into Port Jirador, the hazy air pungent from the smoke.

The city was quiet, save for the snapping and cracking of wood in fires. Along the streets, doors to buildings were shut, windows shuttered. Here and there, more bodies lay on the blood-spattered cobblestones, some human, some Kar'ruk. There weren't as many dead as Kaylina would have expected if an entire army had arrived, but there were enough to be distressing. Even *one* would have been distressing.

"I haven't seen any rangers yet," Vlerion said so softly she barely heard him.

Hand on the hilt of his sword, he gazed around the city, his eyes probing the smokey alleys and doorways.

"They might all be in the castle. If they believed they'd have to defend the king and queen, it might make sense." When she said the word *queen,* Kaylina remembered that she was a wanted woman. They hadn't yet seen any living guards, and maybe people would be too distracted to remember, but she hoped she hadn't made a mistake in coming through the gate with Vlerion. Glad she still had her cloak, she tugged the hood over her head. "Where would the diplomatic party have been housed?"

"The last I heard, they were being taken to the royal castle. That's customary."

Kaylina groaned. The Virts had been after the king and queen. If the Kar'ruk were working with them, part of the deal might be that they help get rid of the monarchs.

"We're heading there," Vlerion said.

A window shutter creaked, the sound startling in the stillness, the taybarri paws much quieter on the cobblestones than horse hooves. It opened a few inches, and a woman with a sooty face peered out. She didn't call out to them; she just watched them.

The herd of taybarri passing through with only a couple of riders had to look peculiar. A few other doors opened partway, people inside also watching.

At least everyone hadn't been killed. Kaylina thought Vlerion might pause to question someone, but the taybarri didn't slow down, and she didn't know if he could have stopped the herd if he wanted. They loped over a bridge spanning a canal, then down the boulevard that passed Stillguard Castle.

From blocks away, the purple glow from its tower was visible, even in daylight. Kaylina didn't expect to spot many bodies near the castle. After all, even during normal days, it didn't get many visitors. To her surprise, numerous armored Kar'ruk lay dead in the street outside the courtyard wall.

One Kar'ruk wasn't quite dead and lifted his head at the sound of taybarri claws clacking on the cobblestones.

A purple beam shot out of the tower window, startling Kaylina. It burned into the head of the Kar'ruk, causing a final jerk and groan before he slumped down. Fully dead?

Kaylina swallowed as Vlerion's gaze shifted toward the tower.

"I… didn't think the plant could do that. Or had the *power* to kill that way." She'd assumed the vines were its only method of attacking and that someone had to be on the castle grounds for them to reach.

"Maybe you've *given* it that power," Vlerion said.

"The honey water is supposed to be a fertilizer, but it doesn't have *that* many nutrients."

Besides, what kind of nutrients could make a plant capable of shooting deadly beams?

The druids were an extremely powerful people, Seerathi spoke into their minds. *The sentinel protects its grounds from enemies.*

"No kidding," Kaylina murmured, recognizing the word the plant had used for itself.

The taybarri passed on the far side of the street from the castle, maybe worried that they too would be targeted. Hopefully not with Kaylina riding among them. After all, the plant had marked her and wanted her alive.

When she glanced at her hand, she thought she glimpsed the brand glowing green, as it had in the vision, but when she blinked, the glow was gone. Maybe it had been her imagination.

The first sounds of battle drifted to their ears. They came from the plateau and the royal castle.

Seerathi roared in that direction as the herd crossed a final bridge. *Young taybarri are up there.*

"Rangers should be up there too," Vlerion said. "Defending the king and queen."

None opposed them as the herd traveled up the road to the plateau. At the top, the portcullis at the gate was not only down but blocked on the far side. By furniture? Crates? Doors? Maybe all. The jumble of wood denied view of the courtyard on the other side.

Outside the walls, uniformed guards crouched behind shields and hastily erected barricades. Using bows and crossbows, they fired at the top of the crenellated walls. The rangers and their taybarri had to be in the courtyard or the castle, but why wouldn't they unblock the gate to let help in?

Kaylina didn't see anyone on the walls and wondered what the men were shooting at.

Two guards with ropes ran forward, swinging grappling hooks upward to catch them on crenelations. As the men started climbing, swords belted at their waists bumping against the stone wall, the archers covered them, shooting arrows through the empty air above.

It was a confusing sight until two horned Kar'ruk heads poked into view, their outlines blurry and wavering but visible. At least to Kaylina. The archers, she realized, couldn't see them and were guessing where their enemies might appear.

Shields toward the archers and axes raised, the Kar'ruk advanced on the climbers.

"Look out!" Vlerion barked.

One Kar'ruk lifted an axe to cut a rope. The other raised a ranged weapon that looked like a mix of a blunderbuss and a crossbow. Both wore the hide tabards of the diplomatic party.

"Some diplomats." Sling already loaded, Kaylina took aim.

The Kar'ruk with the axe succeeded in cutting the rope as the climbers glanced back at Vlerion's warning. The blade sliced through, and one man fell.

Kaylina's round struck the other Kar'ruk in the hand before he shot his firearm, and he jerked back. Unfortunately, he didn't drop the weapon. Scowling, he swung it toward Kaylina.

She hurried to load another round. But Vlerion had a knife, and he hurled it at the Kar'ruk. Thanks to the berries, he could also see the foe, and he struck with accuracy, the blade landing in the invader's throat. The ranged weapon fell from the Kar'ruk's grip a moment before he tumbled off the wall. He hit the ground next to the climber, who'd managed to land on his feet. The man cursed and leaped back, probably close enough now to see through the camouflaging powder.

"Thank you," Kaylina said to Vlerion, shifting her aim to the remaining Kar'ruk on the wall.

The invader was ready this time and ducked. Her round whistled past his horn, disappearing into the courtyard.

"Cover me," Vlerion told her.

"Okay." Later, Kaylina would remind him that she didn't love taking orders from people, but this wasn't the time.

Vlerion leaped from the taybarri's back and sprinted toward

the remaining rope dangling from its hook. The climber had jumped down when his comrade fell.

After a glance back at Kaylina, Vlerion skimmed up the rope. The remaining axe-wielder sprang into view again, ready to cut it.

Kaylina hurled a round. Behind the barricade, the archers also loosed arrows. Even though they couldn't see the warrior, they could guess where he was. Not only the sling round but two arrows caught the Kar'ruk in the chest. Under the assault, he staggered, but he clenched his jaw with determination and swung downward with the axe.

Kaylina swore as it cut through the rope, but Vlerion lunged, catching the wall before it gave way. As he pulled himself up, the wounded Kar'ruk hefted his blade to aim for his head. Kaylina loosed another round. It caught the warrior in the ear, making him hesitate for a split second.

That was all Vlerion needed. He rolled onto the wall, springing to his feet with his sword in hand.

The cracks of firearms rang out from inside the courtyard. Since the rangers usually stuck to swords and bows, Kaylina worried those weapons belonged to more enemies, enemies who might be aiming at Vlerion as he faced off against the Kar'ruk on the wall.

"We need to get inside," Kaylina called to the taybarri, the guards, or anyone who would listen.

"We've been *trying*," one of the guards growled. "They blocked the gate before we knew there was trouble inside, and they keep shooting down our climbers."

"Where are the rangers?"

"Some were inside when this all started, but most got called out to the countryside. The Gavatorin estate was attacked and started burning in the middle of the night, and King Gavatorin ordered a bunch of men out to defend it, even though Captain Targon objected. *Everyone* objected."

"We all saw this coming," another guard growled. "As soon as those phony diplomats arrived."

Clangs rang out on the wall, axe and sword meeting as Vlerion battled the Kar'ruk.

Kaylina lifted her sling in case she got an opportunity to help, but Levitke startled her by surging toward the portcullis. Kaylina grasped a handful of fur to keep from losing her balance. Around her, other taybarri also rushed for the gate, some roaring a battle cry.

But with the sturdy portcullis closed, the only way inside was by climbing the high wall. Or so Kaylina thought. Several of the taybarri wrapped their jaws around the iron bars. Muscles flexed under Kaylina as Levitke pulled. They *all* pulled.

Iron wrenched and whined.

"Keep them covered!" an archer shouted, the men again loosing arrows.

More blades clanged in the courtyard. Vlerion must have jumped down—and found more enemies.

The iron bars didn't bend under the taybarri assault, but stone and mortar gave. Wood and chains snapped, and the taybarri backed up, pulling the now-detached portcullis with them.

More taybarri surged past Levitke, battering at the obstacles that had been pushed in front of the portcullis to hide the courtyard from view. They made short work of them, butting with their heads and shoulders to shove crates and furniture aside.

As soon as the way was clear, Levitke flashed to get past her fellow taybarri and into the courtyard first. The lurch surprised Kaylina, but she still had a grip on Levitke's fur.

They appeared in the open courtyard amid numerous castle guards lying on the ground. Dead, Kaylina assumed at first, but one lifted his head, eyes bleary, as if he couldn't keep them open. Were these people... asleep?

Shards of ceramic and glass littered the courtyard. Someone

had thrown containers around. Containers filled with a concoction that could knock people unconscious?

On the far side of the courtyard, double doors stood open, one ripped half off its hinges.

Kaylina had been that way before and knew it led toward the royal quarters and other important areas of the castle. Bangs, clanks, and clangs rang out from within, promising fighting was going on inside. The rangers? A few taybarri roars came from the wide hall beyond the doors.

Silence fell in the courtyard as Vlerion finished off a Kar'ruk he'd been battling. There weren't as many invaders around the courtyard as Kaylina had expected. Only two, one that Vlerion had killed, and another that the taybarri had trampled.

As with the Kar'ruk on the wall, the ones inside wore hide tabards. The dead in the city had been protected by chainmail, like the Kar'ruk in the preserve. Maybe their duty, like their allies lighting fire to the countryside, had been to distract the guard and rangers while the diplomats attacked from within the castle.

Sword bloody, Vlerion nodded toward Kaylina, then ran for the open doors. Kaylina started after him, but he halted abruptly. Kaylina raised her sling.

Vlerion backed up instead of continuing inside. He kept his sword raised, squinting into the hallway at shadows that stirred.

Numerous blurry Kar'ruk in tabards, their forms hard to see, thanks to the silvery powder, walked out. Among them were the females who'd been riding in the litter.

They'd been disarmed, and the reason soon became clear as Captain Targon, Jankarr, and three other rangers strode out behind them, bows and swords pointed at the Kar'ruk backs. Five taybarri with their heads up and tails swishing also followed. They looked proud of themselves, like they'd been instrumental in capturing the Kar'ruk. Given how hard it was to see the camouflaged invaders, they probably had been. Unlike humans, they had other strong senses to rely upon.

"You're late, Vlerion," Targon snapped when their gazes met.

With a gash on his forehead dripping blood into his eyes, the captain looked crabbier than ever. *Many* of the rangers had wounds.

"We were collecting allies and, with luck, deterring an army," Vlerion said.

"*Another* one?" Targon waved toward the walls, maybe indicating the estates besieged outside of the city.

"They're proliferating this spring."

Kaylina didn't know for certain that they'd deterred the army she'd only seen in her vision, but she did suspect that if that many Kar'ruk had shown up, the city would have been razed by now. The diplomatic party might have been expecting a lot more backup to arrive. Kaylina shuddered, glad it hadn't.

"This year is off to a dreadful start." Targon's sour expression turned toward Kaylina. "You learn how to be respectful yet, Korbian?"

Before Kaylina could decide on an answer, several beleaguered guards jogged out of a doorway, their bloodstained uniforms and begrimed weapons promising they'd also seen battle. One noticed Kaylina and jerked to a stop. He pointed at her and whispered to his comrades.

She tensed, afraid she would have to again flee the castle. Intense weariness weighed down on her at the thought of spending another week in the countryside, hiding from the authorities. She'd helped the kingdom. *Again*. Couldn't these people pardon her?

"Stand down, Sergeant," Vlerion said coolly, stepping close to Kaylina.

He'd also noticed the guards and their reaction to her.

"Lord Vlerion, that girl is—"

"An *ally* to the kingdom and a ranger in training."

The guard shook his head, but before he could say anything else, the elder taybarri female who'd been communicating with them all along padded into the center of the courtyard and lifted her head. *I am Queen Seerathi, representing the taybarri of the Northern Tribes, and I have come to speak to the rulers of the Zaldor Kingdom.* She looked toward the captured diplomatic party. *I will also address the representatives of the Kar'ruk Confederation.*

34

I prefer to face an enemy who attacks me with a blade; the enemy within is insidious and sneakier in his assault.
~ Ranger Founder Saruk

After the taybarri's announcement—the telepathic words apparently conveying to all present—the guards who'd been contemplating arresting Kaylina stood back to wait. A messenger ran into the castle. Vlerion remained at Kaylina's side, his sword in hand, his dangerous gaze promising dire consequences if anyone approached her.

Targon and the rangers had come over to stand beside Vlerion, but they'd sheathed their weapons. Targon stood with his arms folded over his chest.

After greeting their elders, the ranger taybarri had joined the herd, standing almost like bodyguards for their queen. Their queen who hadn't mentioned her rank at any point during their journey, at least not that Kaylina had heard. She couldn't tell if

Vlerion had been surprised. He was busy looming beside her and looking fierce.

Would King Gavatorin or Queen Petalira come in person to greet Seerathi? They'd allowed the Kar'ruk diplomatic party to stay in the castle, so there had to be some royal rules about receiving representatives from other nations and treating them cordially. Far *too* cordially, in the case of the Kar'ruk.

While they waited, Kaylina glanced often at the guards and wondered if she should try to slip away when they weren't looking.

"Should have saved some of that powder for me," she murmured.

"You will not be attacked while I and these rangers are present," Vlerion said, but his face was grim. He had to acknowledge that if the king or queen ordered the rangers to stand down and let Kaylina be taken, he would be bound by his oath to do so.

Targon tapped a pocket in his uniform, pulled out a folded paper, and handed it to one of his men. Kaylina couldn't hear what he said, but the ranger trotted through the double doors and into the castle.

Soon, upper doors opened, and guards stepped out onto a balcony overlooking the courtyard. They carried raised swords, but their stances appeared more ceremonial than battle-ready. However, their uniforms were rumpled and askew, so they clearly hadn't escaped the attack unscathed. By now, everyone in the castle looked frazzled.

Queen Petalira and King Gavatorin stepped out onto the balcony. Their hair was combed, their clothing straight, but they also looked rattled by the morning's events.

Nonetheless, Petalira's gaze skimmed alertly over the taybarri. Gavatorin's eyes were more confused as he peered down at them. He glanced at the rangers, then looked toward a man standing in the shadows near the guards keeping the Kar'ruk restrained.

Since Kaylina had only seen Spymaster Sabor through a crack in Targon's office, it took her a moment to recognize him. He nodded at the king, who nodded back while looking a touch relieved.

"One of his keepers," Vlerion murmured, "though I understand there are a number of people running things now that he's gone senile."

Kaylina started to answer, but the queen's gaze had shifted to the rangers, and she frowned when she spotted Kaylina near them. Her eyes narrowed.

"She hasn't forgotten you," Targon noted mildly.

"It's my perky personality," Kaylina said. "People remember it."

Targon glanced at her chest. "Perky something."

Vlerion glared at him, and was that the faintest growl?

"Easy, boy," Targon told him. "Your savage side is showing."

The taybarri queen started speaking telepathically, and that pulled Petalira's gaze back to the furred visitors.

After repeating her name and introducing the other taybarri elders, Seerathi said, *We have come at the request of Lord Vlerion and Kaylina Korbian. She came deep into the mountains to seek us out, requesting that we help Zaldor in this fraught time.*

"Vlerion and who?" The king looked blearily around.

Kaylina resisted the urge to shrink back or hide behind Vlerion. She hadn't expected the taybarri to mention her, certainly not by name.

Petalira frowned at her again. "Continue, please," she told Seerathi.

Usually, the elders, having grown less aggressive and muscled than our vigorous youth, do not involve themselves in the battles between men and men or men and the Kar'ruk, but, as an anrokk *with excellent honey, Korbian swayed us to listen to her plea.*

Petalira's lips pressed together as she probably thought about how Kaylina's excellent honey had been turned into poisoned mead.

Not by my hand, Kaylina wanted to shout, but she kept her mouth shut. Nobody had brought that up yet. The taybarri probably didn't even know about it.

We came, not to do battle, but to make sure the truth of history is known to all who are now fighting over the right to dwell upon this land.

"What truth of history?" Petalira asked.

The Kar'ruk female leader also asked something but in her own tongue.

Seerathi must have understood both languages, because she continued on without trouble. *As all are likely aware, the Daygarii traveled all through these mountains and this coastal land, interacting with nature and leaving their magical mark on the flora. They also left a few traps and warnings. They did not, however, ever claim ownership of these lands. They commanded only that the handful of preserves they left behind be undisturbed by hunters so that the animals and plants living within could thrive.*

What is less known is that our people once lived in this area. When our numbers were greater, we even claimed this land. What you now call Frost Harbor was a favorite fishing place of ours. We burrowed many tunnels on either side of what you call the Stillguard River. It was, to our people, the Salmon Spawning Pathway—Erestu.

Covetous of the salmon and the easier hunting south and west of the mountains, the Kar'ruk desired this area for themselves. They attacked our people in a season when we were weakened from a disease that plagued our kind. They took advantage, driving us to the south, and they invaded not only the land above but the tunnels where we'd once raised our cubs. That is where they built their catacombs, bricking in what was dirt but which our people had nonetheless created and used for millennia. They occupied these lands until the human gold mining started, and many Zaldorians came to this place and eventually drove out the Kar'ruk. As you recall, our kind aided humans in this endeavor, also desiring to see the Kar'ruk pushed back. Seerathi gazed over at the diplomatic party. *We have heard that the Kar'ruk are attempting to claim a right to the catacombs and the land above them, but this all belonged to our kind before theirs. If we are allowing that claims may be made based on prior occupation, then our claim precedes theirs. They have no right to the mouth of the Stillguard River nor the valleys to the north and south.*

One of the Kar'ruk females said something belligerent. Surprisingly, the other female at her side grimaced and whispered something to her. Did she know the truth of the matter?

Should you venture deeply into the Kar'ruk catacombs and dig, you would find the bones of our ancestors, for we once also used the passageways near the river for burial.

One of the females prodded a male Kar'ruk, the one who spoke Zaldorian. "We believe these statements are made in error, but we will return to our lands to consult with our chiefs and religious leaders on this matter."

Vlerion snorted. "After their invasion attempt, they ought to be put to death. Had we done the same to them, our *diplomatic* party would already be dead."

That might have been true, but the spymaster nodded to the king again, and Gavatorin spoke.

"We will allow the Kar'ruk diplomatic party to return to their lands. Those who have fallen here… their bodies may be taken for your funeral rituals if you wish, and the wounded will be returned to you. Our lenience is only because…" He'd spoken firmly to start with but trailed off, uncertainty wrinkling his brow.

The queen looked at her husband, but maybe she didn't know the answer either. It was an aide who leaned closer to the king's back and mouthed what looked like, "Virts," to him.

"Our lenience," Gavatorin repeated, "is only because we

believe your plot was at least partially instigated by a human element who made promises to lure you here. They are a power-hungry and conniving group who seek to overthrow the throne, and they will be punished for their traitorous ways. Should the Kar'ruk step into our lands again, they will be ruthlessly slain by our mighty rangers." The king looked toward Targon and seemed to include Vlerion in the nod he gave.

Kaylina hoped that no suspicion clung to them, that the crown hadn't taken any stock in the newspapers the Virts had been printing. The king, she recalled, had already known Vlerion's secret.

The Kar'ruk grumbled to themselves, then gathered their dead and headed for the gates. The tight-jawed guards there, many of whom had suffered injuries, didn't step aside immediately.

Only when the king said, "Let them pass," did the glowering men move to do so.

At a finger twitch from the spymaster, numerous guards joined the group, making it clear they would escort the Kar'ruk out of the city—if not out of the kingdom entirely.

As the last of the party passed through the gates, Petalira's gaze shifted back to the taybarri and rangers, settling on Vlerion and Kaylina. Her eyes were cool.

Kaylina tensed, afraid Petalira was about to sic the guards on her. Why had Kaylina so foolishly followed the rangers and taybarri into the castle? It wasn't as if the handful of lead rounds she'd flung had swayed the battle. Nor had she ever believed anything she could do would. Not here, anyway. If she'd been at Stillguard Castle with the plant, she might have convinced it to help, but she doubted it could, even invigorated with honey water, shoot its power across the city to take down foes.

The queen opened her mouth, but someone whispered something from the doorway of the balcony, and she turned before speaking. The ranger that Targon had given a folded paper to was up there, escorted by two guards. He bowed to the queen as he handed her the note and pointed at Targon.

Vlerion looked to his captain, eyebrows raised, but Targon merely folded his arms over his chest again and waited. The queen opened the paper and read whatever was inside.

"Not a love letter, I trust," Kaylina muttered.

Targon squinted at her and gave Vlerion one of his I'm-still-waiting-for-you-to-instill-reverence-in-her frowns.

Petalira lowered the paper and looked at Targon. "Explain, Captain."

"I understand it's a signed note from the one who sold Jana Bloomlong the poison that was used in a bottle of mead delivered to your castle and that the poison maker is willing to answer questions on the matter."

"You *understand*?" The queen's eyebrows twitched.

"My doctor and a young helper spoke with him and acquired the admission while I was busy with the Kar'ruk." Targon twitched a shoulder, as if he was indifferent on the matter.

Young helper? That had to be Frayvar. Would this change anything?

"Jana Bloomlong is a trusted kingdom subject of *decades*." Petalira frowned at Kaylina again. "Was this *young helper* the brother of that one?"

Targon shrugged again. "He was."

As Petalira continued to glower, Kaylina's hope that the note might help faded. Maybe Jana was close enough to the queen that Petalira didn't *want* to believe she'd been at the heart of the plot. Maybe no amount of evidence would change her mind.

As I have stated, Seerathi spoke into the silence, *it is because of the druid-blooded female that we came.*

Though surprised the taybarri queen was defending her when she could have no knowledge of the poisoning incident, Kaylina nodded firmly. Maybe Petalira would listen to another royal.

"Druid-blooded?" Petalira mouthed.

Kaylina didn't nod at that. She still had her doubts.

"Kaylina is not guilty of the crime of which she was accused, Your Majesties," Vlerion said, addressing the king as well, though Gavatorin was watching the last of the Kar'ruk departing and probably hadn't figured out who Kaylina was. "She has helped the crown on two different occasions now," Vlerion added.

Fortunately, Jana Bloomlong wasn't there to accuse him of defending Kaylina because his penis told him to. Kaylina wondered where her mead-making nemesis was. She supposed it was too much to hope that her inn had burned to the ground and she would be forced to retire to the countryside. A far distant countryside.

I have seen into her mind and believe she desires this city and its people to thrive, Seerathi said.

Kaylina winced, hoping the taybarri wouldn't add *so there are customers who can drink her mead and make her famous,* or something like that. If Seerathi truly could read thoughts, she would know what motivated Kaylina. While Kaylina didn't wish any ill on the kingdom or its subjects, she probably wouldn't be risking her life if not for her dream. And Vlerion. He had become very important to her these past weeks.

"Can you also see in her mind if she poisoned mead that was delivered to the castle?" Petalira asked in a neutral tone, lifting the paper. "Or does she genuinely believe that someone else did it?"

The silver-furred head turned, wise eyes locking onto Kaylina.

Panic welled in her. She was innocent, but would her scattered thoughts confirm that sufficiently? Confirm that she hadn't had anything to do with the plot and that Jana had been responsible? That Kaylina would *never* poison anyone and certainly not through her craft?

She couldn't imagine anything more loathsome than deliberately defiling a beautiful batch of mead made from delicious and pure honey from bees who foraged on rare altered plants. What an affront. Jana should have stabbed her own eyes out before destroying mead of such high quality. Jana had even admitted to tasting it. She *knew* how good it had been.

Seerathi's head swung back toward Petalira. *She did not attempt to poison you. She is too devoted to her craft, perhaps egotistically so, to have considered her alcohol an acceptable receptacle for a poison.*

"Uhm." Kaylina wasn't sure *that* would sway anyone. Those weren't the thoughts she should have let cavort through her mind.

Next to her, Vlerion raised his eyebrows.

Kaylina could only shrug and whisper, "It's true. If I was going to poison someone, I'd use shitty wine with the bouquet of used socks."

"Such a *bouquet* would hide poison well," he murmured, amusement glinting in his eyes.

"I see." Queen Petalira didn't sound nearly as amused. After glancing at the note again and contemplatively considering Kaylina for a long moment—one which made Kaylina squirm—she said, "Since the evidence against her was only ever circumstantial, I will dismiss it as insufficient."

"Does that mean…" Kaylina looked to Vlerion.

"She's not going to have you arrested, girl." Targon slapped her on the back.

Kaylina was on the verge of feeling relieved until he spoke again.

"That means you can return to your ranger training."

"Oh, joy."

Vlerion looked at his boss. "She's ecstatic."

"And still irreverent. Oh, joy, *my lord*, and thank you for helping me."

"Yes," Kaylina said as reverently as she could. "Thank you, my lord."

Targon grunted. He was a hard man to please.

"The city will need time to recover, and people may not be dining out for a while," Petalira said, "but you may return to your mead-making business endeavor, Kaylina Korbian."

"Thank you, Your Majesty." Kaylina dipped her head low, then wondered if she was supposed to bow or curtsey or something else.

The gesture must have sufficed because Petalira didn't appear offended. She thanked the taybarri for coming, the king told them accommodations would be made for them, and they both departed from the balcony.

"At least she's not sarcastic with the royalty," Targon said.

"Not until they accuse her of crimes, no," Vlerion said. "She has common sense."

"*Commoner* sense. Unlike those idiots who plotted with the Kar'ruk. You don't get into bed with an enemy like that. The Kar'ruk would have killed the Virts as happily as anyone else. I'm surprised they talked one into perpetrating their so-called beast murders, but I suppose the Kar'ruk are always delighted to kill humans." Targon spat in disgust, called his rangers to him, and ordered them to help the guards check the rest of the castle and grounds for invisible enemies that might yet be lurking.

Vlerion lifted a hand to Kaylina, perhaps to offer a hug or pat of congratulations, but Targon called back, "That means you too, Vlerion. I want you to gather some rangers, get the watchtowers manned again, and make sure nobody is skulking around out there. Oh, and smash that damn press. That newspaper is officially going out of business."

"A ranger is always on duty," Vlerion murmured, then nodded at Kaylina. "I'll come see you later. When you're done making all the honey drops you promised the taybarri."

Kaylina looked toward the center of the courtyard and found Levitke, Crenoch, Seerathi, and the rest of the silver- and blue-furred faces turned toward her.

"Ah. Yes. A priority."

"I should think so." Vlerion squeezed her arm before striding away to assist his captain.

"I'd better find Frayvar to help stir the pot," Kaylina said.

Judging by all the taybarri that padded toward her, she would have an escort to do so.

EPILOGUE

THE GODS GIVE NO GIFTS WITHOUT EXPECTATIONS.
~ "Foundations III" Scribe Menalow

The taybarri waited in the courtyard of ranger headquarters while Kaylina looked for her brother. She glanced back a few times at the antics of the blue-furred youths showing the serene, almost sedate, elders around. More than a few watched her, however, and she knew she would have to make honey drops before getting any rest. Too bad. She felt like she could sleep for a week, if only the world would give her a chance.

She found Frayvar in Doctor Penderbrock's infirmary. It seemed to be his new home. It was even *more* organized than the last time she'd seen it. Someone had added shelves and cabinets above the cots, presumably to provide more room for medical supplies.

Since Frayvar had the carpentry skills of a hippopotamus, she assumed he'd drawn sketches and convinced someone else to do the building. Maybe a ranger apprentice? Given the chaos of the last few days, it was hard to believe someone would have had the time.

"Kay!" he blurted when she walked into the office in the back. "You're alive!"

"I am."

He rushed forward, and for a moment, she thought he might hug her. Instead, he thumped her on the shoulder. Acceptable touching, perhaps.

She resisted her own desire to envelop him in a crushing bear hug. Fortunately, other than greasy hair sticking out in all directions, chin stubble, and bags under his eyes, he appeared fine. Maybe the fighting hadn't made it past the walls of ranger headquarters.

"Based on the garbled reports that made it back, I... wasn't sure you'd make it." Frayvar looked her up and down. "The last we heard, the Kar'ruk kidnapped you."

"And drank my blood, yes. It was an unpleasant experience."

"Ew. That's not hygienic."

"I don't think good hygiene was their goal."

His nose wrinkled. "What *was* their goal?"

"Some kind of ritual in which my blood would... I'm not sure exactly, but some people seem convinced a druid hooked up with some ancestor of ours."

"Of *ours*?" Frayvar touched his chest. "The taybarri haven't been standing at my window looking in."

She started to wave dismissively, but a snuffling noise at the panes made her glance over. Two sets of blue-furred snouts were pressed against the glass, and one silver-furred head also gazed into the infirmary.

"I promised to make them honey drops. Or I might have been bribed to make them. I'm not sure."

"You're not the best negotiator."

"I know. You're the one with business acumen."

"Which makes it puzzling that you keep running off without me."

"Are you upset that I didn't take you along for the blood drinking?"

"No. Being here gave me time to assemble evidence to clear our names." Frayvar gestured toward a desk with two pieces of paper on it. One held a list of ingredients. The other had a sketch of a woman who looked vaguely like Jana Bloomlong. The cloak and hood around the face were accurate even if the rest was rough. "There's a note from the poison maker too. I gave it to Captain Targon. He said he could get it to the queen when there was time."

"He did. Thank you."

"Oh, good. I couldn't tell if he cared enough to follow through. I was lucky Doc Penderbrock was with me. For everything. He and a burly ranger came along when I questioned the paint maker who crafts poisons on the side. You may owe the ranger a kiss as payment, by the way. For scowling imposingly. The paint maker remembered a woman coming in to buy this substance a couple of weeks ago." Frayvar waved at the list of ingredients—a recipe? "He was able to draw her. He also described her in the note and stated how many milliliters she ordered of Special Blend Number Seventeen, as he called it. He wouldn't admit it was poison, but I got the doctor to analyze it, and he said it definitely is. Oh, and the paint maker had seen your portrait on a wanted poster and said that if you give *him* a kiss, he'll go with the authorities to point out Jana personally. Apparently, she was snotty to him, so he didn't feel bound by the dealer-client pact of secrecy that's common in the poison business."

Kaylina scratched her temple. "Why do all these people want me to kiss them?"

"Your allure. Also, I'm trying to conserve funds, so I didn't have a lot to bargain with."

"Except my lips."

"Precisely. Among males of a certain demographic, they're a desirable asset, I understand." He shrugged, as if he couldn't imagine it.

"I've heard that," she murmured. "I appreciate the work you did."

"I should hope so. The city has been in chaos. I barely managed to get out for this research. Most of the time, I had to stay in and organize while planning a couple of additions to our future dinner menu. I made a grocery list. You can help me shop." Frayvar opened a drawer and held his list of ingredients up, the writing much tidier than on the paint maker's.

"There are more items than there were before. Can't you remake what we were going to serve the night of the fire?"

"I can, but that menu was revealed already. I don't want people to think we lack creativity, so I've added a couple of entrées and changed up the accompaniments. I've also talked to local farmers at the early-season market about having fresh herbs and vegetables delivered as soon as they're harvested. I'm thinking of altering my lamb-fig dish to use local ingredients—maybe cherries? I wasn't impressed with the quality of the figs I was able to get. At this time of year, they have to be shipped all the way from the south."

Kaylina had thought the lamb dish delicious, but her brother was a perfectionist. "You were talking with the local farmers while the Kar'ruk were invading the city?"

"Before. There was a brief period of time during which the streets of Port Jirador weren't in utter chaos."

"Other than the garishly murdered bodies that kept appearing by the canals?"

"That wasn't utter chaos. It was a failure of the law-enforcement system, likely brought on by conditions causing understaffed personnel to be overworked."

"It was chaos to the people who were murdered, I'm sure."

The white-haired Doctor Penderbrock walked in, supporting a wounded ranger who gripped his ribs as he limped toward one of the cots. A few more men followed, some of their own volition, some being helped or carried.

Kaylina watched, amazed she'd survived the week with so few injuries. Luck had favored her.

A warm itching sensation came from the back of her hand. The brand.

Maybe it wasn't luck so much as the plant's magic keeping her alive. That would have been more reassuring if the niggling thought didn't keep coming to mind that the thing wanted to use her.

"I need to go check on our leased castle and make honey drops." Kaylina yawned, wondering if she might be able to curl up and finally get some sleep there. Though she'd dozed on the way back on Levitke, it was hard to relax fully when the threat of falling off one's mount was a constant.

"I heard it was, uhm, active in the defense of the city."

"It shot a beam from the tower window and slew Kar'ruk." Kaylina hoped it hadn't killed humans as well. Potential customers might cheer for a cursed castle that slew enemies of the city, but one that zapped kingdom subjects was another story. No matter how enticing the mead and Frayvar's recipes, they wouldn't get anyone through the courtyard gates.

"I believe that fits the definition of *active*."

"As a dictionary reader, you would know."

"Aggressively active. I'd better go with you."

"To have my back in a battle against hostile vines?"

"To run for the doctor if the plant knocks you out again." Frayvar waved toward Penderbrock, who, despite the patients needing care, was walking toward them.

Maybe he thought Kaylina had come because of injuries. He did look her up and down, his gaze lingering on her hand. But he'd already seen *that* injury. Nothing had changed about it, unless its ability to glow in visions counted.

"How's that doing?" Penderbrock pointed at it.

"Weirdly."

He grunted. "About what I expected. I researched a bit on your behalf. Before the Kar'ruk came and gave us something else to worry about."

"Oh?"

"Are there books on the Daygarii that cover magic beyond altered plants? I didn't think to check the library on that matter." The aggrieved look that Frayvar sent Kaylina's way suggested he considered this a deep failing on his part.

"You were busy trying to clear my name," she said.

"Keeping you from being arrested *is* a demanding job, but I should have thought to gather all the history books covering the druids that I could find."

"I happened to have one on the medicinal uses of local altered plants," Penderbrock said. "A chapter at the end mentioned how people used to be marked. Back when the Daygarii walked the world at the same time as men. The text implied only those with Daygarii blood were so marked." He arched his bushy white eyebrows.

"I'm... researching that possibility," Kaylina said, more because people kept bringing it up than because she had plans to do so. So far from home, she didn't even know *how* to research it.

"See what you find. It did say that the marks aren't always a boon." His eyebrows lowered, drawing together in a concerned expression.

"I'm not surprised."

"The druids didn't have a high opinion of humans."

"How come they were *copulating* with them, then?" Frayvar asked. "I assume that must have occurred for humans with Daygarii blood to exist. Unless some sort of experiments were done? Artificial insemination? Delivered by altered plants?"

Kaylina drew back—and crossed her legs. "I don't want to imagine how that could happen."

The usually unflappable Penderbrock also curled a lip in distaste. "I figured some humans might be more appealing than others and have drawn randy druids."

"May I read your book?" Frayvar asked.

"Yes. What I wanted to tell you, Korbian, is that it might be possible to remove that brand. There was an alchemical formula in that chapter for an acid created with ingredients from a number of altered plants."

"*Acid*?" Kaylina drew her hand protectively to her chest.

"It might be worth a scar to make sure you can't be controlled."

Kaylina started to shake her head, the thought of acid bathing her hand horrifying, but she remembered the plant's vision about her killing Vlerion. And his belief that it might have the power to force her to carry out its will. It might be worth enduring the pain to make sure that couldn't happen.

But the brand had also helped keep her alive, and it had led her to seek out the taybarri elders. With trouble finding the city on a weekly basis, she might continue to need its assistance. And to lift Vlerion's curse, she wagered she would need the magic of the druids. She would have to figure out a way to outsmart the plant and use its power to help Vlerion instead of hurting him.

"Should I investigate further?" Penderbrock asked.

"Doc, my leg's about to fall off over here," one of his patients called.

Kaylina shook her head and waved for him to attend those in more dire need of his attention. "I'll keep it for now."

"You might regret that decision." His expression remained concerned, like he thought it was a bad idea to roam the world with the brand.

"It won't be the first. Not by far." Kaylina smiled.

"All right, then." He turned toward the waiting men, though a medical assistant was already tending them. "You sniveling youths, I've seen rangers have entire mountains fall on them who bellyached less."

"Only because it's hard to complain with a mountain crushing you."

As the men continued grousing, Frayvar eyed Kaylina's hand. "Are you sure it's a good idea to keep that? If there's an option to get rid of it?"

"No."

"But you're going to do it anyway?"

"Yes."

~

As dusk settled over Port Jirador, Kaylina and Vlerion stood holding hands on the arched bridge overlooking the Stillguard River downstream of the castle. They could see the courtyard walls and the towers, including the one where the glowing plant resided, its purple glow seeping out into the darkening night, but several buildings stood between them.

This was as close as Vlerion dared come to that plant, and Kaylina didn't blame him for wariness. She was *glad* he understood the danger and wasn't courting it. Though she'd been given the queen's blessing to open the meadery and eating house—Frayvar was already in the kitchen with fresh groceries and his menu plan—Kaylina wouldn't set aside her goal of lifting Vlerion's curse. After all they'd been through together, after all the times Vlerion had saved her, she vowed to save *him*.

Maybe it wasn't a selfless desire, since she was tired of wanting him so much that she ached and not being able to have him. Standing here now, with his calloused hand clasped around hers, his powerful body close enough that she could feel its heat, was as frustrating as it was comforting. She longed to invite him to join her in bed—or have him sweep her off into the woods for a passionate joining under the trees.

"Oh, Vlerion." Kaylina slumped against his side.

"Are you dejected and depressed, despite our recent victory?" His smile had a sad tilt to it.

Many had died—the numbers in the city and out on the estates were still being tallied—so maybe they shouldn't have called it a victory. But at least the fires were out and the bodies cleared from the streets. From what they'd been able to tell, the castle—the *plant*—had only killed Kar'ruk.

"I am a little dejected," Kaylina said.

"Because of the knowledge that humans brought this all upon themselves? Making deals with a deadly enemy instead of working to find a solution that doesn't involve bloodshed? My brother almost prophesied it in his song. Though, I suppose, as a student of history, he knew similar things had happened before and would happen again. It seems to be in our nature to destroy ourselves." Vlerion gazed pensively out at the river.

"Would it be shallow to admit I was dejected because we can't have sex, and I really want to?"

His gaze shifted to her.

"That other stuff bothers me too, but I'm kind of horny right now, and you're..." She turned to press her face against his shoulder, wishing she could wrap her arms around him for a kiss, that he would lean her against the railing of the bridge and take her, not caring if pedestrians passed or not, caring only about their mutual satisfaction.

Vlerion rested his face against the top of her head. "I would also enjoy being with you, but enough time has passed…"

"That it would rouse the beast? I know. Hence the dejection." She leaned back to look into his eyes. "I'm going to find a way to lift your curse."

"So we can have sex?" His second smile was more amused than sad.

Good. They needed some amusement to lighten their moods.

"*Yes.*" Kaylina gripped his arm. "And you know the other reasons. I want you to be safe from yourself and from the beast sabotaging your future so you can fully be the man you want to be."

Vlerion cupped the back of her head. "Thank you for wanting that."

"The curse isn't fair."

"No," he agreed and stroked her hair.

She wanted to scoot closer to him, to press her chest against his, but they both knew where that would lead. They might have stopped the rogue press and taken the Virt journal, but that didn't mean there weren't yet men and women alive who knew about his curse. They had to be careful. The beast couldn't arise, especially in the city.

"As I recall," Vlerion said, "I hesitated when you asked if I would have feelings for you if not for the beast in me being drawn to the *anrokk* in you."

"Yes."

"I wanted to think about my answer, not tell you something that I wasn't certain would be a truth."

"It's fine. You don't have to make any promises to me." Even if she longed to hear him say he would care about her no matter what. That was too much to ask for. "Maybe we won't know for sure—can't know for sure—until the curse is lifted."

"I suppose it's possible that will change our feelings, but, at this moment, I am positive that I care for you and want to be with you outside of any magical allure."

Kaylina looked into his blue eyes, and her heart sang at the statement. It was all that she'd wanted to hear, all that she'd hoped was true.

"I want to be with you too," she whispered. "Not just your allure."

"I know," he said simply.

She snorted. "Of course, because you're haughty and arrogant and full of yourself. You must think *all* women want to be with you."

"Careful. Dwelling on my sexy attributes might overheat you. I'll have to toss you in the river to cool you off."

"You'll take any excuse to see me with my shirt wet."

"And clinging to your body, yes." His eyelids drooped, his gaze shifting toward her chest.

By the moon gods, that look made her hot. She *did* have to worry about overheating around him.

Perhaps thinking something similar, he blew out a slow breath and looked toward the river.

She shifted to stand beside him, only their hands touching. It was safer that way.

As they gazed into the water, she couldn't help but ask, "Was it the taybarri vision that made you realize your feelings? Did you see the reed antennae and finally grasp that you couldn't live without someone so whimsical?"

"You are brave, determined, and loyal to your friends and family. I value all of those things." Vlerion rested a hand on his chest, as if to say he attempted to be those things himself.

That he believed she encompassed all that touched her, but

she vowed to keep her tone—and the moment—light. Otherwise, it would be too easy to lean into him again, to press her body against his while gazing into his eyes...

"But mostly it was the antennae, right?" she asked. "Adding to my allure."

"They *were* alluring."

"I thought so."

"There remains much for the rangers to do in the aftermath of the invasion, so I need to take my leave of you again." Vlerion squeezed her hand, kissed her on the cheek, and stepped back. "I trust you can make it to the castle without a bodyguard. Especially since it has proven capable of defending itself, even beyond its borders." The wary look he sent in that direction promised he wouldn't show up for their grand opening. Not unless she could find a way to get the plant to realize he was a good guy and should be allowed on the premises.

One day, she vowed to herself.

For Vlerion, she nodded. "I think so."

"Good. I do expect to see you at dawn tomorrow."

"Uhm, why?" After all the days of missing sleep, she wanted to collapse in front of the hearth and not stir until noon. Noon *next week*.

His eyes crinkled at the corners. "Now that your name has been cleared, we can resume your ranger training."

"Are you going to knock me off that log into the water again?"

"Maybe." He winked before heading off toward ranger headquarters.

Shaking her head, Kaylina walked down the trail toward the back gate of the castle. Before she reached it, she glimpsed someone standing in the shadow of a tree across the river. Someone *spying* on the castle from under a cloak and hood.

Even without seeing the woman's face, Kaylina knew who it

was. She hoped Jana Bloomlong was fuming because her vile plan had been thwarted.

Before stepping into the courtyard, Kaylina used her forearm and hand to give the woman a rude gesture.

Jana gave it right back.

"Now that the odds are even," Kaylina said as she closed the gate, "we'll see who makes the best mead."

THE END

Made in the USA
Las Vegas, NV
19 November 2024

12041933R00216